The Devil's Cut

Andrew James Greig

Cover illustration: Graeme Clarke
graeme@graemeclarke.co.uk

Published by:
Fledgling Press
1 Milton Road West
Edinburgh
EH15 1LA

www.fledglingpress.co.uk

ISBN 9781912280483

Printed and bound by:
Print on Demand Worldwide, Peterborough

For Shona

...The sleeping and the dead
Are but as pictures; 'tis the eye of childhood
That fears a painted devil.

(William Shakespeare – Macbeth)

PROLOGUE

He should have turned back when the first wave of nausea washed over him, leaving him grey-faced and shaking until the sickness eventually subsided. Instead, here he was, alone, doubled over and retching on the exposed mountain flank. He'd put it down to food poisoning – a queasy stomach offering the first indication that something wasn't quite right an hour into his climb. Now, despite the strenuous effort of the final steep ascent, he was shivering with the onset of a sudden fever. Disturbing geometric patterns whirled in the circling mist as if warning of an imminent migraine attack. The summit was just a few more minutes climb, the path still obvious under his feet from the imprint of boots that had trodden and scraped this way before him. Leaning on a damp outcrop that offered little respite from the chill wind, he wiped his mouth clear of spittle before taking another drink from his water bottle.

"Sod it. I'll just reach the top."

The words were for himself, encouragement to persevere through the veil of shifting pearlescent vapour as he neared the summit.

Once the water bottle had been replaced in his backpack, he focused on the path ahead. With a look of fierce determination, he pushed away from the rock, continuing the journey upwards, leg muscles protesting with each laboured step. Breaths came in deep gulps, synchronised with the placing of each foot. His heart was hammering an uneven rhythm against his ribcage in protest, almost as if desperate to leave the confines of its bone prison. He decided to ignore it – that and the way his eyes insisted on adding curlicues around the periphery of his vision. The sun had long been hidden by the lowering cloud, coalescing into miniature wet jewels on his beard and adding to the cold sweat already beading his forehead. The wind gained in strength as the summit neared, whipping at exposed flesh. At the beginning of his ascent, a gentle breeze had provided welcome relief to his exertions. Here, nearer the summit, the breeze had strengthened into more of a gale and now clawed at exposed raw skin with icy barbs.

The weather never stood still on the mountains, changing so quickly that he knew better than to take off his waterproof – even when the sun attempted to bake him alive. God knows this wasn't the time to take sick, alone on a mountain range at the onset of a Scottish autumn. He berated himself for not keeping in shape. Lugging those extra kilos of body fat up the hills had seemed like a good idea at the start – a well-defined trail easing upwards through the promise of finer weather than could reasonably be expected in late September. An Indian summer it was called. There was a reason it was called that; he once knew why. Now no amount of mental effort called forth the answer. It didn't matter. He just had to reach the top and then he could turn back. An easy path once he cleared the false summit, here at the mountain's upper reaches. The sun was probably still shining further down, away from the clouds that stubbornly hugged the mountain peak. Just a little higher, a few more minutes.

He may as well have been alone in the universe, wrapped in a cold blanket of moisture that conspired at times to obscure visibility to just a few metres. He wondered again at the wisdom of climbing on his own – the swirling mist adding to the feeling of disorientation that followed the sudden onset of his sickness. There were dangerous cliffs here, wander too far off the track and he could easily fall to his death. Foot followed foot, breath followed breath, heartbeat followed heartbeat – until the heartbeat stopped.

He doubled over in agony, clutching at his chest as a giant fist squeezed his heart. His feet staggered randomly off the track as he fought to stay upright, the intensity of pain white hot inside his ribcage.

"Must be a stitch."

The words were forced out from between clenched teeth, giving voice to a comforting lie. He fumbled desperately behind his back to reach the small pack slung over his shoulders, liberating a plastic water bottle, which he upended to drink in urgent gulps. His other hand massaged his chest, trying in vain to unknot the muscle that held him in a relentless grip. At some level of consciousness, he was aware that he was having a heart attack; that he had fallen awkwardly onto the boulders underfoot; that he was dying. Not here. Not now. Not alone. His mind screamed a silent final eulogy through the pain.

Clouds gathered around him – spectral mourners reaching out to hold him in their damp embrace, depositing cold tears on his cheeks as the heat left his body with unseemly haste. The bottle slipped from his weakening grip. Caught by the wind, it bounced from rock to rock before becoming airborne on a powerful gust. It finally lodged in between two boulders; the neck jammed almost horizontally, facing away from the prevailing wind. There was still a mouthful of water left in the bottle, and as the wind veered around the rocks, an errant draft played over the neck – creating an aeolian dirge, which he heard long after his eyesight had faded.

CHAPTER 1
Wake

❝It's how he would have wanted to go."

They sat around a pub table – the one nearest the comforting warmth of an open fire, some distance away from the noise at the bar. The assorted mourners nodded sagely as if hearing some wisdom hidden in such an anodyne statement, pints held close to their chests as they considered the import of the words. Jack McCoach, the focus of their attention, remained silent. For him to have been otherwise would have been noteworthy, reduced as he was to 2.7kg of ashes. He took pride of place, residing in a brushed pewter urn, which occupied the centrepiece of their table. It had been a week since the funeral service. Black clad as crows, they had formed a small part of the congregation, heads bowed respectfully. Singing half-remembered hymns in praise of a deity few there really believed in anymore. The minister had made a reasonable fist of it – praising the family's charitable donations; dropping a few amusing anecdotes into the mix that were tame enough for church.

His wife and son both chose readings from the Old Testament, that rich source of pickings for all occasions. Jack McCoach's wife, Emma, had read the bit about time for dying. What was it? *To everything turn, turn, turn. There is a season turn, turn, turn.* Corstophine stopped the tune running in his head, aware that he didn't have it quite right but that was the gist. He studied his companions, already well advanced in inebriation. Bryan Cobb, the managing director of the firm; Sandy McPhearson, the corpulent finance director, and then Robb McCoach – Jack's son and supposed heir. What was the reading Robb had chosen, stood up there in the pulpit with a voice more befitting a southern preacher? *The Lord is my shepherd, I shall not want. He makes me down to lie. Through pastures green He leadeth me*– something to do with making the bugger's eyes water? No, that's Pink Floyd. Corstophine shook his head in an attempt to bring clarity to his thoughts. He'd had enough.

"Sorry lads, that's me." He held his hands up at the protestations, offers of one for the road, a nightcap. "You'll have to decide what to do with his ashes without me."

"You're a lightweight, Jimmy, gie the man a proper send off!" Sandy's eyes had trouble focusing as he swayed in his seat. Corstophine was put in mind of a bloated cobra wearing a blond wig. Why was he even here with these people? He'd joined the hillwalking club last year, another attempt at finding a life outside of work, an escape from the daily diet of petty crimes that all needed solving. Trouble was these hillwalkers did more drinking than walking.

"Aye, well." Corstophine nodded to the table, encompassing the pewter urn and its dry contents. "That's me!" He placed his glass awkwardly on the table, the hard retort as it impacted punctuating his closing comment.

They watched him as he left, hand held loosely erect as he bid farewell to the landlord. The whole pub let loose a stored breath as the door closed behind him, conversation levels rising as if freed from an unwitting constraint.

Corstophine stood outside in the cold night air, hunkering down into his jacket as he set his feet towards home. The streets of the small highland town were quiet at this hour – too late for the rowdy youths who had earlier congregated at the entrance to the kids' playpark where they shared bottles of Buckfast, cigarettes and stolen kisses. Too early for the habitual drinkers who would soon be weaving random paths back to a lonelier existence once the landlord eased them out the door. He felt an affinity with the streets, a comfort in treading worn paving stones like he had when he was a bobby. How long ago? Corstophine struggled with simple mental subtraction, the numbers refusing to play ball as they bounced from one slurred brain cell to the next. He admitted defeat. Call it twenty-five years, more or less. Twenty-five years since he was as new as his uniform, as polished as his boots. The town had grown in that time; new hotels springing up to cater to a burgeoning tourist trade, eager to sample the rugged mountains surrounding them. They'd brought their own problems: drunken fights as expense accounts encouraged the businesspeople on team-building exercises to excess; stag and hen nights ending in acrimony; walkers, mountaineers and skiers lost on the hills.

It was almost three weeks since he had received a call from the mountain rescue team about a man's body found near the summit of Sgurr Thuilm. There was nothing remarkable about this; the mountain rescue headquarters kept in regular communication about rescues or body recoveries. He'd been talking to the team leader, Dr John Hesketh, during a Zoom conference call earlier that summer. What had it been about? Out of his fuzzy mind emerged a clear picture of the agenda – Emergency Response – Unified Agency Guidelines. All he could remember from the event was Dr Hesketh complaining that lost or injured people were given priority in terms of multi-agency support. Helicopters, Fire, Police, Ambulance, all made readily available in the event of an injury. But if the team found anyone dead on the hills, nobody was interested. As a result, the unpaid volunteers of the mountain rescue team often had the difficult and dangerous job of taking a body off the hill unaided.

He'd seen that for himself that night, standing at the side of a cold, dark Highland track as part of a solemn stationary convoy waiting for the mountain rescue team to appear. They had materialised out of a wild night, head torches bobbing in the air like fireflies, until the orange of their survival clothing caught in the spinning ambulance lights. It had taken six of them to carry the body, taking turns, two about, to clamber down the trail with Jack's heavy weight lashed onto an aluminium stretcher. The team were exhausted, evident in the way they slipped and scrambled down the track towards him. It didn't need the doctor to confirm the guy was dead – swollen tongue hanging out of colourless lips. He looked more like something that should be hanging on an abattoir hook than a human being. Corstophine recognised him straight away, as had the rest of them. Jack McCoach was a larger than life character in every regard, owner of the largest distillery and one of the town's major employers. His wife had been on the phone since three that afternoon, convinced that something had happened to him – insisting they send the mountain rescue out. He'd had to tell her not to worry, Jack was probably on his way home, but she'd sounded hysterical. She'd let it slip that she had an app on her phone that told her where he was, and he hadn't moved from the mountain summit for the last two hours and wasn't answering her calls. He'd sent PC Lamb out to check, and Jack's car was still parked at the foot of the mountain. Then they'd received a call from the mountain rescue. A group of climbers out to bag a double Munro had seen his body just a few metres off the main path when the mist had momentarily lifted. Not that Dr Hesketh leading the recovery team could have helped him – he'd informed

Corstophine that Jack must have had a massive coronary and would have died within seconds.

The body was sent to the coroner anyway, just to keep the paperwork tidy. There, Jack had suffered the final indignity of having his chest sawn open and heart removed, so it could be prodded and poked on a laboratory bench before being sliced into sections. The report had come back as death from natural causes, with weight and heavy alcohol consumption being contributory factors. Corstophine realised the coroner must have removed his liver as well. Exactly how much of him was left in that urn?

A church bell let him know it was 11:00 pm, the sound apologetic and muffled, following the addition of leather pads to the clapper in June. Corstophine glanced up at the clock tower, the hands confirming the bells' announcement. He had some sympathy with the locals who'd been haranguing the council environmental health for years. The bells were never that sonorous, more discordant than tuneful, as if the foundry had offloaded failed bronze casts to those churches with less money. It was far worse when the bell-ringers practiced – or on a Sunday morning when the bell tower broadcast a tuneless cacophony for miles around. How young children managed to sleep through the noise was a mystery.

The thought of children brought his eyes back to a contemplation of the ground. His own children that never happened; a wife that died too young. The case last year that had almost cost him his career. Sometimes being a detective inspector was a cursed job, cleaning up the filth and social detritus that humans leave in their wake.

"You need your bed, James. You know drink always makes you maudlin."

He smiled at the woman whose appearances at his side

became less frequent every year. Her face in its frame of brown curls, looking at him with concern. A face he never stopped loving. A solitary tear appeared unbidden from his eye, and he blinked it away. When he opened his eyes again, she had gone.

"Aye, well. You're right." He spoke the words under his breath, too quiet for anyone to hear even if there had been anyone else on the street. Some words are for the dead, or for comfort when you've nobody else to say them for you. Corstophine fumbled in his pocket for his house keys, turning off into the quiet side street where he lived. Key in the door, he entered a house that was too large, too quiet, and held too many memories.

CHAPTER 2
Séance

"**I** need to see a detective and I need to see one now!"

Sergeant Hamish McKee waved his hands slowly up and down, looking for all the world like a man drowning in slow motion as he ineffectually attempted to calm the woman down. She had marched into the station claiming to have information pertinent to Jack McCoach's death on the mountain – said he'd been poisoned. Insisted she speak to a detective. Hamish tried one more time, picking up notepad and pen and holding them in full view of the reception window as if that might encourage her to speak to him.

"If you can just give me some details, Miss…" His voice trailed off. The woman standing indignantly in front of him had a look in her eye that gave him the strong impression that she probably didn't identify as a Miss. They'd all had diversity training a few months back – Corstophine had somehow managed to attract a far larger training budget than their small station would normally warrant. The word was that he had something over the Assistant Chief Constable who acquiesced to his every request, quite a turnaround from last year when they'd all thought the station was going to be closed. Even PC Lamb had been accepted for a firearms course, swaggering back to the station after a few days with a Taser and holster that he wore on every conceivable occasion. How he'd been able to get past the usual safeguards and checks that weed out the immature or incompetent was still a popular topic of conversation at tea breaks.

The sergeant racked his memory, searching in vain for the correct way to address someone who didn't identify as a Miss – something the sexual diversity training hadn't covered, as far as he could remember. An alphabet of acronyms flew past his mind's eye, LGBTQ+.

Hamish suddenly felt old, too old for all this. First Covid-19 had turned the world upside down, his own parents adding to the daily fatalities as the deadly virus had swept through their care home. He couldn't even be there for them at the end as they had each succumbed. The care home had tried to reassure him, tell him how they had each passed away peacefully; how a carer had held their hands at the end. It was meant to be a comfort, but he'd seen people die; the desperation to pull one more breath, the realisation in panicked eyes as the breathing stopped. The death figures appearing on the TV every evening; thousands upon thousands dying whilst the government applauded their own inadequacies, concealing the true death toll under selective statistics and downright lies. He'd like a few minutes with some of the mealy-mouthed MPs – old-style policing!

With an effort, he brought himself back to the present, facing the woman on the other side of the glass. He struggled to recognise her, which in itself was remarkable for someone who prided himself in putting a name to everyone's face in the town. She was dressed quite flamboyantly. A bright orange jumper had leapt out at him as she entered the police station, white blobs resolving into focus as three-dimensional mice, rendered in wool, frozen in place across her chest. A more subdued skirt in heather hues covered her legs, but her feet were startling in bright purple heels. An attempt at colour coordinating her

17

ensemble with a flowing chiffon scarf in much the same shade of purple was only spoilt by the close proximity of the bright orange wool. The word 'Miss' hung in the air, unattended and ignored until it faded into silence.

"A detective." She repeated the word with a no-nonsense curtness, fixing Hamish with a look that reminded him of one of his primary school teachers who'd taken an instant dislike to the slow-speaking boy in front of her.

"I'll see who's available. Would ye like to grab a seat?"

She turned to inspect the plastic seats behind her. Some unidentified liquid had been spilt on two of them, leaving a dark stain that had spread like a Rorschach test. The remaining seats shared a miscellany of graffiti and knife marks – a clear challenge to those in authority on the other side of the glass.

"I'll stand, thank you." She sniffed, making clear her opinion of the seating choice on offer.

Hamish sighed, impotently replacing pen and notepad on the counter between them, and entered the back office. Corstophine hadn't started his shift yet, his office shut and empty. PC Lamb was out walking his beat – synchronised with all the lassies going to work or taking their kids to school. That left DC Frankie McKenzie, early at her desk as always, bent over her PC and typing a report about the catalytic converter thefts that had hit the area like an unexpected plague. She looked up as Hamish approached, sending him a ready smile.

"Do you know that's ten vehicles this week that have had their catalytic converters nicked? Ten! And those are just the ones that have been reported. I was chatting to the scrappy yesterday – palladium is now worth £1,900/oz, rhodium goes for £21,000/oz – they're worth more than gold! Just a few minutes under the car with a cutting tool and they're away. Bastards!"

"The local scrappie's not dealing?"

"No way. He's not that stupid. No, these are being sent down to Glasgow more than likely. Organised crime wants us to give them some leads but whoever's doing this is too bloody quick. They can nick them in a couple of minutes, nobody knows it's happened until their car sounds like a tractor, and then it's too late."

Hamish thought of the orange woman waiting in reception. "I've got this woman wanting to speak to a detective, she won't say a word to me."

"What's it about?" Frankie's interest was piqued. Not many people were able to get past Hamish's implacable presence at reception.

"She said it's to do with Jack McCoach."

"What about him?"

"You'd best speak to her yourself. Seems to think it wasn't a heart attack."

"What do you mean, not a heart attack? Forensics confirmed it."

Hamish just shrugged in response. This was above his pay grade.

Frankie frowned at her report. It would have to wait.

"Send her through then, Hamish. I'll see her in the interview room."

The woman entered the interview room like a cruise liner entering a substandard port, purple chiffon scarf in her trail like some flag of state. Frankie wrinkled her nose as the unmistakable scent of patchouli oil assailed her nostrils. *Hippie*. The thought entered her head automatically. The small towns around here had more than their fair share of wannabe flower children. They'd made their fortunes in London and elsewhere, then washed up in comfortable houses and farms where they smoked pot and dabbled in the arts. She appraised the woman as Hamish gestured her into the room. Late fifties, possibly quite out of her mind dressed like that. *Bet she's an artist, holidays in Bali, regular at the yoga and acupuncture. Crystal dangler!*

Frankie indicated the chair opposite, noticing as the woman gave it a distasteful look before settling into its plastic embrace.

"How can I help you?" She spoke curtly, wanting to get this out of the way so she could get back to typing her report. "Ms..." Always best to lead with a Ms when in doubt, Frankie thought.

"McCoach. Patricia McCoach. I'm Jack's sister."

Frankie quickly re-assessed her. If she was one of the McCoach family, then she was loaded. Maybe she did have some information, although what could she possibly add to the facts surrounding her brother's unfortunate death?

"And how can I help you, Patricia? Do you mind if I call you Patricia?" Frankie added quickly, seeing the woman's bright red lips draw downwards in distaste.

"It doesn't matter what you want to call me." The words spat out as fast as bullets. "What is important is that you open an investigation into Jack's murder!"

"Murder?" Frankie questioned. She sat back in her seat, eyebrows raised in doubt.

"Yes, murder, young lady. One thing the McCoach family all share is a robust constitution. There's no way under God's heaven that Jack died of a heart attack. My brother was as strong as an ox."

Frankie could see the truth of the McCoach family sharing a robust constitution. The woman was built like a blimp, an orange blimp.

"Let's start by taking down some details." Frankie adopted a businesslike approach, pen poised above notebook as she requested address and contact details. She took the time to study the woman sitting opposite her, pen working on autopilot as it left a neat trail of words across the notebook's page. Patricia was definitely on the wrong side of fifty, crow's feet starting to etch fine lines around startlingly light cornflower blue eyes. The purple chiffon scarf would be there to cover the wrinkles on her neck, riding up to settle under a chin that was well on the way to growing a twin. Her red lipstick had wandered far enough away from the contour of her thin lips to make Frankie wonder if Patricia may have applied her makeup whilst inebriated. The overall impression was one of a woman who had given up the unequal struggle to retain the effortless beauty of youth, resigned to letting herself drift on the prevailing current towards the inevitable.

Frankie decided to put her out of her misery. The cause of her brother's death was clear.

"I'm sorry, Patricia, but the autopsy indicated that your brother died of heart failure. I can get you a copy of the report if that would help put your mind at rest?"

The woman opposite her expelled so much air from her rouged cheeks that Frankie expected to see her visibly deflate. She leant forward, jabbing a finger towards Frankie's face.

"Did you check for poisons?"

Frankie inadvertently recoiled back into her seat to avoid the finger aimed at the bridge of her nose.

"The pathologist would automatically have run a suite of tests for toxins, but there was no doubt about the cause of his death. Both his heart and liver showed signs of wear and tear." *And evidence of heavy drinking – she decided not to vocalise that part of the report.* "I'm afraid the exertion of the climb just proved too much for him."

Patricia's expression went through a number of transformations, ranging between raw anger and doubt before settling on sorrow. A sob escaped tightly clenched red lips as she wrestled in her pockets for a handkerchief, lowering her head to dab at eyes turned newly wet.

"I'm not mad!" The words issued defiantly from the downturned face. She looked up, moist eyes engaging with Frankie's. "I believe he was killed. Poisoned. You have to investigate!"

"What makes you think he was poisoned?" Frankie was genuinely intrigued. It wasn't every day that she had members of the public allege family members had been poisoned. What information could she have?

"He told me," she said simply.

Frankie's puzzled expression prompted an explanation.

"He told me from beyond – in a séance."

OK. This was now officially weird. *Try humouring her, she doesn't look dangerous.*

"I see." Frankie didn't see at all. "What did he tell you?"

"He wasn't clear, the spirits often aren't."

I bet, Frankie thought.

"He said that he'd been poisoned, and that the others had to take care."

"Which others, Patricia? Who has to take care?"

Her wet eyes darted around the room as if searching for the murderer herself.

"The family. He said that he was coming for the family."

Patricia abruptly stood up, a finger jabbing in emphasis with the rhythm of her words.

"I have to go. I'm not mad you know – you have to do something about it!"

Frankie sat immobile as she heard Hamish lead her out of the station, leaving nothing but the scent of patchouli lingering in the air and a deep unease in her mind.

"What was that all that about?" Hamish's head appeared around the interview room door.

"I've absolutely no idea," Frankie replied.

CHAPTER 3
Suicide

Corstophine nursed his head in his hands, forlornly hoping that the additional support might offer some respite to the incessant pulse from deep within his forehead. He had hoped to gently pass the day away, sitting at his desk without doing very much, certainly not having to deal with Frankie's confused report about Jack McCoach's alleged poisoning as soon as he arrived. He wouldn't have felt quite so bad today if he'd stuck to drinking beer last night, but it had only seemed proper to toast Jack with his own whisky.

"She said what?" Corstophine's voice had developed a croak.

Frankie narrowed her eyes, already well aware that her boss was experiencing the ill effects of poisoning himself.

"She said that Jack had spoken to her in a séance and told her that he'd been poisoned, and that someone was coming for the whole family." She waited patiently for the words to sink in.

"A séance?"

She nodded encouragement.

Corstophine removed his hands from his head so that he was able to shake it from side to side. He stopped almost immediately as fresh agony sprang from his temple.

"What the hell are we meant to do with a statement from beyond the grave?"

Frankie remained silent, lifting her shoulders slightly to emphasise her own bewilderment.

"God. I suppose we'll have to make some sort of enquiries. I'll talk to forensics again, see if there's anything they can add." Corstophine waved her away. He'd had enough spirits already without adding to them. The number for forensics was on his speed dial.

"Corstophine. Always a pleasure to hear from you." The voice on the other end of the line was incessantly cheery. The only good to have come out of the string of murders last year was that Corstophine had almost single-handedly ensured that the Inverness forensics department would not be subject to any cost-cutting reviews this fiscal, retaining a full complement of staff for the foreseeable future.

"Aye." Corstophine managed to encompass a lot of information in that single word, notably a clear signal that he wasn't in the mood for any gallows humour. "The toxicology report on Jack McCoach – I want to go over it again."

"The heart attack on the mountain?"

"That's the one. Was anything found in his system that we should have any concerns about?"

"Just a minute, pulling it up on my screen now." Corstophine could hear a distant keyboard clatter down the line. He breathed deeply, feeling faintly sick, and willing the cotton wool to leave his head. The disembodied clattering stopped, replaced by the sound of a phone being picked up.

"Coronary arteries shot, lot of fat around the internal organs, liver damage. Yep – typical heart attack material. Why ask?"

Corstophine decided to keep his source to himself for the moment.

"We had someone come into the station suggesting he may have been poisoned. Did you run a full toxicology on his body?"

The delay in any response told him all he needed to know.

"We gave him a once-over – but there wasn't any doubt about it. Massive heart attack. He would have been dead within a couple of minutes."

Corstophine rubbed his forehead in a futile attempt to shift the pain in his head ,which throbbed in sympathy with his own heart.

"What about any toxins that could have caused a heart attack – did you test for those?"

"Uh. Let me just check."

He knew what the answer was going to be. A corpse is brought in, overweight and in poor physical health. Died during heavy physical exertion. They cut open the ribs, expose the heart to see extensive myocardial infarction. Cut out the heart, section it to confirm the muscle wall has turned yellow as the heart stops pumping oxygenated blood. Pull out the liver just to make it look as if they're earning their keep. Write report. Job done.

"There wasn't anything found." The disembodied voice sounded hopeful, perhaps thinking Corstophine would leave it there.

"Have you still got the biopsies, anything you can run a more detailed toxicology for me?"

"No, sorry. Fiscal released them for incineration. There weren't any suspicious circumstances, cause of death as clear as day."

"OK. Not to worry, probably nothing in it."

He ended the call, deciding to make himself a strong coffee. Jack McCoach was beyond his help now – forensics couldn't do much with whatever was left of him in the urn. A séance! Mumbo jumbo from beyond the grave. Good luck with getting that witness statement approved.

PC Philip Lamb was already making a pot of coffee,

back from pounding the streets. Corstophine had invested in a cafetière not long after making DI, and the rest of the team had soon jettisoned instant granules to join him. It was a small enough price to pay for a decent cup.

"Morning, sir, are you having one as well?" Lamb held the half-full cafetière up in the air as if he was speaking to someone with a hearing impediment.

"Yes, thanks, Lamb. Make it strong – and black."

"Rough night, sir?"

Corstophine grimaced. He must look bad if Lamb could see he was hungover.

"I was at a send-off for Jack McCoach last night – made the rookie error of finishing up with a few of his whiskies."

"Beer before whisky, always risky," Lamb intoned. He took Corstophine's mug and filled it with black coffee, handing it back with a smile.

"Thank you, Lamb." Corstophine couldn't raise the energy to fire off a riposte and took himself back to the quiet of his office. Sipping his coffee, he wondered why Jack McCoach's sister had alleged that he'd been poisoned, and who could she mean was coming for the family? He saw Frankie was sitting back at her desk and tapped on the glass panel dividing his office from the rest of the back room. Frankie looked up, saw his hand waving her in.

"Sir?" She stood in the doorway, one hand resting on the door handle.

Corstophine indicated she sit. Looking up increased the intensity of his headache, probably not helped by the fluorescent lights.

"This woman who was in earlier. What do we know about her?"

"Patricia McCoach, sir?"

Corstophine nodded – gently in case his brain rattled around like a dried prune in its skin.

"Nothing, apart from the fact she's Jack McCoach's sister. She's never been in the station before. I can't say I've seen her around town. It's the first we've heard of her – even Hamish didn't recognise her."

"Find out what you can. She's probably just another fruitcake but I don't want to take any chances. If she thinks there's someone out to get at the McCoach family, I'd rather we knew about it."

"Understood, sir. I'll see what I can find."

Corstophine stared at his screen, opening up the monthly report for crime figures, which needed his attention before he sent it off. He frowned at the list of petty crimes, which was higher than normal for the time of year. As a tourist destination, the town was subject to seasonal peaks and troughs of visitors. They brought the additional baggage of thefts, assaults and motoring offences, along with their eagerly anticipated spending. By rights, the rate should be on a steady decline as winter approached, just leaving the background noise of local miscreants to contend with. He highlighted the crimes that needed attention before the powers-that-be spotted them and gave him the third degree. Top of these were the catalytic converter thefts. Someone must know something. Angle grinders or whatever they used weren't the quietest of tools, surely somebody must have heard or seen something? Then there was the Peeping Tom. Five women had reported seeing someone lurking in their gardens, peering in at bedroom or bathroom windows. If he wasn't found, then someone would more than likely dispense some rough justice themselves, especially as it became widely known a pervert was on the loose.

Corstophine sighed in exasperation at the sordid side of

life that lay exposed in the spreadsheet. Serving as a police officer soon introduced you to those facets of human nature that are normally kept hidden. What drives a man to spy on women in their own homes where they should feel secure, creeping into back gardens? Does the thrill satisfy some urge? Would it nourish a darker need that might lead to sexual assault? Whoever it was, he needed to be found before he did something more serious. Corstophine put the crimes on the team brief. He just hoped to get through the presentation without Lamb making one of his dreadful quips.

"Sorry to disturb you, sir."

Corstophine looked up to see what had caused Hamish to leave his seat at the front desk.

"What is it Hamish?" He asked the question more tersely than he'd intended, the after-effects of his hangover making him more irritable than normal. Corstophine tried a smile to ameliorate the harshness in his tone, the unnatural combination causing Hamish to pause even longer than was usual before constructing his first slow sentence.

"I've just had a call from the railway station. Seems some poor lass has fallen in front of a train. They've asked for assistance."

Corstophine uncurled from the chair he'd slumped into. "It's okay, Hamish, I'll go. No foul play reported?"

"No, sir. Seemingly she just stepped in front of the engine as it pulled into the station. I don't think there's any hope of her surviving. The ambulance and fire service are already on the way."

Corstophine's eyes picked out Frankie and Lamb in the office, switching from one to the other as he decided which one to take.

"Frankie, we've a potential suicide at the train station. Can you come with me? Lamb, you hold the fort."

He wondered at his use of the expression, suggestive of cowboy films from his past before realising that Lamb had recently been slipping western slang into his speech ever since Taser training. He'd have to watch that; it was obviously catching.

They arrived at the station just a short while later, the ambulance and fire engine already sending regular flashes of blue from the emergency vehicles parked in front of the entrance. Corstophine pushed through the crowd impeding progress as they held mobiles aloft to capture the mangled young woman's body that lay across the tracks.

"Put those bloody phones down and give the girl some respect!" Corstophine wasn't in the mood for taking any prisoners today. Frankie joined the station staff, helping to move the crowd back as Corstophine crouched down at the edge of the platform. The other emergency services were already down on the tracks, protective clothing stained with the woman's blood. Two of the ambulance staff looked towards him with an unvoiced question, gesturing with the body bag they held.

"We have to wait for the transport police to arrive. This is their patch by rights – just cover the poor lass for God's sake." He turned away from the sight, screwing the lid down on his emotions.

"Do we have any witnesses?" Corstophine asked the question out loud, searching the faces in the crowd for any response.

"I saw it happen." The voice was quiet, coming from one of the uniformed station staff helping Frankie move back the crowd.

He took in her ashen face, realised she was close to fainting.

"Hold my arm." Corstophine offered a hand as he

approached, felt the tremble in her grip as she held onto him. "Is there somewhere we can sit in private?"

She pointed to a door marked 'Staff', untrusting of her voice. The room held a few chairs and a table; mugs of half-drunk tea and coffee lay on the surface where they had been hurriedly abandoned. Corstophine led her to a chair, watched her as she placed hands on shaking knees. He shut the door, closing off the sound of hushed voices, camera clicks. She looked up at him, tears forming in her eyes.

"She just ran in front of it. I couldn't do anything to stop her. It happened so quickly." The words came in small torrents, forced out before she started to sob – body shaking in wracking spasms.

"It's OK." Corstophine spoke the words automatically, realising it was anything but OK. Even hardened professionals took suicide badly: the waste of a life, the feeling of guilt that they could have done something to help if only they had known.

The shock of someone dying violently in front of you isn't something that can ever be fully prepared for. Trainee doctors at least were broken in gently – given a cadaver, the person's life story told to them before they start, so the donated body is afforded respect. Maybe start with a hand – sawn off, dissected, tendons pulled to make fingers grasp at air; until by the end of their studies each one is given the brain to hold, the weight of it somehow once containing memories, emotions, personality.

The body on the tracks was an anatomy lesson laid out in chaotic and bloody disorder; entrails spread greyly over steel and stone stained red. A human jigsaw that bore little resemblance to the young life this puzzle once contained.

"Tell me what happened. Take your time." Corstophine

waited for the woman in front of him to stop shuddering, held his handkerchief towards her as she raised her face.

"Thank you." Her voice came as a whisper as she dabbed at her eyes, switching his handkerchief to her nose as she blew wetly into it.

She suddenly looked at him, eyes wetly apologetic.

"Oh, I'm sorry."

"Doesn't matter. You keep it." He smiled in what he hoped was a friendly way. "We're issued police handkerchiefs for this very reason."

She smiled weakly back, aware of his poor attempt at humour. The breath she took was deep but not as shuddering as before.

"I noticed her because of the stick. We keep a close eye on anyone with disabilities, just in case they need a hand – but she was a regular."

"Do you know her name?"

"No. But she took the Glasgow train every Monday." She looked up at him, almost pleading from tear-streaked eyes. "That's why I didn't offer to help her. She knew the platform, knew where the edge was. I don't understand why it happened."

Fresh tears started to flow, her shaking hand ineffectually holding his handkerchief against the flood.

"You're not to blame." Corstophine's eyes sought out Frankie through the small window in the room, saw her taking statements from some people in the crowd. "Just take me through it step by step if you're able."

Her shaking eventually subsided again.

"The Queen Street train was approaching. I looked up and down the platform in case anyone was acting strangely." She looked at him hopefully. "It's one of the things we're trained for, you know – in case anyone does anything… stupid."

Corstophine nodded encouragement. "Go on."

"She must have known the train was almost here." She paused, reliving the moment, aware that this was no accident. "She threw herself off the platform. There was nothing anyone could have done! The driver braked but the wheels went over her."

She looked at him in wonder. "There was silence. Just the brakes scraping and the wheels sliding on the tracks. I ran over to see if I could do anything to help but I could only see bits of her under the train – and the blood."

The door opened and the station supervisor entered. Corstophine exchanged a brief nod before engaging with her again.

"That's been a great help. I'll be in touch if we need anything else, you just take it easy. You've had a terrible shock." Corstophine turned to the supervisor. "Can you get me the recording from the platform cameras? It looks like a suicide, nothing anyone could have done."

He made to leave the two of them alone. "You may want to sit with her awhile until she's well enough to go home."

"I'll keep an eye on her, detective, and don't worry, I'll be in touch." He forestalled Corstophine's next words.

"OK. Thanks." The words felt inadequate as he rejoined Frankie; the crowd dissipating as if by magic, but Corstophine knew they merely wanted to avoid getting involved. He had sympathy with that at least. Ahead of him lay the grim task of identifying the dead girl and then having to tell her parents. It was a duty that fell to him as the senior officer, and one that never came any easier, no matter how many times he'd had to impart the news. Somehow, the younger they were, the more it took out of him.

CHAPTER 4
Witches Coven

The large Edwardian house stood on its own in half an acre of land, mostly given over to trees and shrubs through which the original garden designer had woven meandering herringbone brick paths. The front of the house was given over to parking, with a well-manicured hedge kept just above head height and affording privacy from any rare passers-by. The back of the house looked out over a large lawn, illuminated at this late hour by the yellow flicker of flame torches embedded in flower beds bordering the grass. At the centre of the lawn stood an ornate metal ornament; a sphere formed out of curved stainless-steel sections, an arrow piercing the structure and aimed heavenwards at the night sky. A waning moon hung in the cloudless night, a sliver of silver resting crescent-like on black velvet cloth.

Hidden amongst the trees, the voyeur had been watching since before dusk whilst the women decorated the sculpture with yellow sheaves of wheat, branches of rowan, berries shining as red as drops of blood as they caught the last of the sun. A table had been carried out of the house with shared merriment, then breads, wines, apples, and cheeses were brought out to cover the table surface. It had taken a strong effort of will not to succumb to his hunger and raid the table when the women had re-entered the house, leaving the garden prepared for whatever party was to follow.

He stood there undecided. Should he leave now, and

risk being seen by one of the unexpected visitors, or wait until the party was in full swing? He decided to wait.

With the onset of darkness proper, the women filed out of the house, transformed now in flowing robes and foliage crowns. The voyeur's breathing became shallow and rapid, tongue darting over lips turned suddenly dry. He pulled his phone out, set it to record and pointed it at the women in the clearing – this was shaping up to be a rewarding night.

The woman heading the procession wore small horns on her head, silver paint glistening on her cheeks. They joined hands, forming a loose circle around the lawn centrepiece, speaking some words he couldn't catch. As they fell silent, they circled slowly left, completely in step with one another. The circle moved faster, their movements became more wanton, their voices louder. He caught occasional glimpses of thighs and breasts as their loose garments exposed flesh until they may as well have been dancing completely naked around the metal orb. The early evening still retained the warmth of the day, a breeze just gentle enough to rustle leaves and detach early sacrificial victims to winter – curling and pirouetting before impacting the ground with the slightest of sounds. The women suddenly froze – had he been seen? Without any signal that he could detect, they dropped to the ground, all except the woman wearing horns who stood as if in supplication to the waning moon. The women on the ground raised their heads from the cold earth and their arms towards the sky, swaying like some giant pale sea anemone caught in a cross-current. They chanted as one in a low, rhythmic undertone, quite unlike any sound he had heard before.

"Day turns to night, and life turns to death, and the Dark Mother teaches us to dance.

Hecate, Demeter, Kali, Nemesis, Morrighan, Tiamet, bringers of destruction,

You who embody the Crone, I honour you as the earth goes dark, and as the world slowly dies."

Any eroticism he'd felt as the women had danced in front of him evaporated as the words reached his ears. The ritual was more like a display of strength, leaving him feeling emasculated by their strange behaviour. Whatever had just occurred appeared to be over as the women laughed and joked, pulling robes tightly together before heading towards the table to pour glasses of wine. He waited until their chatter was loud enough to cover his footsteps, then made his way back towards the road. Just a short run across the gravel, each step sounding loud to his ears until he reached the pavement beyond. He risked a quick glance behind, and the blood froze in his veins. A dark figure stood at the edge of the trees, red eyes shining unnaturally bright in the glow from the house windows. If they'd raised the devil, he was looking straight at him. His response was primeval. A nascent scream strangled in his throat as his body demanded oxygen to fuel muscles already powering him away from danger. He ran without thought, feet pounding pavement and eyes wide with fear.

PC Bill McAdam was working a late Monday shift, calculating how much the additional 10% uplift would add to his monthly salary, when his interest was piqued by a man running full tilt down the pavement in front of his patrol car. Too late to be catching a train or bus for work, so what was his rush? The guy was running fast, like he was in a panic. He certainly didn't conform to the usual lycra-clad runner that was becoming a more familiar sight on the pavements. The PC shadowed him, cruising quietly behind and checking his rear-view mirror for signs of any pursuit. Nothing. The street was deserted this far out of town. In this area the houses tended towards mansions, large gardens spreading themselves languorously along the road. These occupants didn't take buses or walk, and they certainly didn't run like this. PC McAdam turned on the blues, illuminating the runner in strobing light. He stopped immediately, bent double as if fighting for air and turned to face the police car with a look of relief. McAdam lowered the passenger window as he pulled up to the pavement, taking the time to have a good look as he drew to a halt.

The guy was no athlete, that was obvious from the sound of his breathing. He'd had to deal with people having asthmatic attacks before and they had made less noise than this. McAdam automatically began mentally transcribing details in readiness for writing them up later in his notebook. Age mid 40's: average height, round face, slightly pudgy and sweating profusely. Thinning ginger hair, comb-over hanging listlessly down one side of his head, exposing a circular bald pate. Dressed entirely in dark clothing: black trousers, black jacket, black sneakers. That looked like a black beanie in his jacket pocket. He may as well have carried a placard saying burglar.

"Evening, sir. Can I ask what the emergency is?"

Spittle flecked the man's lips. He wiped them with the back of his hand, his breath coming in tortured bursts.

"They've raised the devil!" The man's voice was hysterical, the pitch high as the words forced their way out of a throat constricted by lack of air.

McAdam had been in the force for long enough that nothing surprised him anymore.

"I see, sir. And whereabouts did you see this diabolical event?"

The man stared wild-eyed back down the road. "The

big house, the one at the end. They're all witches or something."

McAdam checked his rear-view mirror again. Something in the guy's wild stare made him half expect to see somebody in a Halloween costume, it was only a few weeks away after all.

"The last house on the left?" McAdam queried. This was the home address of Patricia McCoach and one of the houses he'd been tasked with keeping an eye on. The team brief mentioned something about a threat being made to the McCoach family, nothing to back it up, just Corstophine wanting their houses checked now and then. "What's your name?"

"Stevie. Steven Lyle." He started shaking.

McAdam turned around, looking back up the road and seeing nothing. Something had spooked the guy.

"OK, Steven. Just take a few deep breaths. What were you doing at the house – are you a friend of the family?"

His eyes briefly held the policeman's before finding the pavement more worthy of attention.

"I'm just out for a walk, nothing else. I must have been mistaken. Sorry to take your time, officer."

Whoever Steven Lyle was, he was as much a poker player as he was an athlete.

"Do you have any ID on you, sir?"

His expression turned to worried in a split second. "Am I under arrest?"

"Not for going out for an evening run – unless there's anything else you'd like to tell me?"

Guilt was written all over his face. "No. Nothing else."

He fumbled in his jacket, extricating a driving licence from his wallet. McAdam took the licence from the comfort of his driving seat, stretching an arm out towards the open window. The photograph matched a younger, thinner and more hirsute version of the man standing awkwardly beside the patrol car.

"12 Strathyre Avenue. Is that your present address, Steven?"

"Yes, officer." He shuffled from foot to foot, shooting worried glances back up the road in between guilty looks at the constable.

"Here you are, sir. Have a pleasant evening." McAdam handed the driving licence back, watching sheer relief flood across his face. "We'll be in touch if I hear there's been anything amiss tonight – just to clear you from our enquiries."

"Oh. No, nothing amiss. I'll be off then?" He spoke as if asking permission, receiving a curt nod from McAdam in return.

He turned off the emergency lights, watching Steven Lyle walking away until he turned a corner and was lost to sight. Pulling his notebook out of a top pocket, Bill laboriously wrote down Steven's details, together with the time and location, before turning the car back to the McCoach house. From the comfort of the road, nothing looked out of place. Five cars filled the drive, lights shone from downstairs windows. He could hear music and laughter coming from the house, nothing that gave him any cause for alarm. He added this to his notebook, just so Corstophine could see he'd taken the brief seriously, before continuing his circuit around the town.

In the shadows a figure watched as the patrol car drove away. He was patient. There would be other opportunities when the house wasn't so busy. He needed her to be on her own for what he had planned.

CHAPTER 5
Box of Spanners

Corstophine left for Patricia McCoach's house immediately after reading PC Bill McAdam's report on Tuesday morning. He had made a note of Steven Lyle's name, not that they had anything on him, but Corstorphine had felt something akin to paranoia ever since hearing of Patricia's bizarre allegation. When she answered his knock, her curious face peering around the door, Corstophine's concerns immediately eased.

"Sorry to bother you, Ms McCoach, but one of our officers was driving past your house yesterday evening and saw a man acting suspiciously. I was just checking to see if everything was alright?"

Patricia had appeared startled for the briefest of moments before fixing him with a piercing stare.

"And you are?" The question snapped at him so quickly he had to replay the words in slow motion to understand her.

"I'm sorry. DI James Corstophine." He held his ID in full view. What was he thinking? He should have started by identifying himself. "I was a friend of Jack's."

Her head inclined to one side, birdlike, inspecting him. The door opened wider. She was wearing a large smock, paint-spattered in colours that matched the multicoloured blouse underneath. A pair of paint brushes were held in her other hand, splayed between her fingers.

"I'm creating," she announced simply. "Come in."

She led the way into the house leaving a waft of patchouli

in her wake. A substantial oak staircase dominated the hallway, stretching up to a half landing illuminated by a stained glass window. Patricia passed the stairs and turned into the first doorway, entering a large room flooded with morning light. It would have been the drawing room in Edwardian days. As he followed her in, Corstophine could tell she had taken the designation more literally. Paintings lay carelessly propped against the walls, one on top of the other. Patricia's perfume fought an unsuccessful battle with the smell of fresh paint and turpentine. Bare wooden floorboards were covered in splashes of colour whilst pots full of brushes and tubes of paint lay on every available surface. A large canvas dominated the room, propped on an easel. She approached the work with the same birdlike intensity she had displayed with Corstophine, head held critically to one side before she darted forward and attacked the canvas with jabbing motions from one of the brushes. Patricia just as quickly stood back to regard her work, DI Corstophine all but forgotten. She placed the spare brush on the table beside her, swapping it for a palette board preloaded with smears of vivid colour.

Corstophine stood in the doorway, casting a quizzical look at the paintings resting against the walls before focussing on the work in front of them. A circle of near naked women stood in a clearing, arms raised towards a crescent moon. Patricia was adding dark streaks in vertical lines, randomly as far as he could tell. She worked with an intensity he found unsettling, almost manic in her movements. *I'm not mad.* The words Frankie had repeated from her interview came back to him as he watched her.

"You came to the station yesterday, talked to DC Frankie McKenzie?"

She paused her onslaught, grabbing a tube of red paint and smearing it directly from the tube onto the canvas before standing back to critically examine the new blotches.

"Yes. Did you find anything suspicious about Jack's death?" She turned to face him, eyes interrogating his with an unsettling intensity.

Corstophine held her gaze, trying unsuccessfully to fathom the hidden message behind her pale blue eyes.

"I'm sorry. Forensics merely confirmed what we'd been told. He'd had a heart attack, more than likely brought on by the strenuous climb."

Her expression remained the same. Corstophine wondered if this might be how a fish would feel under the beady eyes of a heron. A fairly colourful and rotund heron in this case. He dismissed the thought before it could take hold.

"What made you think he may have been poisoned, Patricia?"

"I told the policewoman. Jack told me."

"In a séance?"

"Yes. In a séance. Look, officer, you may not be a believer but there are more things in heaven and earth… I believed Jack when he told me he'd been poisoned. If your forensics didn't find anything, then they didn't look hard enough!"

Corstophine listened uncomfortably. The stuff about messages from beyond was bad enough but she'd hit a nerve with forensics. He was fairly certain they'd not done much of a thorough job either.

"We can't begin an investigation without some hard facts. You mentioned someone was out to get the family – what did you mean?"

It was Patricia's turn to look uncomfortable.

"I just get the feeling something isn't quite right."

Corstophine waited. The silence grew between them like a palpable object, another presence in the room.

"I've felt someone watching me at night. I can't explain it. You know that feeling you sometimes have, and you catch someone looking right back at you?"

"You've seen someone in the garden?"

She shook her head irritably. "No, nothing as simple as that." Patricia seemed to be having an internal struggle, biting her lips to prevent words from escaping. "It's not just me. Emma – Jack's wife – she's felt it too."

"Is there anyone who'd want to harm the family?" Corstophine was struggling to find anything rational that he could act on.

"You'll have to talk to Emma." She said the words with an air of finality. The discussion was closed.

"What will Emma be able to tell me?"

"I'll show you to the door, DI Corstophine."

Patricia martialled him out of the room, forcibly ushering him through the door like flotsam carried before a multicoloured tsunami.

"Talk to Emma!"

The door slammed shut, leaving Corstophine standing bewildered on the driveway and wondering what hadn't been said. Once back in the car, he raised Frankie on the radio.

"What's your location, Frankie, anywhere near the McCoach house?"

"Lamb and I are just patrolling, sir, keeping our eyes skinned for any catalytic thefts. We're about ten minutes away. Is there a problem?"

"I don't think so. I've just had the strangest conversation with your Patricia – she seems to think that Emma may be able to suggest someone who might have it in for the family."

"Is this a credible threat, sir?" Frankie cut straight to the point as always.

Corstophine gave a wry smile. "The whole thing is unsubstantiated, could just be an overactive imagination, but have a word with Emma. See if she's able to provide further detail. It's probably a complete waste of our time but I don't want to take any chances."

DC Frankie McKenzie pulled into the driveway of Jack McCoach's house, PC Lamb beside her, riding shotgun as he annoyingly liked to call it. The drive swept through an impressive avenue of beech trees, leaves in full technicolour reds and yellows as they caught the morning sun. The house lay in ornate gothic splendour in front of them, turrets and spires revealed as they broke cover from the last of the trees. It was a pile worthy of the richest family in the town – designed to impress.

"Bit *Wuthering Heights*." Lamb's comment followed the reveal.

"I think you're going for *Jane Eyre*." Frankie replied.

Lamb's blank expression was evidence enough that this level of literary discourse was wasted on him. The door was opened by Jack's son, Robb. He looked startled to see the police at his door, swiftly recovering to offer them a cheery welcome.

"Good morning. How can I help you? Do come in." He stood back and gestured them inside. "Can I get you tea, coffee?"

"That won't be necessary, sir." Frankie interposed before Lamb placed his order, watching his raised hand lowering out of the corner of her eye.

"I was hoping to have a word with your mother. If she's available?"

"Can I ask what this is about? She's not to be disturbed."

"I just wanted to ask her about your aunt."

A distant scream pierced the house, undulating on and on for what seemed an eternity until it was abruptly silenced. Frankie and Lamb exchanged a glance before returning their focus to Robb. He stood there, unconcerned, not bothering to turn around as a nurse hurried past them before running up the stairs two at a time.

"Is someone ill?" Frankie asked.

"Oh. That's my sister, Phoebe. She has…" he paused, searching for words. "She's not well – mentally. We look after her here rather than leaving her in a hospital."

Robb could see neither Frankie nor Lamb were entirely convinced.

"It's OK, honestly. We've been looking after her for years. The nurse will calm her down." He turned, leading the way down the hall. "Follow me. I'll ask my mother if she feels well enough to join us in the living room."

They followed him down the hall, passing several closed doors before turning into a room larger than the entire ground floor of most modern houses. The windows looked out over the town below, an expanse of lawn dropping down to tennis courts until more trees screened the immediate environs.

"Take a seat, I'll be with you in a minute." Robb smiled before turning sharply on his heel and leaving them alone.

"I'll do the talking. You take notes," Frankie spoke quietly as footsteps sounded in the hallway.

Lamb nodded as Robb reappeared, leading his mother into the room. Emma McCoach would have been a beauty in her youth. High cheekbones still gave her face a model's definition, but now her skin allowed gravity to do its worst. Dark hair held traces of grey, thinning sufficiently to show glimpses of scalp as she self-consciously ran an agitated hand through the loose strands falling over her forehead.

The frown she gave her son as she brushed his helping arm away created a multitude of brow lines.

"I can manage, thank you." Her voice was severe, dismissive. "You can leave us and shut the door on the way out."

Frankie noticed the smile Robb gave didn't reach his eyes.

Emma McCoach pointedly waited until he'd closed the door behind him before addressing the police.

"What can I do for you?"

"Mrs McCoach, Emma – can I call you that?"

Emma tilted her head in agreement.

"I've been asked to talk to you about your sister-in-law, Patricia. Our Detective Inspector, James Corstophine, was talking to her earlier this morning."

"Yes?"

Frankie hurried on. "Patricia suggested you may know of someone who wanted to cause harm to your family. Would you have any idea what she could have meant by that?"

Frankie saw the look that crossed Emma's face before she was able to conceal it. It looked like fear.

"Nonsense. The woman's mad. She has the McCoach curse."

Frankie's interest quickened. "What do you mean by that – the McCoach curse?"

Emma frowned. "I'm sorry, this is not a good time. I'm not feeling well at present, with Jack's death and everything. You'll have to excuse me."

She stood up to leave the room.

"So you're not aware of any threat against your family, anyone who may bear a grudge?"

Emma paused, casting a look over her shoulder. "I wouldn't pay too much attention to anything Patricia says, officer. She lives in a world of her own, sufficiently insulated from the normal cares and concerns of the rest of us to sometimes feel that she has to create her own dramas. We've learned to ignore her for the most part. I'd recommend that you do the same."

"One last thing, Mrs McCoach. Was that your daughter we heard earlier?"

Emma looked trapped, switching her glance between the policewoman and the door.

"Yes. My daughter, Phoebe. She's not entirely herself. You must excuse me – you can find your own way out."

She almost ran from the room, leaving Frankie and Lamb to follow in her wake. Robb was nowhere to be seen.

They closed the immense front door behind them, the sound reverberating around the huge house like someone shutting the door to a tomb.

"Fuck me!" Lamb exclaimed once they were safely back in the patrol car. "Mad as a bag of spanners."

Frankie held her own counsel but couldn't find fault with Lamb's initial analysis.

CHAPTER 6
County Lines

Corstophine met Frankie back at the police station. He motioned her into his office as he sat contemplating the month's crime figures. The visit to Patricia's house had been a complete waste of time, only serving to confirm his initial suspicion that the woman was unhinged – maybe even in need of professional help.

"Did you have any joy with the family?"

Frankie chose her words with care, unwilling to cross the politically correct divide as easily as Lamb managed to accomplish on an almost daily basis.

"I spoke to the wife, sir, Emma McCoach. She claimed not to know of anyone who might hold a grudge towards the family or wish them any harm."

Corstophine picked up on the word 'claim'. "Go on."

"I had the strong impression she was hiding something. When I mentioned Patricia had suggested we speak to her, she looked panicked for a second, before she as good as told us the woman was mad."

"She may have a point," Corstophine added drily.

"That's not all, sir. They have a daughter, Phoebe, who is apparently mentally unwell and cared for at the house by a nurse. We heard her screaming the house down when I was talking to Emma." Frankie thought back to the son's reaction when he was told to leave the room. "Do you know him well, the son? He's in the hillwalking club, isn't he?"

"Why do you ask?"

"Well, nothing to go on here, sir, but there didn't appear to be any love lost between him and his mother."

Corstophine brushed the comment away immediately. "I think you'll find the McCoach family are as miserly with affection as they are with their money, seems to come with the territory. He's just a bit focussed, a businessman like his dad was. If anything, he strikes me as the religious sort. Gave an impassioned reading at the funeral service."

"I see, sir."

Corstophine raised his eyebrows, seeking for anything further. Nothing was forthcoming.

"So, this whole 'somebody's out to get the McCoach family' is a figment of an overworked imagination?"

"Looks that way, sir."

Corstophine sighed. Maybe he was just being oversensitive.

"Alright. Let's get back to something that is real. These petty crime figures. They were through the roof last week, even discounting the catalytic converters. Purses stolen and petty cash nicked from shops overnight. I've a string of reports from the geriatric brigade claiming bogus workers have taken money for jobs that were never done. What's driving this mini crime wave?"

Frankie had a good idea, but no hard evidence to back it up.

"I think someone may have moved in and is pushing drugs, sir. I've not anything substantial to back it up but the patterns are there. We've seen some new addicts appear on the streets and I've had a few parents contact me, worrying about a change in their children's behaviour."

"You think the county line thing has reached this far?" Corstophine found it difficult to believe their small highland town could fall prey to such an urban crime.

"Drugs have always been here, sir. It's just that now the gangs are more organised and hitting us with stronger gear."

He frowned at the crime figures displayed on the screen, as if the reason for them would be listed there as well.

"OK, we'll have the team brief at 14:00. If someone's pushing drugs, we need to nip it in the bud."

He bent back down over his computer keyboard, her signal to leave.

"Sir." She closed the door.

PC Lamb was also at his desk, smoothing down his hair as he checked the small mirror he kept beside the monitor. Frankie resisted the urge to pass comment.

"What's the old man saying?"

"I don't think DI Corstophine would appreciate being referred to in that manner, Phil."

Lamb shrugged, unconcerned. "Are we doing anything else with the McCoach family or is that it?"

"Just keep an eye on them whenever you're in the area. Both houses." She sat at her desk, logged on and wrote up the visit to Emma's house. "We've enough to do without having to chase unsubstantiated claims."

At 14:00, Corstophine called them all together for a weekly briefing. Frankie and Lamb stayed at their desks, Sergeant Hamish McKee vacating his usual post at the front desk to join them. PC Bill McAdam stood near the kitchen, anxious to make his first coffee of the day as his shift started.

"Thanks, everyone." Corstophine fiddled with his laptop until the latest crime figures appeared as a graph on the large office wall screen. "These are the most recent figures and as you can see, we've had a bit of a crime wave. Frankie's thinking there may be a gang pushing drugs – keep your eyes open for any dealing, especially around the railway station. It's a favourite spot for pushers. I want us to run two-man patrols for the next few weeks, just in case."

PC McAdam raised a hand. "Does this mean I'm off nights, sir?"

"No, Bill. In fact, I'd like Phil to join you, starting Thursday late shift so you have back up. Can you manage three days late shift starting Thursday, Lamb?"

"Anything to help old Bill, sir." PC Lamb replied enthusiastically. PC McAdam's expression managed to convey both long-suffering and threat as he fixed Lamb with a stare.

"OK. It means we'll be spread a bit thin on the ground for the next week or so, but if we're to stand a chance of catching these characters, we'll have to work in pairs. Has anyone any concerns to raise?"

McAdam raised his hand again. "Do you want me to check up on the guy I saw acting suspiciously Monday night, sir?" He consulted his notebook, "Steven Lyle?"

"We've had no reports of any crimes committed in the area over the weekend and I checked on Patricia McCoach myself this morning. He doesn't show up on the database, so nothing for us to do there. If we see him prowling around again, then we'll maybe have another look at him. No, we need to concentrate our efforts on finding any drug pushers. Ask the usual suspects, see if we can't get some info. If there's organised crime moving into the town, I want them found and dealt with."

"Sir," the team chorused with one voice as Corstophine made his way back into his office. An email notification chimed as he shut the dividing door. It was from Robb McCoach.

Hi Jim,

we've decided to scatter my father's ashes on the summit of Sgurr Thuilm, seeing as how he never made it to the top. Planning on going this Thursday, then we're going to do some hills, make a two day trip out of it and camp out in the bothies. Thought my dad would have liked the idea of leaving part of himself on each peak. If you can get the time off, you'd be welcome to join us. There's three of us so far, Bryan and Sandy are coming along. Let me know if you can make it.

Best,
Robb.

Corstophine frowned. It would have been a good opportunity to do a bit of hillwalking, but the possibility of the town falling prey to organised drug dealers was not something he could ignore. He typed a response, expressing his regret that he couldn't take the time off and wished them good weather. On second thoughts, he added that he'd try to make the first peak with them, take most of Thursday as paid leave and see them off from Sgurr Thuilm. He pressed send, watching the screen as the email went its electronic way. He didn't really think he could cope with being stuck in close proximity with the hillwalking club members for more than a day anyway – this was as good a compromise as he could muster.

The exercise will do you good, Jamie, and you really should try harder with people. I'm not going to be around for ever.

He glanced over to where his wife stood, looking down

at him with that sad smile she used whenever she gently castigated him for his social failings.

"Aye, lass, I know," he voiced to himself as her image faded from memory. What troubled him more than anything was the difficulty he had in remembering her face – the features blurring indistinctly into an insubstantial image whenever he struggled to bring her back into any kind of focus. *I'm not going to be around forever.*

He leaned back in his seat, staring up at the office ceiling in contemplation. The last year had been the strangest time any of them had lived through. First the murders, then the Covid-19 virus arriving without warning, leaving streets deserted and the police left with nothing to do except turn tourists away and enforce social distancing. Since the lockdown had eased, crime had quickly returned and then surpassed pre-pandemic levels as unemployment rocketed and businesses folded. The compulsory wearing of face masks had proved a boon to the criminal fraternity, making it socially acceptable to conceal identity in shops, garages, even banks. The whole country gave the impression of turning into the Wild West – perhaps Lamb's ready adoption of cowboy memes was prescient.

The past year had seen people isolated from friends and family, their older relatives cut down by the merciless progression of a virus nobody could cure. No wonder the suicide rate had increased. The thought of suicides brought the image of the young woman's body back into focus, carelessly broken and eviscerated by the train's steel wheels. He'd seen too many deaths – and yet this one threatened to stay with him. Why would a young woman throw herself under a train? Didn't she have people who loved her, have any hope for the future? Corstophine sighed and focussed on his computer. Sometimes the job demanded too much of him, too much from all of them.

CHAPTER 7
Artwork

Patricia's eyes snapped open. Thick curtains obscured any light from the distant streetlamps, so all she could see of her bedroom was inky blackness. What could have woken her? The faint outline of the room came reassuringly into focus as her eyes grew accustomed to the darkness. She strained her ears to catch any sound that was out of the ordinary. Was that someone else breathing? Her eyes opened wider in an unconscious effort to penetrate the darkness. There was her large Victorian wardrobe, the mirror showing as a lighter shade of black. There, the bulk of her chest of drawers. There, next to her bed, was that someone standing over her? She dismissed the thought as a night terror, persuading herself that maybe she was still asleep, that this was but the precursor to a nightmare. The figure suddenly moved, so quickly she had no time to pull her arms out from under the covers. She was too frightened to scream, her throat paralysed with shock. Too slow to react as something hit the side of her head with such force that she blacked out immediately, spiralling into a darkness so deep and profound that no vestige of consciousness remained.

In her bedroom, the intruder turned on a light. Patricia lay on her bed, head twisted at an awkward angle following the force of the blow. He dropped a heavy cosh onto her prostrate body, then with a tenderness that contrasted utterly with his previous action, gently straightened her head back into position on the pillow, smoothing her hair down so she looked completely at rest. For a long moment, he stared at her face, searching for something he scarcely understood before leaving her unresponsive body and running quickly downstairs. In the drawing room, he reached for the two paintbrushes left soaking in a jam jar, returning to her bed where he knelt over her body. With delicate care, he lifted an eyelid, exposing the white of an eye rolled back into her head and forced the brush handle past the initial resistance into the jelly-like liquid of her eye, until the tip impacted into bone and muscle. With careful precision he repeated the process until two slender wooden sticks protruded from each socket, the eyes pierced and leaking clear fluid and blood onto the pristine white linen pillowcase underneath. He admired the contrast of red blood on white bedding, enjoying the slow flow of blood tears gently issuing out from ruined eyes. Reluctantly, he left the room, walking quickly back down the stairs and entering the drawing room before gathering up her latest canvas. He returned for the easel, setting the canvas reverentially into place within easy reach of her body.

Working carefully and without haste, he pulled the sticks wetly from her eyes – spinning them around to offer bristles to blood-filled sockets. Once fully loaded with gore, he applied broad red strokes to the canvas. Line after bloody red line trailed viscous liquid across the painting, primed again and again from the red wells in her face. Finally satisfied that the artwork was complete, the brushes were once again replaced in their macabre paint pots. He casually wiped his hands on a turpentine-soaked rag as he admired his work, turned the bedroom light off and left the house once more in complete darkness.

Patricia lay deeply unconscious until long after the sun had risen, blood coagulating darkly around her head. At

9:30 a.m. the cleaner arrived, surprised to find the front door ajar but supposing Patricia was out in the garden. She shouted a welcome, heard no response and let herself in. It was the same daily routine: clean the hall, ignore the drawing room where Patricia did her 'creating', tidy up the kitchen and wash up the cups and dishes left on the counter before making her way up the stairs. Now equipped with duster and polish, she set to cleaning the bannister, exclaiming with some annoyance at the dark smudges left on the wood. They took a lot of hard rubbing and extra polish before she was able to remove them. Now for the carpets. The vacuum cleaner was plugged in and she started working her way around the ground floor before tackling the stairs. Still no sign of Patricia. Nothing to concern her, Patricia often spent hours in her garden. At the top of the stairs, she rested for a moment, old bones exhausted by the effort involved in heaving the hefty vacuum cleaner upstairs. Time for the bedrooms. She knocked on Patricia's bedroom door just in case she was still in bed and, getting no response, pushed the door open wide before it knocked against the easel. *Don't say she's starting to paint in her bedroom – even more work for me to do!* The thought died as she took in the sight in front of her. Her screams shattered the morning as she fled down the stairs, running out of the house and along the driveway until she could run no more.

Corstophine knew a major incident had occurred by the look on Hamish's face, moving unnaturally fast to push open the door to his office without bothering to knock.

"It's that Patricia McCoach woman. One of her neighbours has just called. Patricia's cleaner is in hysterics, saying she's been found murdered in her bed."

Frankie leapt up from her desk, grabbing a couple of

forensic suits from the cupboard and joined Corstophine as he left his office.

"Call forensics, Hamish, we need them there as soon as. Check with the hospital, see if anyone's called it in, and if not, make sure they send a team immediately. You have the address?"

"Yes, sir, in the log. The caller said they've already sent for an ambulance."

They left the station in a rush, hitting the siren before they'd even left the car park. He hoped to hell it was a burglary gone wrong, someone just lashing out in a panic when they were discovered. At the back of his mind, he replayed Patricia's statement – the words Frankie had typed up following her interview. *He said he was coming for the family.*

An ambulance was already waiting in the driveway when they arrived. Corstophine and Frankie pulled on latex gloves before taking the stairs two at a time, pulling to a halt at the sight waiting for them. Two medics were working on Patricia, heart monitor beeping a steady accompaniment to their urgent staccato speech. A large white bandage waited in one of the medic's hands as she waited for the other to carefully extract bloodied paintbrushes from each socket, a wet squelch accompanying each reluctant release against the suction of clotting blood, before laying them on a surgical cloth. She raised Patricia's sightless head in readiness for a bandage to be applied before acknowledging the detective's presence.

"We'll be another ten minutes at least. She's had a bad head wound, maybe even a broken skull, and there's no telling how far these wooden brushes went in. We need to stabilise her before we can move her." The medic didn't even bother looking round, concentrating instead on attending to her patient.

"Will she able to tell us what happened?" Corstophine didn't hold much hope for a positive answer, his attention fixed on the horrific sight in front of him.

"She's out cold. Trauma wound to the side of her head, possible brain damage – she'll not be talking for a while." The medic indicated the cosh lying on the bed, glanced back down at her patient and started wrapping the bandage around Patricia's head. Corstophine dragged his eyes away as the pristine white bandage stained red.

"Check the house, Frankie. I'll see if I can find anything in the gardens – there's nothing we can do here until the medics are through." Corstophine felt sick at the sight in front of him. For someone to blind her with her own paintbrushes, this either had to be personal, a psychopath, or both. They met back up on the landing, confirming neither had detected any sign of an intruder.

Corstophine took up position beside the bedroom door, trying to make sense of the macabre scene in front of him. The ambulance paramedics were still working on Patricia, the stained bandage taking the place of two bloody paintbrushes. A drip had been inserted into her arm, oxygen mask over her face. They carefully lifted her onto a stretcher, drip placed on a metal hook as they manoeuvred the body out of the door.

"Is she going to make it?" Corstophine saw her facemask mist with breath.

"Too early to say. We'll get her stabilised. As long as she doesn't suffer complications from the head wound, she should pull through."

"Her eyes?" Frankie asked.

A shake of the head confirmed that Patricia was never going to be able to see again.

"We need to get suited up." Corstophine followed the medics out of the house. Another car pulled into the drive as they left, the driver giving Corstophine a cheerful wave as he parked.

"Hello, Corstophine, what have you got for us this time?" He recognised the driver – one of the newer forensic technicians from Inverness. Paul, or Peter. It didn't matter.

"You must have broken a few speed limits?" Corstophine replied, genuinely puzzled how anyone could have arrived from Inverness so quickly.

Paul or Peter pulled on his protective forensics clothing, grabbing a camera and watching the body being loaded into the ambulance with interest.

"I live locally. I was just on my way to work when they called me. Can I check the victim?"

"You'll have to do that later." Corstophine forestalled him before he moved in on Patricia, the look of disappointment at losing a valuable source of evidence clear in his face. "She was attacked in her bedroom, top of the stairs, first left."

Corstophine took his time pulling on the forensics oversuit, replaying the scene in his mind's eye. It wasn't something he was likely to forget in a hurry. Whoever had attacked her had deliberately blinded the woman. Was that so she couldn't ID the assailant or some sort of deliberate mutilation? They made their way back up to the scene of crime; the white-suited forensics technician standing over her bloodied bed, checking photographs on his camera.

"You have everything you need?" Corstophine was anxious to check the bedroom.

"Aye. Don't touch anything, we still need to dust for prints and try for any DNA. Someone will be with us in the next hour." He pointed to the two wooden brushes, lying in a pool of congealing blood on a surgical wipe. "What's with the brushes?"

Corstophine explained as the camera was brought back

into play, the brushes taken from a variety of angles as if the guy was entering a photography competition.

"Are you done?" Frankie wanted in as well.

"Aye. I'll wait in my car for the van to arrive."

The technician left the room, gathering the cosh sealed in a clear plastic bag. An ambulance siren started up in the driveway. Corstophine crossed over to the bedroom window, watching as the ambulance exited onto the road and accelerated away. He replayed the scene of the medic pulling each paintbrush out of her eyes, the sound of clotting blood reluctantly loosening its hold. He felt momentarily faint, holding onto the window frame for support.

"Jesus!" Frankie almost gagged. The iron tang of blood competed with the smell of turpentine and medical wipes, but it was the painting that had caught her eye. The scene showed women dancing semi-naked around a figure in a woodland setting. The figure had been painted roughly in red, daubed over some garden sculpture that had previously taken central position. The primitively rendered figure was undoubtedly a devil, red horns sprouting from an evil head. A forked tail left no room for interpretation.

"Is that her blood?" Frankie pointed at the figure, the paint still wet in places where it had been applied thickly.

Corstophine stared at the painting. It was the one she'd been working on when he had visited her yesterday. The figure in red was new.

"Looks like it, Frankie."

"What sort of person does something like that?" She asked the question rhetorically, not expecting an answer.

"Someone who's either out of their head on drugs…"

Frankie waited in vain for Corstophine to finish before mentally filling in for him, *or just completely mad.*

"What are your thoughts?" Corstophine turned away

from his contemplation of the vandalised artwork. Frankie dragged her eyes away from the blood-streaked canvas to look him in the face. She noticed new lines around his eyes, a world-weariness in his expression she had not seen before.

"I'd say it was premeditated, sir. I don't think this is the behaviour of an opportunistic thief. Whacking her across the head may be construed as an act of panic but this..." She didn't have to spell it out for him. "Patricia mentioned that someone was out to get her – the entire family. Do you think she knew the attacker?"

Corstophine had been thinking along the same lines.

"We need to talk to her, if and when she's in a fit state. In the meantime, I want to have a word with her sister-in-law – Emma McCoach. You said that you thought she was hiding something?"

Frankie hesitated. Emma had known something, she was sure of it. Something that had frightened her.

"We need to inform her about Patricia, sir. Maybe if we both went?"

He nodded in agreement. "I also want to interview that character that McAdam found running away from here two nights ago."

"Steven Lyle, sir."

"Aye. Didn't McAdam mention something about him saying Patricia had raised the devil?"

The red figure in the centre of the canvas held their attention once more. Corstophine took a picture with his phone before calling the station.

"Hamish. Is Lamb doing anything useful? Forget that – just send him out to Patricia's address with a roll of tape. We need to keep the place locked down until forensics finish up. And get hold of that character Bill stopped the other night, Steven Lyle. I want him in for questioning."

CHAPTER 8
Happy Families

Emma McCoach took the news of Patricia's attack badly. She was already sitting when Corstophine informed her of the assault, grabbing her son's hand with a grip so tight that her fist had turned as white as her face. She hyperventilated as if she was trying hard not to pass out.

"Poor Patricia. Is she badly injured? I have to go and see her! This happened last night?"

The questions came in a rush, sharp intakes of breath providing the punctuation.

"They were taking her straight into surgery, Mrs McCoach. I don't think she'll be seeing anyone for a few days." Corstophine groaned inwardly. He hadn't mentioned the full extent of her injuries, which was just as well, given such a crass comment.

"I'm sure you'll be able to visit her in a day or two," Frankie smoothed over his obvious discomfort. "I'll ask the hospital to let you know directly once she's out of surgery."

Corstophine shot Frankie a grateful glance. "Patricia mentioned to DC McKenzie that someone was out to get the family. Do you know anyone that might have wanted to harm her?"

"My mother was asked this yesterday. There isn't anyone who would want to harm any of us." Robb interjected before his mother could reply. "We're one of the largest employers in this town. The distillery has employed generations of families over the years and given them a good living. Why would anyone want to harm us?"

It was a question that Corstophine wanted answered as well. Emma had avoided his eyes after he'd asked the question, content to let her son have his rant. What was it she didn't want to say?

"Could I possibly have a glass of water?" Corstophine asked Robb directly.

"Of course. I'll just be a minute." His mother reluctantly loosened her grip as he made to leave them alone. Corstophine waited until he was out of earshot before making his move.

"Mrs McCoach – Emma. I know this must have come as a shock, so soon after Jack's death, but is there anything you can think of that might help us in our enquiries? Any threats or incidents? Had Jack made any enemies?"

Emma raised her eyes from contemplation of the carpet, fixing Corstophine with a face suddenly devoid of any expression.

"My husband was a good man, officer. He worked tirelessly to provide for his family and for this town. You'll not find anyone who has a bad word to say about him."

"Why would Patricia have told us that Jack had been poisoned?" Corstophine persevered.

"What?" The word snapped back at him.

"She told us that it wasn't a heart attack; that he'd somehow been poisoned on the mountain." At least he had her full attention now.

"Why haven't I heard about this? Do you have any proof?"

"Don't upset yourself, mother." Robb had entered the room, handing Corstophine a glass of water with a look indicating he knew he had been sent out on a ruse. "What's this all about, Jim? Is there any evidence to back up such a claim?"

Corstophine let the unwelcome familiarity pass. "Your aunt made a statement when she came into the station. She believed that your father died of poisoning, not a heart attack."

"Well, that's ridiculous. The autopsy said it was a heart attack, didn't it?"

"Yes, that was the outcome of the report. I'm just trying…"

"Then I'd rather you didn't upset my mother any further. Aunt Pat has her flights of fancy and I'm sorry if she's been wasting your valuable police time. Thank you for letting us know about her. If there's nothing else, we'd appreciate being left in peace."

Corstophine placed the glass down on a table, the water untouched. A thought that had been attempting to gain attention crystallised in his head.

"When we checked your husband's backpack, it had been opened. Was there anything missing that you noticed, anything you would have expected him to take on a hike?"

Emma frowned, searching her memory as she mentally unpacked the rucksack.

"I don't think so," she said eventually. "Nothing that I can think of at any rate. He always took the least with him that he could get away with." She smiled, a fleeting curvature of thin lips. "He always complained he had enough weight to drag up the hills as it was."

Corstophine nodded, exchanging the briefest of smiles in return. "I didn't notice any food – or drink. Did he not carry some provisions with him when he went?"

"I don't see what possible relevance this can have to my aunt's attack. Can't you see mum's still recovering from the shock of my father's death?" Robb took a step towards

Corstophine, interposing himself between the detective and his mother before placing a comforting hand on her shoulder. She reached up to pat it, then clasped his hand in hers.

"It's alright, Robb, they've a job to do and we must help as much as we can." She looked Corstophine directly in the eye, taking a deep breath before continuing. "Jack would have packed a bar of chocolate or something, he called it his emergency rations, but he always had a sweet tooth. The only other thing he would have carried was a bottle of water." Her eyebrows drew down in puzzlement. "He wouldn't have dropped any litter on the mountains, but there weren't any wrappers or a bottle in his rucksack. They must have been lost when he passed away."

The last words came out as a croak, fresh tears appeared in response to her picturing his last moments alone on the mountainside.

"I'm sorry to have to ask you this, Emma, but can you describe the water bottle to me?"

"Really Corstophine! Can't you see she's had enough?" Emma looked up to her son, patting his hand to quieten him down, accompanied by an almost imperceptible shake of her head.

"Plastic. Just a plastic bottle," she answered.

"No, wait." Robb interrupted, "He took one of my bottles. It had the distillery name on it."

Corstophine's interest quickened. "What bottles are those?"

"One of Robb's ideas for starting his own brand of bottled water. His father didn't think it would catch on, but he liked the bottle design." Emma sounded dismissive.

Robb glared at her, angry at the extended questioning or upset because one of his business schemes had been disregarded so easily. Corstophine decided to leave it there.

"Thank you for your time. Sorry to have disturbed you, Mrs McCoach." Robb led the way to the front door, holding it open for the two police officers to leave. Corstophine paused on the threshold, his face held close to Robb. "One last thing. Can you tell us where you were last night?"

"Do you honestly think I had anything to do with the attack on my aunt?" Robb almost shouted his indignation.

"We have to cover all eventualities, Mr McCoach. If you can help us eliminate you from our enquiries, then we can spend more time looking for the real culprit."

Robb glared at them, unsure how to react.

"I was here, working on a gin infusion I'm developing for the distillery" He pointed down the drive towards a log cabin that Corstophine had taken for a garage. "We have a small still that I use for trying out different botanicals." He stopped, seeing the frown developing on Corstophine's brow. "Flavourings." He continued, "I was working there until late. Our cleaner stupidly used bleach or something to clean the equipment. I had to clean it all thoroughly before it could be used again so it must have been around 11:30. Then I went to bed."

"Can anyone substantiate your story?" Frankie questioned.

Robb scowled for a second until he regained his composure. "You can ask Angela. She's the night nurse, comes on duty at 11:00."

Frankie dutifully wrote the name down in her notebook. "Do you have a surname, her contact details?"

"Ask Glenlochy Healthcare. They run the private health hospital in town and supply the medical support staff my sister requires. If that's all?"

"Yes. Thank you, Robb. You've been most helpful."

Corstophine stepped down from the doorway, hearing the door slam behind him.

Back in the patrol car, Frankie peered up at the house windows trying to catch a glimpse of the sister as Corstophine strapped himself into the driving seat.

"You think he might have been the one who attacked her, sir?"

"I don't know, Frankie. You can never tell with families. Sometimes resentment builds up over years and finds release in an act of mindless violence. You just have to look at the crime statistics to see how many assaults are from family or friends."

He started the car, pulled around the turning circle to face back down the tree-lined drive. "Check his alibi with this nurse – Angela. While you're at it, see what you can find out about the daughter. I'm not comfortable with the idea she's being kept locked up in some bedroom."

"Will do, sir."

They drove in silence until clearing the entrance gates and back onto the road. "Did you mention the painting to forensics, sir? The figure painted in her blood?"

Corstophine swore under his breath. "No. I'd have thought it was bloody obvious but you're right. I'll call them when we're back at the station." Corstophine checked the time. "They'll be at the scene another hour or so yet."

"Was there a point to questioning them on the rucksack contents, sir?" Frankie was genuinely interested, wondering where Corstophine was going with that line of enquiry.

"I'm just keeping an open mind about the poisoning allegation. Probably just nonsense, but if he was poisoned, then maybe his food or drink was tampered with."

"But if there's nothing left in the rucksack, sir…" Frankie let the words trickle to a stop.

"No. Probably nothing we can do about it, Frankie.

Best concentrate on this lunatic who attacked Patricia, but we need to eliminate the family as suspects first."

CHAPTER 9
Madness

Robb watched until the patrol car disappeared, hidden by the trees lining the drive. "What the bloody hell?"

The question was directed at no-one in particular. A short rant against life and all the curved balls it sent his way. The mention of the word poison had thrown him – his father had died of a heart attack, pure and simple. That's what the coroner's report had stated, that's what he'd expected. Why had Aunt Pat taken it into her head that her brother had been poisoned was anyone's guess – but to take that to the police? Then for his aunt to be attacked in her own house and for him to be a suspect. "Christ almighty!" The words were issued with less of a religious fervour than as a straightforward curse. Could things get any worse?

"Robb. *Robb!*" His mother's voice came quavering down the hall, then stronger as he didn't respond.

"Coming, mother." One last glance out of the door's leaded window reassured him that the police had gone – for now at least. His mother remained sitting in the same position, her face unnaturally white. "What is it? Can I get you some water?"

Her eyes met his, ice meeting fire.

"What do you know about this? Jack's poisoning and Patricia being attacked?" She stared at him unblinking, accusative.

Robb was completely thrown now. For the police to consider him as a potential suspect in Patricia's attack –

well, family members are always in the frame, aren't they? But for his own mother to think along the same lines. His anger returned.

"How can you even think that?" He took a step towards her, thought better of it and turned away to stand at the French windows looking out over the town. His fingers clenched and unclenched at his sides as he attempted to calm down. The last thing he needed to do now was to engage his mother in a row. He couldn't be sure that he would not lash out at her if they started one of their arguments in earnest and that would only add fuel to the fire.

"You've never loved your father! I wouldn't put it past you to have poisoned him just so you could get control of the company. Well, I'm telling you that this will be over my dead body!"

His mother stormed off, leaving Robb alone with his rage. *Don't tempt me.* The thought leapt into being, causing him to bite his tongue before the words came out. *Why me? Why did I have to be born into such a crazy fucked-up family?*

He opened the French doors, suddenly desperate to breathe in some fresh air. A step took him onto the stone veranda that extended almost the entire length of the ground floor. Romanesque pillars stretched upwards at intervals, providing structural support for the upper floor and fulfilling a secondary purpose as anchors for vines planted by some optimistic predecessor. They curled around the stone pillars, holding tight onto the masonry with aged thick arms – brown and wrinkled as if clinging to life itself. Across the ceiling could still be seen traces of the wires that had provided the initial handholds for eager young tendrils. Now it was as if a forest had been lifted up to the roof, lush foliage making full use of the south-facing veranda. He remembered playing here as a child in another life. Adventures in tropical climes – losing himself, sometimes for days on end, in a world of imagination. His parents saw him as a dreamer, unreachable. Left to his own devices in a land they had no way of reaching. Perhaps if his father hadn't been so involved in his work, his mother so focussed on the beautiful daughter lost to madness – perhaps then they might have realised that Robb, too, was in desperate need of an anchor. Instead, he had been left to ride out the treacherous waters of adolescence, cast adrift without map or compass.

Robb slammed the front door as he left the house, the violence of the act providing some small release to the anger bottled up inside him. His car waited on the drive – a green Morgan open top with personalised number plate. It was a present from his father when he had turned 18, before the incessant arguments that turned them against each other. He climbed into the driving seat, looked at the small distillery shed before starting the engine. His attempts to persuade his father to try gin manufacturing was the source of one of their arguments. They wouldn't even have had to wait ten years before turning a profit, like they did with the single malt whisky. God, they could even use grain alcohol and just add the botanicals as he had demonstrated time and again in the shed. Use the same bottling plant with fancy-looking bottles and the money would have piled in.

His father had just laughed at the idea, given him the small still to 'play with', and then the entire board had followed his father's lead in criticising the taste, the look and then the whole business plan he'd spent a year putting together. Chastised him for not realising that independent gin distillers were springing up in every corner of the country, swamping the market with amateur produce at grossly inflated prices. He had patiently explained, as if to a child, that this was a bubble about to burst, and no self-respecting distillery would be stupid enough to commence gin manufacture at this point. Maybe after the market had suffered the inevitable collapse, they could look at it again. The condescending bastard! Gravel sprayed as he released the clutch, twin exhausts issuing a challenge as the car leapt down the drive.

At least he'd turned a healthy profit with the alcohol hand sanitiser. Who would have known a pandemic was around the corner, with an accompanying market for overpriced bottles of cheap alcoholic gel? They'd had to give him grudging respect for turning surplus pallets of grain alcohol into pure profit. The manufacturing process was simplicity itself: just add aloe vera gel, a few drops of essential oils and then bottle to feed an insatiable market. If only they'd at least tried his idea for the own label gin brand – the distribution and trade contacts were all in place. Now his father was out of the way, he could try again and the more shares he had, the bigger his voice at the board meetings.

Inside the house, Emma sat weeping in her chair, the nurse returning to the spare bedroom she had been allocated, Phoebe spaced out in her bedroom.

Emma McCoach wept, but was it for her husband she mourned? She missed his comforting presence, that smell of his in particular – he carried the scent of the distillery in his clothes, on his skin. But did she miss him in the way one misses part of one's soul? That question had re-presented itself for appraisal every day since he had died, and every day she put off answering it. Except today. Curled up in her favourite armchair, body convulsing with sobs, she faced the question and answer head on.

CHAPTER 10
Schizophrenia

Frankie left Corstophine at the station and headed out of town towards the business park, looking for the offices of Glenlochy Healthcare. They occupied the first floor of a modern office suite, all bright yellow bricks and angular geometric blue glass that reflected the surrounding mountains like a child's kaleidoscope. The ground floor was occupied by some pharmaceutical company, offering a business symbiosis of some kind she supposed. She'd not had any reason to visit this business park before. Built within the last year, the scars of its birth were still evident in the lacklustre landscaping – raw mounds of earth sculped into unnaturally smooth shapes with a nascent coating of monocultured grass. To Let signs adorned many of the buildings as the retreating economy failed to materialise into the full occupation the developers had hoped. Twin hammer blows of Covid-19 and a bungled Brexit had left the park more of a white elephant than anything else. The tenants already here had most likely taken full advantage of the regional development fund before it was cut – financial inducements put into place to seduce new industry to the area.

She entered the revolving door at the entrance, took the steel staircase up to the first floor and rang the buzzer. She could see a young woman look up from her desk in the offices beyond the glass, not bothering to conceal her irritation at having to raise herself out of her seat to answer the door. She took off a set of headphones, dropping them onto the worksurface and nonchalantly walked over to press the door release buzzer.

Frankie let herself in, facing a counter displaying brochures on homecare, private health, and respite homes.

"Can I help you?" The young woman managed to ask the question whilst clearly conveying the wish not to help her at all. She started looking at her nails, feeling the edges with a finger to check if they required filing.

"I'm DC Frankie McKenzie, from the local police station. Can I speak with your office manager?"

The receptionist appeared startled, much as if she had forgotten Frankie was standing in front of her. "What's this about?"

"I'd rather just talk to your manager if that's possible?"

"I suppose." She lifted one end of the counter to allow access, pointing a manicured finger towards a waiting area. "Take a seat. I'll get her for you."

Frankie sat, reaching for one of the leaflets lying on the low table in front of her. This one extolled the benefits of the care company respite homes – fully serviced rooms available for a minimum period of one week, complete with carers and meals. She did a doubletake on the cost – from £1500 a week in a basically furnished single room. The McCoach family must be paying out at least that every week for 24-hour home care.

The insouciant receptionist returned, moving a bit faster on her feet this time, with a stern middle-aged woman in tow.

"I'm sorry, Morag wasn't too clear what it was you wanted PC…"

Morag stood next to her boss, her face a study in ennui.

"DC," Frankie corrected. "DC Frankie McKenzie. I wonder if we might be able to talk in private?" She stood, matching height with the manager and cast a deliberate glance towards the receptionist.

"My office is right along here."

They entered a small, functional room. A filing cabinet dominated one corner, crowned by a rubber plant in desperate need of water. The ubiquitous computer screen took central position on a desk, picture window looking out over conifer clad hillsides. The manager bustled around the intervening desk, retrieving notepad and pencil from a drawer whilst indicating that Frankie take the only other chair.

"Has someone put in a complaint?" Her painted brows drew down in irritation as she leant back in her seat, fixing Frankie with a stare that she must use on her staff. The accent wasn't local, sounded more Edinburgh than anything else.

"No, this is just a routine call." Frankie saw the brows lift as a look of relief flitted across her face. "I'm here to talk to one of your staff, just to confirm a statement given by one of your clients. Shouldn't take more than a minute."

The manager adopted a businesslike manner, preparing to wield the pencil on the blank notepad. The flourish she made in sweeping the pencil off the table put Frankie in mind of a matador facing a bull. "Who is it you need to speak to?"

Frankie pulled out her notebook, rather more mundanely than the theatrical movements opposite. "I've only been given a first name." She consulted her notes, confirming the name she already held in her memory. "Angela. She works nights for the McCoach family."

"Angela Henderson. She doesn't start work until 11 p.m. She won't be coming in here at all today."

Frankie added the surname to her notes. "That's not a

problem. Do you have her home address? I'd like to have a word with her."

The manager's eyes narrowed with suspicion. "Can I ask what this is about? It's not our policy to hand out staff contact details without due cause."

Frankie sighed inwardly. She'd met the type before – officious, obstructive. "I'm afraid this is part of an ongoing investigation so I'm not able to provide any more information. Suffice to say Robb McCoach mentioned that Angela started work at 11 p.m. last night. I just need to confirm that with her."

"Well, I can do that for you here." Fingers tapped a staccato rhythm on the keyboard. "Yes, here you are. Angela signed in at 11 o'clock exactly at the McCoach house."

"How can you be sure?"

"All our staff have an app on their phones. They scan a QR code at the client's address on arrival and departure – it's how they clock in and out. Each time a member of staff does that, it sends a notification through to our server. Keeps everyone straight and makes sure they get paid accordingly." She smiled, a hint of smugness about the efficiency of their IT systems written across her face.

"Does the app report the physical location of the phone as well?"

The painted eyebrows headed south once more. "We don't use the system to spy on our staff."

Frankie doubted that. The plethora of smartphone apps, vehicle trackers – all companies kept a close eye on their employees these days, if only to wring the last scrap of profit from them. "Can it be used to report actual location?" She persevered, sounding as if she had a genuine interest rather than pursuing a line of investigation.

"Well, yes. If we have to." The answer came reluctantly.

Frankie scribbled the details in her notepad. "OK, thanks so much for your help." She pulled a worn business card out of her notepad, handing it over the desk. "Could you ask Angela to call the station when she's free, just so we can close the paperwork?"

"Robb's not in any sort of trouble, is he?" Her eyes held a calculating look as her imagination ran through any number of possible scenarios.

"No. Nothing like that." Frankie kept her tone deliberately light. "We just have to eliminate him from a line of enquiry. It's really nothing at all, just to keep the paperwork straight." She attempted a conspiratorial tone. "You know what it's like with paperwork, dot the i's, cross the t's."

The manager nodded, suddenly seeing Frankie as a fellow administrator bogged down with needless tasks that had to be completed every day to keep head office sweet. "Tell me about it!"

Frankie stood up to leave, the manager rising quickly to her feet to reach the door first.

"One last thing," Frankie asked. "What's wrong with Robb's sister? I heard some dreadful screams from her last time I visited."

"Oh, she suffers from schizophrenia. We have to keep her fairly heavily sedated otherwise she could harm herself. It's so good of the family to care for her rather than put her into an institution. Such a sad case." The frown returned, Frankie suspected this was more like her normal expression and that it took her an effort to keep her eyebrows raised. "I'm not supposed to pass any client information on, strictly confidential. But seeing as how you're the police…" She let the sentence hang – sufficient justification for a professional slip.

"I understand. It won't go any further – could you ask Angela to call?"

"Yes, of course." The manager appeared flustered, most likely annoyed to have revealed more than she should.

Frankie was ushered out with undue haste, earning one last bored glance from the seated receptionist before the door closed on her. As she made her way back to the patrol car, she went back over the exchange. Nothing there to raise any suspicions, the nurse by all accounts had arrived when Robb said she had. Most likely, she would be able to substantiate him being there all night if she was working a night shift. Neither she nor Corstophine seriously thought he would have attacked his aunt anyway – just following procedures and filing the paperwork as she'd said. The schizophrenia, though, wasn't that something that's meant to be inherited? And Patricia's repeated mantra that she wasn't mad?

CHAPTER 11
Peeping Tom

Corstophine stood in front of the crazy board in the incident room. The McCoach incident had suddenly grown wings and flown, no longer a flight of fancy but a real case, complete with horrific injuries. He had a sinking feeling that this was just the start, that whoever was responsible for the attack on Patricia McCoach could have designs on the rest of the family. Taking up a dry black marker pen, he wrote Patricia's name at the top, near the centre of the board. To the left of her name he added that of her brother, the recently deceased Jack McCoach. Not that he was officially the victim of any crime, but Corstophine had a premonition that might change. To the right of her name went Emma McCoach, at this stage neither a victim nor a suspect. After a moment's hesitation he wrote Robb's name under his mother's, then added the daughter's name, Phoebe. Two faint lines traced a connection of some kind to the parents, Jack and Emma. Corstophine selected a red marker and connected Robb to Patricia, at this stage a person of interest rather than a suspect until his alibi was confirmed. He added the name of the late-night runner that PC McAdam had intercepted, Steven Lyle, as another red line connected to Patricia.

Motive was always key to solving any crime. Sure, there were motiveless crimes: common assaults, random attacks, but the injuries inflicted on Patricia made it more likely this was premeditated. So, what motive would drive someone to murder Jack and blind his sister? Corstophine frowned in concentration. The most obvious factor was their shared wealth and ownership of the distillery. He had no idea what the value might be, but it had to run well into the millions, and that amount of money could turn even the most law-abiding citizen into a criminal if they saw an opportunity to grab a slice for themselves. Who would benefit from Jack's death? The contents of the will had become common knowledge soon after the beneficiaries had been announced, a symptom of small-town society. Emma, Robb, Phoebe and Patricia had all featured heavily in the dispersal of the estate. Could the attack on Patricia have been a botched murder attempt? The blow to her head was powerful enough to put her into a coma, any harder and the bleed on her brain might well have been enough to finish her off. But if her assailant had merely wanted to kill her, why bother putting out her eyes?

Corstophine shook his head. There had to be something else, something he was missing. If Jack had been poisoned as Patricia alleged, two big ifs as far as Corstophine was concerned, then that would suggest a woman being the murderer. Not that Corstophine fell into the common trap of believing poison was a girl's best friend. The last Scottish crime statistics he had reviewed still had murder by a sharp object top of the list, closely followed by blunt force trauma. But historically, poison was a favoured method of choice for women, a damn sight more effective and a lot less messy than physical assault, especially if your target was a lot larger and stronger than you. Trouble was that with Jack's body no longer available for post-mortem and the official cause of death being listed as heart attack, how was he meant to put any meat on the bones of that theory?

Meat on the ashes! He smiled as his wife's voice sounded softly in his mind. She had been able to lighten even the worst of the job when she had still been with him. He was grateful for her voice now. The gaps between hearing her, seeing her, had become longer. One day he feared she'd no longer be there at all. *I'm not going to be around forever.* That was the last thing she had said to him just days ago as he weaved a drunken path back home from Jack's wake. Even as he thought of her, she faded, leaving just a faint remembrance of her perfume behind. Is this how we all leave this world? Corstophine wondered. Our faces blurring out of memory's focus, the sound of our voices forgotten until just a dying trace of our scent holds in the air?

He shook his head again, angry with himself for drifting off into reverie when there was a job to be done. Motive for Jack's death? Most likely the money and the distillery, and that placed Robb directly in the frame, maybe his mother too. Phoebe, the mysterious mad daughter locked away in an upstairs room like some character in a gothic novel, he couldn't see how she could have any involvement at all. Maybe Jack's death was a simple heart attack, in which case the motive could have nothing to do with the distillery after all. Corstophine sighed in frustration. There really wasn't anything he could do until forensics came back with whatever they had found at Patricia's house and that could take weeks.

"Excuse me, sir." Hamish's slow words interrupted the DI's thoughts. Corstophine turned towards the desk sergeant, framed in the reception doorway. "I've got Steven Lyle waiting to see someone. You asked me to get him in for a chat?"

"He's keen. OK, send him through to the interview room. Is Lamb still with forensics?"

"Yes, sir."

"And Frankie's off talking to the private health

company. You'd better sit in with me, Hamish, see if we can find out what Steven was up to at Patricia's house the day before her attack."

Corstophine settled into the interview room, cued the recorder and waited for Hamish to make slow progress with Steven Lyle in front of him. He was reminded of an arthritic sheep dog, well past its prime, corralling a single frightened sheep into the pen.

"Take a seat, Mr Lyle. Thanks for coming in so quickly." Hamish slowly sank into the seat beside him like a shipwreck settling onto the ocean floor.

"Do you mind if I call you Steven?"

"No, not at all." Steven attempted a confident smile. He failed.

"I'm going to record our conversation, if you're happy for me to do so. You're not being charged with anything at this stage, so it's entirely voluntary."

Steven nodded, his face a picture of worry.

"I'm sorry, Steven. I need you to say yes to confirm you're giving me permission to record this conversation."

"Yes." His voice came out as a quiet squeak.

"Would you like some water, Steven?" Corstophine worried that his voice wouldn't be loud enough to be caught on the recording.

"No, I'm OK."

"Good. Sergeant Hamish McKee present, DI James Corstophine interviewing. Your name for the record?"

"Steven. Steven Lyle."

"And your address?"

"12 Strathyre Avenue."

Corstophine checked his notes to confirm the details. "Tell me, Steven. What were you doing on Monday evening when our officer, PC McAdam, stopped to provide assistance? You told him that 'they'd raised the devil'. Would you like to elaborate on exactly what you saw?"

Steven Lyle swallowed nervously. He didn't want to be here in this brightly lit room, facing two stern policemen, but the sergeant hadn't given him much choice when he had been contacted earlier that morning.

"I was out for an evening walk." He faltered as the two faces opposite expressed a look of incredulity, Corstophine's eyebrow taking a well-travelled route skywards.

"PC McAdam's notes state that he saw you running down the road at full tilt, looking as if you were trying to get away from someone." Corstophine tried a gentle reality check. This particular interviewee looked so nervous any strongarm tactics could send him over the edge.

"I wasn't doing any harm," he answered plaintively.

"What were you doing, Steven? There's no rush, just tell us in your own words. Just be sure that you tell us the truth – otherwise you'd be wasting police time and that's a criminal offence."

"Oh God. This won't come out, will it? I knew I shouldn't do it but after my wife left me, I've just felt so alone…" Steven started crying, reaching into his pocket to pull out a large blue handkerchief to wipe his eyes.

The sergeant exchanged a look with Corstophine. This could drag on a while.

"Can you get Steven a glass of water, Hamish, whilst he composes himself?"

Hamish made his way out into the main office, filling a glass from the tap. Corstophine took advantage of the time that his languorous sergeant took to finish the simplest task by observing Steven as he cried into his handkerchief. Unless he was a consummate actor, there's no way he could have been responsible for causing Patricia's horrific injuries. The sergeant returned with a glass, putting it down in front of Steven without bothering to disguise a look of disgust. Corstophine motioned him back to sit beside him with a flick of the head – Hamish was old school, grown men weren't meant to cry.

"I've just felt so alone since my wife left me. I came home from work one day and she'd left me a note, said she couldn't stay with me any longer." His eyes were like a puppy's: big, brown and begging forgiveness for some transgression he couldn't comprehend. He quickly looked away from Hamish, finding no comfort in the sergeant's hard stare, to focus instead on Corstophine.

Corstophine nodded, gently encouraging him on.

"It started as an impulse really. Taking underwear off washing lines. I knew it was wrong, but it reminded me of her, the feel of it." He made a conscious effort to focus on the here and now. "I saw a woman – when I was in my back garden. She was half undressed, standing in full view of the window. I've never done porn, prostitutes, anything like that. It became an addiction. Over the last few months, I went out again and again, different gardens, different windows. I collected all sorts of underwear. I don't really know why. They are all in June's wardrobe. It made everything seem a bit more... normal somehow."

"What did you see the night PC McAdam stopped you?" Corstophine pressed harder, anxious to try and find any lead into the McCoach assault. "What did you mean by raising the devil?"

Steven paled at the memory. "I was passing the house, late afternoon. I normally wait until dark, but I could see the rear garden was mostly woods. I decided to hide there, find a good spot to see the windows. Then all these cars turned up. All women. I shouldn't have stayed, but I couldn't risk being seen, especially as they were all busy in the garden – putting out tables and chairs. It looked like they were having a party. When they finally went back in the house it was dark enough to get away, but I wanted to see what they were doing."

"And what were they doing, Steven?"

He swallowed nervously, taking a sip from the glass Hamish had left on the table for him. "They came out dressed in robes. One of them had horns on her head. It was like some sort of witch's coven or something. They danced in a circle, praying, I think. Then they finished and started on the food and drink. It was too weird for me, so I left. The noise they were making made it safe for me to get away."

He stopped at that point, puppy dog eyes seeking approval.

"What did you see to make you run, Steven? What was this devil you said you'd seen?"

He visibly trembled in front of them. "I looked back when I reached the pavement, checking I hadn't been seen, and then I saw it."

Corstophine waited patiently – he could hear Hamish sighing in exasperation beside him.

"There was something looking at me from the edge of the woods, something tall and black with shining red eyes." He lost the puppy dog expression, became earnest, desperate to be believed. "It wasn't human, it was a devil. They'd raised the devil!"

The two policemen looked at him, exchanged a glance with each other and then back to regarding Steven as if he was in need of psychiatric help.

"You don't believe me, do you?" Steven's voice was plaintive.

"Oh, I believe you've been responsible for causing a great deal of distress to a number of women locally."

Corstophine said tiredly. Another dead end – still, at least that's the peeping tom found. He turned to Hamish. "Charge him with theft."

Steven's face turned ashen as the full import of his actions became apparent.

"It's up to the courts whether you're put on the sex offenders register. If you want to avoid prison, I'd leave washing lines and other people's back gardens alone from now on." Corstophine stood up to leave, speaking his intention for the benefit of the recording when Steven put his phone down on the table.

"I filmed it – it's all here."

CHAPTER 12
Uisge Beatha

Robb drove at speed, desperate to escape the stultifying limits of the small town he called home. The open road beckoned, engine growling in pleasure as the Morgan was unleashed, mountains and lochs forming a scrolling panorama to accompany his churning thoughts.

He had hoped that his life would drastically improve once his overbearing father was gone. Nobody to belittle his schemes for the distillery, to treat him like a spoilt child. When the will was read out in the solicitor's sombre office – the extended family gathered around the large oak desk like impatient vultures – he had expected majority control of the distillery to be handed to him. Instead, his father had split his shares five ways between himself, Emma, Phoebe, Aunt Pat and someone whose identity the solicitor was unwilling to divulge. Everyone there had the same thought, a mistress that Jack had sequestered away somewhere. A final slap in the face from beyond the grave, another taunt letting Robb know he wasn't capable of the job, and a final insult to his wife.

That at least went some way to explaining his mother's increasingly bizarre behaviour. She had taken to locking all the doors and windows ever since the police visit – following up on Aunt Pat's crazy allegation that someone was out to get the family. He loved his aunt dearly, she was the only close relation who had ever expressed any real affection to him and his sister, but they all knew she was eccentric – too many drugs back in the sixties, too many drugs now! On more than one occasion, he'd caught the aromatic tang of marijuana in her 'studio' as she hastily stubbed out a reefer. Christ knows why she was being supported by his father anyway. Robb had walked in on several arguments between his parents, so involved in shouting at each other that his presence wasn't noticed. It was via these exchanges he had learned that his father had purchased Patricia's house for her, that she was on a comfortable allowance. As long as there was enough money to go around, he couldn't see the problem. Jealousy, he guessed, another woman in her life. He laughed out loud. Now she had real competition, a mystery woman with 20% of the shares. No wonder she was upset!

And what was the point in giving Phoebe any shares? She was completely catatonic, locked in her bedroom, drugged up to her eyeballs. What a waste of money and influence. He slammed the steering wheel in disgust, causing the car to veer dangerously on the twisting road, then it bucked like a wild animal as he overcompensated. Chastened, Robb reduced speed. This would not be the best time to have an accident.

But what could he do now? Without the controlling shares that he had expected to come to him as son and heir, the distillery was still run by the board of directors. The family now all had seats, except for Phoebe, of course, and her voting rights had been passed to his mother in the will, failing which they passed down to him. Even if his mother died, he still didn't get free rein with the board. Bryan Cobb, the managing director of the firm, and Sandy McPhearson, the finance director, both had equal voting rights with the family shareholders.

Robb's eyes left the road for a moment, taking in the mountain peaks as they caught the autumnal sun, setting the bracken-covered slopes alight in red hues. The planned trip to scatter his father's ashes on the peak where he had died was this Thursday, just two days away. He didn't have much time to put everything in place.

It was dark by the time Robb eventually returned home, car headlights sweeping a floodlit path over the mock gothic architecture of the family home. He checked his watch, 10:30. It would soon be time for the nurses to change shifts. His mother's bedroom light was on. Good! She'll be getting ready for bed, no need for any arguments or wild swings of emotion. Since his father had died, she was either clinging on to him like a drowning woman or accusing him of more outlandish acts each day. Patricide was only the latest accusation. He could see she was lining him up as Aunt Pat's attacker. The thought gave him some cause for concern, what if there was someone out to get the family? He checked the driveway before opening the car door, at the same time berating himself for being caught up in the hysteria surrounding Patricia's attack. Just a robbery gone wrong, she'll be fine. A knock on the head might even be good for her, knock some fucking sense into it for once.

His mood lifted, but he still retained the sense of being watched as he opened the main door, nervously looking over his shoulder as he entered the house. Robb shut the door behind him with a sense of relief, closing out any number of terrors that roamed the night. The afternoon nurse came down the stairs as she heard the door, peering down into the hallway before recognising Robb and offering a slight smile of recognition. He watched her as she turned around, watched her as she climbed back up the staircase, watched her for longer than he should.

The drinks cabinet beckoned. He'd had a shitty day and this was one way of closing it down. The mahogany cabinet stood in the dining room, carved dark wood imported at great cost from Africa at a time when slaves provided a better return for the investment in stowage. His ancestors had some part to play in that, he knew, a significant part of the family fortune derived from the slave trade. It was never mentioned, not today. Instead, society held onto the imagined conceit that inherited wealth was earned without recourse to morally bankrupt practices – that the UK was a beacon of racial equality.

Robb poured himself a decent measure of the distillery's 12-year-old, crystal glass catching the contents and mirroring them back in fragmented golden facets. He raised his glass to the ceiling – to his mother in her sterile, loveless and now lonely bedroom; to his sister in her padded and lonely hell.

Uisge-beatha – the water of life. The only medicine that soothed his incessant headaches, took away his lost hours, kept the dark dog of despair on a tight leash.

"Slàinte mhath." Robb aimed the Gaelic toast to those above him, and to those beyond reach. The whisky burned a smooth path down his throat, placed warm hands over his heart. He sank into a reclining chair, glass firmly held in his hand, and emptied his mind to allow the alcohol free access. He could accomplish so much at the distillery if only he held the power. The rest of the family, the board – what did they know? Stuck in some Groundhog Day where nothing was ever allowed to change. The same products, the same methods, year after year after endless bloody year.

The doorbell sounded in the hall. Robb checked his watch, confirmed it was time for the nurse changeover and placed his whisky glass on the low table beside his chair. Quiet footsteps sounded on the stairs, eager to leave. A hurried conversation came on low female cadences, the words bubbling as fast as a highland burn. A quick laugh. The shutting of the front door. A moment's silence. Robb felt the quickening of his pulse, the anticipation almost a physical weight upon his stomach.

"The polis wanted a statement from me today." Angela knew where to find him, near the source of the whisky. She was around twenty-five, blond hair pinned back in a sensible bob, wearing a private nurse's uniform that she somehow managed to wear provocatively. Intelligent eyes probed his, searching.

"What did you tell them?"

She offered Robb a conspiratorial smile. "Said you were in all night." Her eyes closed slightly, as if by that simple process she could see the truth more clearly. "Were you?"

"Of course, where else was I going to be?" The words were issued with an undeserved fervour. He had gone to bed last night not long after she had arrived. Seen the flicker of disappointment cross her face as he refused the bait she'd delicately offered. He could almost read her mind as she reassessed the quarry, selecting another fly to flick across his slow flowing river. *Where else was I going to be?* The self-interrogation bothered him. Where were any of us once we fell asleep?

Angela laughed lightly, as if he had said something that had amused her. "Alright for those that don't have to work for a living." She inclined her head upstairs, towards the bedroom, caught his eye in a brazen look. The message unmistakable.

Robb feigned ignorance in the language of courtship, picked up his glass.

"I'd better check on sleepyhead. Make sure she's comfortable." Her voice contained barely disguised disappointment.

"Sure. I'll be going to bed soon. I've had a rough day."

She nodded, gave a tight smile and left the room.

His eyes followed the sway of her hips, the animal in him subdued – for now.

CHAPTER 13
Outdoor Sex

Corstophine arrived early to work Thursday morning, even managing to beat Frankie to the station, which was a rare occurrence. Sometimes he wondered if there was anything other than police work in her life, the hours she spent at her desk. He logged onto his computer, checked his emails and opened the attachment sent from Steven Lyle's iPhone. He'd had to wait for the file to be scanned by some IT department buried in Police Scotland headquarters and be given the all clear.

It didn't look promising. Shot at night on a shaky phone and framed in a vertical letterbox, the view displayed the lawn behind Patricia's house. Corstophine could make out the metal sculpture that featured in her painting, catching reflections from flaming garden torches embedded in flowerbeds. That must be Patricia in the lead, dressed in a white robe like all the other women dutifully following in her wake. Any attempt at dignity was ruined by a set of toy animal horns attached to her head. He was instantly reminded of his one foray into amateur dramatics, an unedifying episode which made the toes inside his size 11 shoes curl at the memory. Corstophine swiftly returned his attention to the video on his desktop. The women had by now gathered in a circle, the sculpture forming the epicentre. He struggled to find the control to increase volume, dragging a slider across the screen with his mouse. Whatever words they spoke sounded like gibberish, overlaid with heavy breathing, which he supposed must come from the cameraman. They whirled faster around the circle, occasional glimpses of white flesh becoming more prevalent, encouraging faster panting from the voyeur until they fell to the ground. Only Patricia remained standing, her arms raised towards the sky. He heard the chant they spoke in unison, the heavy breathing quiet for the moment. That must have been the end of whatever ritual he had just witnessed, as they gathered their robes more tightly together and sauntered towards tables set with food and wine. The level of chat and laughter reached levels more befitting a group of twelve women who were out on a social, despite their odd dress code. The view slipped sideways as Steven made to turn off the camera, catching trees jolting at crazy angles. Just before the picture went dark, he thought he saw a figure in the trees. Corstophine freeze framed until he caught the image. The screen displayed a blurred figure looking at the camera from about 15 metres away, the eyes catching his attention as twin points of red light. There was insufficient detail to make out the face, height could be anything from 5' 8" to 6' 2", build appeared normal. Nothing he could use for ID.

"Damn!" Corstophine had hoped to catch a glimpse of Steven Lyle's so-called devil, but at least it corroborated his account of the evening and that certainly gave credence to his claim that he wasn't the only voyeur hiding in Patricia's woods that night.

"Who the hell could that be?" Corstophine voiced the question out loud. No answer was forthcoming from the deserted station. He pressed print and the indistinct image regurgitated from the printer, blurred and almost lost in the darkness. It would have to do. A handy magnet held the image onto the crazy board, taking up position next to Steven Lyle's details. Corstophine stood back to admire his handiwork. Could this be Patricia's attacker, and if so, who was it?

He turned around as he heard the office door open, Frankie's face cautiously appearing as she checked who was in before her.

"Morning, sir. I thought I was the only one daft enough to arrive before 8 o'clock. Has anything happened overnight?"

"No, nothing like that. I just wanted to get an early start before I join Robb McCoach and a few hillwalkers. I said I'd climb Sgurr Thuilm, over by Glenfinnan, with them and see his father's ashes being scattered on the summit." Corstophine indicated the newly printed frame grab from Steven's video. "I've had Steven Lyle's video given the all clear, it looks like he was telling the truth. He wasn't the only one hiding in Patricia's garden."

Frankie stood next to him, peering more closely at the figure. "Can't make out much. Definitely someone there, though. Any ideas?"

Corstophine shook his head. "I've nothing to go on, but whoever he is, there's a good chance he was involved in the attack."

Frankie's eyes narrowed as she focussed on the photograph, her nose just centimetres away from the wall. "Strange how the eyes have caught the light. You certain it's a man, sir?"

Corstophine considered the photograph as if seeing it for the first time. "No. You're right – it could be a woman. If it wasn't so bloody dark!"

"And blurred," Frankie added.

"Aye." Corstophine agreed. "It's really no bloody use at all."

"Did the video corroborate Steven's description of the women doing some sort of ritual, sir?"

"I've got the footage on my computer. Come through to my office." Corstophine led the way, turned the monitor towards Frankie and replayed the video. They watched the short film in silence, the women's chanting and Steven Lyle's heavy breathing forming the soundtrack.

"Looks like Patricia is part of a coven, sir."

"Is that actually a thing, Frankie?" Corstophine's voice expressed doubt. The last witch in Scotland was some poor woman from Dornoch who was put to death in 1727. He only remembered about her because he had used the case for a history project when he was still at school. Janet Horne was suffering from senility, and her daughter had deformities of the hands and feet – caused by her mother riding her like a horse to see the devil – or so the magistrate had decided. That was sufficient for her to be covered in tar, paraded through the town on a barrel before being burnt alive. The daughter managed to escape, a fact that had impressed the young Corstophine as he imagined her running for her life away from an angry mob on her deformed feet. He had managed top marks for that project.

"Yes, sir." Frankie's voice brought Corstophine back to the present. "There's even websites where you can get in touch with your local coven in case you want to try it out."

"Isn't that just an excuse for outdoor sex?"

Frankie felt uncomfortable as the conversation drifted towards matters she considered best left private, but then she realised that Corstophine might have a point.

"There's twelve people in a coven, generally, unless they have a high priest."

"You appear to know an awful lot about witches, Frankie. Is there something you're not telling me?"

Frankie ignored Corstophine's teasing.

"There's twelve of them in the video, including Patricia."

"And your point is?" He was genuinely puzzled.

"They're all women, sir."

Corstophine struggled to see where this revelation was taking them. "I'm sorry, Frankie, I still don't see what you're getting at."

"What if Patricia isn't interested in men? She's never married, as far as we know. What if we're looking at a crime of passion? What if it was a woman who attacked her?"

Corstophine raised both eyebrows. "Hit her hard enough to send her into a coma and put out her eyes?" His voice expressed his incredulity.

Frankie shrugged.

Corstophine sighed heavily. "You could be right."

He sat down at his desk, spinning the monitor back into position. The lack of any leads into Patricia's attack was getting to him. One blurred photograph, a peeping tom and a dysfunctional family – he needed something better than this.

"Frankie. Pay a visit to the hospital and see if Patricia's in a fit state to be questioned. I'll chase up the SOC team, see if they've anything for us to work with. You'll have to cover with Hamish today. Lamb and McAdam are working late shift to find these catalytic thieves and catch a drug dealer if they can."

"Yes, sir." She paused in the doorway. "I was reading up on catalytic thefts, sir. They make a habit of waiting until the garage has replaced a unit, then hit the same car again. It might be worth their while staking out a likely target, one parked out in a quiet road?"

Corstophine nodded. "Good idea. Can you pass that on to them? Thanks, Frankie." He stared at the computer screen, willing the blurred and underexposed photograph to resolve into someone recognisable until the phone rang.

"DI Corstophine?"

He recognised the voice. "Hello, Dave, what have you got for me?"

Dave Anderson had been with the Inverness forensics team ever since Corstophine could remember – a quiet, studious man, more at home with a microscope than a telephone.

"We've managed to identify eight different people from samples found in the attacked woman's bedroom."

"No fingerprints?" Corstophine asked, more from hope than expectation.

"Plenty. Those on the paintbrushes or canvas are too badly smudged, so nothing yet directly linking the assailant to the scene. We're more hopeful for the cosh – I'll let you have the results."

Corstophine sighed in exasperation. This was exactly what he had feared, another drawn out investigation without any obvious suspect in his sights.

"Dave, you don't happen to have the contact details for that forensic psychologist? She gave a talk at the police conference last year – something to do with profiling the Glasgow serial killer?"

"The shrink from Carstairs?"

Corstophine nodded. "That's right! I couldn't remember where she was from. Do you have a name or number for her?"

The line went silent except for random mechanical clicks. "Got it here. Dr Sharmila Mallick – she's on the hospital website. Do you want me to send you a link?"

"No, I'll track her down now I've got her name. Thanks, Dave."

"You thinking of asking her for some help?"

"That's the plan. She may even have come across someone with the same MO. It's worth a shot anyway."

"Good luck," Dave offered. "I'll be comparing swabs

from the family and friends, so we can eliminate them from the genetic profiles we've identified at the scene of crime. I'll hopefully get an initial report out to you later today."

"That's a great help, although I'm hoping this Sharmila Mallick can help with the elimination. So far the only suspects in the frame all have alibis." He ended the call, turning to his computer and pulling up the staff pages for the state hospital in Lanarkshire. Corstophine sent off a quick email, feeling more like a man risking it all on a roll of the dice and knowing that luck was not on his side.

CHAPTER 14
Princess or Dragon?

The voices were quiet – for now. Phoebe listened intently, holding her breath to detect the quietest of sounds. Nothing. Just the regular surge of blood in her ears, usual stirrings from the house. She could hear the nurse in the next room turning the pages of her book, the wind attempting access through the gaps in the sash window frames. Phoebe stared out of the window from her seat, seeing the tops of the trees bending in submission, bowing to a stronger force. Silent times came more often now.

She tried standing, holding onto her chair for support as her balance fought against the cumulative effects of her medication. After a while the floor settled, completing a metamorphosis from stormy sea. She crossed quickly to the window and pressed her palms against cool glass, an invisible barrier. Her breath misted on contact with the cold surface, the world growing more like an impressionist painting with every exhalation.

Green. Blue. Yellow sun searing her eyes until the tears ran down her cheeks. Water offerings for a burning world. Phoebe's hands raised to her dampened cheeks, slender fingers tentatively offered to lips, a saltwater tribute from her eyes.

It hadn't always been like this. As a child she was allowed to have invisible friends. Her fantasy world indulged as make-believe. As she grew older her friends deserted her, aware something was wrong. They grew afraid of her. The voices let her know that they talked about her, laughed at her, plotted against her. She became a loner, a lone wolf. The things they said hurt. Her parents could not be trusted. Her brother even less so. She was the wounded wolf, survival at all costs.

The first time she hurt someone was in primary school. How old was she? The face that she saw reflected in the window grew younger – six, seven? The girl had laughed at her, something Phoebe had said in response to an internal voice, forgetting to not speak aloud. It was too difficult, deciding which voices were real and which voices were only inside her head. The girl's stupid face was contorted with laughter, finger pointing. Sinister had told her what to do. The voice from her left side was always louder than Righteous, the voice that advised caution, holding her back, telling her to ignore the other voice. Sinister's voice, the dark voice, had made her grab the scissors, made her stab them again and again and again into the girl's fat ugly face until it ran red. The screams just made her stab harder, until the scissors hit bone and sent shock waves back along her nerves.

Then it was the hospital, the concerned faces, the drugs. Years passing as weeks. Slack face unrecognisable in mirrors until she was no longer allowed mirrors. The last face she saw in a mirror wasn't hers. Someone else was in the mirror, staring at her – always watching her. She would look away then slowly slide her eyes back towards the glass. Whoever she was, Phoebe caught her slyly watching, waiting for the moment. Sinister told her to break the glass, use the shards to stab and tear and wound. Righteous told her it was just her reflection. Fist broke glass. Cut hands left red trails. The wolf had fangs.

She had been left alone in her hospital room, door locked from outside. With nobody to attack, Sinister told her to cut and slash her own flesh. Light fought dark, darkness won. Her arm and stomach were tattered threads of hanging flesh by the time they reached her. White uniforms stained with her blood.

When she returned from intensive care the mirror had gone and her flesh bore cuneiform scripts, death white against her olive skin. It was a message, one only she would be able to understand, with help from her voices.

She stared around her as if seeing the room for the first time. This wasn't a hospital. This was her bedroom, her childhood bedroom scourged free of anything that could be used to harm. The window glass was so thick that light lost the energetic part of its spectrum, the high frequency violet and indigo blue fading partway through the toughened pane, leaving green as the dominant colour. It was like looking under the sea at a drowned landscape, trees now caught in tidal currents that pulled at them so they appeared as an underwater kelp forest.

She glanced back to her chair, a throne for a captive princess. On the seat were jewels: green, blue, white, red. They lay in a line where she'd hidden them from sight. Sinister had told her days ago to pretend to swallow them with the cup of water, had told her how to conceal them under her tongue so that when she obeyed the command to open wide the tablets had gone. Righteous was growing weaker as the medication passed through her body. Soon, she'd only have the one voice and sanity of a kind would prevail. But first she had to hide the tablets.

The floor was devoid of any coverings. Bare wood amplified each step. Wolves tread carefully, silently. The pills collected, fed one by one through the hole in the wood where a knot had shrunk and fallen into the dark void between floor and ceiling.

She regained her seat, contemplated the underwater world outside and bided her time.

Above her head the hoist waited. A metal rail led the way to her bed for when her body lay unresponsive, unable to manage the few steps when the chemical cosh had been administered. This nurse was lazy, preferring to dose her into some sort of oblivion so she could read books undisturbed in the adjacent bedroom. The night nurse was even worse, a cursory check at the beginning of her shift then locking the door until morning meds. Phoebe could hear her waiting in vain for her brother each night before closing her own door on loneliness and disappointment.

Her perfect lips curled upwards in a smile until the wolf took over, teeth bared in a warning snarl. Sinister had returned. He had important things to tell her, secrets about the nurses: what her mother was planning to do with her; warning her about her brother. She was not to take any more of the tablets they gave her. Poison weakening her body and mind. Hide them, fool them, make them pay for locking her in this room. Make them all pay.

Righteous tried a counter-narrative, a voice of reason. His voice was weak, barely discernible above her breathing. Each day without the drugs he grew weaker and weaker. Sinister's snarl became triumphant. He was in the ascendant, his day would come. Sinister started to tell her what was written in the cuneiform scars in her flesh, a secret message that she alone could understand.

It had taken all of Jack McCoach's influence and a fair amount of money before he was able to have his daughter back. The antipsychotic medicine had helped of course, silencing the voices – silencing her voice until the clinical psychiatrist was satisfied she was safe to be released. Phoebe had left one prison for another, rarely leaving the house and never alone. Never alone. That had been one of the conditions of her release; continuous supervision, a daily diet of pills. On good days she had free run of the house, was even allowed out into the garden to feel the sun on her skin. On bad days they bound her in chemical captivity. Barely aware of her own existence, she lay on the bed, head too heavy to lift and hair wet from the drool that slid from slack lips. The smile returned. How could they not understand she was never alone? Sinister and Righteous were always with her, whispering conflicting advice in each ear, drowning out the lesser voices that struggled to be heard.

In her seat, Phoebe strained against the armrests, muscles tensing then relaxing. Legs forced down harder and harder to the floor until her pelvis raised off the chair. This was the workout regime Sinister had instigated, strengthening muscles slack from inaction, toning stomach and shoulders, building strength whilst all the time she appeared inactive, docile.

Whilst Phoebe concentrated on her exercises, Sinister fought a continuing battle with Righteous. This was a struggle that had been going on for as long as she could remember, the voices arguing and shouting at each other in between urgent whispers telling her what to do. What not to do. She was quite adept at tuning them out now, all except those urgent whispers that caught her unaware. At some level of understanding she was aware that Righteous was sounding weaker, more desperate, whilst Sinister had a triumphant edge. Muscles tensed, relaxed. Phoebe listened with dispassionate interest as Sinister continued the slow and calculated murder of Righteous inside her head, one neuron after the other.

She heard the key jangling long before the lock was turned. Phoebe slackened in her seat, allowed her head to fall to one side, lowered her eyelids. Day nurse in her crisp blue uniform opened the door, cautiously checking before entering.

"How's Phoebe? Would you like to go to the toilet?" She asked the question as one would a child, arm held out to offer support.

Phoebe smiled in return, taking care not to allow her wolf smile to show. She held onto the proffered arm, allowed herself to be raised out of her seat and acted weaker than she really was. Followed day nurse to the toilet. She read the writing on her arm as she peed – Sinister patiently explained what each scar represented, told her what the future held. She nodded in understanding. None of this was her fault. The trickle of urine slowed to a halt, leaving the sound of silence pressing against her ears like an oppressive force. She listened intently, head to one side in an effort to pierce the all-enveloping silence. Nothing but the high whistle of eardrum stretched tight inside her skull.

"I'd like to walk in the garden awhile." Voice plaintive, little girlish.

Day nurse's eyes narrowed imperceptibly, appraising threat.

"I'll help you down the stairs. Do you need a coat? It's colder than it looks."

"I'm fine," Phoebe answered. Her smile appeared genuine, friendly.

"Come on, then. We'll take a stroll around the lawn until you feel tired."

They climbed slowly down the sweeping staircase, Phoebe's arm held captive in the day nurse's grip. In her imagination they were descending from the princess's tower cell. Phoebe's smile remained; day nurse hadn't realised she was arm in arm with the dragon. The princess had been eaten a long, long time ago.

CHAPTER 15
The Ashes

DC Frankie McKenzie stood next to Patricia's prostrate body, watching the slow rise and fall of the thin hospital blanket, which offered the only indication that she was still alive. A white bandage covered her eyes, wrapped enough times around her head that she resembled an Egyptian mummy abandoned before the job had been fully completed. The doctor had tersely informed Frankie that the patient was being kept in a coma until the swelling inside her head reduced, before double-checking the drips and breathing tubes a nurse had adjusted under his watchful gaze.

The hospital, Patricia's home for at least the next week, was a white concrete monolith. It always put Frankie in mind of an oversized Swiss ski lodge, perched incongruously up on the hill above the railway station. The window of Patricia's airless room looked out over the sea loch some distance below, sunshine glinting on wave crests like a picture postcard. The attendant doctor and nurse had given Frankie a cursory glance as she entered the room, bending back to their patient.

"When do you expect her to regain consciousness?"

The doctor gave the impression of a man too busy to talk, turning towards her with barely concealed irritation. "It's too early to give a definitive answer. There was a bleed on her brain, which luckily stopped before we had to operate on her skull, but I'm not expecting her to be ready to talk for at least 3 days." He paused, sparing a quick glance back at Patricia before continuing, "If she can talk."

"Do you expect her to be brain damaged?"

"Head trauma is notoriously difficult to judge. I'm hopeful she'll pull through, but don't be surprised if she can't remember the event or days beforehand. Short-term memories are always the first to go. Then there's the loss of eyesight. She'll be needing help. A lot of help. Not an interrogation!" The tone in his voice was sufficient for Frankie to realise she wasn't welcome.

She persevered despite his irritation. "Can you ensure we are notified as soon as she regains consciousness? Whoever did this needs to be found and put away before anyone else gets hurt."

"I'll ask the nursing staff to contact you when she's in a fit state to receive visitors. Now, if you don't mind, I've a job to do."

Frankie watched the doctor as he swept out of the room, stethoscope swinging across starched shirt. The nurse followed in his wake, sending an apologetic look towards Frankie. She exchanged a tight smile in return before pulling out her notepad and making a note to come back in three days. On her way out, she stopped at the ward reception where a staff nurse had provided directions to Patricia's room. The same nurse still sat at the desk, flicking through a pile of paperwork and scrawling indecipherably on each sheet. She looked up as Frankie stopped in front of her.

"Has Patricia McCoach had any visitors, any family members since she was admitted?"

"Not that I'm aware of. She's still being kept in a coma and we don't generally encourage bedside visitors to intensive care – unless the prognosis isn't good. Then family are notified so they can say their goodbyes."

Frankie nodded. The nurse's bedside manner had adjusted so they could talk as one professional to another, both well enough acquainted with death to not treat the subject as taboo.

"What about telephone calls, anyone calling in to see how she's doing?"

The nurse looked puzzled for a moment, taking a few seconds to reflect before answering. "No. No, we've not had anyone call." Her voice expressed surprise, as if only just realising how unusual it was for no-one to enquire after a patient's health. "You would have thought her family would be in touch, wouldn't you, after what's happened?"

Frankie thanked her for her time and made her way back to the patrol car. As she drove out of the car park, she found herself in agreement with the staff nurse. Although the family had just suffered a bereavement, it seemed strange that they hadn't called the hospital. What that meant was anyone's guess at the moment, but she would have to let Corstophine know.

Corstophine had left the station immediately after sending an email to Sharmila Mallick. It was at best a long shot, asking the state hospital if they had a record of anyone committing a similar double blinding, but he needed to identify a suspect quickly.

The road to Glenfinnan only took twenty-five minutes, a quiet drive along the A830 following the shores of Loch Eil and running alongside the railway line connecting Fort William to Mallaig. Corstophine tried his best to enjoy the promise of a fine day in the hills, but a passing train reminded him of the recent suicide and the father's anguish when he had broken the news of his daughter's death. When he and Frankie had tried to leave her distraught father, he had stopped them from going – pointing out his daughter's photograph on the mantlepiece. He had told them how proud he was of her, how well she was doing at the Glasgow Conservatoire. He steadfastly refused to use the past tense, insisting they look at the photograph in its cheap frame, which he'd thrust almost aggressively into Corstophine's hands. His daughter straddled a cello, face bent down towards the instrument in concentration, hand caught in mid flow pulling the oversize bow across the strings.

"I'm sorry for your loss." The words were spoken automatically, parroted in Pavlovian response and mirroring the words he'd spoken to Emma McCoach at the church service a few days ago. He knew fine well that the words were inadequate, but what else could he have said? The girl's father had watched them leave, his empty eyes meeting Corstophine's when he glanced back at the house. The father had stood motionless, his expressionless face that of a man who had lost all reason to live. Corstophine had driven away concerned that the father might commit suicide himself, but there were limits to what he could do – and social workers had too much on their plate to be bothered with a grieving parent.

It was in this state of unsettled distraction that Corstophine pulled on his hiking boots in the company of three other hikers, parked in a gravelled layby on the banks of the River Finnan at 9 a.m. They were just a few miles from where he had waited for Jack McCoach's body to be carried down the mountain a month previously.

Robb and the distillery's MD, Bryan Cobb, were regular enough hillwalkers but Corstophine was surprised to see Sandy McPhearson had joined them. The man was struggling to pull on his boots, foot raised awkwardly on the tailgate of his estate car as he groaned with the unaccustomed exertion. How he was expecting to manage the mini expedition that Robb had planned, God only knew.

"I've had to pack his ashes in this Tupperware container." Robb held an orange plastic tub up for them all to view, "I couldn't fit the urn in my rucksack."

Three faces turned dutifully to regard Jack McCoach's temporary resting place – grey ash clearly visible through the clear plastic lid before it was unceremoniously thrust into the top of Robb's backpack and sealed tightly closed.

They exchanged a shared look, faint surprise at the choice of container mingled with the struggle of attempting some sort of reverence for a plastic tub.

"Aye well, you don't want to be lugging anything too heavy up there." Sandy McPhearson might have been referring to himself as his eyes took in the route ahead of them. At this point, the path was obvious: a metalled road following the River Finnan towards the railway viaduct that dominated the glen. Sandy swept his blond hair back from his forehead, causing Corstophine to wince as he willed the suspected hairpiece to stay put. He laid an internal bet with himself that Sandy and his hairpiece would part ways before they reached the first summit, nodding in self-confirmation as a cool breeze strengthened off Loch Shiel as if to gently encourage them onwards.

"You two been to the same sale?" Sandy directed his question at Robb and Bryan, both sporting the same outdoor jacket in subdued yellow.

"Wish it was in a sale!" Bryan replied. "I asked Robb to recommend a jacket and he suggested this one – almost £200!" He compared his to Robb's. "Hadn't realised we'd bought the same colour. This mustard wouldn't have been my first choice, but they'd almost run out of stock."

"Sunrise Yellow," Robb corrected. "Everyone ready?" He had assumed the role of team leader.

A chorus of ayes responded, followed by the shutting of car boots and multiple clicks as car remotes were triggered. Packs were strapped on, adjusted and the small party started up the private road.

They had readily assumed a formation, Robb setting a measured pace to accommodate for Sandy's level of fitness, with Corstophine and Bryan Cobb bringing up a leisurely rear. They walked in relative silence, apart from Sandy puffing like one of the steam trains that transported Harry Potter fans across the Glenfinnan viaduct high above them.

Corstophine took the time to appreciate the view, morning sunshine making a sporadic showing between racing clouds. A few older walkers were on the path with them, overtaking their slow-moving convoy with cheerful greetings and comments on the weather as they drew level. Walking sticks tapped staccato beats on the metalled road, announcing each walker's presence before they arrived, aluminium poles waved in acknowledgment with a swordsman's flourish as they walked ahead. When their small party reached closer to the bubbling waters of the River Finnan, the sun was mirrored back to them in broken stars.

It was the promise of sunshine that had decided him – a day without rain being a rare enough event in late October, besides which he might be able to talk to Robb when his guard was down. Someone in the family must know what Patricia's attack meant or who might have been responsible.

"There's a horse and cart entombed in one of these pillars." Bryan gestured above their heads as they passed under the West Highland Railway viaduct, literally within touching distance of soaring stone columns, each crowned in over-engineered Victorian arches.

Corstophine's poetic mood suddenly deserted him. "Is that so? I thought they'd discovered it was the viaduct at Loch-nan-Uamh?"

"No, definitely here. These supports are hollow by all accounts and the poor beastie slipped as it carried building materials across the railway. Too difficult to get it out so it's still here. Somewhere."

Bryan's eyes followed the line of stone pillars, trying unsuccessfully to guess which one held the unlikely time capsule. Corstophine couldn't be bothered to argue the point.

"I heard that Jack might have been poisoned?" Bryan's question caught Corstophine unaware. He'd asked quietly enough that the sound of Sandy's laboured breathing, several paces in front, covered anything they said.

"What gave you that idea?" Corstophine fixed Bryan with a look that Frankie termed his 'inquisitorial stare' – not that she'd ever shared that with him.

"Emma told me you'd been around to question her."

Corstophine held Bryan's eyes for an uncomfortably long time, wondering how close a relationship he might have with his ex-employer's wife.

"It's an allegation that's been made without any substance, and not something that we're taking seriously. I'd be grateful if you didn't spread it around – for Emma's sake if nothing else."

"No, of course." Bryan's dismissal came as a reflex, closing down the conversation before it had a chance to begin. He studiously concentrated on the path underfoot, but Corstophine caught the quick sideways flick of his eyes as he checked for any reaction.

Fishing was one activity Corstophine hadn't yet tried.

For a man enveloped in loneliness, the thought of standing thigh deep in slow flowing water watching an artificial fly drift past him on the current was too familiar a metaphor. He did, however, share some of the essential qualities that marked out the successful fisherman compared to those who merely embraced ennui as a hobby.

"Do you know Emma well?" Corstophine set a friendly tone, aiming his fly with precision.

Bryan took his time before responding, studying the bait.

"I've known the McCoachs ever since I started at the distillery – must be near twenty years now. We used to be regular visitors, my wife and I. Emma is a wonderful cook, you know, she'd put a lot of professionals in the shade. Her loin of venison in a sloe gin and blackberry glaze…"

Bryan shook his head in admiration as he drifted off into a reminiscence of meals past.

"Used to?" Corstophine gave the lightest of touches to the line, caused the fly to dance across the water.

Bryan looked puzzled for a second until he'd replayed the conversation back again.

"Yes. When my wife left me, it just became too awkward."

He turned to Corstophine offering a tight smile. "People generally don't want to spend their evening with a morose divorcee – not the best of company."

"I'm sorry." Corstophine found he could only too easily relate to that statement.

They continued in silence, broken only by the rush of water as the River Finnan cascaded off small waterfalls marking its snaking progress down the glen – that and the regular exaggerated exhalations Sandy made with every breath. Corstophine wondered again at the wisdom of taking the man up any hill; the path they followed was a well-maintained road, scarcely any incline at all.

The road ended just ahead. They had reached the Corryhully Bothy, a low-lying stone building nestling beside the river and sheltering in the company of a few straggly firs. Almost without them realising, the mountains had drawn closer – the rounded and ragged peaks of Sgurr Thuilm and Sgurr nan Coireachan hinting at the true wilderness beyond. Corstophine studied the skyline, drinking in the Gaelic names as if the native sounds connected him in some meaningful way to the land.

Sandy's laboured steam-engine breathing reached tortuous levels as the party drew to a halt.

"Do you want to stop for a minute?" Robb's concerned voice rose above the puffing and panting.

"No, no. I'm absolutely fine. Just a bit of a climb." Sandy's immobile stance gave lie to his words, his red cheeks ballooning out with each breath.

"We can stop off at the bothy for a bit if you'd like, we've come quite a way." Robb glanced down the track to Corstophine and Bryan.

Corstophine rested on his stick, polished oak smooth under his hands. The stick was a birthday gift from his colleagues, the wood refusing to conform to standard walking stick vernacular. It twisted and turned along its length like the clues in a typical investigation before reaching the ground. Hidden in the handle was a shot of whisky, he hadn't asked what brand, but they knew him well enough for it to be a single malt. Lamb had joked that it had taken a while before they'd settled on the ideal stick for him, and although he had laughed good-humouredly with the rest of them at the time, he still couldn't see what was funny about it.

Sandy's breathing returned to a more normal rate. "No need, I'm alright now. Ready for the next slog."

"We'll be staying here tonight anyway," Robb pointed towards the bothy. "No point in carrying everything up the hills. Why don't we dump the packs and I'll just take the essentials in mine?"

Sandy's face brightened at the thought of losing his backpack, and with a surge of newfound energy he positively bounded across the small bridge that led to the bothy – releasing the straps as he went.

Corstophine waited for them to rejoin him. He had no intention of climbing the second mountain and spending the night with them. A slow ascent of the first munro to see Jack's ashes away, then back to his car well before he lost the daylight.

CHAPTER 16
Glasgow Train

"Corstophine's taken the day off. He's gone hillwalking." Hamish's ponderous announcement welcomed Frankie back to the station as he peered at her from over the top of his computer screen at reception.

"Aye, he said he was making the best of the weather. Don't blame him – there won't be too many days like this before winter arrives." Frankie waited patiently for Hamish to operate the door release to the back office.

"We've had a delivery from forensics, they've sent us preliminary results from Patricia McCoach's house." Hamish lifted a large manila envelope off the counter before activating the door, the harsh buzz letting her know the lock had been released.

Frankie took the envelope in passing. "Thanks, I'll have a look at it."

She checked the other desks, wondering briefly where PCs Lamb and McAdam were, before remembering they were both working a late shift.

"Better not be any major incidents," she announced to an empty office as she took her seat, pulling open the envelope and laying the contents out on the desk. The reports gave a factual account of Patricia's injuries, citing the two paintbrush handles as being instrumental in causing her blinding. There was plenty of DNA left on the brushes and the cosh, sufficient for the forensics lab to rule out the samples taken from immediate family and others at the scene. No matches from the police database either. They'd lost access to the Europol database since the UK government had pulled them out of Europe without agreeing any sharing of police information, something Frankie knew would bite them in the butt one day.

God, I'm starting to think like Lamb talks! Frankie realised her daily exposure to PC Lamb's recent affectation of Americanisms was having an effect. She shook her head in denial before studying the report with interest: trace DNA markers indicated a good possibility that they were dealing with someone from the local region, but they needed more than that to go on. She shut the file with a sigh. This investigation wasn't suggesting any short cuts.

What did they have? A possible connection to Patricia's brother, Jack McCoach – assuming he hadn't died of natural causes and that was a big assumption. That at least would bring the family and their ownership of the distillery into focus. Why blind her and use her blood to paint on the canvas the assailant had carefully carried upstairs and set up in her bedroom? That would suggest more than a random attack, something more personal or someone seeking retribution. For what though?

Frankie started scribbling on the spare notepad she kept on her desk, circles containing Patricia and Jack's names joined by lines leading to cloud shapes. The distillery occupied one cloud, Jack's family another, then random lines leading to empty clouds. She sat back in her seat and critically viewed the diagram before admitting that it told her nothing. She needed something else to go on and just had to hope that something didn't turn out to be another mutilated person.

She gazed longingly out of the window, autumn sunshine painting the town in a golden light. Just a couple more hours before her shift ended. It was too good a day to spend in the office, Corstophine had had the right idea taking to the hills whilst the weather stayed like this.

"I forgot to say, the stationmaster said the CCTV was available to view if someone can collect it?" Hamish's head had appeared around the door.

Frankie grabbed the patrol car keys and headed out the door, calling to Hamish in passing.

"I'll go and see if I can spot any drug dealing while I'm there."

"Now, don't go putting yourself in harm's way." By the time Hamish's pedantic way with words had reached a conclusion, Frankie was already out of earshot. Hamish's head shook slowly as he wondered at the impetuousness of youth, before checking his police radio was charged and working, in case she needed help.

The train station car park brought back the recent memory of the young woman's suicide. Frankie had been handed a purse as the ambulance crew zipped the body into the bag. Inside was a plastic season ticket identifying the woman as Sarah Keir and an almost unrecognisable photograph. They'd found her address easily enough, then she and Corstophine had driven the short distance to knock on her parent's door.

The father had opened the door, stated just he and his daughter lived there. Frankie had asked him if they could talk inside, seen his skin pale as the implication of having two serious-looking police officers arrive on his doorstep sank home. They had watched him collapse in on himself as Corstophine told him what no parent ever wants to hear, seen him act in denial of any possibility his daughter could be dead, and left him drained of hope – a husk of a man.

She wiped the memory from her mind. Life was full of shit like this, you either closed it down or it got to you in the end. A constant drip feed from the darker side of human existence. Corstophine's drug of choice was whisky – a nightcap, he termed it, but they both knew it helped dull the senses sufficiently for sleep to come.

The stationmaster's office was a small room constructed as an afterthought behind the ticket office. One window overlooked the main entrance, the other window gave a limited view of the two platforms. His uniform had seen better days, unidentifiable stains dotted the jacket whilst his shirt gave the impression of having been slept in. Judging by the slightly offensive stale odour permeating the confined space, Frankie suspected he rarely changed his clothes.

"Let me just run the footage, it's here somewhere." His voice became muffled as his head sank below the intervening desk, accompanied by quiet curses and exclamations as he bumped into the furniture. Frankie turned around in her seat to view a row of monitors on the back wall, displaying views of the station concourse and platforms. One of the screens blanked, then disconcertingly displayed one of the platforms with passengers walking backwards at speed as he searched for a date stamp.

"There." His head reappeared, glasses readjusted as he smiled encouragingly at her.

Frankie watched the monitor. The scene had frozen in time, people caught awkwardly in mid-stride or staring at phones. The video started again and she saw the young woman standing alone some distance back from the platform edge. The train hadn't reached the station yet, the benches still filled with commuters too tired to stand. A couple of men passed by the woman; her head inclined towards them as if in response to some comment before they walked out of camera range.

"Keith Tunstall. I wonder what you're up to?" Frankie

had spoken quietly to herself, but the stationmaster queried her.

"What? Sorry, didn't catch that."

"No, it's nothing, I just recognised someone on the platform." She kept her attention fixed on the screen. Keith's face was split by an unpleasant grin, shared with the guy he was with before she lost them both to view. Her attention once more on the woman, seeing her hand brush her cheeks with a repetitive motion. Was she crying? She was too far away to see in any detail. She held a stick in her left hand, leaning on it for support as if she was disabled or recovering from a leg injury. There followed another minute of nothing much happening until the benches started to empty as passengers moved towards the platform edge. In the corner of the screen, she could see the train pulling in, already moving fairly slowly as the driver gradually applied brakes to bring the carriages to a halt. Her eyes focussed on the young woman, watched with the pain of foreknowledge as she suddenly sprinted forward and threw herself in front of the engine, saw the body bounce like a rag doll before the train rolled over her as if she offered no impediment to progress. Frankie saw the platform passengers once more frozen in inaction with only the train displaying any motion. The train driver's face was clearly visible through the front windscreens, mouth open and eyes wide with shock. Frankie had seen enough and stopped the footage before the crowds gathered around, horrified yet strangely excited at the scene in front of them.

"That was the Glasgow train, wasn't it?" Frankie asked the question with a steady voice, ignoring the quaver that threatened to affect her speech.

"Aye, there's a ten-minute break before it goes back again." The stationmaster hesitated, adjusted the grimy collar of his once white shirt. "But not this Monday. The driver had to take leave. It's standard practice when you get something like this, it throws the whole network into disarray." He said this as if the woman's suicide was an affront to the efficiency of the ScotRail network.

Frankie refrained from using the retort she favoured. "Can you give me footage from the other cameras covering the next ten minutes? If you have cameras covering the main entrances too, that would be a big help."

"Is this really necessary? It's fairly clear to me the girl just ran in front of the train, like!"

"Yes, we need to be absolutely sure when there's been a death."

The stationmaster grimaced, eyes holding doubt as to the veracity of her statement but proceeded to rummage around under his desk for a few minutes until eventually producing a memory stick attached to a ScotRail lanyard.

"I'll need it back." He held it close to his chest until Frankie agreed that it would be returned as soon as they had finished with it.

"She had a stick," Frankie queried more for her own benefit rather than for the stationmaster, "but she ran in front of the train?"

All she received in return was a disinterested shrug.

"OK. Thanks for your help, I'll get this back to you as soon as I can."

Frankie left his office, glad to breathe in air that wasn't tainted by sourness and headed back to the patrol car. The drug dealers could wait, even the presence of a police vehicle parked in the station car park would be enough for them to move elsewhere for the moment. She patted her pocket, confirming the presence of the memory stick and headed back to the police station. Frankie knew exactly how she would be spending the last few hours of her shift.

CHAPTER 17
Munro

The hillwalkers continued up the track with a lighter tread once the backpacks had been stowed in the bothy. Corstophine only had a small pack, space enough for some sandwiches, water and additional clothing. He'd been too long in the force to consider leaving his pack unattended, even for the few hours the climb would take. The unwritten code that anyone using a bothy would never interfere with another hillwalker's possessions didn't wash with him, but then constant exposure to the worst that humanity had to offer tended to have that detrimental effect.

The tarmac road had turned into more of a rough track several kilometres back, a slight incline still following the river Finnan along the valley floor. Sandy was noticeably more voluble now that his breathing had returned to a less desperate fight for air, and he began to engage Robb in a never-ending monologue about export tariffs and EU trade barriers. Corstophine made a mental note to avoid ever getting into a conversation with the man and instead attempted talking to Bryan, but he'd turned positively monosyllabic since Corstophine had started quizzing him on how deep his relationship went with Jack's wife. Walking in relative silence at least gave him the chance to enjoy the solitude of the mountains, watch the play of clouds chasing shadows over the lower flanks. He found himself responding almost spiritually to his surroundings, a penitent dwarfed by the dimensions of this natural outdoor cathedral. A few deer were grazing ahead of them, suddenly alert as they scented danger, then slipping silently into the shelter of trees. The track dipped down into water and they detoured to cross over a rickety wooden bridge, several of the floor struts missing and the whole edifice swinging alarmingly on wire ropes. Sandy inched across as if one wrong move would most likely result in his death, rather than an undignified soaking in the water below.

The mountains surrounded them on all sides now, a low-lying conifer plantation screening the immediate slopes on their right. They had lost the warmth of the sun as it dipped beneath the bulk of the ragged skyline, throwing the glen floor into shadow. Corstophine took advantage as they regrouped after the bridge crossing to join Robb, leaving Bryan and Sandy to bring up the rear where Sandy's conversation had progressed to holiday destinations. They reached the end of the track and Corstorphine recognised the location where they had waited for Jack's body to be brought down from the hill.

"We just have to climb up to this ridge and follow it up to Sgurr Thuilm." Robb's outstretched finger indicated an obvious muddy path trodden into the grassy slope and Corstophine's stick became more than a fashion accessory. As they followed the track upwards across boggy grassland, Sandy's breathing regained its stentorian volume. This was the beginning of the climb proper, and within minutes Corstophine and Robb had left the other two stragglers so far behind that Sandy's breathing could no longer be heard.

Corstophine tried an easy opener. "How's your mother coping? It can't have been easy for her these last few weeks."

"She's been alright, on the whole. We had a few tearful

moments when I caught her unawares. We're not the most demonstrative of families." Robb stared fixedly ahead. "There's an awful lot of paperwork when someone dies; funeral arrangements, wills, notifying tax authorities, legal stuff. Bloody nuisance to be honest but it takes your mind off the awfulness of what's happened."

"Has she anyone to talk to? I mean, with what happened to Patricia, it's good to have a close friend or two."

"Bryan's been very supportive. He's been over a few times now and she seems calmer after he's visited."

"Do you know Bryan well? I know you probably meet him mostly through work, but he seems a nice enough guy."

Robb nodded in agreement. "Bryan's the only member of the board that ever shows any interest in my ideas. The rest of them always followed Dad's lead and closed down every idea I have."

"What ideas were those?"

"Well, things like the gin production. Other distilleries have turned to gin when there's been a slump in sales and have made a killing. The turnaround is in weeks as opposed to years for whisky."

"Was the distillery in any sort of financial trouble, sales not doing well?" Corstophine's detective nose was twitching.

Robb turned to face him with a look of slight incredulity. "Every industry has gone through a slump in the last year! First, the economy closed down due to the pandemic, then it took almost the entire year before anyone started drinking in public again with social distancing in place, and to top it all they totally messed up Brexit. It's a wonder any industry has been left standing!"

"I take your point." Corstophine agreed. "The surge in long term unemployment has certainly given us more to do with all those idle fingers looking for easy cash." He thought of the mini crime wave hitting the town. "So why not go with your idea for the gin?"

"Oh, Dad was saying it would just be one more product in an already swamped market." Robb checked the skyline, automatically taking note of the weather as any experienced hillwalker would do. He thought for a moment before continuing, "Point is, everyone and their dog was starting a distillery. You just buy the alcohol in bulk and add flavourings, it's really not that difficult, then you add a massive mark-up and presto! Cashflow coming into the business. I still think it was worth a go."

"What else did you try?" Corstophine spoke with genuine interest. His experience of the whisky manufacturing process was slim at best, but he enjoyed the end product. It wouldn't hurt to learn a bit more about it as they climbed.

"The gin was my main idea. I've a small distillery at the house to infuse botanicals. I was experimenting with different flavourings. When that idea was scrapped, I started using the infuser to flavour water. We have our own water supply at the distillery and more than enough to serve another lucrative market, especially somewhere like China. They love the idea of pure Highland water but again, the competition is huge. That's why I started trying out flavoured water and had a batch of bottles made with the distillery branding."

"Sounds like a good idea." Corstophine tried flattery to keep him talking.

"Yes, I thought so too." Robb started to warm to Corstophine. "Bryan came up with some flavouring ideas as well. Now the old man's gone, I may just suggest the bottled water idea again."

Robb pushed ahead up the hill, leaving little air to waste on conversation. Once they reached the top, Corstophine was not in the least surprised to see the real summit some distance ahead, along a broad ridge with steep drops each side. It was not a path to take in poor visibility. His appreciation of the mountain rescue team went up another notch, imagining them negotiating this track in darkness whilst carrying Jack's heavy body. He stopped for a minute to catch his breath, looking behind to check on Bryan and Sandy making slow progress up the hill. In front of him lay the summit of Sgurr Thuilm, and beyond that lay the Knoydart hills – mile after mile of true wilderness. He followed in Robb's footsteps, now a good 50 metres in front of him. Somewhere along this last section was where Jack's body had lain, hidden by the mist. Corstophine's eyes swept over the vista opening up all around him as he neared the summit; there were worse places to die.

The wind assisted Corstophine up the last 100 metres, picking up strength as he neared the exposed summit. Robb already had his thermos out, sitting in the lee of a cairn that offered some respite from the wind. Corstophine spied a rock that would suffice as a makeshift seat and joined him, removing his backpack to liberate sandwiches and water. They sat in companionable silence, content to rest after the exertion of the climb and view the hills and lochs spread out beneath them. Corstophine reflected that Jack McCoach had almost made the top, his heart giving out just a few minutes shy of the summit. Would he have lived if he'd completed the climb, had the chance to recuperate before the less arduous walk down?

A new note entered the soundscape of wind cutting through gaps in the pile of boulders, a repeat of the steam engine he'd heard at the beginning of their climb. Sandy collapsed rather than sat, his face an unhealthy shade of purple as he fought for air. Bryan let go of the arm he was holding, an expression of quiet relief etched on his face at reaching his destination without having to cope with another heart attack.

"Made it then?" Robb may have been trying for encouragement but to Corstophine it came across as disdain. Sandy rolled his eyes in some sort of response, unable to speak for the moment. Bryan settled into place, completing the quorum on top of the mountain, accepting the plastic carrier bag Robb extracted from his pack.

"Some view!" Bryan spoke between gulps of water from his bottle, screwing the top back down tight before securing it between two rocks at his feet.

The comment went unanswered apart from nods and indecipherable grunts. Sandy had recovered sufficiently to request his rations from Robb's pack, who handed a large plastic lunchbox and water bottle for Corstophine to pass over. He held the bottle in his hand, turning it to inspect the distillery crest and name on the label.

"Is this one of your bottle designs?" Corstophine found he was almost having to shout above the wind.

"Aye, I only made a small batch so these will be collector's items one day!"

Corstophine passed the bottle over to Sandy, who desperately gulped the contents down before tearing into his lunchbox. They remained like this for ten minutes or so, until leg muscles threatened to cramp. Robb was the first one to make a move, stretching up out of his makeshift seat and presenting his father's ashes with a flourish.

"We'd better do it."

The words were simple but effective, causing them all to stand as one and form an impromptu semi-circle with Robb in the middle. The small group positioned themselves away from the likely course the ashes would take, Sandy sealing his lunchbox lid firmly against inadvertent contamination.

126

"Well, Dad, we've taken you to the top." Robb had lost his southern preacher delivery, sounding more like a child who has only just realised they've lost a parent. "These were the hills you loved. You were born within sight of these mountains. Lived, worked, loved and died in their embrace. I hope you find peace here."

He tipped a handful of ashes out of the Tupperware container, the orange tub lending an almost absurd tragi-comic feel to the proceedings, and a swirl of dust followed the winds towards the Knoydart peninsula. Only a small portion of the ashes landed on the actual summit, coating the rocks and slipping down between the gaps.

"Aye. Peace." Bryan echoed the words and they bowed heads in respect.

"Right, we'd better press on to Sgurr nan Coireachan if we don't want to be coming down in the dark." Robb assumed his team leader role once more, packing the orange tub back in his rucksack along with assorted bottles and packets. He sounded too enthusiastic, covering for the tremor in his voice.

"I'll wish you all a safe onward journey," Corstophine held up a hand in farewell. "I'll just take in the view here a while longer, then head back to the car. What's your plan for tomorrow?"

"We'll be staying at Corryhully bothy tonight, then we're planning on driving back down the road to climb Streap if the weather holds up. We may spend the night at Gleann Dubh-Lighe bothy if it takes a while." Robb's eyes strayed towards Sandy in silent admonition.

Corstophine watched them as they retraced their steps, hearing snatches of Sandy's voice as the wind veered towards him. He regained his seat, padding the cairn with his spare jacket to protect his back, and enjoyed the solitude. Since his wife had died, he'd become self-sufficient out of necessity, learning to live with himself, cope with everything life threw at him.

"For God's sake – listen to yourself, man!"

There she was, laughing good-naturedly at him as he sat on the top of a wind-swept mountain, eyes crinkling with merriment. He smiled in return, even as she faded from his mind's eye, but it was enough. With a last lingering look over the wild landscape beyond and a lighter heart, Corstophine packed his rucksack and headed back down the trail. The wind veered from the south as he started his descent, coming at him from the west, which he took as a good omen. He'd only walked a short distance down the trail before a new note entered the soundscape of wind moaning around stubborn rock, a faint flute-like tone coming from his left. Intrigued, he climbed cautiously down from the ridge to investigate and found the source. Caught between two rocks was a plastic bottle, the open top catching errant drafts of air as they swirled in eddies around it. He recognised the distillery design from Robb's water bottles and, with mounting interest, realised there was still liquid left inside. Corstophine eased it out from between the rocks, holding it carefully in his handkerchief as it was placed within his rucksack and carried down the hill.

CHAPTER 18
Taser Taser

Frankie ran the video footage from the railway station cameras, paying particular attention to Keith Tunstall whenever he appeared on screen. The segment where he made some sort of comment towards the girl was no clearer, but whatever exchange had occurred caused Keith and his companion great amusement. She watched stony-faced as the girl ran in front of the train, saw the phones raised above heads for the most advantageous view, felt the crowd's shock and excitement as they flooded towards her death like crows to carrion.

The station staff ran into the frame in a panic and peered over the platform edge before looking away in horror, then positioned barriers to screen off the sight. Disembarking passengers filed past the scene, craning necks to see what had happened to jolt them to a halt, pretending not to raise phones for a snap as they hurried past.

At the exit, she saw Keith Tunstall reappear, his dyed blond mop of hair making him an easy target to spot. He was still in the company of his weasel-faced friend and heading out of the station concourse in a rush before the emergency services arrived. He carried a large blue rucksack on his back, which hadn't been there when he had first arrived on the platform.

Frankie reran the video to watch the passengers disembarking from the Glasgow train, taking a screenshot when she identified someone carrying the same rucksack. Unless Keith was planning on doing some travelling, what did he need a rucksack for? More to the point, what was he carrying? She had her suspicions.

Voices from the front desk announced the arrival of PCs Lamb and McAdam, starting their late shift together. She wondered how long Bill McAdam would be able to survive a shift with the younger constable before something gave.

"Are you feeling lucky, punk?" PC Lamb held his Taser in a threatening stance, legs slightly spread, and lips curled in a sneer.

"Put the bloody thing down, Phil! It's not a toy." Bill McAdam had the look of someone whose limited store of patience was close to exhaustion. "Hi, Frankie." He gave her a tight smile of welcome as he made a beeline for the coffee. "Much happening today?"

"Hi, Bill. No, all quiet on the western front." She watched PC Lamb struggling to replace the Taser back in its holster, half hoping that he'd shoot himself in the leg. He'd volunteered for the 24 hour Specially Trained Officer programme months ago, and Corstophine had given him the go-ahead. Christ alone knew why, maybe he thought Lamb had matured since first joining straight from police college. It hadn't escaped Frankie's notice that Lamb had gone out of his way to cut down on the quips and jokes that had been his trademark. She knew this was Lamb's way of progressing towards the firearm unit – it fitted with his cowboy delusions but nobody up the bloody ladder had realised.

"Don't!" Bill's tone let her know he'd had enough of western references.

Poor bastard. He had an eight-hour shift in front of him, trapped in a patrol car with the younger constable.

"Corstophine's taken the day off, hillwalking with that club he's in. They've taken Jack McCoach's ashes, they're going to scatter them on the Munro he was climbing."

Frankie spoke as she pocketed her mobile, logging off from her computer as she prepared to finish for the day. She picked up a sheet of paper, handing it over to Bill as he poured milk into his coffee mug.

"These are the cars I reckon are most likely to be targeted in the next few days. They've all had new converters fitted and are parked out in the street, easy pickings."

"Thanks, Frankie." The rich aroma of freshly brewed coffee brought PC Lamb over to join them.

"Is this going to be a stake out?" His young face positively shone with enthusiasm, oblivious to the death stare PC McAdam sent his way.

"I'll leave you to it then." Frankie's smile was not shared by PC McAdam. "Mind how you go now, y'all."

She left the station with a light tread, imagining the two of them working a night shift together.

PC McAdam took a sip from his mug, frowned at PC Lamb's back and concentrated on reading Frankie's list. They were all vehicles that had recently had their catalytic converters replaced, parked in the street as she had described. He selected a Toyota Prius from the list, if only because he'd seen more of these cars being targeted than any other brand. Frankie had left additional information: the preferred tools of the trade being a car jack and electric saw; average time to remove, under two minutes.

"Shit!" PC McAdam realised that coming across one of these thefts as they drove around the town was going to be extremely unlikely.

"Looks like you're going to have your stake out after all. Finish your coffee, we're going to spend the next few hours undercover."

"Like a detective? Are we getting changed back into civvies?" PC Lamb asked in incredulity.

"Just get in the car as you are, Phil. There's undercover, then there's under cover."

They parked up within view of PC McAdam's chosen target, slotted in between a row of cars on a side street that hid them from any cursory view.

"Now what do we do?"

PC McAdam tilted his seat back into a reclining position and folded his arms.

"Now, Phil, we wait. Quietly."

"How long for?"

PC McAdam's eyes rolled back in his head, looking for divine help. It wasn't forthcoming.

"As long as it takes. Just shut up and keep your bloody eyes open."

PC Lamb checked his watch. It was past six and the traffic was noticeably quieter as the last of the commuters headed back to the warmth of their homes. The sun had set over an hour ago, streetlights now fully lit and bathing the roads in LED white. The few pedestrians hurrying past bent their heads to the pavements, tightly wrapped in jackets and coats against the chill wind announcing winter's approach. Those few passers-by who noticed the two constables observing them swiftly turned their heads back to a contemplation of the pavement, each one a study in guilt attempting innocence.

The hours dragged by, marked only by house lights showing in windows all around them and the electric blue flicker of TV screens casting their spells upon the occupants. PC Lamb reached for his phone, automatically searching for social media updates, only for McAdam to tell him in no uncertain terms to put it away. It was then that a small van caught their attention, slowly cruising down the road before stopping just in front of the Prius.

Both constables became alert as two occupants exited the vehicle. Lamb made to leave the patrol car, but McAdam laid a restraining hand on his arm.

"Wait for a bit, we need to catch them in the act." He removed his arm, adjusted his seat back into an upright position and checked that his cuffs, PAVA spray and baton were in place.

They watched intently as a trolley jack was removed from the back of the van, shoved under the Prius and the vehicle tilted up on one side. The second man disappeared from view, diving under the car.

"I'll take the guy standing guard." PC McAdam indicated the character standing by the car, his face turning this way and that, searching the road for any approaching traffic. "You take the one under the car. He should be easy enough laid flat out in the road for you."

They opened the patrol car doors as quietly as they could. PC McAdam left immediately, bent almost double as he used the parked cars for cover. Lamb struggled to replace his Taser in its holster, he had been playing with it whilst waiting in the car. By the time he had managed to get out of his seat, PC McAdam was already onto his man, twisting one arm behind his back before he'd even realised the constable was there. PC Lamb ran down the street towards them, all thoughts of concealment forgotten as the two men's curses filled the air. He wasn't too concerned with McAdam's struggles, there weren't many people who could fight him off, given his size and enthusiasm for a 'bit of physical'.

His accomplice slid out from under the car before Lamb had a chance to reach him, springing to his feet and walking menacingly towards the two grappling men.

"Let him go, ya bastard, or I'll cut your fucking arm off!"

The sound of a high-powered electric saw suddenly filled the air, and Lamb realised McAdam was in real danger. In normal circumstances, the constable could easily have taken the two men on, but with his hands literally full as he attempted to cuff his struggling captive, he was an easy target. PC Lamb struggled again with the Taser holster, almost tripping over his own feet as he closed the distance between them. Finally, he was able to release the fastenings and had the weapon in his hand.

"Stand still!" he shouted. "Taser Taser Taser!" PC Lamb pulled to a breathless halt and aimed the weapon squarely at the man's buttocks, using a visible rear cleavage to line up the laser sight. The rules and regulations for when it was appropriate to use the weapon ran through his mind in a blur, then instantly forgotten as his target span around with the electric saw and came at him. His finger squeezed the trigger in an automatic response, causing the lower of the twin barbs to embed itself in his potential assailant's more delicate parts. The assailant's expression turned from naked aggression to stunned shock as 50,000 volts coursed through his reproductive organs. The electric saw slipped through unresponsive fingers, hitting the tarmac mere seconds before its owner, his legs crumpling as they turned to jelly. The gun stopped arcing after five seconds, leaving the human target lying in a foetal position, hands cupping his manhood and strange mewling sounds coming from his mouth. His partner in crime stood unresisting in PC McAdam's grasp, mouth hanging open in shock.

"We'll need a medic to remove that barb." PC McAdam spoke as if what had happened was an everyday event, but his eyes betrayed his amusement. He efficiently finished locking his prisoner's wrists in cuffs before reaching for his radio and requesting a medical response team be sent to their location.

PC Lamb applied cuffs to unresisting wrists, basking in the glow of a job well done. His prisoner slowly uncurled, quiet now except for short, tortured breaths, then spoke in broken sentences, his voice at least an octave higher.

"I'll fucking sue. Shooting a man in the balls, what the fuck! I'll press charges!"

PC Lamb waved the X2 Taser in his face.

"The only one pressing charges around here is me. You shouldn't have turned around, should you?"

PC McAdam swept a practiced eye over the two of them and decided nothing was going to kick off for a good while.

"Come on you, in the back of the patrol car." He glanced back towards PC Lamb and his incapacitated victim. "Keep an eye on him, Phil. I don't think he's going to make a run for it, not whilst he's still hardwired to a Taser."

PC McAdam only walked a few steps towards the patrol car before his unrestrained laughter echoed down the street. PC Lamb looked around him. Curtains were being twitched open, and the more adventurous souls had appeared on doorsteps, their faces illuminated by the mobiles they held up like religious offerings. He stood up straighter, adjusted his cap, which had lost its regulation angle. This could make the front page!

CHAPTER 19
Sarah

Corstophine checked the holding cell where two sullen faces looked up as he opened the peephole. He closed the flap with a sigh.

"You have to hand it to the boys, that's a result. Have they been charged?"

"Aye, the paperwork's on my desk." Sergeant McKee stood at his side, consulting a sheaf of documentation. "There's outstanding arrest warrants on both of them. Glasgow's sending their boys to pick them up."

"Even better!" Corstophine rubbed his hands with satisfaction. Not only had they closed down the catalytic converter thefts, but they'd managed to avoid the tedious work of processing the two criminals for the Procurator Fiscal's office. That was a ton of paperwork he'd just sidestepped.

"Well done, Hamish. Good work!"

"Just one thing, sir." Hamish had waited until they were out of earshot of the cells.

Corstophine felt his momentary euphoria fading away. "What is it, Hamish?"

The old sergeant hesitated, searching for the appropriate wording, and failing.

"It's just there was a medical callout, sir, following Lamb's Tasering."

"Why, was one of those jokers suffering from a heart problem or something?"

"Not exactly, sir. You see, PC Lamb was aiming at his back – the one carrying the offensive weapon."

"The electric saw?" Corstophine queried.

"Aye, the electric saw. He was about to have a go at Bill and well, Lamb shouted out a warning then fired the Taser. But he'd turned around and received the shock in his balls, sir."

"I see." Corstophine tried to picture the scene. "Well, keep an eye on him, he'll not be our problem for much longer." He turned to enter his office, pausing at the door. "You'd better tell PC Lamb to make sure his notebook agrees with Bill's, just in case there's any comeback."

"Will do, sir. I'll catch them when they're in later today."

Corstophine sat at his desk, switching on his computer with a wide smile. He keyed the speed dial for forensics.

"Corstophine! What can we do for you today?" The voice was incessantly cheery – what was it with the forensics team, did exposure to the chemicals they routinely used make them all high?

"I've a bottle of water I'd like you to look at." His eyes focussed on the plastic bottle on his desk, distillery crest displayed across the neck. "I found it near the top of Sgurr Thuilm."

"Ah, the heart attack."

"Yes. Jack McCoach. I've reason to believe this was his water bottle."

"What do you want us to do, check it for fingerprints?"

"Yes, and analyse what water is left inside for anything that may have caused his heart attack."

"You think someone poisoned him?"

"I don't know what to think. Let's just say I'm taking care of all eventualities."

"OK, I'll ask Paul to swing by and collect it on his way to work. He lives local to you."

"Paul." Corstophine wrote the name on his pad. He knew it was Peter or Paul. *Sure it wasn't Mary?* He started at the sound of his wife's voice in his ear, scarcely hearing the forensics officer finishing the call. She was still there then. He felt a sense of relief that her voice was still making itself heard after so many years. She had been a constant presence for years following her death; her voice, her face, her smell appearing at random times in his thoughts. Was this what it was to be haunted? He sat in silent contemplation of the water bottle. Better to be haunted by someone you love than to never see them again.

The knock on his door prevented any further philosophising. Frankie entered his office following his call to enter.

"Morning, Frankie. The boys had a result last night."

"Yes, sir. By the sounds of it, they'll not be keen to come back in a hurry."

Corstophine's face creased in a smile, causing her to think how much better looking he was without that permanently haunted look he had about him.

"At this rate we'll have no crimes left to solve!"

"No, sir. Talking of which, I collected the CCTV from the railway station yesterday. Oh, I forgot to ask, how was your day yesterday? Get to the top?"

Corstophine nodded. "Aye. The weather held up as well, grand views from up there all the way across Knoydart. I left them to it, just did the one peak and back to the car." He pointed towards the water bottle on his desk. "I found this up there and there's still some water left in it."

"Is that Jack McCoach's water bottle, sir?"

"That's what I believe. Forensics are dropping by to pick it up and run an analysis. We'll see if Patricia's séance has any basis in fact."

"Well spotted."

"It was more the sound it made."

"Sorry, sir?" Frankie's puzzlement was almost comical, adding to Corstophine's good mood.

"The wind changed direction whilst I was up there. I heard it blowing over the open neck of the bottle and I couldn't work out what I was hearing, so I went to investigate and found it jammed between two rocks. Bloody lucky. If it hadn't been trapped there, it could be anywhere by now."

"The deep Pacific Ocean trench, sir. That's where they reckon most of the world's plastic ends up."

"Yes, well, wouldn't be much use to anyone there." Corstophine logged onto his computer, eager to clear up another string of crimes on his patch. "Was there anything you wanted, Frankie?"

"Yes, sir. I was checking the video footage from the suicide."

"Sorry, yes. I went off at a tangent about the hillwalking, you were telling me. Anything out of the ordinary?"

Frankie wondered at what point in Corstophine's career a young woman's suicide had become ordinary. "A couple of things, sir. First, there's this interchange I spotted just before she died." Frankie handed over a still from the video, a pixelated shot of the two youths walking towards the camera with the young woman in the background. Corstophine squinted his eyes at the photograph, causing Frankie to wonder when he was going to admit he needed glasses.

"Keith Tunstall, if I'm not mistaken. Nasty piece of work. He's been in a few times for various offences. Who's the bampot?"

"Don't know, sir, be easy enough to find out."

"Why are you showing me this?" Corstophine's

eyebrow raised in its familiar interrogative fashion. He knew there was more to come.

"He'd spoken to the girl seconds before this still, looked to me she was crying after he left. He may be the reason she ran in front of the train, sir."

Corstophine focussed on her eyes, trying to read her. "That's not enough for us to pull him in, Frankie."

"But this could be, sir." She placed a further two photographs in front of him, showing the blue rucksack on one passenger's back and then reappearing on Keith Tunstall's back as he left the station.

"OK." Corstophine held both pictures up as if they held more information that could somehow be extracted by staring at them more closely. "What are your thoughts?"

"Drugs, sir. I think what we're seeing here is a mule passing over the drugs to Keith."

Corstophine leant back in his seat. "Is he in that league? More your thuggery and small-time burglary, wouldn't you say?"

"I think it's worth looking at, sir." Frankie held her ground.

"OK." He thought for a moment. "This happened on when, Monday?"

"That's right, sir, it was the Glasgow train."

Corstophine's brows angled down in thought. "You could be right, there's nothing more common than a backpacker here in the Highlands. But how is Tunstall distributing the drugs? He's not turned up on any stop and search." He wrote the name in his notebook. "We should pay him a visit."

"That's what I thought, sir." She paused, seeing him return to a scrutiny of his screen. "I've arranged for the formal ID at the mortuary this morning; expecting a call any minute."

Corstophine raised his head, concern etched in new lines surrounding his eyes. "I can take it if you've other work you need to do?"

"It's OK, sir. I'd prefer to take this one."

"Thanks, Frankie."

She left, taking her seat in the main office. If they caught Keith Tunstall red-handed, that might be one of the drug runners dealt with, but unlike Corstophine she didn't think that would be the end of the problem, not in the least. It was like the mythological Greek Hydra, cut off one head and another two grew in its place. The suicide, though, the poor girl deserved more than to be left as just another statistic.

The arrival of two Glaswegian coppers she'd not seen before took her attention. Hamish led them down to the holding cell and she watched as the trio returned, accompanied by the two cell occupants. One was walking strangely, as if he was treading tenderly on eggshells. The prisoners' sullen looks contrasted with those of the happiest policemen she'd ever seen, even the normally dour sergeant's face was split with a wide grin. The door closed on them, just as Frankie received a call from the mortuary. The girl's father was on his way to make an ID.

Frankie stood on one side of the glass, a white body-shaped sheet covering whatever lay on the steel table on the other side of the mortuary viewing screen. Sarah Keir's father had given one terse nod when the sheet had been pulled back to expose her face. He'd brushed off Frankie's attempts to console him, slamming the door in a barely contained rage before storming away. She collected the paperwork, before thanking the mortuary staff for preparing the girl's body in preparation for the father's visit. He would not have wanted to witness what lay under the rest of the sheet.

Rage wasn't an unusual reaction. Most people collapsed in tears, holding onto each other for mutual support, taking comfort from the living. The dead girl's father was on his own; all his dreams lay on that cold slab. Rage was fine.

Corstophine had seemingly written off the girl's suicide, an open and shut case as far as he was concerned, but Frankie refused to draw a line under her death. Keith Tunstall had a part to play in her suicide, she was sure of it, and the poor lassie deserved justice. Once back at her desk, she started with social media, searching for anyone with the name Sarah Keir. Frankie clicked on the first hit, checking each photo against the scan of the girl's ID. The quality wasn't great, but it was enough when taken together with geographical data to discount every hit she found. After an hour's fruitless search, she had to conclude Sarah Keir had no social media presence, and that in itself was of interest.

That left Sarah's friends and tutors at the Glasgow Conservatoire. That picture of her on her father's mantlepiece where she was bent over in concentration, playing a cello. Frankie pulled up the website, searched for the cello tutors and pulled out a couple of names. She checked Corstophine's office, watching him bent over his own screen. This enquiry was taking her off-piste and she didn't necessarily want him to know what she was spending her valuable police time investigating. Corstophine stood up even as she watched him, pulling on his winter jacket and carefully collecting the plastic water bottle from his desk.

"I've someone to collect from the Glasgow train, Frankie," Corstophine called as he passed through the office. "I'll keep an eye open for anything suspicious while I'm there."

CHAPTER 20
Streap

R obb McCoach opened one eye, alerted by a curlew's call, even as the haunting sound faded away into the chill charcoal light of early dawn. He lifted his head, still heavy with sleep, and contemplated the dim outlines of the two other incumbent forms sleeping in the bothy. They resembled pupae, wrapped in their sleeping bags and sharing the basic sleeping platform. The comparison intrigued him, until his imagination failed to conceive what metamorphosis the two middle-aged directors might undertake.

He'd had a terrible night's sleep, punctuated as it was with the snoring emanating from Sandy McPhearson's gaping mouth, and had elected to stay at the far end of the building to sleep on an old sofa next to the fireplace. They had lit a fire there last night, making use of the paper and kindling left by a previous occupant and soon had a good blaze going. Bryan and Sandy had each packed a bottle of the distillery's finest, offering toasts to Robb's father and each other until they reached a state of contented incoherence. Robb had sunk into silence, listening to the two older men's inebriated conversation, watching as their gesticulations cast surreal shadows in the firelight. When they finally decided it was time for bed, Robb realised he was too drunk to stand and fell asleep in the comforting glow of the fire's embers. There he had suffered dream upon dream, his father a constant and disapproving presence as Robb failed again and again at ever more fantastical tasks.

They had reached the Corryhully bothy shortly after six p.m., as the fading evening light turned everything monochrome. Robb had managed to chivvy Sandy down from the summit of Sgurr nan Coireachan, completing the Corryhully horseshoe in a little over nine hours. None of them wanted to be trying the descent once the light had faded, so it had required little in the way of encouragement to make good progress down the hill. Once they had arrived back at the bothy, Sandy had collapsed in a ruddy heap, chest heaving and leaving him no energy to talk, a happy state of affairs that Robb and Bryan had taken full advantage of as they heated a meal on the portable stove. The previous evening had begun in quiet conversation: shared anecdotes about his father, plans for the distillery, companionable silences.

Robb had woken in the darkest hours, alerted by the absence of Sandy's snoring. His eyes failed to penetrate the darkness, but he had heard two sets of breathing apart from his own; one accompanied by muffled snorts and sniffles, almost as if Sandy was attempting to kick-start his snoring off again.

They had another day's hiking ahead of them. Most of his father's ashes had been distributed on the two Munros they'd climbed yesterday. Not that there was much likelihood that any residue of his father remained where his ashes had been so carefully scattered, the shifting winds had stolen them before they had even touched the ground; a grey cloud carried off to dissipate in the air, becoming more indistinct by the second. If this was Jack McCoach's ghost, then it had been shredded and cast off into the wilderness. Is this what his father would have wanted?

Robb still didn't have an answer when dawn finally arrived, the bothy windows turning as grey as his father's ashes before a crow called a harsh good morning from the ragged few pines taking shelter behind the building's low stone profile.

He lit the portable stove, poured the last of the water into a saucepan and headed outside into the cold dawn. The ground was hard with frost, freezing his bare feet as he pissed into the lee of the wind. Grey clouds cloaked the mountains, no sign yet of the sun that the two-day forecast had promised. It was OK, though, nothing to concern him – they would be fine to make the next climb as planned, sleep in the next bothy then home again for Saturday.

"Morning!" He shouted louder than was strictly necessary as he re-entered the bothy, jolting the recumbent figures into movement. Both sleeping bags stirred, folding as legs were drawn up, bulging as arms attempted to stretch. Robb watched to see which chrysalis would hatch first as he made himself a coffee.

"My God, that's the most uncomfortable bed I've had to endure for many years." Bryan emerged, his nose poking out from under the sleeping bag hood to test the air. It twitched as he smelt the coffee, encouraging him to pull himself free and stand on the cold earthen floor. Sandy took longer to awake, fighting to extricate himself from the tighter fit his bag presented until he emerged bleary-eyed and triumphant into the world.

They both regarded Sandy in silence as he stood free of his sleeping bag, contemplating the day ahead whilst dressed only in garish boxers and a t-shirt proclaiming the benefits of Ibiza as a holiday destination.

"Is that t-shirt yours, Sandy?" Bryan was trying, unsuccessfully, to envisage the finance director sharing the resort with hordes of drunk and drug-fuelled randy teenagers.

"What, this?" Sandy gazed down at his stomach, bulging out to present a Mercator projection of palm trees with 'I took a pill in Ibiza' in a font size far larger than the designer had originally intended. "My son gave it to me as a holiday present."

"Tasteful." Bryan pulled on his trousers, hurrying through the open bothy door. "I need a piss."

Robb poured hot water into the last mug, offering it to Sandy.

"Are you OK for the last hill today?"

Sandy had upended the mug and was apparently pouring near boiling water down his throat with no ill effect.

"Aye, why not." He stretched his shoulders back, before sitting back down on his bed and pulling on his trousers.

They left the bothy as they had found it, making sure the door was secured against any inquisitive sheep and headed back down the Land Rover track.

"We're lucky to have had the place to ourselves," Robb broke the silence.

"Aye well, the stag stalking season has only just ended. There's probably not that many people keen to be mistaken for deer by some short-sighted London toff." Bryan set the pace, striding back down the metalled road that began a few hundred metres from the bothy as if keen to leave his hangover behind. Sandy seemed completely unbothered by last night's alcohol consumption, striding along beside them as garrulous as he'd been the day before.

They reached Sandy's estate car in just over an hour, dumping bags in the boot before driving past the Glenfinnan monument that stood in lonely commemoration at the head of Loch Shiel.

"And there's plenty of daft buggers who would still

follow him today." Sandy's conversation had moved on from accountancy.

"Is that such a bad thing?" Bryan caught Sandy's meaning, following the pointed finger he crooked towards the lone Highlander's statue.

"Is it a bad thing when two thousand Scots died at Culloden? When an entire nation still suffers because of the vanity of one man!"

"You need to put it into historical context, Sandy. It's no use trying to attach modern sensitivities to events that happened in 1746."

Robb let their voices wash over him in the back seat. By the sounds of it they were going over a tried and tested argument that had been rehearsed many times before. He stared unseeing out of the window, drifting off into a waking dream where he held the controlling shares in the distillery. It wasn't so fanciful. His Aunt Pat might well die in hospital, his mother wouldn't be there forever and his sister Phoebe, well, he'd be the judge of that. There were just the missing shares his father had left in the will to account for, some woman he had kept secret from them all. Not that it really mattered, Robb would still end up with the lion's share, but it wouldn't hurt to find the missing 20%.

A bit like the whisky process itself, he mused, the 2% lost every year as the amber fluid matured in casks. The Angel's share. By the time they bottled a 10-year-old whisky, it had already lost 20% to evaporation.

Robb struggled unsuccessfully to picture his father reclining on a cloud, white wings draped around his shoulders and whisky glass in hand. His vision shifted groundward as the corpulent angel proved too heavy for the insubstantial cloud, tumbling down until he arrived in the fiery bounds of hell. His father's ruddy complexion better suited the flames, leering up at him as he raised an amber glass heavenwards. The Devil's cut – the alcohol absorbed by the wood of the cask itself – that was more appropriate.

The car swerved to avoid a post van exiting the Glenfinnan visitor centre. Robb caught the driver's eyes as his hand waved an apology. He pulled himself back upright in his seat, adjusting the seatbelt, which had pulled into his neck.

"Fucking posties!" Sandy's exclamation came as he glared angrily at the rear-view mirror. "They're a menace on the roads."

"No harm done," Bryan responded. "He braked when he saw you. You alright in the back, Robb?"

"Aye, I just have to remove my face from the window."

"I should pull over and give him a piece of my mind!" Sandy wasn't letting it go.

Bryan looked at Sandy askance. They had known each other since school, and he was about as menacing as a limp lettuce. Sandy had been a podgy kid, slow at sports, useless in a fight but always good at maths. In the hard barter of the school playground, a transferable skill such as an ability to complete maths homework for the alpha males proved a useful asset.

"Just forget it, Sandy. Look, we're here already. Turn off this track on the left."

The car swung off the road, hitting a pothole which caused the car to bounce, accompanied by a metallic clunk coming from the suspension. Suitably mollified, Sandy reduced his speed to a crawl and they crept the last few metres up the rough track to park in a gravelled section overlooking the main road.

Robb stretched once he was out of the back seat, opening the tailgate to retrieve his pack.

"There you go, said it wasn't far." He watched as the other two levered themselves from their seats, occasional groans advising him that their bodies hadn't recovered from the previous day's strenuous activity.

"Is this one a Munro as well?" Sandy looked up the track ahead with some trepidation. A gate barred the route from any vehicle seeking an off-road adventure, and a notice board displayed one of those simple maps that managed to provide no useful information at all.

"Near as makes no difference," Robb responded. "Streap's just 5m short, so it's officially a Corbett. We need to go back to the road for a 100 metres or so to join another track. That will take us to Gleann Dubh-Lighe Bothy, where we can dump the bags and spend the last night." He raised the orange Tupperware container into the air like a Catholic priest elevating the host. "Let's do it."

The three started back down the track, packs once again strapped into place on their backs. Sandy turned back after a few steps to check he had securely locked the car doors, satisfied by the electronic wink from the indicators in response to his keypress. He missed the opportunity to give the postie a piece of his mind, joining the others at the side of the A830 as the post van sped away out of sight in the direction of Fort William.

CHAPTER 21
Forensic Psychology

Corstophine waited in the train station car park, keeping a watchful eye on anyone wearing a rucksack. Like most cops, he had developed a sixth sense that alerted him to anything worthy of closer inspection. None of the backpackers he spotted caused him any concern. A couple of chimes from the station PA announced the imminent arrival of the Glasgow train and Corstophine unwound his lanky frame from the patrol car.

There weren't that many passengers on this connection, too near the middle of the day for any commuters, too late in the season for tourists. When autumn drew to a close, the entire town took a deep breath and prepared for hibernation. Some of the tartan tat shops closed down entirely so their owners could escape somewhere warmer to while away the winter months. Locals finally found seats in bars and cafes, crimes tended towards domestics and vandalism as darker nights encouraged darker behaviour.

He spotted her immediately. Sharmila Mallick was the only passenger whose skin tone didn't match the pallor of bleached bone – marching purposely along the single platform, overnight bag slung over her shoulder. She was almost as tall as he was, eyes catching his as she headed for the platform exit.

"DI Corstophine?" Her voice carried the unmistakable modulation of a Glasgow accent.

"Aye, you must be Dr Mallick." Corstophine held out his hand to receive a strong grip in return.

"Sharmila's fine. Still weird isn't it, handshakes?" She looked at her hand once it had been released, as if she was searching for any Covid-19 residue.

Corstophine wasn't sure how to respond to such a query. Sure enough, it had taken them long enough to return to anything approaching normality following the pandemic.

"I've a bottle of hand sanitiser in the patrol car?"

She gave him a wry smile in return. "It's OK, officer."

"Call me James." Corstophine turned away from her to cover his momentary embarrassment. "The car's this way." God, he had just met her and here he was behaving like an awkward teenager. "You said you have family here?"

"My mother. She's in care now, big place out on the Inverness road." She found she was speaking to his back and increased her stride to catch up.

"Are you mixing business and pleasure then?"

She caught his eyes as she drew level. "I wouldn't call it pleasure, James. She's had dementia for a while now."

"I'm sorry."

"Don't be, it's no-one's fault. Just a symptom of living longer than our allotted three score and ten."

They reached the car and Corstophine offered to take her bag.

"It's fine, I can manage, thanks." She held the bag close to her chest as she settled into the passenger seat, stowing it by her feet as she strapped in.

They drove out of the station, Corstophine quiet with concentration as he extricated the car from where it had been almost blocked in by another vehicle. Once clear of the car park and back on the road, he turned to view her profile.

"It's good of you to offer to help with this investigation."

"I'm not actually here in any official capacity. I visit the care home infrequently, more out of a sense of duty than anything else. It just makes the trip a little less painful if I have something else to concentrate on." He saw her mouth tighten with emotion before she caught him observing her.

Corstophine swiftly switched his attention back to the road ahead, momentarily flustered at being caught looking. "Do you want to go over the details now, or can I drop you somewhere?"

"Might as well see what you've got. I may not be able to add anything, James, just to warn you at the outset. There's nobody on our records with an MO involving blinding and art."

Their brief conversation terminated as he turned into the police station car park and he led the way to the front entrance. The office was quiet as they arrived. Hamish occupying his usual seat at the front desk.

"This is Dr Sharmila Mallick, Sergeant Hamish McKee" Corstophine offered as way of an introduction. "I'm hoping she can shed some light on Patricia's assailant."

She offered the desk sergeant a fleeting smile as they swept past into Corstophine's office.

"Please, take a chair." She looked around the office as Corstophine started laying out crime scene photographs on the desk. A filing cabinet provided the only furniture, apart from the desk that lay between them. Through the glass wall divider, the general office was deserted, three desks awaiting the return of occupants who had left touches of their personality behind.

"I may not be able to offer you much assistance here, James." Sharmila caught Corstophine's enquiring look. "My job is to work with other professionals to understand what environmental or clinical conditions drive someone to commit crimes. We then work on changing behavioural norms by altering perceptions or applying medication. It's not like it is in television dramas where I give a cursory glance at the scene of the crime and tell you to look for a one-legged Irishman with a penchant for marshmallows."

"I wasn't expecting that level of detail." Corstophine locked eyes with her, the awkward silence holding until they both smiled at the incongruity of the situation.

He continued arranging the photographs on the table between them, the canvas with a devil drawn in Patricia's blood taking the centre. "The assailant knocked her unconscious as she slept in her bed, then deliberately blinded her with her own paintbrushes before adding his own artistic interpretation." Corstophine pointed to the crimson figure in the middle of Patricia's last canvas. "That was painted with her own blood. He left the brushes embedded in her eye sockets."

Sharmila gave silent thanks that the medics had arrived before the photographer. A picture showed two bloodied paintbrushes lying on a surgical bandage where the medics had placed them. Her imagination filled in the missing detail.

"Is there anything you can tell me, anything here that I can use to help me find whoever did this?" Corstophine's voice betrayed a hint of desperation.

She studied the photographs, moving them all to the sides of his desk until just the painting remained.

"Does anyone know what was originally on the picture, here in the centre where it's been painted over?"

"Aye, I saw her painting it the day before she was attacked. I'd called in to check if she was alright, one of our PCs had stopped a guy acting suspiciously near her house, Monday night. She'd called in here Monday morning and basically stated that she and her family were under threat. She wasn't making much sense to be honest, but I asked everyone to keep an eye on the family's houses, just in case. It seems she runs a witch's coven and the guy we stopped had been spying on them dancing half naked around this garden ornament..." Corstophine stopped, aware of the incredulous expression opposite him. "Small Highland towns aren't as staid and boring as people fondly imagine!"

He thought back to Patricia daubing paint on the canvas. "The painting is a representation of them dancing around the lawn. There's a metal sculpture of some sort in the middle – quite modern art, curves forming a sphere with an arrow pointing upwards." Corstophine paused as a new thought came to him. "Bit like the male sex symbol." His finger transcribed an imaginary circle in the air between them, culminating in a flourish as his index finger cut the circle and pointed heavenwards.

Sharmila pursed her lips as if deep in thought, but her dark eyes betrayed amusement as Corstophine's erect finger detumesced in front of her.

Corstophine saw her attempting to keep a straight face and immediately made the connection as her eyes followed his lowering hand.

"Does the fact he's painted a devil in her own blood have any meaning?" He blurted out the question to cover his momentary embarrassment. Psychologists – attaching meaning to the most innocent of gestures.

She picked up the remaining photograph, angling it towards her eyes as if there was a hidden detail waiting to be discovered.

"Religious iconography is a common meme in some psychiatric states. We often find patients suffering from psychosis will blame their actions on angels or devils who tell them what to do." She looked directly at Corstophine, the humour now replaced with seriousness. "The mind is a delicate thing, James. Those who enjoy robust mental health are often dismissive of those who don't. But it only takes one event, or seemingly insignificant chemical imbalance, to cause major changes in personality and behaviour."

"Like LSD?" Corstophine ventured.

"Sure. The American military tried using it as a means of interrogation, of breaking people. Aldous Huxley explored how his mind performed once freed from the normal strictures of neural processing – the Doors of Perception: Heaven and Hell."

"Like our devil?"

"Like your devil," she confirmed, glancing back at the picture. "Thing is, James, it's easier to control people than you may think. Religion is a well proven case in point. Or take state operatives, murdering on command. There's a reason army training uses the same tried and tested methodology to take a normal human and turn them into a killing machine. The truly frightening fact is that populations are easier to manipulate than individuals once you have access to the right levers and buttons. You think social media is just an innocent pastime?"

Corstophine cast his mind back to recent history, seeing a pattern emerging that he hadn't noticed previously. "I'd not thought about it."

Sharmila returned her attention to the photograph, pointing at the rough depiction of a red devil. "The artwork your assailant added, it's a message. He's deliberately left it in full view next to the scene of his attack. All we have to do is decipher it."

"Have you any ideas?" Corstophine's voice held an optimistic edge, desperate to find some sort of lead to Patricia's attacker.

She pursed her lips again, narrowing her eyes in

concentration. Corstophine found himself studying her a little too intently and switched his attention to the table.

"I'd say the assailant knew her; I'd say the attack was pre-planned and the blinding was either because she'd seen something, or he never wanted her to see anything ever again. There's a connection between her and the assailant." She sent him a quizzical glance. "Is there any history of mental illness in the family?"

Corstophine thought of Patricia telling them she wasn't mad, of Phoebe locked in her room. "There's a daughter, Patricia's niece, who's kept locked in her bedroom. I think she's schizophrenic?"

Sharmila looked doubtful. "Schizophrenic? And they keep her locked in a bedroom?"

"So I understand. We were told she's kept under 24-hour care and heavily drugged for her own safety. I was a bit doubtful about it myself, but the DC checked with the private healthcare company who look after her and it all appears above board." Corstophine saw Sharmila's expression. "Is that normal?"

"No. If she has to be so heavily sedated and kept locked up, then no, it's not normal. What's the name of this healthcare company?"

"Glenochy Healthcare. They're based here, in the town. The girl's name is Phoebe –Phoebe McCoach."

Sharmila's fingers tapped a quick note onto her mobile. "I'll look into it. Now, back to the photograph."

She squinted at the photograph as if there was a clue in the picture trying to tell her something. Sharmila shook her head in frustration, feeling the thought that was tantalisingly close slip away. "The devil represents something personal. Maybe it's to do with witchcraft?" She sounded doubtful. "Do you mind if I take this and have a closer look? I'll be leaving Sunday evening, I can get it back to you before then."

Corstophine considered her request. By rights, any forensic evidence, including SOC photographs, should remain secure. Against that, he had to balance the fact that she had expertise that wasn't normally available to him.

"You'll not make any copies or show it to anyone?"

"No, James, I deal with evidential material on a regular basis. I'll be careful."

He nodded in return, watching as she slipped the photograph into her bag.

"I'll be in touch."

Corstophine escorted her back to the front desk, holding up a hand in farewell when she glanced back at him at the door. Her enigmatic smile remained long after she had gone, reminding him of a far older painting.

CHAPTER 22
Funnelling

Frankie had drawn a blank. The lecturers at the Royal Conservatoire of Scotland hadn't responded to her voicemails and she was loath to commit to an official email. There was something about the young lassie's suicide that had touched a nerve, perhaps because she had selected such a public place as the train station – cameras and people everywhere.

When she and Corstophine had looked over the platform edge, they saw the train had run over the girl, almost severing her torso in two. Sarah's face, though! The girl had stared sightlessly towards the sky, her expression strangely at peace amongst the carnage of her ruined body. There was no doubt it was a suicide. The station CCTV clearly showed Sarah running across the platform of her own volition. But something had caused her to take her own life, and Keith Tunstall was involved, she was sure of it.

Frankie logged off, grabbed a notebook off the desk and retrieved her coat. Her shift finished in an hour, giving her plenty of time to pay Tunstall a visit. It wouldn't do any harm to see what that lowlife recalled about seeing Sarah at the train station, and she could shake him down about the drugs that were circulating around the town.

She let Hamish know where she was going and took the remaining patrol car. The sunshine lent an almost summery feel to the late afternoon, as long as she ignored the chill breeze coming off the steel grey waters of Loch Linnhe.

The surrounding mountains loomed over the town; their brown backs bent double in readiness for the coming winter as they shed their green summer coats. It wouldn't be long before they sported snowy caps, attracting the mountaineers and thrillseekers like moths to an icy flame.

Once she had left the main thoroughfare behind, the streets shrugged off their veneer of gentility, becoming progressively meaner as she entered one of the council schemes. The town always put her in mind of a film set; the buildings mostly large and well maintained as they plied a B&B trade on the major arteries, then once behind their facade the real town revealed itself. This street of semi-detached houses valiantly attempted an air of gentility with manicured hedges and lawns, only to be let down by uncaring neighbours whose flaking paint and abandoned gardens provided an instant glimpse into the character of those who lived therein.

It was perhaps the most decrepit house on the street that Frankie parked outside, a child's bike rusted and forgotten in the jungle that comprised the front garden. The sight instantly depressed her, the metaphor for a lost and abandoned child only too reminiscent of her own failure to conceive, the fault line that had broken her marriage in two. She pushed the memory back into whatever corner of her mind it had sprung from and knocked smartly on the front door.

Frankie spotted a grimy net curtain twitch and waited patiently for someone to answer. After giving the occupant a minute to respond, she rapped again, knuckles impacting painfully against wood. Still no response. She flicked open the letterbox, releasing a foul odour, which was a synthesis of takeaway food and stale cigarettes. It was overlain with that sour note that always accompanied dwellings where the occupants couldn't be bothered with anything as banal as basic hygiene. The hallway was strewn with rubbish. A clear path meandered through the middle like an animal trail in undergrowth, discarded cartons and plastic cups shared space with discarded clothing. Propped carelessly against the wall, a new blue rucksack rested incongruously in its setting. She noticed it was empty, the nylon collapsed in on itself. Whatever had been packed inside was nowhere to be seen.

"Anyone at home?" Frankie attempted shouting through the open letterbox, ears tuned for a response. "This is the police." She added this piece of redundant information more for the benefit of the neighbours. It was always a good move on occasion to let people know that the police actually exist, it kept them on their toes. Silence returned her call, and she straightened up to stare at the net curtains for another sign of movement.

Frankie considered leaving a note but decided that would be a waste of her time. With a swift backwards glance at the window, she made her way back to the car. Not enough evidence to raise a search warrant, she would just have to wait until she met the wee bampot on the streets.

She knew the family well. Most of them had had dealings with the police at one time or another. They were traveller stock, fiercely protective of family and kin but lacking any real regard for settled society. Frankie had no issue with the majority of travellers she met; those still living a nomadic lifestyle despite having swapped colourful caravans and horses for Transits and flashy upmarket caravans. They washed up locally, following the soft fruit harvest north, which still had need of tireless pickers, before overwintering in dedicated caravan parks or council houses. Keith's family had abandoned the nomadic lifestyle a generation back, for whatever reason, and were constantly causing trouble. The father was doing a stretch inside following a spot of GBH, the mother hadn't been seen for years and now just Keith lived here, and he didn't want to answer the door.

Inside the house, flat out on the kitchen floor and with his hands roughly tied to his sides, Keith Tunstall was in no fit state to answer the door. His ability to shout was severely compromised by the large plastic funnel shoved down his throat, and his widening eyes betrayed the dawning comprehension of what awaited him. A trickle of blood pooled like red treacle on the filthy lino under his head, pulsing weakly from a head wound and dyeing a matted clump of his blond hair dark red. He'd attempted to move his head when he regained consciousness, but found it was jammed between two piles of breezeblocks. Something held his chest to the floor. When he tried raising his head, the plastic funnel forced itself even deeper down his throat, the gagging reflex making him lower his head to avoid being sick. His throat felt raw, almost as sore as the side of his head.

He had known the guy at the door, just one of the weak bastards the Glasgow muscle had persuaded to deliver drugs. He wasn't a threat and they had an effective hold over him by threatening his kid. Long as he did his bit, everything was sweet. Drugs delivered, no risky dealing on the streets and even better, the daft bastard didn't even want any money; he just wanted his kid left alone.

The last thing Keith expected as he led the guy into the kitchen was the bone-jarring impact of a heavy metal cosh swung with some force against the back of his head. His legs had crumpled like rubber bands before he had blacked out.

When he came around, he could see his attacker at the kitchen counter, bags of white powder being carelessly poured into a jug: cocaine; heroin; benzos; methadone. There must have been a few thousand quid's worth of product in that jug. Keith's concerns at that point were for the Glasgow mob who'd recruited him. They weren't going to be impressed with him being so careless as to lose a few thousand profit. In fact, they were probably going to make his life very unpleasant unless he managed to find a way out of his predicament.

When he heard the front door knock, the unmistakable sound of police at the door, all movement stopped. He pulled as much air into his lungs as the constriction across his chest would allow, just as the guy shoved a dirty dishcloth into the funnel and left him on his own. When the second knock came, Keith realised he had to attract attention before this maniac did something worse to him. Despite his best efforts, he couldn't make a sound and was struggling to breathe until his attacker returned to pull the cloth out. Keith's forlorn hope that the police visit might serve to scare the guy off was in vain; he went back to opening drug wraps at the kitchen counter.

Keith needed to make him take this fucking funnel out of his mouth and untie him. He managed a croak, the sound surprisingly loud in his ears as the funnel amplified the weak noise. The guy ignored him, concentrating on ripping open more of the week's deliveries and pouring them together until the jug was half full of grey and white powder. It was only when he stopped with the wraps and opened the bottle of cheap cider that Keith finally began to understand what was coming.

The contents of the jug absorbed the cider, turning into a grey sludge that fizzed as the cider level rose higher up the glass. Keith tried to escape then, ignoring the pain in his throat as he swung his head side to side in increasingly frantic movements. The breezeblocks stayed put; all he had managed to accomplish was to flay his scalp. His feet stayed immobile too, he could feel the strap that bound his ankles firmly to the floor. Another panicked croak escaped the funnel before the jug was upended and the entire contents poured down his throat.

Keith fought hard not to swallow, felt the narcotic stew bubbling out of his mouth, entering his nostrils. He coughed, struggled for air and took a gulp. The alcohol hit him first, sending fire across exposed nerves where the end of the plastic funnel had removed layers of skin. The sudden lancing pain caused him to gasp, but instead of air he drew the funnel contents into his lungs.

After that it was a straight contest between drowning and overdosing. Keith even managed to break the straps holding his ankles to the floor as his body reacted violently to the chemical cocktail. Then the benzo and heroin mix must have hit because he lay there like a dead man, beyond caring whether he lived or died. His assailant watched him die without expression, feeling cheated that Keith's last few minutes of life were apparently painless. He put the now empty jug back on the kitchen counter, then moved quickly over to Keith's prostrate body before landing a heavy kick between his spreadeagled legs. Keith's fingers clenched in response, opening and closing in a rapid semaphore of pain. His assailant gave a tight smile, the bastard could still feel something. That would have to do.

CHAPTER 23
Party Time

The police station was quiet when Frankie returned. Hamish had left his favoured position at the front desk and it looked as if Corstophine had decided to call it a day; she could see him tidying up his desk through the office windows. The two constables must have left for their evening shift. Frankie spotted PC Lamb's comb left behind on his desk and wondered how he would be able to manage a shift without tending to his hair. She smiled at the thought of PC McAdam working a few late shifts with Lamb. Two less well-suited personalities would be hard to find, although according to the old desk sergeant they had bonded following the arrest of the two Glaswegians last night.

She wrote up her abortive visit to Keith Tunstall, marking it as a drugs enquiry. After a moment's contemplation she added seeing the blue rucksack in the hall, seemingly now empty. Somehow, they were distributing the drugs around town, someone or some people were dropping off the wraps and collecting the cash. How the hell were they managing to do that without being spotted?

Frankie frowned. It was already past the end of her shift, but something didn't add up. On a whim, she logged back onto her computer, sparing a glance at Corstophine's crazy board while waiting for the aged operating system to creak into life. The police weren't known for adopting the latest software; their IT department had only recently and reluctantly waved goodbye to Windows XP for God's sake! No wonder the criminal fraternity were increasingly exploiting the virtual world for ill-gotten gains and mostly getting away with it. Frankie was put in mind of cops on penny-farthings chasing the bad guys in Lamborghinis, a manic upright piano soundtrack accompanying her imagination.

There hadn't been any additions to the enquiry board since Patricia's attack on Tuesday night. No new names added to join the rest of her extended family who shared the whiteboard with her. Was there a connection between that isolated and horrific act of violence, the suicidal girl and the drugs? None that sprang to mind.

She searched the police database for the two individuals the Glasgow police had taken into custody. The charge sheet listed firearm offences, causing her brows to draw down even more as she read on. These two nasty bits of work were associated with the Glasgow drugs trade, acting as muscle for one of the hardest drugs families in the city. There was plenty of violence in their pasts, but nothing to indicate they had given up the day job to concentrate on catalytic converter thefts.

Frankie leant back in her seat, staring at the ceiling tiles above her head. The hired muscle must be here in town on behalf of their Glasgow drug overlords, that was the only logical conclusion. If they found that they weren't needed to squash any competition, or use the art of gentle persuasion on anyone, then they were effectively idle. And idle hands...

Corstophine called out to her as he was locking his office door behind him. "Goodnight Frankie."

"Sir! Before you go. I've just been looking at our Glaswegian thieves on the national crime database. They've a strong connection to the drugs trade, especially the same Glasgow family that has been implicated in setting up county lines in other towns."

Corstophine stood beside her, squinting at her screen. Frankie held her tongue, the comment about him getting his eyes tested unvoiced.

"You think these two characters were acting in the same capacity here?"

"I think it's quite likely, sir. They probably found they had time on their hands since there's no real competition for them here. I think these two have been kicking their heels. There's no need for anything heavier than the occasional physical threat here, certainly no need for firearms."

"They weren't carrying?"

"Nothing found on them. And being arrested on the street means there wasn't anywhere to conceal a weapon. No, I think they've had time to diversify and work on their own initiative. A couple of hundred quid for a few minutes under a car is a good return and doesn't cross any line that their bosses would care about."

Corstophine nodded. "Makes sense. I couldn't see why they'd travel all the way from Glasgow just to trash a few exhausts, but if they were staying up here until the drug sales were running smoothly then it makes a lot more sense. Lucky thing Lamb tasered one of them, it may have been a bit of a handful dealing with two thugs like these. Any idea who they're dealing with locally, not that Keith Tunstall boy?"

Frankie hesitated. Corstophine didn't believe that Tunstall was up to running a drugs cartel – he'd make a good mule, but did he have the ambition and intelligence to run a drugs op?

"I think we should pay him a visit, sir." She noticed his eyebrow rising and hurried on. "I've just come back from his house. I noticed the blue rucksack that we spotted on the CCTV lying in the hallway, except now it's empty. I think he may be running the show for the Glasgow bunch."

"Did you speak to him? Go inside the house and have a good look around?"

Frankie shook her head. "Nobody answered the door, but someone was in – I saw the front curtains twitch."

"I don't know, Frankie. By all accounts the boy's an idiot. This is out of his league."

"Not necessarily, sir. The Glasgow connection have traveller links."

Corstophine's expression changed from doubting to calculating in a split second.

"Then they'd be happier dealing with one of their own, even if he isn't the brightest tool in the box."

"Especially if our two characters were helping him set up and applying gentle persuasion where needed."

"Not that gentle!" Corstophine hesitated, checking his watch. "Look, this can wait until tomorrow. Why don't you and I pay him a house call first thing, say nine? Chances are he'll still be in his bed at that time."

"Love to, sir."

Corstophine pulled on his coat, searching in his pockets for keys. "I'll see you tomorrow then. Have a good night, Frankie."

"You too, sir."

She turned off all but a few of the station lights and locked the main door behind her, seeing Corstophine's hand raise in farewell as he drove out of the car park. Frankie returned the wave, wondering how good a night he'd be having on his own in an empty house before realising that she was in the same sad boat.

Sod that! Frankie decided there and then that she'd take herself off to her local, meet up with some old friends. She keyed her mobile as she crossed over the car park towards her car. Friday night, it used to mean something, and she wasn't ready for a life of microwaved ready meals for one just yet...

Corstophine called in at the Indian takeaway on his way home, ordering chicken tikka masala and hoping to hell they weren't using American meat, not that there was any reliable way of telling nowadays. The other customers waiting for their orders all avoided his eyes, finding something of intense interest on their mobile phones or on the cheap TV playing a muted 24-hour news channel. Was it that obvious he was a cop? Even the takeaway wanted rid of him – his order leapfrogged the queue.

Once home, Corstophine collapsed on the settee and forked the food straight out of the plastic tubs. The TV news was the same every night: America and China trading insults instead of just trading; some celebrities he didn't recognise with their brief marriage on the rocks; government borrowing up; employment down. Was it really any wonder at all that the police were being used as sticking plasters to cover the open wounds in society?

Why not stop watching the news, Jamie? You could watch a film instead.

His wife stood behind him, her face etched with concern. He couldn't see her. He didn't turn his head because she wasn't there, not anymore. She was right, though, about the news. Even for those like himself who only watched the news for the comfort of hearing another voice, it was increasingly propaganda. Detectives soon learn who's lying or they find themselves eased out of the job.

His eyes flicked towards the whisky bottle, then towards the mantlepiece clock that kept better time than it ever had before. Did it really matter if he started drinking before seven o'clock? It was just a silly rule he'd placed on himself to avoid taking that road to ruin. An internal struggle commenced, for and against.

His mobile rang before he could pass verdict and he squinted at the display to bring it into focus. The number wasn't one he recognised. Who would call him this time on a Friday evening? He hit the TV mute and answered the call.

"Corstophine." He spoke abruptly, ready to give any telesales short shrift.

"James. It's Sharmila, Sharmila Mallick?" She stated her name like a question and waited for a response to the query.

"Oh, Sharmila." Corstophine realised his tone may have been abrupt. "I wasn't expecting a call from you until Sunday. How can I help?"

"I was hoping I could help you."

"In what way?"

"The case you asked me to look at. I think I may have spotted something about the painting. Do you want to meet up and grab a drink? I'm staying at the Royal Hotel."

Corstophine checked the time again. The clock on the mantelpiece sounded unnaturally loud in the silence. "That's not far from me. Is eight o'clock good for you?"

"Make it nine. I'll be in the lounge."

"Nine it is, look forward to seeing you." He winced slightly – no need to add the last bit.

"Hmmm. See you then."

Corstophine held the phone against his ear until he was certain the call had ended, then swiped though to the most recent photograph he'd taken. There was Patricia's painting, there was the figure painted in blood. He zoomed in until the devil filled the screen. Was it even meant to be a devil? It was the sort of painting a child might manage: sticklike appendages providing a rough approximation of a human figure. He'd made the assumption it was meant to be a devil partly based on the voyeur's fanciful description of the other interloper in Patricia's garden that evening, but it could be anything. Corstophine tried viewing the picture from different angles without success. Whatever the psychologist had spotted eluded his eye, and that bothered him more than it should.

Sharmila's extended 'hmmm' response bothered him as well. Did it mean she was looking forward to seeing him, and what should he make of that? Was he reading too much into it? For a man no longer used to swimming in waters such as these, he was already out of his depth. Corstophine could sense his wife's pitying expression as he hurried upstairs to freshen up. *Easy on the deodorant and aftershave.* He heard that clearly enough.

CHAPTER 24
Devil's Advocate

Once they'd left the car safely locked, Robb led the way along the estate track. He forced a fast pace before the morning air had lost the last remnants of the night's chill, their warm breath creating miniature clouds around their heads. The deeply rutted track accompanied a small river which tumbled energetically over small waterfalls at their side, each one making itself known by a muted roar as they approached. The three of them walked in companionable silence, enjoying the play of sunlight as it filtered through the thinning leaf canopy. Startling red and yellow leaves stood out against the deep blue of the sky, the weather forecast for once proving accurate. Sporadic birdsong and the last hardy red admirals enjoying the mild autumn sunshine added the soundtrack and visuals. From somewhere deep in the forest a stag bellowed a primeval warning to other males as they began their yearly, testosterone-fuelled rut. At one turn in the path they came across a lone red deer hind, standing directly in their path before leaping with balletic silence into the safety of the woods. This late in the year there weren't too many flies: the voracious midges which preferred to envelope each unfortunate victim in a cloud of near invisible flying piranhas; or the larger cleg which landed as softly as a feather then painfully bit through clothing and skin to drink blood like a miniature vampire.

Robb was enjoying himself. Here in the mountains, he was the one in charge. Having spent years hillwalking with his father, he was completely at home amongst these monuments to geological turmoil. The ragged contours that held the three of them cupped in giant stone hands were as familiar to him as skyscrapers to a New Yorker.

Sandy had resumed his noisy breathing, making a theatrical performance out of the mundane ability to draw in a breath and exhale. His face glowed, but not in a good way – his ruddy cheeks had spilled colour from his bulging neck, up past two loose chins until his scalp assumed a traffic light red under his blond mop. Through some arcane magic known only to a select few hairdressers his wig had lasted the course, hanging on during yesterday's ascent when the wind had attempted forcible removal on more than one occasion. Robb smiled inwardly as he pictured the overweight accountant holding onto his head as if fearful his hair was about to undertake an airborne adventure of its own.

Sandy was struggling to keep up but enjoying taking in the views and wondering how he had managed to live in such a beautiful part of the world without ever venturing beyond the common tourist destinations. Yesterday's climb up Sgurr Thuilm and Sgurr nan Coireachan had been a revelation for him. He'd thought that he knew the land of his birth, but as natural as the mountains surrounding his hometown were to him, this was the first time he had ever set foot on them. Sure, he'd managed a spot of Scottish skiing, taken the gondola up the Nevis range when the snow was in a fit enough state, but he had never been out on the mountains proper. The hillwalking club Jack McCoach set up years ago was unique in that few of the members had ever climbed anything more demanding than a flight of stairs. Jack had probably envisaged that his innate love of the mountains would transfer to all those who joined; pictured himself leading enthusiastic groups up more and more challenging ascents. Instead, the local businessmen and corporates from within his own distillery had joined, encouraged no doubt by wives anxious for them to perform another type of climbing up the social ladder, of which he represented the highest rung. In the end, the hillwalking club had had entirely the opposite effect to the one he fondly imagined. The members met irregularly in pubs where they planned expeditions, always for some indeterminate time in the future, always accompanied by a skinful of drink. Perversely enough it was probably the hillwalking club Jack McCoach instigated that had contributed to his own death; the regular consumption of alcohol reducing his own fitness to the point where climbing the Munro proved too much for his body.

Robb took a right fork, some two miles along the estate track, crossing a bridge over the river and they soon spotted the bothy as the trees thinned out. The building had only recently been restored, a new roof and no sign of the fire that had razed the single storey to the ground in 2012. Inside, new pine panelling offered a warm welcome as light poured in from the two modest windows and twin skylights overhead. It was a step up from the previous night's accommodation, and they dropped off their backpacks in the largest room with a smug feeling that they'd reserved the best accommodation for themselves. This room had a fireplace and sleeping platform, and the three of them looked forward to sharing the last bottle of whisky later on in front of a warm fire. Although bothy code had a strict 'don't touch' policy where other people's kit was concerned, Robb hid the last whisky bottle in the guttering to one side of the porch door. Some temptations prove difficult to resist.

Before considering the comfort of a warm fire and whisky, they had a hill to climb. Sandy started a garrulous conversation with Bryan once free of the weight of his pack, leaving Robb several paces in front of them, relieved that he wasn't the one being subjected to another tirade on American trade tariffs. Robb still had his pack, now full of his companion's waterproofs, food and drink for the climb, but it weighed a lot less than it had at the start. He filtered out Sandy's voice until the words lost all import, just a background hum that joined the sound of running water and the soft whisper of wind tugging at remaining leaves. His father's ashes, those that remained, he planned to leave on Streap's summit. It wasn't the highest hill. Truth was, it wasn't even a Munro, but his father had loved the view across to Loch Arkaig from the summit and Robb felt it was a fitting location for his final resting place.

They passed through a gate at the forest's limit and saw the true extent of their journey laid out in front of them. A green glen dotted with trees led the eye up towards a sequence of peaks, each one higher than the next until Streap's summit proclaimed it had every right to be considered a true mountain.

"Is it far?" Sandy's question put them both in mind of a child's plaintive voice. Distances were deceptive once freed of clues to perspective. No houses, pylons or anything obviously man-made met the eye. No trees afforded scale once the glen floor was left behind. Robb wondered how they would both feel if he told them that Streap was in easy reach of yesterday's two hills. He'd avoided trying to manage all three summits in a day with two people whose fitness levels were in doubt, preferring instead to spread the summits over two days. One thing his father had instilled in him was an awareness that even this close to civilisation, death waited for one wrong step, one mistake. The pity was that his father hadn't taken someone with him on his last fateful climb.

They'd had one of their 'fallings out' that day. Robb couldn't even remember what the argument had been about, just that he'd felt guilty about leaving his father to walk the hill on his own. If there was only the one thing that had drawn the two of them together, made him feel as if the years had dropped away, it was their shared joy of hillwalking. Instead, he had watched him drive off that morning, seen his father give one long lingering look at the house as if pleading for Robb to join him before the car was lost to sight down the drive. That was the last time he had seen him.

"Streap. Is that it?" Sandy asked again, aiming a finger accurately enough at their destination. A few fat yellow clouds hung almost motionless in the sky, neatly framing the mountain's peak.

"Aye, it's not too far." Robb thought of the final stretch to the summit. "If you find it too much of a struggle you can always just stop and wait for us. We have to come back the same route."

Robb saw Sandy's face visibly light up. "No, I'll be fine, I'm sure." He patted an ample midriff. "I think this hillwalking's doing me the power of good!"

"OK then. We follow this track for a while longer, then we need to cut up to the west. It gets to be a bit of a climb, so we better get moving."

Bryan fell into place next to Robb, ostensibly to talk about his ideas for gin production but he had a suspicion it was to avoid listening to Sandy's extended monologues.

"You know your father held you in high esteem, don't you?"

Robb's attention faltered at the mention of his father. His foot landed awkwardly on a stone and he swore as he almost twisted his ankle.

"That wasn't an opinion he ever shared with me. Quite the opposite."

Bryan adopted a fatherly look, or something that he hoped was a close approximation. If he was to continue seeing Emma, then somewhere along the way he'd have to reach some sort of accord with her son.

"Jack told me himself how much he appreciated your attempts to deliver new business, the gin and the bottled water. He gave you a hard time, I know, but it was because he wanted you to understand how difficult it was to enter these markets. In many ways he played Devil's advocate."

Robb concentrated on the ground in front of him. Twisting an ankle out here with two novices wouldn't be very clever, especially higher up where he needed to be sure-footed.

"Sometimes he played the bloody devil himself." Robb immediately regretted his outburst but there wasn't a delete button in real life. If only there was.

"Don't be too harsh on him, he meant to do what was best for you. For all the family, as well as for the business. It's just dealing with the cut and thrust of the corporate world…" Bryan paused as he searched for the right words. "You can understand how difficult it is to leave all that behind even when you're with family. The stress, the daily battles. Business is a lot like warfare and if you want to succeed you don't take prisoners!"

Sandy's theatrical wheezing had gone up a notch and Robb turned around to see how he was. He'd fallen back 10 metres whilst they were still on fairly level going. How he would fare further up the hill was anyone's guess.

"Well, I wish someone had told him we were on the same side."

Bryan didn't come back with an immediate response.

"What do you make of Corstophine?" Robb deliberately changed the subject.

"How do you mean, as a person?"

Robb nodded, wondering in what other way he could be considered. "Aye, do you get along with him?"

Bryan walked in silent contemplation for a while. "He keeps himself to himself, taciturn you might say. He seems alright but there's always the inescapable fact you're talking to the police. It tends to make a lot of banter off limits."

A bird of prey called overhead, the sound like a shepherd whistling commands through his fingers. Another call responded, too far away to see but in the same trilling language, quite unlike a raptor's normal keening call.

"Red Kite." Robb explained, seeing Bryan's confused expression. He stopped and pointed up at an unmistakable red body and forked tail as the bird effortlessly sailed over the glen. They both watched it until was lost from view, leaving them with another fainter call that reached them from somewhere already far distant.

"Wish I could bloody fly!" Sandy's voice came from nearby. He'd closed the distance between them.

Bryan's dubious expression as his eyes traversed their obese companion made it abundantly clear that Sandy lacked the necessary aerodynamic qualities required for flight.

"Probably safer with our feet firmly on the ground," Robb interjected diplomatically before Bryan had a chance to comment. He set his eyes on the ridge to their left. "We're best to head up to the ridge rather than keep going along the coire. It looks an easier route but that's a difficult climb at the end and hard going over the rocks."

Sandy released a long drawn-out breath, emulating a

steam train pulling out of a station. "I thought we'd stop for a rest?" He sounded hopeful.

"We don't have time. As it is, we'll have to go some to make the summit and back to the bothy before it gets too dark." Robb set off with renewed enthusiasm up the grass flanks of the ridge, leaving the two of them exchanging a resigned look.

"What's a coire anyway?" Sandy had sufficient lung capacity left to ask the question.

"The corrie." Bryan gestured towards the hollowed-out glen directly in front of them. He continued his description as Sandy's sweat-drenched face hadn't changed its querying expression. "Coire is the Gaelic for pot or cauldron. The Ice Age scooped out this valley as glaciers flowed down from the surrounding mountains. They tend to be pretty steep at the end where the corrie meets the mountain, probably why he wants to climb up here instead."

Sandy's resigned expression was sufficient excuse for Bryan to catch up with Robb, leaving the steam train lumbering noisily up the tracks behind him.

It took Sandy two hours before he wheezily made the ridge, collapsing in a wet heap next to Robb and Bryan where they'd stopped to view his progress.

"Why don't you wait here?" Robb suggested. "You get a great view of Loch Beoraid over to the west." He removed his backpack to retrieve the plastic repository of his father's ashes, took off his jacket then placed the backpack beside Sandy. "We'll just follow the ridge up to the end, scatter the last of Dad's ashes and rejoin you in a while." He offered his jacket to Sandy. They needed to make up time on the last climb and he didn't need the additional layer of clothing. "You can have this to sit on if you want?"

Sandy nodded, unable to talk and dislodging beads of sweat that flew off his eyelashes and nose. He watched as the other two headed along the ridge, making better progress without him, then folded Robb's jacket and stuffed it inside his rucksack to make a pillow.

Robb and Bryan hardly exchanged a word as they powered up the long section towards the summit. The ridge undulated up and down several times before the final stretch lay in front of them, Bryan growing increasingly concerned as the ridge narrowed. A latent feeling of acrophobia made itself known as the drop became more vertiginous each side of the narrow arête. Brian concentrated so much on keeping his balance on the path that he almost walked into Robb, standing facing him head on.

"Are you sleeping with my mother?"

Bryan felt a chill run down his backbone. There was a time and a place to have a conversation like this, and balanced on a narrow track with certain death awaiting him either side was not ideal.

"Look, Robb, this isn't the best place to have this talk." He swayed as the wind gave him a gentle push, feeling ice form at the bottom of his stomach.

"I think this is exactly the place we should have this talk, Bryan." Robb turned easily on his feet to gesture at the peak just a few more minutes climb away. "This is where we're laying the last of my father's ashes. Don't you think he'd prefer us to be honest with each other?"

Bryan's heart was in his mouth as Robb spun back to face him, unconcerned at the fall awaiting one wrong step.

"I can't talk here. Can we at least get to the top?" Bryan's voice now had a pleading tone.

"I just need to know, Bryan. I heard Corstophine talking to you yesterday, and I hadn't thought much about it, all those visits you made after my father died. Then I started putting two and two together; how my mother's mood changed whenever you'd been around. Those days when you appeared at breakfast. Like an idiot I thought you'd just arrived that morning but of course you'd stayed the night. How long has this been going on?"

Bryan had the totally irrational vision of him dancing on the mountain's tightrope to the song that was a hit in his youth. The world tilted. Shit. He needed to sit down before he fell down.

"Your mother and I have been good friends for years, Robb. There was nothing planned. I just tried to comfort her as best as I could, and one thing led to another." The words came out in a panic. "I'd never do anything to hurt Emma, you have to believe me. We were going to tell you in good time it's just that this…"

"This is maybe a little too soon after my father's death?" Robb completed the sentence for him. "He's been gone less than a month!"

Bryan swayed like a drunk under Robb's furious gaze.

"Look, we can talk about it later. I'm losing my balance." His voice betrayed the panic that showed in his face.

Robb stared into his eyes, seeing the fear. He could easily push him to his death or feint a move, that would be sufficient to send him plummeting down. Another death. Would it resolve anything? The police were already trying to pin Aunt Pat's attack on him. Then there was this whole thing about his father being poisoned, ¬would that be laid at his door as well? If Bryan took a tumble here, what were the chances Corstophine would think he was responsible?

"You're right," Robb conceded. "I just needed to know. Let's get these ashes done and pick up Sandy before he finishes all the food."

Bryan's weak smile was his only response.

CHAPTER 25
Cognitive Dissonance

The Royal Hotel was a cherished institution in the town, cherished in the same way a maiden aunt, smelling of lavender with an undernote of urine, might be regarded within a family. In its heyday, over a hundred years ago, it had provided a comfortable stay for the new breed of tourists brought this far north by the novelty of the steam train. Now, overtaken by brash new hotels featuring swimming pools, gyms and wi-fi it just managed to cling onto its elevated position with an air of increasing desperation. The Covid-19 pandemic hadn't helped of course. Edwardian hotels such as this were reliant on a steady stream of older tourists arriving on coach tours, eyes too weak to see the faded grandeur, palates incapable of differentiating local fresh produce from the defrosted gloop they were served. The absence of any tourist trade for the best part of a year had turned the hotel from an ailing geriatric to a barely functioning zombie. Why Sharmila had chosen this place over the more modern chain hotels was a mystery.

Corstophine exchanged a greeting with the manager at reception, passed through into the resident's lounge and spotted her immediately. Sharmila sat near the fireplace, a glass of white wine on a table beside her chair and her attention focussed on the book she held. She looked up as he approached, placing the book down next to her glass.

"James. Glad you could make it." She stood, holding a hand ready for his.

"Please, don't get up." Corstophine protested. He took her proffered hand, the grip as firm as he remembered. He looked around as she returned to her seat, catching the eye of a young waiter. "Can I order a pint of IPA?"

"Room 27." Sharmila held up a key fob, the overlarge wooden label imprinted with black digits that could easily be read from the other side of the lounge. She ignored Corstophine's protestations, watching him with barely disguised amusement as he sank so deeply into his seat that he grabbed the arms to avoid hitting the floor.

"My seat did the same to me." Sharmila's smile was infectious. "I think the springs gave out last century." She retrieved a bag from the side of her chair and extracted the photograph Corstophine had taken of the artwork, before laying it on the intervening table.

"You said you'd found something in the drawing?" Corstophine prompted.

The young waiter returned, Corstophine's pint presented on a cloth-covered tray with a flourish worthy of the finest champagne.

"Thanks." Corstophine took a long sip from the glass, trying not to notice the beer was warm and flat. The table surface offered no resting place, his glass hovering over the photograph ineffectually before Sharmila removed her book to create a space.

"Thanks," he repeated, somewhat inanely. She slid the book back into her bag, giving him the opportunity to surreptitiously wipe his mouth clear of any froth that might have adhered to his upper lip.

"There are a few salient images in the painting that I only noticed after giving it quite a bit of study." She passed the photograph to Corstophine. "First, take a look at the trees painted on the right."

Corstophine screwed his eyes partly shut to bring the

photograph into sharper relief. He knew that he needed glasses, but resented acknowledging that his eyesight was beginning to deteriorate. The trees had been painted in dark colours, primitive brush lines forming a sombre vignette surrounding the dancers illuminated by flaming yellow torches. He'd not given the perimeter of the painting any close attention; the eye being drawn effortlessly to the natural centre of the work, now overlain with Patricia's own blood.

Sharmila gave him a while before coming to his help, leaning over to extend a slender finger which traced an outline delicately over the edge of the photograph.

Corstophine was increasingly aware of her proximity, her scent. It took him a few moments before he was able to concentrate on the photograph and see anything of note among the muddy hues, and then he saw it!

Hidden in the dark shadows was the suggestion of a figure, the merest hint of something other than trees or natural foliage. His eyes began to ache with concentration. If only the light in here was better.

Sharmila passed over her phone, the light already on as if she'd just read his mind.

"This might help."

He took her phone with a grateful smile, holding it so the cold LED brought the photograph into greater clarity. There was a dark figure standing watching the dancers, almost concealed behind layers of paint, but once he had seen it Corstophine wondered how he'd ever missed it. The eyes held his attention. Why would Patricia have painted two specks of red?

"How did I never spot this? Patricia must have known she was being watched that night."

"We term the process of visualisation the bidirectional hierarchical network model."

Corstophine's blank expression prompted further explanation. Sharmila took a sip from her glass and regarded him steadily.

"The process by which we see and interpret the world is actually much more complex than you might think. Most people fondly imagine that we see what we see, and if they ever wonder about the process of seeing, they simplistically visualise a pinhole camera and the brain as the photographic plate. Most people don't even realise that the eye forms an upside-down image on the retina, so the brain has already manipulated reality before we start."

Corstophine reached for his pint. This had the makings of a mental marathon.

"There's a whole area of science dedicated to cognitive processing, but basically the process of seeing and understanding can be broken into distinct sections. The visual cortex, that area of the thalamus that processes input from the retina, allocates visual information in a hierarchical sense. Horizontal lines generally attract low attention, diagonal lines require more."

"How's that even a thing?" Corstophine queried.

Sharmila's head tilted, paradoxically increasing Corstophine's awareness of how attractive she was.

"They've run brain scans to detect activity whilst subjects view different diagrams. My own interpretation is that the primitive brain saw diagonal objects as potential intercepts, predators moving in on prey. The brain automatically assigns higher import to such visual clues for self-preservation."

Corstophine wasn't sure he saw at all but nodded for her to continue.

"As information proceeds through the cortex, neurons appear to be tuned to various patterns. So, for example, the ease in which we see faces in clouds or in tree trunks.

The mind is attuned to facial recognition patterns, perhaps overly trained you might say."

"Not in my experience." Corstophine thought of the many requests made, asking the public to describe an assailant or robber which invariably resulted in an anodyne description.

Sharmila carried on, evidently warming to her subject. "What has only recently been discovered is that the higher brain functions actively modify the raw input from our visual senses. There is about five times as much information being sent back down to the thalamus in response to the information being received."

A blank look was the only response Corstophine felt able to provide. At this stage he was beginning to wonder if she would suspect there was a clinical absence of neurological activity happening inside his head. "What does that actually mean?" Corstophine ventured, taking a deeper sip from his tepid pint in case that helped his understanding.

"What it means is that our cortex is altering the visual input from our eyes before it even gets to our consciousness. In other words, you're not seeing what is in front of you, you're seeing what your mind tells you is there!" She finished enthusiastically, waiting for Corstophine to respond.

"I'm not sure I get your point." He struggled with the concept of his mind telling him what to see instead of faithfully presenting what was in front of him. How would such an interpretation even play out in the field of detective work?

"I know it's difficult. Have you ever seen those diagrams of a duck that looks like a rabbit, then it's a duck again? Or the old lady who turns into a young lady?" Seeing

Corstophine's head beginning to shake side to side she hit upon another example.

"Look." She'd retrieved the book back out of her bag and was quickly thumbing through the pages. Corstophine read the title where it showed between her fingers, *Cognitive Dissonance*. She stopped with an air of satisfaction and turned the page towards him. Half the page displayed the logo for the Brazilian world cup in 2014. The green, yellow, blue of Brazil formed an abstract football atop a trophy.

Corstophine realised he had probably just failed a test. "I'm sorry. I just see a football trophy in Brazilian flag colours."

"How about a face palm?"

He looked again. Sure enough, the logo clearly showed someone holding their face in their palm, appropriately enough following Brazil's abysmal performance that year.

He laughed, impressed by the trick she'd so neatly executed.

"Here's the thing, James. You'll never be able to unsee the face palm again. Your brain will always interpret that logo in the same way from now on. It's a simple example, I know, but it shows you that there's a lot more going on than you may realise whenever you see something. This is why witnesses are generally unreliable. The mind constructs the narrative for them. As a scientist I know that the mind works to predict reality from sensory input. If something isn't right, then the brain tries again and again until it can make sense of the data. It effectively changes reality until it fits into a well-defined pigeonhole."

She pointed to the photograph again. "Can you see the figure in the trees now?"

Corstophine spotted it without any difficulty. "Yes, there at the edge of the woods."

Sharmila waited for the realisation to dawn.

"I saw it straight away!"

"Exactly, and you always will with this picture because your mind has detected the pattern of a man in that random mess of lines and brush strokes."

"You said a few salient images?" Corstophine asked.

She nodded. "First, look more closely at the graffiti your assailant left on the original picture. You've described it as a devil, but this is another instance of your mind creating a narrative out of what are really random shapes. The devil is often represented in red, and this is a trope originating from medieval illustrated manuscripts where Satan is often wreathed in the flames of hell. I don't think that this represents a figure, but I do think it serves a purpose."

Corstophine was intrigued enough to leave his pint temporarily untouched. "What purpose? Patricia's assailant deliberately carried the painting into her bedroom, increasing his chances of being caught. He set it up on an easel and then blinded her with her own paintbrushes to make his mark. You think it was just a random mess?"

Sharmila mused for a while, looking at the photograph with him. "It's possible there might be a message contained within those markings. Flames, a vertical stroke for each potential victim? Impossible to say. The main reason he's obliterated the centre of the picture is to hide his identity."

He looked at her, thinking he'd misheard.

"Hold the picture at arm's length."

Corstophine followed her instructions now feeling slightly foolish.

"Make your eyes go out of focus so the picture is more of a blur." She gave him a few seconds. "Now look for a face filling the centre of the canvas."

He struggled for a few seconds, managing the out of focus bit with ease but seeing nothing other than the dancers forming a rough circle as they contorted around the garden ornament. Corstophine was about to admit defeat when he saw it, the dancers formed the outline of a face; flying robes described eyebrows and eyes.

"I can see it." Corstophine said quietly. "The circle is a face, these are the eyes. He's blotted out the nose and mouth. He's hidden his identity."

"Exactly!" Sharmila's delight was clear. "He saw his own face in the painting because his brain was used to seeing himself. It must have given him a shock when he realised his victim knew who he was before he'd even attacked her."

She finished her wine, replacing the glass on the table and searching for a waiter. "Do you have a picture of the painting before it was vandalised?"

"No. I saw her working on it but there wasn't any reason to look more closely at the time."

"Shame. At least it lends credence to the idea that she knew her attacker." Sharmila spotted a waiter and beckoned him over. "Another one, James?"

He was tempted. The evening had been an eye-opener so far. He'd learned things he had never imagined and the parallels to his work as a detective had given him food for thought. Then Sharmila herself, was he only imagining that she was more interested in him than a mere meet between professionals?

His mobile interrupted, and his eyebrows drew down in irritation as he checked the caller. PC Bill McAdam, what could he want?

"I'm sorry, will you excuse me?" Corstophine accepted the call, turning away from Sharmila. "McAdam, you are aware this is my time off?"

"Sorry, sir, but I thought you ought to know." The metallic voice sounded breathless. "It's Keith Tunstall. We responded to an anonymous call. He's dead. We found him nailed to his kitchen floor with a funnel full of drugs rammed down his throat."

CHAPTER 26
Black Doctor

Robb tipped the last of his father's ashes over Streap's untidy cairn with little formality. A portion was immediately taken as an offering by the wind, carried effortlessly towards the distant glittering waters of Jack's beloved Loch Arkaig. The rest trickled down between gaps in the cairn's boulders, burying themselves back into the land of his ancestors.

Robb bowed his head, catching Bryan copy his stance from the corner of his eye. He didn't bow his head for any religious reason; a Christian God held little sway in these ancient mountains. He bowed his head for forgiveness. Robb didn't expect absolution, not here, just the chance to tell his father one last time that he loved him and that he was sorry.

As for Bryan. Well, he and his mother deserved each other. She had never loved his father. She had never loved him or Phoebe. She'd managed to circumvent that innate biological imperative of a mother to offer unconditional love to her offspring, avoiding the inconvenience of giving anything of herself away without expecting a return on her investment. He could guess at what magnetism had attracted the two of them together following his father's death – Bryan's seduction by Emma's fading beauty and her lust for his wealth.

They had walked back down in silence. Robb fighting the unexpected tears that threatened his vision as he negotiated the mountain's sharp arête. Now he no longer had the ashes, he had nothing of his father left, just memories that shamed him. Bryan's thoughts were concerned with how he was going to break the news to Emma that Robb knew about the two of them. He felt as if he was negotiating two knife-edges at the same time and wasn't sure which of the two balancing acts was causing his stomach to perform cold somersaults.

Sandy was in good spirits as the two of them hove into view. He was sprawled out on the ground in the late afternoon sun, the abandoned rucksack forming a pillow for his head.

"I've left your pieces." He said this with the triumphant air of someone whose character had been tested to the limit by the proximity of temptation and yet had heroically resisted.

"We'll eat as we walk." Robb's terse response drew a calculated look from Sandy as he heaved himself up off the ground.

"Everything OK?" Sandy had not survived school without developing his own personal radar, reading trouble before it came anywhere near him.

"We're fine Sandy, just tired." Bryan's words were unconvincing. "We should get on, the sun's getting low."

Sure enough the sun was sinking towards the horizon. Sandy might have been enjoying the warmth of full sunshine but further down the glens were already in full shadow, with patches of creeping ground fog shadowing the valley floor.

The return journey was a lot faster than the ascent had been, once they had cleared the steep section down from the ridge. Sandy had only then realised how steep his ascent had been and inched down like an overweight ballerina, feet delicately placed to avoid loose stones. When they eventually saw the reassuringly solid rectangular presence of the bothy, the daylight was almost completely away.

"It's an unusual name for a building – Gleann dubh-lighe," Bryan ventured in an effort to break the pall of unnatural silence that had followed them off the mountain.

"Gleann an lighiche dubh translates as Glen of the Black Doctor."

They waited for Robb to add further detail to his comment, but he had entered the building ahead of them. Bryan and Sandy shared a shrug before following in his footsteps, the light from his torch randomly flickering around the room before Robb anchored it to a hook on the wall.

"Isn't there a paraffin lamp or something?" Sandy was relieved to see his pack where he'd left it, hurrying over to check the contents were still in place.

"This place burnt down a few years ago. The estate doesn't encourage anyone leaving anything too flammable behind." Robb retrieved another torch from his pack, offering it to Bryan. "Do you want to collect some firewood from the plantation? We just need a few sticks to get the fire going. Someone's already left a pile of logs here."

Bryan left them, checking in on the second room to see if anyone else would be joining them that night. The other room remained empty, not much chance of anyone else taking it this late in the day. He left the bothy, heading towards the nearest trees to gather kindling.

Sandy watched the firefly glow of his torch as it bobbed away into the distance, then turned back to confront Robb.

"You two have an argument or something?"

Robb looked up from the floor, assembling the camping stove in readiness for their last meal. Two tins of stew lay in wait next to the battered saucepan he'd packed.

"It's a personal thing, Sandy." He attempted to close the conversation down before it began, adding emphasis by forcibly attacking the tin lid with his Swiss knife.

"I didn't mean to pry. It's just you were both very quiet when you came back. I thought maybe something had happened?"

Robb sawed with more violence until the lid was severed, then poured the contents into the awaiting saucepan. He reached for the second can.

"We had a chat about some personal issues. Nothing for you to be concerned about. It's all sorted."

"OK." Sandy knew when to back off. He concentrated instead on finding the most comfortable spot for his sleeping bag.

"Can you fill this up with water?" Robb held an empty water bottle up for Sandy. "There's a burn just along the track, you'll be able to hear it from the door. Take the torch, I'll have enough light from the stove." He struck a match and the stove responded by casting a blue light into the room as the gas caught fire.

Sandy took the bottle and torch, leaving Robb bent over the recalcitrant tin. The last remnants of a red sunset had almost bled away as he left the bothy, leaving a faint memory of its passing on the highest peaks. He glanced upwards, hoping for a full moon to appear and shed its benevolent silver glow but only the stars were on display, more becoming visible as the sky darkened. Sandy had never realised there were so many stars in the night sky. There must have been thousands of tiny pinpricks of light showing as a broad band stretching from horizon to horizon, random shreds of cloud insufficient to cloak the Milky Way. Outliers twinkled, some in colourful hues. He recognised the Big Dipper by its bent saucepan handle shape, Cassiopeia as a giant W in the night sky. It was with an effort of will that he dragged his attention away from the heavens, listening instead for the sound of running water. Over there! He moved cautiously, sweeping the ground in front of him with the torch beam until he found the source.

Sandy lowered the water bottle into the fast-flowing burn, trying not to imagine what the quiet rustling sounds all around him might be. Were adders likely to be active this time of year? He swept the torch around nervously with his free hand, trying to see underneath the dying bracken. When the explosive crack from a nearby rifle reached his ears, Sandy dropped the water bottle and torch in shocked reaction. His wide eyes darted from hill to hill as he followed the echoes from the shot, instinctively remaining close to the ground to avoid being hit.

"Who in hell is hunting at this time of day?" Sandy's voice came as a whisper, strangled into horrified silence as an unmistakable human scream split the cold evening air. That was Bryan's voice, he would swear to it – but making an animal cry unlike any noise he'd ever heard. He held his breath, ears straining as the glen fell silent. The dropped water bottle made hollow, plastic sounds every time it encountered a rock on its escape down the burn. Sandy found himself hissing at it to keep quiet before he realised that he would be drawing attention to himself by doing so. The torch lay a short distance away, the beam illuminating the heather. Should he shout out, let the hunters know there were people here? Why hadn't Robb appeared? He must have heard the shot. He would know what to do. Sandy lowered his head and started crawling on his hands and knees through the bracken, all concerns about adders forgotten in his desperation to keep out of sight. He just needed to get away from the torch; inside the bothy where he'd be safe.

Robb had leapt to his feet at the sound of the shot. His first thought was that these were poachers – the red stag season had only just finished and although hinds were now fair game, no-one in their right mind would attempt lining up a kill when the light was almost away. He stood framed in the open doorway just as Bryan's sub-human cry reached his ears, cut short as if he'd suddenly run out of air. The realisation that Bryan had been shot ran like ice in his veins, swiftly followed by the realisation that they could all be in danger. Even with dusk falling a hunter wouldn't mistake a man for a deer, especially through telescopic sights. If someone was using hillwalkers for target practice, he was making that task a lot simpler by standing stock still in a doorway, outlined in the stove's blue glow. Robb's legs initially refused to move, until sheer panic drove him back inside where the stone building offered protection against any stray bullets. He was just in time. The bothy door splintered as he pushed it shut, followed by the percussive ricochet of a bullet rebounding off the stone walls. His ears were still ringing when he caught the explosive snap of the rifle shot, fractions of a second later. Whoever it was, he was close.

On the floor, the stove's steady blue flames suddenly appeared unnaturally bright. If someone wanted to come up to the windows and shoot him, he was a sitting duck. Robb stopped himself from turning off the gas and letting whoever was out there know that he was still alive – maybe if he kept quiet they'd assume he was dead and leave? What about Sandy, though? He was still out there fetching water. Did he have the presence of mind to lay low? Moving as quietly as he could, Robb crouched down beside the door and away from the windows, holding the small Swiss knife like an inadequate toy in his hand. He strained to listen for any movement from outside, head so close to the slightly open door that errant drafts tugged at his hair. The world had fallen silent after the second gunshot, every creature in the glen frozen in place in case they were the next target. Above the low moan of wind attempting to access the bothy he heard a weak voice carried on the breeze.

"Help me."

The words were so quiet Robb imagined they were created from his imagination, whispered in anguish. That was Bryan's voice – he'd swear to it.

"Help."

It came again, even weaker this time, as if the act of breathing out the word was a monumental struggle. Robb bit his lip so hard he drew blood. He had to help him – he couldn't leave him out there to die. He steeled himself to run out of the bothy, make a zig-zag towards the woods where Bryan surely lay. His fingers stretched towards the edge of the door, preparing to pull it open, when from the direction of the woods came an insane laugh, made all the more terrifying as the last of the evening light faded away on a dark crimson horizon. "I hope you die slowly, Robb McCoach. You'll pay – your family's going to pay."

Behind the bothy door, Robb felt the colour draining from his face. He'd been dismissive of Aunt Pat's dire warning that someone was out to get the family; had treated it as another of the woman's mad eccentricities. Whose voice was that? Robb ran through a sea of faces, adding individual voices as each came into focus, in a desperate attempt to match the maniacal laugh. Nobody. He literally had no idea who it could be or why they wanted him dead. All he knew was that someone was out there with their rifle sights aimed at the bothy. He reached into his pocket, hands trembling so much he had difficulty in retrieving his mobile, aiming a shaking finger to switch it into life. The screen display showed no signal. No chance of reaching anyone this far from the nearest mast. Robb switched it off, frightened that the blue glow would attract the hunter's attention.

Minutes passed – just the sound of Robb's heavy breathing unnaturally loud within the confines of the bothy entrance. Outside, the last of the daylight had all but leached from the sky, the mountains and forest merging into one featureless darkness. A whisper of cold air crept in from the partially open door, adding to the chill that had begun in his stomach then spread over his skin when the first shot rang out. Robb's legs were threatening to cramp despite the constant shaking that had taken hold of his limbs, an unconscious reaction to the fear that had him gripped in a vice. He had been squatting close to the floor in readiness to run for so long that he was in danger of falling over. He decided to risk a quick look outside, moving forward with some difficulty just as the heavy sound of running footsteps approached.

Caught off-balance, Robb backed away from the door and sprawled onto his back, his leg muscles finally giving in to spasm as he made the sudden movement. He managed to hold onto the Swiss army knife, the point aimed squarely at Sandy's panicked face as he threw open the bothy door, tripping over Robb's legs in his desperation to find safety. A bullet hit Sandy just as he fell, slamming into his shoulder with enough force to spin him around. He landed on Robb like a dead weight, his corpulent body pinning him to the flagstone floor. The sound of the shot seemed to fill the small stone building, rebounding from wall to wall and leaving Robb temporarily deafened.

He had to free himself before their attacker reached the door. Robb dropped the inadequate knife, grabbing hold of Sandy's shoulders; recoiling as he felt the first drops of warm blood fall wetly onto his face, then with adrenaline-fuelled muscles rolled the body over until he could clamber out from underneath. Sandy responded to the rough treatment with a low moan, lying where Robb had pushed him on the cold flagstones with short breaths bubbling in his mouth.

"Stay there," Robb whispered, not knowing if Sandy was even conscious. "I'll jam the door shut." His eyes searched the bothy for inspiration, focussing on the pile of logs. As quickly as he could, Robb pushed the bothy door closed, dropping the catch and deadening the sound of its metallic closure with his fingers. Keeping low to the floor, he carried the largest logs and lined them up until they formed a makeshift barricade against the door, preventing it from being pushed open from outside. The physicality of the action provided a welcome outlet for his pent-up adrenaline, moving as quietly and as quickly as possible. It was the best that he could do.

Sandy lay on his back, jammed against the wall with his face screwed up in pain and one arm hanging from his shoulder as if it didn't belong there anymore. Under his torso the stone floor pooled black with blood.

"I've been shot!" The words came wetly out of Sandy's mouth, spoken in denial and disbelief. His hand rose awkwardly from the floor, searching for his bloody shoulder then falling back down as if the effort was too great. "It fucking hurts!"

Even in the flickering blue light from the gas stove, Robb could see it was a serious wound. Sandy's breathing came in short, tortured gasps – each one accompanied with an ominous bubbling from somewhere deep in his lungs. His eyes wetly searched Robb's face. "You've been shot too?"

Robb struggled to understand what Sandy meant, touching his own face as he felt a drip run off his chin. He stared stupidly at his red-stained, outstretched fingers then realised it was Sandy's blood.

"No. I'm OK," he whispered urgently. "Lie still and keep quiet. I'm going to try and stop the bleeding." He pressed his palm with as much pressure as he dared over Sandy's wound, feeling his fingers warm with blood. Sandy responded with an animal whimpering before he passed out from the pain, only his laboured breathing indicating that he was still alive.

Robb strained to detect any sign of their attacker coming closer above the steady hiss from the stove, and Sandy's struggling breath. There was silence, even the constant wind that played around the building held its breath. He struggled to hear Bryan's weak voice through the closed door but it was useless. What could he do? They were trapped inside the bothy, about as isolated as it was possible to be, with some homicidal maniac shooting at them with a high-powered rifle. Robb had seen for himself what one of those bullets could do to a fully grown deer – if Bryan had been hit then he didn't stand much of a chance. Expanding bullets for deer hunting were designed to inflict maximum damage as they passed through a body, resulting in a clean kill as long as the animal was hit in the chest. Bryan might stand a chance if the bullet had gone straight through his flesh ¬– but the sound he'd made before it was suddenly choked off... Robb didn't want to think about it. They had to think of their own survival.

They lay in silence until darkness finally laid claim to the land; the stove spluttering the last of its light and leaving them in a black so profound they may as well have been buried underground. Sandy was still breathing raggedly, giving Robb some hope that his lungs hadn't been too badly damaged when the bullet had hit him. He stirred from under Robb's hand, regaining consciousness and weakly attempted to raise his head before the effort proved too much.

"Here, press your hand down as hard as you can." Robb guided Sandy's hand to the wound. "I need to get the first aid box. Did you see anyone when you were out there?" Robb spoke in an urgent theatrical whisper, climbing to his feet and massaging his legs where muscles had knotted into hard lumps under the skin.

"I don't know. Is Bryan OK?" The words came out in a hushed staccato, laboured breaths interspersing each short statement. Both men stared at the blackness where the door was, as if expecting Bryan – or someone else – to come through at any moment.

"I think he's been shot. I tried to help him but just missed a bullet as soon as I opened the door," Robb whispered in response. "What do you mean you don't know – did you see anyone or not?"

Sandy hesitated. "Something stood up as I crawled through the bracken. It was looking for me." His hand sought Robb – clutched his clothing. "I saw its eyes, they glowed red. It wasn't human."

Robb felt the tremble in Sandy's arm, heard the terror in his voice. He had to try and remain calm, despite the rapid beating of his heart, if only for Sandy's sake. He felt for Sandy's hand, gently prised it off and returned it to the wound – guided by the slick blood covering the hole in his shoulder. "Keep the pressure on." Robb hoped Sandy couldn't feel the obvious tremor in his own hands.

"Do you think he's coming to finish us off?" Sandy's eyes were wild. Robb could see the whites of his eyes even in the dim lighting offered by the starlight coming through the bothy skylights.

"I don't know. Whatever happens, I'm going to have to try and stop your bleeding," Robb added as a hushed afterthought.

The long night stretched in front of them, they had no defence save for his small knife and neither of them knew who or what was out there.

CHAPTER 27
Drugged

Corstophine pulled up outside the most rundown house in the street. It wasn't too difficult to find. The combined police and ambulance emergency lights had turned the location into a strobing disco, minus the music but complete with static crowds. He pulled on forensic gloves and overshoes, feeling the assembled crowd shift focus onto him as a fresh diversion in the ongoing entertainment. Curious faces stood attentively on garden paths, the more brazen thrillseekers thronging the pavement nearer the ambulance in hopeful expectation of catching a good look at a dead body. Clouds of strongly scented smoke billowed from electronic cigarettes, making the whole area smell like a dysfunctional orangery.

A sigh of frustrated disappointment came from the cheap seats as the ambulance staff exited the building without the eagerly awaited corpse in their possession.

"Body bag job," one of them said to him in passing. "We're waiting on forensics."

Corstophine nodded in acknowledgement and entered the hallway, checking the front door for signs of forced entry before picking his way past the paraphernalia clogging the passage. There was the blue rucksack Frankie had spotted through the letterbox. He hoisted it from a hanging strap to check the weight. It certainly felt empty. A spattering of blood on the wall where the violence had begun caught his eye, then the smears of dried blood where a body had been dragged along the floor towards where

Lamb's face peered at him from around a kitchen door. He let the rucksack drop back on the ground, buckles hitting the floor like small firecrackers.

"Sir, in here, sir." Lamb swept his arm in a theatrical flourish, keen to show off the latest exhibit.

The exhibit wouldn't have looked out of place in a modernist art gallery. Keith Tunstall lay stretched out on the floor as though re-enacting the crucifixion, packets of drugs and their spilled contents surrounding his body. If Tracey Emin had been commissioned to design a piece incorporating drug paraphernalia, murder and a kitchen, it would look like this. Once Corstophine was able to tear his focus away from the plastic funnel that remained jammed in Keith's throat, it was the dead man's eyes that drew his attention. They bulged unnaturally from their sockets, staring at the ceiling with an expression of abject horror from a head entombed between two piles of breezeblocks.

"What have you found?" Corstophine addressed both constables, but he focussed on PC Bill McAdam. The older constable stood in the back doorway, letting the cold night air blow the worst of the smell away from him.

"I couldn't see any sign of forced entry, sir. It looks like whoever did this was let into the house via the front door and left the same way. There are signs of a struggle in the hall." McAdam crouched down, pointing out the arc made by the back door as it had swept a path through the powdered drugs coating the floor. "We came in this door, it was already open, but there were just the one set of footprints coming in, leading directly to the countertop with the breadbin and then straight out again. I took a photograph on my phone before we entered, sir."

Corstophine's eyes sought out the breadbin, found it with the lid lying on the counter beside it. One set of footsteps stood out in sharp relief on the powdered floor. He could see the breadbin was empty.

"Who called it in?" He crouched down by the most obvious footprint, placing his car keys next to it for scale and took a shot on his phone. There were other prints underneath, less obvious and mostly obscured by Lamb's footprints. Corstophine held back his anger, forensics might still be able to rescue a print. He'd have a quiet word with Lamb about protecting the scene of crime later.

"It was a 999 call, sir. We responded within minutes. I may be wrong, but I think it was whoever found him like this. They described the scene fairly accurately."

Corstophine nodded, reaching out to feel Keith's body. There was still some residual heat, although that might have been from the ambient temperature in the kitchen. His arm was stiff, evidence that rigor mortis had taken hold. That would put his time of death anywhere between three and eight hours ago, but forensics would be able to give a more accurate estimate.

"Any ideas as to what was in the bread bin?" Corstophine ventured.

"I'd say money, sir. There are still plenty of wraps and packets of drugs left behind so they weren't so interested in those." McAdam again. PC Lamb was staring at the corpse with a horrified intensity from the hallway and keeping unnaturally quiet.

"Are you alright, Lamb?" The young PC had taken on the same grey hue as the powder coating the floor.

"I'm fine, sir." Lamb's answer lacked conviction.

"Perhaps you could ask the circus crowds outside whether any of them heard or saw anything."

"Yes sir, right away, sir." Lamb left the kitchen with

the air of a man escaping one of Dante's levels of hell, retrieving his notebook from his top pocket as he went.

"Do you think it's a drugs war, sir? Someone wanting in on this patch?"

Corstophine's eyebrow raised in contemplation of McAdam's question. "It's certainly a possibility, Bill, although they'd not leave this amount of product around unless they were disturbed."

He considered Frankie's suggestion that the two Glaswegians they'd nicked for the catalytic converter thefts were there as muscle. If a rival drugs gang had found out the town was wide open, then they might have been tempted to move in, but why make such a theatrical spectacle of Tunstall's death? It had the makings of a revenge killing.

"What do you know about him?" Corstophine tilted his head towards the spread-eagled corpse.

"Just that he's one of the local troublemakers. I never had him down as a drugs pusher, more as a petty criminal with a penchant for the physical." McAdam paused for thought before adding, "I didn't think travellers dealt drugs particularly, doesn't go with their culture."

"I think the criminal element have moved on from clothes pegs, Bill. If it generates ready cash then drugs are fair game, along with people smuggling. Damn sight more profitable than laying dodgy driveways."

A welcoming shout sounded from the hallway, followed by the appearance of a forensics suit.

"Been trampling all over the scene of crime again, lads?"

Corstophine nodded a welcome. "See what you can find. There are well-defined footprints in the layer of dust on the floor in here, looks like the murderer's footprints underneath. I'd work on the assumption that's a cocktail of narcotics littering the floor, so watch yourself."

The forensic officer pointed to his mask. "I'm safe but you two ought to leave."

Corstophine realised he'd been holding his breath. "Keep an eye on the back door, Bill. I'll ask Lamb to look after the front." He turned his attention back to the forensics technician, pointing a finger at the body. "Can you deal with him first, the ambulance guys don't like to be kept waiting."

Corstophine turned to leave, the flash of a camera announcing that forensics had started to document the SOC.

"Oh, we found some interesting chemical traces in your water bottle," the technician commented conversationally as he started tugging away at the funnel, finally managing to release it with the accompaniment of a wet groan from the corpse. He caught Corstophine's surprised expression. "Air pressure. His lungs had formed a vacuum, or it could be decomposition gases." He tentatively sniffed the air as if searching for bad breath.

Corstophine thought back to the mountain, the water bottle jammed between two rocks, and Jack McCoach's body slung on a stretcher like so much dead meat.

"What did you find?" He asked the question, not sure if he wanted to hear the answer.

The technician was busy releasing the straps anchoring Keith's body to the floor. "That's it!" He stood over the corpse with an air of satisfaction. "They'll have to be creative how they carry him out or they'll never get him through the door." He turned his attention back to the detective. "I'll send the report to you tomorrow. The water contained high concentrations of Taxine-derived alkaloids, taxane-derived substances and glycosides. If your hillwalker drank the rest of what was in the bottle, then he would have had a large enough dose to kill him."

Corstophine attempted to process the information. These terms might mean something to a forensics technician or a doctor but meant nothing to him.

"Any idea where these taxaloids might have come from?"

"Taxanes and taxines." The technician corrected. "Yes, taxus baccata. The European Yew."

"You're saying someone filled his water bottle with yew tree extract?"

"The leaves, aye. It only requires 3mg or so to do the job. I haven't seen a case of yew poisoning for years." His tone picked up with obvious enthusiasm as he started getting into his stride.

"But there weren't any leaves in the bottle." Corstophine was struggling to understand how the poison came to be in the bottle.

The technician scooped up a portion of the sludge still left in the funnel, carefully depositing it into an evidence bag which he sealed before writing on the label. "No, but it was in a fairly pure form. I'd say whoever did it had to extract the compounds and concentrate them before adding them to the water."

"Is that a difficult process?" Corstophine asked.

The technician considered for a brief moment, seemingly unconcerned by the corpse underneath his feet. "Someone would just need to soak the leaves in ethanol, maybe agitate the mixture then filter and let it evaporate. It's fairly crude but effective."

"Would alcohol work?" Corstophine was picturing the wooden shed in the McCoach garden, Robb's artisan distillery.

"I don't see why not." His voice was muffled, head bent down in inspection of Keith's open mouth. Corstophine looked away as the technician pushed a long-handled swab down the throat.

"Thanks. Can you send the water analysis to me first thing tomorrow? Plus whatever you find here. Ask the mortuary to fast track this for me, will you?" Corstophine left forensics collecting samples of grey sludge from Keith's throat and sought out PC Lamb working his way through the crowd.

"Has anyone seen or heard anything?" Corstophine asked, already knowing what the answer was going to be.

"No sir, nothing yet." PC Lamb's colour had returned to more of a ruddy hue, as best as he could tell in the streetlight's unnaturally white illumination.

"OK. Keep an eye on the front door. Usual procedure, nobody in or out unless they're meant to be here." Corstophine walked back to his car and sat watching as the ambulance crew awkwardly manoeuvred a body bag out of the premises. Flashes of light accompanied them as the residents prepared their own social media commentary. *Everyone's a bloody pundit these days.* The thought came and went. There were two sides to that particular coin. Everyone had the means to record events, even transmit them in real time. That played merry hell with the legal process but then again, the police were often provided with evidence that otherwise would never have been available before the advent of the ubiquitous mobile phone.

Where did this leave his investigation? This death looked like a drugs turf war at first glance, although the method of killing was over the top. Could it be a warning to other dealers not to take some of the product for themselves, or cut it even further with talc or rat poison? Being found stapled to the floor with a load of hard drugs shoved down your windpipe would be a lesson few would be likely to forget. There wasn't any immediate connection he could see to Jack's death, or the attack on Patricia. But the poison in Jack's water bottle? Corstophine hadn't really expected anything to be found; the pathology report had clearly stated heart attack. So, if someone had killed him, who was in the frame?

Patricia had to be a suspect, if only because she had seemingly known that her brother had been poisoned. Corstophine didn't give any credence to voices from beyond the grave, which was ironic given his continuing dialogue with his dead wife. He understood the difference though. His wife was gone, gone for good. What remained were his memories, and his imagination of how she once had been before cancer took her away forever. Her voice was a continuing comfort, her presence none the less real for living inside his head.

The other members of the family had to be considered as well: Robb, with his distillery and artisan bottled water manufacturing was a prime candidate, Emma and her possible love interest, Bryan Cobb, who'd been evasive when questioned on yesterday's hike. The daughter he could discount as she was under 24-hour care and as far as he could tell, locked inside the family house. But if Patricia was a suspect, who had then attacked her and why?

The ambulance pulled away from the kerb, lights still flashing but the siren silent as it took Tunstall's corpse to the forensics slab. Corstophine pulled away from the kerb, following the ambulance down the street. Already the onlookers had started to melt away, all excitement over for the moment. He saw them drifting back to their houses, waiting to be mesmerised by the flickering screens until bed, exchanging one type of coma for another until the cycle repeated for another day. At least Keith had provided some stimulation for once, marked the day as one to remember.

You're no better, James. You've only been marking time since I've been gone. Treading water.

Corstophine glanced in the rear-view mirror, not really expecting to see anything other than his own tired grey eyes staring back at him but strangely disappointed not to see her.

"Aye." He sighed, a long, drawn-out breath as if he'd been storing it for years. "You're right, I know."

He parted ways with the ambulance as they reached the main road and drove home with a feeling of regret that he hadn't been able to have that next drink with Sharmila. At least he still had the single malt waiting.

CHAPTER 28
Old Pretender

The Old Pretender was a favourite watering hole of Frankie's. The pub was just off the High Street and presented such minimal and unwelcoming frontage to any passing trade that tourists mostly passed it by without even realising it was there at all. The more observant took one look through the grimy windows where the older clientele sat in silent contemplation of their pints, responding to any inquisitive face with well-practiced gurns, and decided to give it a miss. Perversely, the lack of any marketing material or A-boards announcing its presence had ensured its survival; the regulars were all locals and so it had weathered the Covid-19 tourist famine that had decimated so much of the competition. Inside, the layout resembled nothing more than ancient stables that had been left over from the time of the pub's eponymous name. Individual stalls stood back-to-back, wooden benches upholstered with tartan, tables that had seen generations of drinkers. The dim lighting and well-worn tables, each in their own secluded stalls, were almost purpose-built for meeting social distancing guidelines. It was a strange quirk of fate that the obscurity of the place, together with the ability of drinkers to hide themselves away in relative privacy in hidden nooks, attracted such a wide variety of punters. The police preferred it to the flashier chain pubs because they could talk shop without being overheard, thanks to the landlord doubling duty as a DJ with eclectic tastes, all of them loud enough to make eavesdropping an impossibility. For exactly the same reason the local criminal fraternity also enjoyed drinking there; alongside just about every other walk of life who preferred an authentic drinking experience to the chain pubs elsewhere.

Frankie often mentally compared the place to an African watering hole: lions and antelope sharing a drink under truce conditions; always keeping an eye open but with the understanding that they were all off duty. She had made a bit of an effort, applying makeup and putting on her 'party clothes' as she liked to call them, and used the walk to the pub to clear her head at the end of the day's work. Pushing open the door, she was met with the pungent aroma of humanity and stood for a second to let her eyes adapt to the dim lights. Chrissie Hynde was singing from the speakers, telling her she was special in that quasi-sultry tone that gave The Pretenders their unique sound. *Appropriate enough*, she thought, given that her hand was already picking through the change in her purse for her first drink. The choice of beverages was more limited here. None of your fancy cocktails, just straight beer from the pumps or shots from the upturned spirit bottles behind the bar. She'd once seen a bunch of young students march in and confidently order Strawberry Daqs in brash American tones. She had been too far away to hear the barman's response, but they had quickly filed out a lot more sheepishly than they'd entered. Frankie's G&T was placed on the bar before she even had a chance to order it, her outstretched hand offering money declined. The barman pointed to a woman sitting at the end of the bar and Frankie's improving mood suddenly took a backwards step.

"Hello, Frankie, good to see you out socialising." The voice betrayed her French origins. Josephine Sables was the reporter for the town's only newspaper and Frankie knew how adept she was at flushing out everything that happened in their small Highland town.

"I've nothing to give you, if that's what this drink's for." Frankie laid down the ground rules before they started. She looked around to find the rest of the girls she'd arranged to meet and waved a greeting to let them know she was coming.

Josephine checked behind her, seeing the welcoming hands as they dropped back down.

"I'm just being friendly, Frankie." She pouted slightly as if offended, then swept her dark hair back from her face to expose her high cheekbones to their best advantage. "I saw you as you stood in the door, thought you might just like someone to talk to. I didn't know you were here with friends. It's OK."

She shrugged in that peculiarly Gallic way, an exaggerated pulling up of the shoulders before releasing them slowly back into place.

Frankie suspected the reporter wasn't in the least bit offended but felt a wave of shame at being so abrupt.

"I'm sorry. No, it's kind of you, thanks." Frankie raised her glass to her lips, the gesture mirrored as Josephine raised a large glass of white wine in response.

"Slàinte mhath." The Gaelic for 'good health' came with a distinct French accent. Frankie felt the reporter's eyes on her as she drank, lowering her glass to meet the reporter's amused look head on.

"I hear you have caught the catalytic burglars." Josephine said the words as if she was trying out a headline, head tilted to one side then upright again.

"Yes, two of our constables arrested them yesterday evening. Word gets out quickly."

Josephine nodded enthusiastically. "Yes, and I have some great photos from the public. Electrifying!"

Frankie curled up slightly inside. *Not the Taser shot, surely?* "Well, as long as your readers know we are working hard to keep the town safe."

"Of course! We always work with you, as you know."

Frankie wondered how she could extricate herself from this conversation without being too offensive.

"Well, it's great to bump into you. Thanks for the drink, can I get you one in return? I've arranged to meet some friends so I'd better dash."

"No, this is enough for me. Maybe some other time?" She smiled disarmingly. Frankie could have sworn that she'd even batted her eyelashes.

"OK. Well, enjoy your evening." Frankie made to leave, stopping as she felt the insistent touch of a hand on her arm.

"Just one thing before you go."

Frankie gave a fair imitation of one of the old men's gurns in response. "What is it?"

"How is Patricia McCoach? I hear she was badly injured in the attack at her home."

"You know I'm not able to comment on an ongoing investigation." Frankie attempted to close her down.

"Yes, but being blinded. That's not normal, is it?"

"Who told you she was blinded?" Frankie knew what the answer was going to be before Josephine touched the side of her nose twice in reply.

"We have to protect our sources." Two dark eyes held Frankie's in a combative stare. "Should we be worried there's a psychopath creeping around the streets at night?"

Frankie needed to close this line of questioning down. She could see the headlines being written as they talked.

"That's a bit hysterical even for the Courier." Josephine's

expression remained unchanged. Frankie tried again. "We have strong forensic evidence. Whoever did this will be caught, I can assure you. Finding Patricia's attacker is our main focus."

The hand left her arm.

"That's good to hear, I'll let our readers know."

"Aye, right." Frankie started walking away.

"What about Keith Tunstall?"

Frankie paused mid-stride. What was she talking about?

"What do you mean, what about Keith Tunstall? What's he got to do with anything?"

Josephine gave another Gallic shrug. "Just that he's been found dead of a drug overdose this evening. Thought you might have known something about it." She returned to her drink, deliberately turning her back on Frankie.

Christ! This woman knew more about what was going on around town than she did! If only the police had access to her lines of information.

"That's news to me." Frankie retorted.

Josephine turned back to face her, a smile etched deeply across her face and forming small dimples underneath her cheekbones. "That's what we do, Frankie. We are the news."

Frankie left her at the bar, offering a silent curse as she joined her friends. Her buoyant mood had deflated, and she tipped more of the alcohol down her neck in an effort to regain it.

"How's that boss of yours, Frankie? Is he still on the market?" The woman beside her asked with a twinkle in her eye and the slightest hint of desperation in her tone.

The other women quietened their chatter to hear Frankie's response. She was put in mind less of a pack of cougars than something much more deadly, a group of women approaching middle age all on the lookout for an available man, still in possession of his own teeth and with a reasonable income.

"I'm not sure, he seems to have lost interest." Frankie felt protective towards Corstophine, there was no way she'd throw him to this lot. They'd eat him alive.

The woman beside her turned her mouth down in disappointment.

"That's a shame, it's been so long since Katie's had a man, she's worried it's going to heal over!" The voice came in a harsh trill from the other side of the table and the women collapsed in laughter, arms flailing like windmills.

Frankie smiled with them. It was going to be one of those nights, no holds barred and men the focus of most of the barbed comments. She quickly finished her glass as the next order was taken, watching as the reporter half raised a hand in farewell as she left the pub.

A weasel-faced man took her place at the bar, waving a fistful of notes at the bartender in an effort to jump the queue. He looked familiar, and he didn't dress as if he normally had that much money. The barman ignored him, dealing with his customers in strict order. 'Ordinary People' was playing, the night's soundtrack having a definite retro vibe. She took out her phone, pretending to check the screen and took a surreptitious shot of the guy at the bar. Frankie might be off duty, but like most cops, she was never really off duty.

She had asked for a double, tipping the contents down her neck in an effort to catch up with her companions. Before the night was over, she intended to get quite drunk. Frankie shared the same medicine as Corstophine, and alcohol was a sure-fire method of forgetting the worst of the week's images etched in her memory.

CHAPTER 29
Idle Hands

Corstophine stood in front of the crazy board, hand thoughtfully stroking his chin. He'd added Keith Tunstall's name to the right of the whiteboard, quite separate from the attack on Patricia McCoach. Forensics would be coming back with their report in the next hour or so, and from the tech's comments last night he was hopeful for some good fingerprints at least. There was still nothing substantial from Patricia's attack though, and by the sounds of it they'd still have a few days wait until she was out of her coma. There was just one thing worrying him about the two cases; in each instance the attacker had coshed their victims to knock them senseless before performing further atrocities. It was only a matter of luck that Patricia wasn't dead, although whether she would feel that way when, *if*, she recovered…

Hamish made an appearance, his quizzical face cautiously poking around the main office door to see who had opened up before him. He wasn't particularly surprised to see the DI working on a day off. Corstophine pretty much lived in the station.

"Morning, sir. Early start?" He moved with ponderous intent towards the small kitchen area, feeling the kettle to see if it had already boiled.

"Morning, Hamish. Yes, I had a call from Lamb last night. One of our druggy pals has been found dead with a funnel full of narcotics shoved down his throat."

"I'm sorry to hear that." Hamish proceeded to turn on

the kettle, a complete lack of concern anywhere to be seen in the look he gave the DI. "Coffee, sir?"

"Thanks. You don't know him, do you? Keith Tunstall? Lives on the new scheme."

Hamish slowly nodded as he carefully measured out two scoops of ground coffee into the cafetière.

"Aye, I've had dealings with his dad before he was put away for GBH. The apple never falls far from the tree."

Corstophine pursed his lips. The sergeant had only recently attended diversity training, a two-day course at the police college down in Tulliallan Castle, Kincardineshire. The aim was to break down misconceptions that lay the police open to complaints about racial profiling; or dealing with the minefield that gender fluidity brought to the table. The old sergeant had made it clear what he thought of the course but had attended anyway. When he returned, the only change that Corstophine had noticed was an inability to know how to address any member of the public when they turned up at the front desk. Any new face was subject to a painfully long period of observation before the sergeant decided upon a term of address. The slight hope that he'd be treating anyone from the traveller community with the same respect as he would the general public was a forlorn one. Corstophine could sympathise in this instance, though, Keith Tunstall was a nasty piece of work, and someone had put out the garbage.

"You're not wrong in this case." Corstophine puzzled at the similarities between the two separate attacks. "You don't know of any connection between the McCoach and Tunstall families I suppose?"

Hamish brought over a mug of hot coffee, the smell of it enticing so early in the day.

"Thanks, Hamish." Corstophine took a sip and enjoyed the taste as it rested in his mouth for a brief second. *How did people manage before coffee?* The thought slipped away along with the liquid, burning a path down towards his stomach.

Hamish had been standing with a look of concentration etched on his face, his own coffee untouched and still held in his hand.

"No sir, I can't imagine any way those two would be connected. Have you found something linking them?" He peered short-sightedly at the whiteboard to see if any links had been added, McCoach to Tunstall.

That's two of us needing glasses. Somewhere along the line he'd have to accept that his eyes weren't what they used to be, but Corstophine railed against the thought of growing older, growing weaker.

I think you may have peaked already, James. His wife, poking fun at him as always. He smiled to himself, pleased to hear her voice again.

"No, Hamish, just similarities in the way both victims were attacked. It's probably coincidence."

Hamish made his deliberate way to the front desk, foot placed in front of foot almost as if he was making a parody of leading Keith's funeral cortège. Corstophine watched him go, wondering how much longer the old copper would stay in uniform. He turned back to the crazy board just as Hamish called out a welcome to Frankie.

"Morning, sir. Wasn't expecting you in today. Is this because of Keith Tunstall's murder?"

His eyebrows both took a short journey heavenwards.

"How did you hear about that? Have you been working a night shift as well?"

Frankie felt as if she'd been working nights. The girls had overdone the drinking, moving on from the wines and half pints towards the inevitable shots and leaving her with a tongue that didn't feel like her own anymore. She ran it experimentally around her mouth, feeling the fur attached to the inside of her cheeks. Definitely her tongue.

"No sir. I met our favourite reporter last night in the Old Pretender, she was pushing for information."

Corstophine pursed his lips again. He had an ambivalent relationship with Josephine Sables, realising that in many ways they needed each other. "I'll talk to her." He paused, constructing a timeline in his head. "When was this? What time did she mention Keith's murder?"

Frankie forced her brain into action. It had been perfectly comfortable just nursing a hangover up to that point.

"Must have been just after eight, sir. I'd just arrived, and she had a drink waiting for me at the bar. She started by asking me if we'd made any progress on the Patricia McCoach case. She knows about her being blinded." Frankie said the last few words with a degree of trepidation. Corstophine had wanted to keep the details of her injuries quiet for as long as he could but keeping a secret in this town was almost an impossibility.

Corstophine nodded and Frankie was relieved to see he didn't seem overly concerned.

"It had to come out sometime. Did you tell her we were giving it our full priority, not to make a song and dance about it?"

"Yes sir, I think she'll handle it discreetly."

"That's something I suppose." Corstophine sounded resigned. Whatever the Courier printed was out of his control.

The rest of the journalist's conversation came into reluctant focus. Frankie decided it was best to get all the bad news out at once. "She also implied that they have a photograph of Lamb tasering the Glaswegian on Thursday night. I think they're going to use it in today's paper."

Corstophine raised his eyes towards a God he knew for a stone cold fact didn't exist.

"Oh shit!"

Frankie stood still, undecided whether to leave for the sanctity of her desk.

His eyes came down from a contemplation of the infinite, resigned to an acceptance of reality. "It can't be helped, everyone's a bloody photographer these days."

She looked at the whiteboard, seeing Keith's name standing in isolation on one side.

"When did you hear about Keith's murder, sir?"

Corstophine smiled to himself again. Frankie might be hanging but her brain was still functioning.

"I was called by Lamb just after ten p.m. They responded to a 999 call from a local number. Someone was indiscreet enough to use their mobile. We'll be able to track them down if they haven't used a burner."

"Two hours after Josephine Sables mentioned it to me!"

"Interesting. I think we need to have a word with Josephine. Whoever told her knew about his death hours before the emergency call was made."

"Could be the same person, sir?"

Corstophine nodded. "That would be the most likely, unless it was a sideshow and they charged admittance!"

Frankie wasn't sure if he was joking. Another thought surfaced from the clouds fogging her brain.

"There was someone at the bar I recognised. I think it was the same guy we saw walking with Tunstall on the railway station CCTV. I took a shot of him on my phone – wait a minute."

She pulled her mobile out of a pocket, opening the photographs and expanding the shot until a face filled most of the screen.

Corstophine squinted his eyes to bring it into focus.

"Looks like the same individual right enough."

"I've kept that bit of the suicide footage on my PC, sir. I can run a comparison."

An eyebrow began its journey north. "Why have you kept that, Frankie? You know we're not meant to hold on to any CCTV footage that's not evidence. The last thing we need is the ICO at our door."

Frankie quickly thought on her feet. She knew her investigation into the girl's suicide wasn't authorised.

"I thought it might help any case we could bring against Keith for drug dealing, sir."

Corstophine searched her face. "OK. See if it's the same guy and we'll track him down."

She turned towards her desk.

"One more thing." Corstophine's voice stopped her.

Frankie turned sharply on her heel mid-stride and then wished she hadn't as the room swam alarmingly. She anchored herself on the floor and presented what she hoped was an alert face back towards the DI.

"I had a preliminary verbal on the water bottle I found on Sgurr Thuilm."

"The one missing from Jack McCoach's backpack?"

He nodded. "It contained enough poison to kill him."

"Jesus!"

"We're going to have our work cut out, Frankie. Two murders and the attack on Patricia." He turned back to the crazy board, adding a childlike representation of a tree next to Jack's name.

Frankie felt ice forming in her veins. "Why the tree, sir?" She hoped it had nothing to do with the deaths they'd worked on last year.

"It was from a yew tree, the leaves. Someone went to the trouble of distilling the poison and bottling it."

Corstophine stayed looking at the board, his back to

her. She knew what that meant. Robb McCoach was the main suspect.

"Which case do you want me to focus on, sir?"

Corstophine was back to stroking his chin, feeling a phantom beard under his fingers.

"Robb McCoach will be returning home later on today from scattering his father's ashes on the hills. I don't want to move on that until forensics come back with the full report later, which should be in the next hour or so. Find out who weasel-face is. With a bit of luck we can close that case down if he knows as much as I think he does. In the meantime, I'll get a search warrant for Robb's distillery. We'll pay him a visit after lunch."

Frankie took a detour around to the front desk, showing Hamish the same shot of the sharp-faced individual. He squinted at her phone until the face swam into focus.

"Aye, I know the lad."

"Who is it, Hamish?" Frankie asked with a degree of impatience. It was like trying to squeeze blood out of a stone dealing with the old sergeant.

"That's Frank Currie's boy, Stephen. Everyone calls him Weasel. I know his father." He took a slow sip from his mug before continuing. "He's an absolute waste of space. Don't think he's ever done a day's work in his life. I've never known anyone so bone idle." A thought made its tortuous way to the surface; she could almost detect its progress from inception to vocalisation.

"He lives a few doors down from that Keith Tunstall. He's not done anything stupid, has he?"

"I don't know, Hamish. I think he may have information about Keith's murder."

He nodded slowly as if she'd confirmed something he'd known all along.

"Idle hands." Hamish spoke the words in a sepulchral tone.

She waited for more, but the sergeant had switched on his computer, sat on his favoured perch at the front desk, his fingers laboriously typing his password one slow finger after the other.

"I've a name and address, sir." Frankie returned to find Corstophine still staring at the crazy board like a man in a trance.

"Good work!" He appeared genuinely surprised at the speed with which she'd tracked weasel-face down. "Then I suggest we pay him a visit."

Corstophine checked his mobile, pulling out a phone number from his messages. He offered an increasingly rare smile to Frankie.

"I have the mobile number that called 999 last night." He waved his phone towards her. "I'll ring him when we have him in front of us. It should shorten the interview process."

CHAPTER 30
Bothy Nights

Sandy's breathing was becoming more ragged and the wet bubbling had returned from somewhere deep within his lungs. Robb needed to look at the wound, but both torches were outside and what if the hunter was still out there? It had been almost an hour without further incident – enough time, Robb reckoned, for their assailant to have either finished them off or to have left them alone to die. He decided to risk opening the door, quietly moving the stacked logs away and operating the catch slowly to avoid giving any hint that there was anyone left alive in the bothy. His eyes had grown accustomed to the feeble silver light thrown down by the stars, sufficient to make out the trees standing stark against the Milky Way. Over by the burn a dim but steady light shone into the bracken. It must be his torch – the one Sandy had taken to fetch water. Robb watched it carefully, sensitive to the slightest movement that would betray somebody was holding it, before calculating it was safe enough to fetch it. He crossed the short distance to the burn, doubled up and feeling terribly exposed. If the hunter had him in his crosshairs, then he was as good as dead.

The relief Robb felt once he'd retrieved the torch safely was short-lived. Now he was even more of an obvious target, his light an advertisement to anyone looking to shoot him. He put the fear aside, making towards the woods where Bryan had been headed before the shots had rung out. The torch beam made little impact, weakened light from the fading battery catching a ground fog rising like curling wraiths from the cold earth. Robb swung the light from one side to the other, searching in vain for any sign of Bryan. He risked calling his name, a stage whisper that would only carry a short distance. Every few paces, he stopped and listened for any answer to his call. The only responses were the natural utterances of the woods: invisible rustlings, the faraway crack as something heavy trod on dry sticks, an owl's mournful call.

The chill running down Robb's back wasn't entirely due to the cold night air. He felt as if a target was painted on his back, expected his body to be slammed by the impact of a bullet at any moment. His mobile lay heavy in a trouser pocket – useless out here in the shadow of the mountains, far from any signal. He swept the torch beam over the ground at his feet, hoping to see a recent footprint or sign that someone had been this way. Yellowing pine needles carpeted the ground, keeping their own counsel. *He only had to collect some kindling at the edge of the wood. Why would he have gone any further in?* The thought came into his mind as a surge of anger hit him; anger at not finding Bryan; anger at whoever had attacked them. Robb welcomed the anger – it replaced the debilitating fear of some nameless, red-eyed entity hunting him in the wild.

The forest had taken on a malevolent air as the trees thickened, tendrils of mist reaching out to trap him in serpentine coils. He felt he was being watched by something dangerous and evil. The beam reflected off something as he swung the torch around, a glint of metal in the dying bracken. Bryan's torch. Robb pocketed it before straightening up to see further. There! A booted foot, almost lost in the undergrowth. With a sense of growing foreboding, Robb walked slowly forwards, the torch beam picking out Bryan's crumpled corpse. There was no chance that he had survived. He lay face down in the bracken, an enlarged exit wound visible in the tattered material forming red curtains around the dark hole in his lower back. It was a miracle he had lived long enough to cry for help. Robb stared at the red mess of his back, saw the outstretched arm reaching towards the bothy for help that never came. Not that any amount of help would have been able to repair the slaughtered meat that had been a living human just hours previously. He could feel bile rising in his throat and turned away, holding a palm against his mouth to prevent bile from desecrating the body.

There was nothing he could do here, but he could still help Sandy. Robb ran quickly back to the bothy and now that he had some light, was able to inspect Sandy's wound; setting one torch on the floor close to his prostrate body and using the other to search in his backpack. The knife still lay on the flagstones where it had been dropped, and Robb used the blade to cut away Sandy's jacket – trying not to waken him from the semi-conscious state he'd drifted into since being left alone. Sandy stirred back into consciousness as his jacket and top were being prised away from the wound, reluctantly releasing their grip on the blood that had formed a hard, dark crust on his skin.

"It's OK, take it easy." Robb reached out for his backpack, retrieving a green first aid box and selecting a sterile gauze bandage. "This may hurt."

Sandy cried out in pain as Robb gently washed the worst of the blood away, revealing the entry wound in the top of his shoulder.

"I'm going to have to turn you over, Sandy, see how bad it is." As gently as he could, Robb rolled Sandy onto his good side, cutting the rest of his clothing away from the larger hole torn in his back.

A weak scream accompanied the move, then cursing as cold water stung the wound causing Sandy to try and move away from the all-enveloping raw pain.

A firm hand forced him back down. "Just a minute, Sandy. Hold still and I'll get a bandage on you, we need to stop the bleeding." His patient resorted to panting wildly as Robb taped a sterile dressing over the wound. Blood still pulsed weakly from under the dressing as Robb pressed down again in an attempt to staunch the flow.

"It doesn't seem to have done too much damage." Robb spoke encouragingly, as much for his own benefit as for Sandy. "I think the bullet passed straight through without breaking up." He realised Sandy's arm was at a strange angle and tried adjusting it, only for Sandy to scream in pain.

"Sorry. I think it's broken"

"I need water." Sandy's voice was weak, coming as more of a croak but Robb was relieved to hear him speaking and poured the last of his water into a mug, holding it to Sandy's lips as he sipped. He took the opportunity to look at his patient. Beads of sweat covered his skin, bits of dead bracken were woven into his hair. The flow of blood had stopped – giving Robb hope for the first time that Sandy might not die in this isolated place.

"I have to find the other water bottle, Sandy. I'll just be a minute." He turned to leave the bothy again, only to stop in the doorway as Sandy called out.

"Is Bryan alright?"

Robb shook his head, catching Sandy's eyes so he understood.

"I'll fill up the bottles, then I have to go and find help as soon as it's light enough to see where I'm going."

"What about whoever's hunting us?"

Robb left the question hanging. He didn't have an answer that would encourage either of them. What he did know was that he was the intended target, and Bryan, wearing an identical jacket may have just saved his life. He returned to the burn, the water bottle giving away its location as it circled a small pool downstream, knocking against the larger rocks damming the flow of water. He filled it, replaying the conversations he'd had with Bryan like a disjointed film reel. It didn't seem possible that he was dead, even though the image of his bloodied corpse, lying crumpled into the ground, repeatedly flashed in front of his eyes. Was he dead simply because he wore the same jacket? He'd not even wanted that colour – he had called it mustard instead of sunrise yellow. Robb screwed the water bottle lid down, eyes darting nervously around like prey. Why was he even recalling his anodyne comment about the specific colour of Bryan's jacket when he had an entire lifetime of experiences to remember the man by. Was it because he'd never see another sunrise again? Would any of them? Robb headed back to the bothy, heart beating fast as he shut the door and squatted down next to Sandy, pulling the sleeping bags over his bloodied and semi-naked chest in an attempt to keep him warm.

As the night passed, Robb watched the sky gradually lighten through the bothy windows. They'd not slept a wink, Sandy imagining movement outside the door and insisting Robb replace the log barricade. Every noise, creak or whisper of wind served to startle them back to full awareness whenever they did manage to briefly close their eyes against the dry itch of tiredness.

The revelation of Bryan's inopportune relationship with his mother was the least of his worries at the moment. Who wanted him dead? He ran through a list of friends and acquaintances, testing each as one might a hypothesis, searching in vain for any cause that might result in someone wanting to attack him in a lonely mountain bothy. Why was someone trying to wipe out members of the McCoach family, one by one? To get their hands on the distillery? It seemed far-fetched and one of the most likely beneficiaries of that theory was lying dead in the bracken.

Robb concentrated, trying to ignore the possibility that someone might still be waiting for an opportunity to kill him. If Bryan had wanted control of the business, and shacking up with his mother was part of that plan, then removing the other shareholders would certainly be in his interest. Maybe Bryan had poisoned his father? The policewoman's bizarre allegation began to seem more real, especially as his father would have been a major obstacle to Bryan's getting it together with his mother, Also, the shares all reverted to her if other family members died. It was too improbable. But then, what if an attacker was looking for someone wearing the same colour jacket? Bryan had been wearing an identical jacket and it was dark, easy to pick the wrong person. He dismissed the thought to dwell on more urgent concerns. The hunter's shouted threat had made him realise his sister and mother were also at risk, and here he was, trapped in a bothy, hours away from being able to protect either of them.

Once the sky had lightened sufficiently to discern mountain from sky, Robb climbed out of his sleeping bag, took the few steps towards the window and cautiously looked out at the world. He could see the beginning of the forest, looming black, some distance from the bothy, but no evidence of anything moving in their immediate vicinity.

"Can you see anything?" Sandy's voice scarcely managed to escape his throat, curled up on the floor and almost hidden under the sleeping bags as if that offered a refuge against the unknown.

"No, I can't see anyone out there."

Sandy groaned in pain as he attempted to sit up.

"Take it easy, Sandy, try and rest." Robb attempted to speak reassuringly as he searched in his first aid kit. "Here. I've got some paracetamol. It may not do much, but it should take the edge off the pain."

He held two tablets to Sandy's mouth, tilting his head forward so he could sip from a mug of water.

"Thanks." His voice sounded weaker than Robb would have liked. Fresh blood stained the dressing. He had no choice but to leave him, miles from any mobile signal and with a potential madman prowling around.

"I'll fetch you some of the stew. You'll have to eat it cold, the gas ran out."

Sandy managed to eat a few mouthfuls of the cold stew. Robb crouched down on the floor beside him, feeding spoonfuls into his mouth whilst his worried eyes returned repeatedly to the windows, imagination running riot as to who or what might be looking in.

Robb felt the walls pressing in on him. He felt as trapped as a caged animal, with some complete homicidal maniac out there wanting him dead. What was going on? First his mother more or less accusing him of poisoning his own father, then Aunt Pat being mutilated in her own bed. The chilling thought returned to him. Perhaps it was the same person. There was no doubt now, someone really was out to get the whole family. He desperately tried to remember the policewoman's words when she had spoken to his mother, something Aunt Pat had said. He shook his head in denial. It made no sense. What had any of them ever done to make someone kill them? Robb had no answer.

"I'm going to get you some help." Robb patted Sandy's good hand, placing a full water bottle beside him. "I'll be as quick as I can, I promise." Pocketing Sandy's car keys, Robb slipped off into the early dawn, gently pulling the bothy door closed behind him.

Outside the bothy the land stirred into life as the sky lightened imperceptibly. A few deer raised cautious heads as Robb's figure disappeared into the woods, then returned to grazing the last of the season's fresh grass. Like a dying breath, the land released the last of the night's cold air, mist held captive close to the ground. Written against the charcoal sky, the first curlews sketched a path, calling their burbling song to the wilderness.

Sandy heard their wild call and realised how alone he truly was.

CHAPTER 31
One Ring to Find Them

Corstophine found himself parked outside the same house as the previous night, blue and white police tape now daring anyone to pass the gate, or the gap where a gate once stood. Frankie sat beside him, reading the house numbers before identifying Stephen Currie's house and pointing it out to the DI.

"OK, Frankie. I don't think he's likely to make a run for it, but you knock on the front door and I'll stay hidden at the side of the house, just in case I have to head to the back."

They left the patrol car, Corstophine positioning himself where he could reach either door in a hurry and nodded for Frankie to knock.

A dishevelled lump of a man eventually answered the door, dressing gown held around his pot-bellied waist and a face that expressed surprise that anyone was out of bed this early on a Saturday morning.

"What is it?" he asked in a belligerent voice before catching sight of the patrol car. "How can I help you?" This time he attempted more civility, only spoiled by yawning widely in Frankie's face.

"I'd like a word with your son, Stephen. Is he at home?"

The lump appeared startled for a second, swivelling to look up the stairs behind him.

"Aye, he's still in his bed. What's he done?" Eyes blinked at her, clearing blurred vision and hoping that DC

McKenzie was a mirage. He looked disappointed when she remained there on his doorstep.

"Nothing that we know of," Frankie replied honestly. "We're hoping he may be able to offer some insight about your neighbour."

She tilted her head in the vague direction of Keith Tunstall's house.

"Ah." If Frank Currie was attempting an intelligent response, he was failing. His eyes searched around his own head in search of inspiration and finding none, spoke in the manner of one resigned to dealing with whatever life threw his way. "I'll get him for you."

He turned his back on her, white flesh from his thighs catching her unwelcome notice as the dressing gown billowed out. "Stevie! It's the polis wanting a word with you, get your lazy arse downstairs!"

The lump shambled down the hallway, turning into the kitchen where she could hear the sound of a tap filling a kettle. Vague groans and muffled thumps emanated from up the staircase until the rodent-like features of his son peered suspiciously from around a corner.

"Morning, Stephen. I wondered if you'd be able to help us with our enquiries about your neighbour, Keith Tunstall. I believe you two knew each other?"

Stephen's eyes followed a similar circuitous exploration in search of a way out of the dilemma he was faced with, and much like his father, he failed.

"Alright. Let me put some clothes on." His head slipped back around the corner of the landing from where he'd been observing her, and Frankie breathed a sigh of relief that she hadn't been exposed to the full Monty.

They waited patiently, Frankie at the door, Corstophine at the side alley until reluctant footsteps announced Stephen's descent down the stairs.

234

Corstophine rejoined Frankie and they regarded the character leaning on the door frame in front of them. Stephen Currie gave every impression of having been trolleyed the previous night. His sunken bloodshot eyes peered out from under a greasy matt of hair. Something that looked suspiciously like dried vomit still stuck to his receding chin. They could smell his breath from where they stood, and both took a step backwards in search of a more fragrant source of oxygen.

"Morning, Stephen. I'm DI Corstophine and this is DC McKenzie. I was hoping you may be able to help us with our investigations into your neighbour, Keith Tunstall?"

Stephen stared at Corstophine, his mouth hanging open in surprise at how he'd managed to appear next to Frankie. He switched from one to the other to confirm there were now two of them.

"I didn't really know him, to be honest."

He looked at them hopefully, face expressing anything but honesty, holding onto the doorframe in an effort to stop himself from swaying.

Corstophine smiled at him, eliciting a toothless grin back as if Stephen had just discovered a new pal.

"So, you didn't know he'd been attacked in his house?"

Stephen attempted to shake his head, the movement more like someone had loosened his neck sufficiently for his head to fall off. His weasel face pinched in concentration as he attempted to focus back on his new friend.

"Nah, first I knew of it was when you lot turned up."

"Were you here all last night then, Stephen?" Frankie joined the questioning. She and Corstophine were experienced hunters in bringing down prey much more dangerous than this drugged-up creature.

Weasel's eyes performed their random walk.

"Nah, I was down the pub most of the night." He brightened, the rose-tinted memory of a night well spent foremost in his thoughts.

"So, it couldn't have been you who called the emergency services around ten p.m. last night?" Corstophine's disarming smile remained fixed in place.

Weasel had more success shaking his head this time.

"No, mate. Like I said, I was down the pub." He smiled in satisfaction.

"Thanks for your help, Stephen." Corstophine made as if he was leaving, turning back to see Weasel's surprised face at having rid himself of two troublesome coppers so easily. "One last thing, have you got a phone number so we can contact you again, just in case we need to get in touch?"

His spare hand, the one not glued to the door jamb, made jerky progress to his jeans pocket. A look of intense concentration crossed his narrow features as he dug around, before the idiot grin returned as he produced a mobile with a flourish.

Corstophine hit the dial button on his phone and watched with satisfaction as Stephen's phone started ringing in his clenched hand, the strains of *Scotland the Brave* becoming louder as his hand unclenched. He attempted to focus on the screen before holding it close to his ear.

"Just a minute," he advised before lowering his mobile so he could hit the answer button.

"Who is it?"

Corstophine almost felt sorry for him as he watched Stephen's puzzled features listening to an electronically delayed response.

"This is the police, Stephen. I think you're going to have to accompany us to the station."

It took a few tortured seconds for Weasel to understand

it was Corstophine on the phone to him, his attention switching back and forth between phone and detective before realisation dawned.

Once they'd dealt with the procedural small talk of him not being under arrest and how he was accompanying them of his own free will, they left his father standing in the doorway with a mug of tea in his hand, watching as they took his son away. Frankie had the strong impression that he was glad to be rid of him for a while. She opened her window, forcing the sour tang of their passenger back towards the rear of the patrol car.

In the interview room, Weasel looked decidedly ill at ease. There was a cold sweat beading his forehead, visible under the lank clots of greasy hair that formed a fringe. He'd asked for a cigarette several times already and the lack of any instant fix was getting to him.

Frankie ran through the preamble once the recorder was running, Weasel confirming his name and address in increasingly sulky tones.

"So, Stephen. How come it's your mobile that made the 999 call last night, advising the emergency services that Keith Tunstall was dead and tied to his kitchen floor, with a funnel of drugs in his throat?"

"Dunno. Maybe someone stole ma phone when I was in the pub."

"Then returned it to you?" Frankie quizzed.

It was almost comical watching Weasel try to construct a narrative that would fit the facts.

"Aye, that's right. They must have put it back in ma pocket after dialling 999."

Corstophine couldn't even find the enthusiasm to raise an eyebrow. "So, if we check the call triangulation it will confirm you were at the pub?"

Weasel puzzled over what a call triangulation might be,

but accepted the call would have been from the vicinity of the pub.

"That's where I was." He sat back in this seat, pleased to have fooled the two detectives so far.

Corstophine made a note to check the mobile location, writing carefully on his notepad so Weasel would wonder what notes he was taking.

"And any fingerprints we find in Keith's kitchen, say from the bread bin, wouldn't match yours?"

The smug expression was wiped off his face in an instant.

"I haven't been anywhere near his bread bin. Told you, I don't know the guy. Say hello if we meet in the street but I've never been in his house. Never!"

Corstophine nodded. "Are those the shoes you wore to the pub, Stephen? They look like fairly expensive trainers."

Weasel frowned at the sudden conversational shift, looking for the trap. "Aye, well. I've been treating myself since I've been working so hard." He stretched a leg out so Corstophine could admire his footwear. "Burberry."

Corstophine stared at the proffered shoe. Even Frankie craned her neck to view the article. It looked ridiculous on him as far as she was concerned, a huge thick sole that must have added an inch to his height, some tartan pattern on top with Burberry printed across it just in case the branding wasn't obvious enough.

"Very nice." Corstophine offered by way of a comment.

Weasel relaxed into a self-satisfied smile again. "Aye, well, I earned it, didn't I?"

"How did you earn it, Stephen? From what I understand, you're claiming the dole." Frankie played the bad cop with practiced ease.

His irritation at having his good mood regularly punctured shone through. "None of your business, hen."

Corstophine summed up. "So, Stephen, to wrap all this up. You've never been in Keith Tunstall's house, hardly know him, in fact. And it wasn't you who called 999 from your phone?"

"That's what I said, isn't it?"

Corstophine nodded slowly, making another comment on his pad. "In that case I'd like to ask you to stay with us for an hour or so until we get the fingerprints back from forensics. Is that OK?"

Weasel looked panicked, his eyes performing what must be a regular nervous dance around his head.

"You can't keep me here. I know my rights. You can't keep me here unless you arrest me."

Weasel faced them with more defiance than he felt, noticing that Corstophine's smile had taken on more of a sinister appearance.

"You're right of course. So, Stephen, you can either stay here at your great inconvenience for an hour or so until we've corroborated your story, or I'll charge you as an accessory to Keith Tunstall's murder. Which will it be?"

CHAPTER 32
Seven Is a Prime Number

Phoebe woke to another day. She had slept through the night without any troubling dreams, any dreams at all which was in itself an unusual occurrence. For a long while she lay in bed, arms held tightly to her sides whilst staring at the blank, white ceiling. It was, she thought, like looking into a void where visions formed of their own volition. Random marks, scuffs, imperfections in the decorator's brushwork rearranged their outlines to create incredible visions. Mostly these were faces. Once she'd found a serpent writhing towards the central ceiling rose, mouth gaping in readiness to swallow the light whole and set the darkness free. She had favourites: the dwarf's face with the lascivious leer; the thin man on a bicycle who always frightened her for reasons she could never understand.

Now her mind was free of the drugs, she found it harder to create a menagerie of fantastical creatures. She used to find the process of creation effortless, whole worlds had sprung into being across the tabula rasa of her ceiling as she stared entranced. Stories and narratives played out in the theatre of her mind. At least she shared a set of tenets, as did the God she had been taught about as a child, a list as meaningful as the ones she remembered were once written in stone.

Open the doors of creation
Breaketh out the popcorn

Obey the Prime Directive and Do Not Get Involved
Shit happens, Get Used to It
Who gives a Flying Fuck Anyway?
Me Me Me Me Me
Hey! We're all going to die so, really, what the Fuck?

Seven made a much more suitable number than ten, so she had always stopped there, Phoebe's Seven Commandments (with some help from Sinister and Righteous). Seven is a prime number; seven pieces of heaven in Fry's Chocolate Cream; dance of the seven veils; seven deadly sins; the world created in seven days.

The ceiling remained uninspiring this morning, so much so that Phoebe was tempted to take the row of pills concealed under her pillow, if only to kickstart her imagination again. She resisted the impulse. Climbing out of bed, she carried the row of multicoloured pills over to the hole in the floor and fed them, one by one, into the nothing space. The nothing space must be totally out of its head by now!

She quietly laughed, a gentle sound that wouldn't wake night nurse. She didn't like this night nurse, not at all. This night nurse never let her watch the TV that was her only source of information. The world could only be improved if night nurse no longer existed in it. She crossed over to the window where the garden waited patiently for the sun to rise high enough to burn off the dew that shone on the lawn like discarded jewels. Cobwebs draped across the corners of her window that never opened; deadly drapes and swags designed by a master murderer with a penchant for taking interior design outside. When a fly landed in a web, she would watch it in fascination, observe as it struggled to escape. They both knew the score, she and the fly. This was silent music, but music, nevertheless. Bass notes from the radial attracting the spider's interest, then the higher pitch melody from the spiral exciting the builder to action. Size, position, strength, all contained within the musical score until the inescapable crescendo.

Phoebe was a fly. Phoebe was caught in a web. Phoebe knew it was time to change the tune. From now on, she was going to play the spider at its own game.

Downstairs the hall clock struck seven. Seven deep gongs. There it was again, seven, the universal constant. She climbed back into bed and waited with eyes closed. On the landing, a door opened, and a light tread betrayed someone walking to the bathroom. Night nurse. She'd be peeing, brushing, slapping on makeup for no-one to see. Hiding the spots, painting her eyes, painting over her smell. Then back to her adjacent bedroom, pulling on the starched uniform, checking her watch.

Phoebe heard the key turn in her bedroom door, heard night nurse standing over her.

"Good morning, Phoebe. How are we today?"

How many people did she think Phoebe was? Not how are *you* today, always how are *we*. How many people was she today? It was a good question. She listened intently, inside ears for inside voices. All gone. All quiet. She opened her eyes, slowly. Remember the music. She didn't want anyone to realise the tune had changed – especially night nurse.

"There we are. We are a sleepyhead this morning." She was holding two plastic cups as she always did. She or others like her. They were mostly interchangeable. Night nurse morphed into day nurse, into someone completely different yet exactly the same. One cup for the tablets, one cup for the water. She allowed night nurse to raise her head off the pillow and reached out for the cup of pills.

Quick tilt into mouth, pretend swallow. Oh, that was a good gulp. Her throat noisily constricted and swallowed air as the pills slipped under her tongue.

"Good girl. Now, here's your water to wash it down."

Phoebe gave her a grateful glance, sipped at the water. This was the difficult bit, this was where the skill lay, avoiding washing any pills from under her tongue. She opened her mouth wide like a fledgling and was met with the juicy worm of approval.

"There. Now let's get you to the bathroom and dressed for the day. Can you manage to get out of bed without my help this morning?"

Oh, no. Phoebe needed help every morning. The drugs stopped her muscles behaving, as they all went on strike. Sapping her strength, keeping her weak.

She allowed herself to be half-lifted out of bed, held onto night nurse until they reached the toilet where she was closely watched as she lowered herself down onto the seat with the aid of the toilet frame. Night nurse shut the door and Phoebe peed noisily. An explosive fart added to the ensemble of noises. Phoebe tried not to laugh at the thought of night nurse screwing up her face in disgust. She dried herself on the toilet paper, flushed the toilet. Night nurse hurried in to check that no tablets bobbed around in the disappearing vortex, then, satisfied all was well, helped by putting toothpaste on her brush.

Phoebe played the part of a young woman under a chemical cosh with skill worthy of an Oscar, but then she had been training for years.

When the changing of the guard occurred, Phoebe was sitting in her chair as was the custom. Day nurse unlocked the door, looked in, shut the door and went to sit in the nurse's room where she'd surf social media all day. Phoebe could sometimes hear snatches of tunes, dialogue. Sometimes the day nurse would laugh out loud. Sometimes, like today, day nurse didn't lock the door. Silly day nurse!

Downstairs, she could hear the cleaner as she let herself in. The cleaner was a trustee, she had the code to the key safe. The washing machine sprang into life in the room underneath, sloshing and groaning like some mechanical monster finishing a meal. Soon the hoover would start up, working its inevitable progress around the house, up the stairs, through the bedrooms. It took all morning. In a while her mother would surface, shower, spend hours in front of her mirror. She'd never look in on Phoebe. She didn't want Phoebe to exist.

It was mutual, so Phoebe held no grudge, no hard feelings. Her father though, that was a different matter entirely. Her father had loved her. That love was strong enough to force through the chemical clouds and sustain enough of her to keep her from going as mad as they thought she was. She missed him. Her brother had told her that he'd died, that he'd never return. Her brother had cried in front of her, huge sobs that he tried to muffle under his arm. That had made her sad, not her father's death, after all *Shit Happens*. No, it was her brother not realising she was there in front of him that hurt. He saw only the slack-jawed body, the dull eyes. Even he couldn't see how desperate she was to escape.

Never mind. Sinister had talked to her, told her what she had to do. Since she'd stopped taking the tablets Sinister had rejoiced, crowing with pleasure that he'd finally silenced Righteous for good. No more wishy-washy, goody-goody-two-shoes telling them what they couldn't do. But just when Sinister had reached his ascendant, she'd taken back control. Sinister had accepted that, at first; he thought that together they could accomplish great things.

Night nurse falling down the stairs. Mother burning to death in her bed. Running away together into the jewel encrusted world outside the window.

She'd almost felt sorry for Sinister as he started to fade, almost felt sorry as his voice grew increasingly desperate, then furious, then pleading. Almost.

For the first time, Phoebe only heard Phoebe in her mind. Phoebe had plans to make, she had things that needed to be understood. Phoebe sat in her chair, muscles tensing, pushing, relaxing, whilst in her mind she began to unravel the tapestry of her life. Each thread carefully unwoven and analysed, unpicked for study.

Things were not looking good. She had been treated as if she were mad, locked up, drugged as a child.

Those doctors in white coats – guilty.

Her parents – guilty.

That fat, ugly girl – guilty.

It was time to pay the piper, time to change the tune.

In the corner of the web the spider waited patiently, eight eyes on watch, eight legs feeling for the music. In the web, the fly landed as soft as a thought, avoiding any glue that served to trap its wings.

Eight against seven. Not really a fair contest, not really a fair contest at all!

Seven is a prime number.

CHAPTER 33
Odyssey

Robb didn't dare take a torch in case the lunatic who had shot them was still out there and saw the light. He hunkered low, following the track across the exposed open ground until reaching the relative cover of the trees. Water bubbled in the nearby burn, covering the skitter of stones following each clumsy footfall. Now he stepped more cautiously, his senses straining to detect anyone lying in wait. The sky had lightened imperceptibly, hinting of a dawn yet to come. It was too early for birds to commence their song, yet overhead a pair of curlews made an early start towards the west, their shimmering call sharp in the rarefied air. Crouched down at the entrance to the forest and away from the safety of the bothy, Robb was having second thoughts.

The world was depicted in dark grey monotone this early in the morning, an hour before the sun's elongated reach could bring first red light to the day's palette. Robb spared a backwards glance for the bothy he'd just vacated, attempting to make out the building's geometric outline. Once inside the forest he knew he'd struggle to keep to the path – he could only just make out the outline of the gate which was literally within touching distance. It would be madness to try and walk that path in pitch darkness. An ancestral reminder of the dangers inherent in a dark forest set his skin crawling, yet he had to reach a point nearer the road where his phone could find a signal. Sandy needed medical help, and he needed to warn his family that someone was out to kill them.

Searching the ground under the nearest trees, he felt rather than saw a fallen branch, small enough to carry yet strong enough to offer some protection in case he was attacked. Thus armed, Robb unlatched the gate as quietly as he could and set off down the forest track. The dark was oppressive once out of reach of the open sky, pressing in on him with an almost physical force. Eyes straining to the limit of their ability, Robb made cautious progress, his arms extended in front of him like a blind man, feet feeling the ground at each step. He was alert to every movement, every sound. The impact of his own feet on the track underneath sounded deafening in the silence.

Mountains caught the first hint of sunrise, peaks gradually revealing themselves as rose-tinted against a sky turned more grey than black. The meagre improvement in visibility encouraged Robb to faster movement, able at last to discern track from trees. He'd only managed thirty minutes slow progress before his foot landed awkwardly on a stone, not large enough to see but sufficient to twist his foot over onto its side. The sharp tug of a ligament tearing sent a searing pain along his nerves, bringing an involuntary curse to his lips. He lifted his foot in response, standing on one leg whilst testing how much damage he'd done. It didn't appear too bad, the ankle rotated without much pain. Robb set it gently back down on the ground, careful to avoid the errant stone that had twisted his ankle. The pain immediately shot back up his leg as he shifted his balance onto the damaged ankle, causing him to put all his weight back on his one good foot.

"Fucking hell!" He cursed almost silently, the exclamation more a release of frustration and fear than anything else. Robb knew he'd not be able to move easily, even with the light gradually improving. A two-hour walk would most likely take at least twice that time, and if he twisted his other foot... The stick he carried wasn't long enough to use as a crutch, he'd need to find something else to help support his weight. He suddenly regretted leaving his torch with Sandy, at least he could have used it to search each side of the track.

The forest stirred into gradual life around him as he paused. Leaves betrayed a passing dawn breeze, the rustling running through the trees without a care for the earthbound. In the distance a stag bellowed a warning, the low notes travelling unimpeded through an inversion layer until Robb could have sworn the animal was almost on top of him. He had to find a stick capable of supporting his weight or he wouldn't be able to move at all. Retrieving his phone from his jacket, he checked how much charge was left. The screen glowed with a ghostly blue luminescence and he made covert use of it to search into the forest. There was no knowing if the attacker was looking for him even now, and a brighter light would be visible for miles.

Moving off the path presented its own problems. Sharp branches conspired to impale him whilst the ground held more traps than the path, sudden dips and random roots trying to pitch him over. When he eventually found a suitable branch, he gently lowered himself beside it, breaking off unwanted side shoots and hoping there wasn't anyone around to hear the sharp reports. Eventually he had something that would suffice and tested his weight on it as he levered himself back into a standing position. The stick bent slightly, and the end of it sank some distance into the soft, moss-covered ground, but it held.

Now it was just a case of working his way the few steps

back to the rutted track, then the rough miles until he reached Sandy's car and a mobile signal. Could things get any worse? Robb left the question hanging.

Progress was painfully slow, literally. The track had been used quite recently by heavy vehicles, most likely Land Rovers carrying well-heeled hunters closer to where the herds of deer could be found. The gamekeepers preferred to pick out the weaker animals, the old or infirm or those stags that were never going to amount to much. They steered their clients away from the majestic animals, the twelve-pointed Royal stag or the sixteen-point Monarch, unless the hunter paid. Everything had its price.

Robb had been on a shoot. Once. He had been taken by his father, as a young man, to hills much the same as these. That had also been early in the morning: crossing the heather-clad mountain flanks, keeping upwind of the herd, remaining below their line of sight. They had fallen prostrate on the ground following an urgent sign from the gamekeeper, until they lay almost buried in the fragrant heather. His father had reverentially handed him the high-powered rifle as if it were a religious artefact, watched him intently as he lined up the chosen animal through the crosshairs. He remembered the oily smell of the metal, the smooth feel of the wooden stock, the hard kick on his shoulder as the bullet left the muzzle. The gamekeeper had watched silently through his binoculars, praying for a clean shot but fully expecting to have to apply the coup de grâce after tracking some poor crippled animal's blood trail for miles. Instead, the stag had folded in on itself, neck throwing antlered head towards the sky.

They had congratulated him, told him he was a natural, a marksman. Instead of pride, Robb had felt sick. The herd scattered seconds later, time for the sound of the shot to reach them. Those nearer the kill ran first, alerted by the dull impact of bullet on flesh and bone. He'd approached the animal with a feeling of self-loathing, revulsion at his own actions in ending a life. The only uplifting moment had come when he realised that it was a clean kill, the large, dark eyes already dull with death. At least he wouldn't be asked to finish the poor beast off. He'd stood impassively as the gamekeeper dipped fingers in the wound, dragged blood across his cheeks. Now he was marked. It was a rite of passage, the taking of an innocent life.

As Robb staggered from one deep tyre rut to the next, he hoped to hell he wasn't just waiting to be finished off. Above him the sky was beginning to lighten and through gaps in the tree canopy he caught sight of hundreds of geese, each following the other until the skein formed lines of wavering Vs. Their call encouraged him to keep going, to keep moving. Now that the path was becoming more visible, he was able to take faster strides; good foot and stick then hop forwards, carrying his damaged ankle like some cumbersome attachment. Every time his injured foot touched the ground it sent pain shooting up his leg. There wasn't any possibility of putting any weight on that foot and now the hand holding the stick was beginning to blister.

With the slow advance of dawn, so the forest stirred into life. His eyes flicked towards every sound. Every shadow held the outline of a man waiting to end his life. Robb knew his attacker could be lying in wait, a telescopic sight tracking him as he walked or waiting for him to cross the next clearing up ahead. The first he'd know about it would be his head exploding, or his chest opening up as the bullet exited. Spinning him around with the force of the blow until his neck craned for one last look at the sky before death brought a permanent night.

Robb stopped, took deep breaths and persuaded his

imagination to stop this free-running horror show in his mind. The reality of his situation was bad enough without looking for even worse outcomes. He wrapped his handkerchief around his blistered hand, gripped hold of the makeshift crutch and studied the track ahead. Now that it was slowly getting lighter, he could see where the ground was rutted, could see where his best path forward lay. The burn was close now, running nearer the track and changing tone as it tumbled down small waterfalls. Was it only yesterday he'd hiked up this trail so easily?

He had to keep moving, ignore the protestations of pain from his body and walk as best he could. The car was only a few miles away. He just had to reach it and then he'd either have a phone signal or could drive until he reached help. Robb tried not to think what might be happening at the bothy, tried not to imagine what might be happening at home. Just walk, one step at a time.

CHAPTER 34
One Call

The preliminary forensics report arrived soon after Hamish had taken Weasel to his cell. Corstophine read the email, printing off the pages until he had a small pile of A4 awaiting collection at the printer. Top of the list was the drug dealer's death, and he didn't need to read the fingerprint analysis to see those were Weasel's prints all over the back door handle as well as the breadbin. The footprint was almost certainly Weasel's as well. He'd asked Hamish to make sure Stephen Currie's shoes were removed before placing him into custody – and the aromatic article he held in his outstretched hand matched the print exactly.

The other prints were either Keith Tunstall's or belonged to his murderer. Corstophine frowned as he viewed the unidentified fingerprints. Whoever had decided to execute him at or around 16:00 yesterday hadn't bothered wearing gloves. If this was a hit organised by Tunstall's Glasgow overlords then it had been an amateurish job, with no regard for the forensic arts. Any hitman or woman knew enough not to take those sorts of risks if they wished to avoid an early end to their career. Either that or whoever it was just didn't care. It was the 'didn't care' option that troubled him.

The cause of death came as no surprise. Keith Tunstall had more drugs in his system than the average Russian dissident. The only question the pathologist had been unable to conclusively answer was whether Keith died from a drugs overdose or from choking to death. Either way, whoever had upended the narcotics and rough cider into the funnel and down his throat was guilty of murder. A paragraph on the contusion Keith suffered to the side of his head caught Corstophine's attention. Blunt force trauma, single heavy blow from behind – hard enough to have knocked him unconscious.

The resemblance to Patricia's attack was too much of a coincidence. Corstophine didn't believe in coincidences, very few good detectives did. He scanned through the printouts before finding the initial report into Patricia's SOC. There were so many fingerprints found at her house that forensics had arranged them in serried rows across two pages. A few had already been marked as belonging to Patricia, her comatose body providing the prints, or to the traumatised cleaner. Robb McCoach's prints had been found in a few locations, including her bedroom; but Corstophine needed the prints left on the cosh he'd seen casually left on her body – thrown down like a declaration of war.

Corstophine nodded to himself as he carefully compared the prints. Whoever had hit Patricia with enough force to cause a brain haemorrhage was the same suspect who'd finished Keith Tunstall. He had no doubt that the fibre particles and DNA samples still undergoing tests would confirm that they were dealing with the same assailant. The only problem with this discovery was trying to work out what possible connection there could be between the two cases.

Picking up the relevant pages, he entered the main office and placed the sheets in front of Frankie.

"See any matching prints?"

Frankie switched her attention away from the computer

and picked out the similarities from the tables of fingerprints in seconds.

"These ones here, and here. They look like matches to me, sir. Whose are they?" Frankie asked, wondering why her boss was looking more concerned than satisfied to have made progress.

"That's just it, Frankie. Whoever it is, he hasn't triggered a match on the database, so we're dealing with an unknown. More than that, these are the prints found on the cosh left on Patricia's body and the ones that forensics took from Keith Tunstall's funnel."

"You're joshing me!"

Corstophine's expression told her that he wasn't.

"Whoever this is, Frankie, he's somehow connected to Patricia McCoach and Keith Tunstall. We need to work out what that connection is before he moves onto his next victim."

"You think there's going to be more, sir?"

Corstophine nodded. "Whoever it is, he's not bothered about us finding his prints. That tells me he either doesn't expect to get caught or doesn't care if he is caught." He frowned in concentration, brows drawn so low that Frankie could see the worry lines etched across his face.

"And that would suggest we're dealing with someone who's settling a score," Frankie offered.

"That's my interpretation. Someone who no longer cares about the law, or the consequences of their actions." He looked directly at her. "And that means we have to find out whoever it is fast because we're dealing with someone who doesn't care how this all ends."

"You don't think this has anything to do with someone out to get the McCoach family?" Frankie suggested. "Did forensics manage to find any usable prints on Jack's water bottle?"

Corstophine shook his head. "It had been out in the open too long, Frankie, nothing of any forensic value apart from the contents. It was definitely Jack's bottle, though. Robb only had a few of those plastic bottles made with the distillery logo on them." He glanced towards the crazy board. Keith Tunstall and Weasel both needed to be added, and an unknown assailant tying the whole lot together.

"What was it Patricia knew?" Corstophine voiced the question that had been gnawing at him ever since her attack. Frankie didn't have an answer. He checked his watch. Robb McCoach should be well on his way home by now and he'd had the search warrant approved.

"Let's deal with our character in the cells and see if he can't shed some light on any connection between them."

Weasel sat in the interview room as if he belonged there. Corstophine viewed his assumed swagger with an experienced eye. Some people broke down as soon as they were arrested, spilling information in the hope that their interviewer would be so overcome with gratitude that they would let them walk free. Some attempt to brave their way through the process, when all along they're shitting bricks. Weasel was in the latter category.

"You sure you don't want legal representation, Stephen? It is your right."

"Nah, I'm OK. I haven't done anything, so there's no need. Is there?" Weasel attempted a hard man look, his features adopting a collage from a bunch of B-movie actors that had caught his imagination.

"Suit yourself." Corstophine had no time for games. He placed the prints down on the table like a card shark presenting a winning hand.

"These are your fingerprints, and these are the ones found on Keith Tunstall's back door and also on the empty breadbin. This is a footprint taken from the kitchen floor, and this is a photograph I took of your shoe sole. See any similarities?"

Weasel's mouth opened and closed repeatedly as he looked from one print to the other. Frankie watched him dispassionately as he worked through his options. In many respects, he was a fish out of water, his gaping mouth merely reinforcing the stereotype.

"Then we'll have the DNA analysis to add to this, and whatever we find in your home when the search warrant comes through." Corstophine piled on the misery, building up the pressure without even having to break a sweat. Frankie knew what was coming, she almost felt sorry for the lad. Not sorry enough to stop her from joining in.

"Then you managed to get so drunk in the Old Pretender on Friday night that you told the newspaper reporter you'd found Keith dead on the kitchen floor, hours before the 999 call, which will be traced to the same location." Frankie added the snap she'd taken of Weasel at the bar. A nice touch, she thought. Corstophine caught her eye and almost winked.

"When we pull the banknotes that you spent in the bar, we'll find traces of drugs along with your fingerprints, won't we, Weasel?" Frankie added. "Same as on the money you took from Keith's breadbin that we're going to find in your house."

"Would you like to try telling us the truth now, Stephen, or would you prefer to be charged with the murder of Keith Tunstall?" Corstophine added the final flourish.

They watched as his bravado evaporated in front of them.

"It's not like that! I never killed him!"

Corstophine adopted his avuncular expression, the

kindly face of a man only wanting to help, to sort out a terrible misunderstanding.

"Tell us what really happened, Stephen, in your own time."

Weasel spilled the goods faster than a capsized cargo ship. When they had a detailed timeline of when Keith had been found, and what Weasel had opportunistically appropriated for himself, Frankie just had one question that still demanded an answer.

"One last thing W…Stephen." Frankie corrected herself before using his nickname again, no sense in kicking a man when he's down. "What did Keith say to the girl on the station platform? The one who threw herself under a train."

A puzzled look appeared on his face as he attempted to connect Frankie's question to the investigation into Keith's death. "I dunno," he said at last. "Something like 'you're such an ugly cow, it's lucky you can't see yerself in the mirror'."

He smiled at the memory. It was one of Keith's better jokes. "Somethin' like that anyway." The realisation that those words might have led to the girl taking her life moments later only then seemed to occur to him.

"Nothin' to do with me, hen. I never said anything"

Frankie said nothing. Weasel was already beneath her contempt.

"I'm charging you with obstructing the law; concealing or transferring the proceeds of drug trafficking and the acquisition, possession or use of proceeds of drug trafficking. I recommend you ask for legal representation before we have you back in here, when I expect to add to those charges."

Corstophine called for the desk sergeant. "Take him back to the cells, Hamish. I'll need to talk to him later."

He called after the old sergeant as he left the interview room with Weasel in his care. "He's allowed the one call."

"Sir, one call. Come on, laddie. Your dad's not going to be very pleased when he hears about this now, is he?"

Weasel's expression confirmed Hamish's analysis.

Corstophine shouted after the retreating sergeant, "Give McAdam and Lamb time to search his house before he makes that call."

"Understood, sir."

CHAPTER 35
Gin Making

Corstophine left a note for the two PCs to search Weasel's house. They were due back on shift in half an hour, not enough time for him to apply for a search warrant, so they'd have to ask his father for permission to enter. Failing that, he let them know they'd just have to force an entry and he'd play the securing evidence card. It wasn't ideal, leaving the constables in charge of the search, but he and Frankie both needed to have a proper look around the McCoach house and have another chat with Emma.

When they arrived at the McCoach house, it was Emma who answered the door, welcoming them both in like old friends, except Corstophine noticed her calculating look as she recognised who they were.

"Sorry to bother you, Emma, but I was wondering if we could have a look around Robb's small distillery in the shed? He's not here is he, back from his expedition?"

"No, not yet. He should be here soon." Emma appeared distracted, thrown off balance but quickly recovering her composure. "Why in heaven's name do you want to be looking around Robb's shed?"

Corstophine attempted a reassuring smile. "We're just following a line of enquiry, making sure we haven't overlooked anything."

Emma folded her arms. "I don't know. I have to go out soon, can't it wait until Robb's back home?"

He gave her a reluctant look. "We really need to look now. Do you have a key?"

"This is such an inconvenient time!"

Corstophine ran out of patience. "I have a search warrant, Emma. I'd prefer not to have to use it but if you're not going to help, I have no other choice."

She looked startled then, eyes widening in disbelief. Her arms dropped uselessly to her sides. "A search warrant?" Emma echoed the words in disbelief. Search warrants applied to another class of people. The criminal class.

"What exactly are you investigating, officer? Is this to do with the attack on my poor sister-in-law?"

"We have reason to believe there may be a connection."

"Well, this is most irregular." She turned to face back into the house. "Come this way, the key's in the kitchen."

They followed her inside. The house smelled of polish and cleaning materials, and as if on cue, Corstophine saw a woman busily wiping down the kitchen surfaces as they entered.

"Thank you, Sandra, that will be all for today." Emma spoke to the woman in the effortlessly superior way an employer might deal with a servant. Mock civility barely disguising the inequality involved in the transaction between the privileged and the not so lucky. She handed over an envelope which the woman took, keen eyes appraising Corstophine and Frankie and realising they were the police.

"Thank you, Mrs McCoach. I'll be back on Tuesday."

Emma waited until she'd left the kitchen before opening a drawer in the central island, selecting a key and holding it up for inspection before offering it to Corstophine.

"I was hoping you'd come with us, Emma. We don't want to damage anything by mistake."

She considered for the briefest of moments. "Yes, of course. You're not going to take long?"

"No, we'll just have a quick look and then be off." Corstophine reassured her.

They followed Emma in single file back through the house, Corstophine taking up position beside her as they walked down the drive.

"These really are magnificent grounds. They must keep you busy. My own garden is much more modest but takes hours every week to keep it under control."

Frankie walked behind them, finding Corstophine's claim to be any sort of gardener difficult to comprehend. His front garden consisted of stone chippings in which a few abandoned plant pots waited forlornly to fulfil a purpose.

"Oh no, we have a gardener in to deal with all that." Emma responded as if Corstophine was an ingénu in the workings of large houses and their estates. "It's almost a full-time job." She looked around as if seeing the gardens for the first time. "We don't really make any use of the grounds. If it wasn't for the privacy, I'd sell them off for housing."

They approached the log cabin that Robb had pointed out as his distillery. It looked as if it had been built fairly recently, the ground around it still bearing scars from the builder's efforts. She raised an arm, key held ready in her grasp.

"That's a beautiful pine tree, must be a few hundred years old." Corstophine stopped to admire a tree that was anything but beautiful. The trunk and branches resembled a torture victim, twisting and curling around each other for protection or comfort.

Emma looked at him as one would an idiot. "That's a

yew tree. There was once a graveyard here, three hundred years ago, long before this house was built."

Corstophine nodded wisely, his expression unchanging. Frankie smiled inwardly, her keen eyes searching Emma's face as she spoke.

"Local legend has it that it was planted from seeds taken from the Fortingall Yew – one of the oldest trees in Britain."

"Goodness." Corstophine said inanely, turning to inspect the tree more closely. The turn of the key in the lock announced Emma's opening of the shed door.

The interior was dominated by a miniature version of the huge copper stills he'd seen inside the distillery. This one was almost small enough to put in the back of a car. The place was immaculate, every surface sparkled as Emma switched on the lights. A strong smell of bleach pervaded the air.

Frankie felt disappointment welling up as she surveyed the interior. The place had been cleaned within an inch of its life, next to no chance of forensics finding anything in here.

"He keeps it very clean," she mentioned conversationally.

Corstophine didn't need to catch her eye, they were both thinking along the same tracks.

"Well yes. Anything concerned with foodstuffs and preparation has to kept spotlessly clean," Emma responded. She stood to one side to allow the two detectives room to look around. Corstophine made a direct line towards a cardboard box holding plastic bottles, taking one out to view it more closely. The bottles had been emblazoned with the distillery crest, exactly the same as the one he'd found on the mountaintop.

"Is this the same bottle that Jack would have had in

his backpack?" He held the bottle up towards Emma, eyebrows raised in his familiar interrogative stare.

She appeared flustered. "Probably. I don't know. Robb kept trying different flavours out on him for his bottled water idea. It was never going to catch on, but Jack indulged him. Jack indulged both of them." Emma didn't bother trying to conceal the bitterness inherent in the last few words, spitting them out.

"You don't happen to know which flavour water your husband took with him?" Corstophine asked conversationally. "On his last climb?"

He could see the thought taking hold in her face before she answered.

"You think Robb had something to do with Jack's death?" She spoke in a curious mix of denial and confirmation. Denial of a mother believing that her son could do anything as terrible; confirmation that it was something she'd suspected.

Corstophine was nonplussed. He'd hoped to read Emma as easily as a book but she was giving him mixed signals. He hoped Frankie was picking up more from her than he was.

"Robb's not necessarily a suspect at this time, but I found Jack's water bottle and it contained traces of something that shouldn't be there."

Emma reached behind her to steady herself against the log walls, her face visibly turning pale.

"You mean he was poisoned, like Patricia said?"

"As I say, Emma, we're exploring all possibilities at the moment. It might just have been an accident. Who else has access to this shed?"

"No-one. Only Robb ever comes here to play at being a distiller." She swallowed, mouth working to produce enough moisture for a throat turned suddenly dry. *"Poisoned!"*

Frankie left Corstophine to attend to Emma, standing awkwardly beside her with an arm outstretched as if for comfort. The shed was empty of any produce; no bottled water, gin or hand sanitisers. Frankie searched the floor, hunting for anything that could be evidence. The place was as pristine as a weapons grade biological laboratory.

"Let's get you back to the house." Corstophine spoke soothingly as Emma's tears ran silently down her cheeks. "It's come as a bit of a shock, I'm sorry."

Frankie took the key from Emma's unprotesting hand and locked the shed behind her, following the two of them as they headed back. In an upstairs window, a movement caught her eye. A young woman stared down at her, palms held flat against the glass like someone offering a benediction. She smiled shyly at Frankie, who responded by raising a hand in salute.

"We'll be off, Emma. I'm sorry to be the one bearing this news, I know it's the last thing you needed to hear." Corstophine had stopped by the patrol car. "Can you ask Robb to come to the station as soon as he returns? We'd like to ask him some questions."

"I'll be sure to pass that on, officer." Emma's voice was emotionless.

"You remember when Patricia said there was someone out to get the family?" Corstophine asked before Emma reached the front door. She hesitated, head towards the ground as if in grief. When she raised her eyes, the tears had gone.

"Yes." The single word was spoken in a flat tone.

"Have you had any thoughts as to who Patricia could have been talking about, who might want to harm your family?"

She stared coldly at the two detectives, one foot on the step leading up to the imposing front door.

"No, officer. As I said, Patricia is quite mad, you'd be well advised to ignore anything she says." Emma turned her back on them, shutting the door with more force than was required. An emphatic end to that particular conversation.

When Frankie looked back up at the window, the young woman had gone.

CHAPTER 36
Doctor's Fix

Frankie replayed their visit to Emma McCoach as Corstophine drove the short distance back to the police station. She knew he'd made the link between the yew tree and the poisoning, but forensics would struggle to find any residual evidence in that shed. Had it been deep cleaned with that in mind, or did Robb keep it that way as a matter of course?

The early morning sun had been covered by steel grey skies, stretching all the way to the surrounding mountains. The streets had turned two dimensional as shadows were erased by the diffuse lighting, colours leached from the scene like an old photograph left too long in the sun. Autumn was already well advanced: trees held onto a few stubborn leaves; streets empty of tourists – just the few Lowry-like figures bent away from the unseasonably cold wind heading off Loch Linnhe. The town was preparing for hibernation.

"What did you make of it, Frankie?"

Corstophine brought her out of her reverie with a jolt. "It's difficult to say, sir. I thought she didn't come across totally legit when you said you'd found poison in his water bottle."

"Thought she over-reacted?"

"Yes, sir." Frankie considered for a few seconds. "Emma McCoach strikes me as a fairly unemotional sort, I thought maybe she acted out the distraught wife scene."

"It did feel a bit out of character," Corstophine agreed. "Still, guilty until proved innocent eh, Frankie?"

Frankie smiled grimly at one of their in-jokes. "Aye, sir."

"She's still not wanting to tell us who might have it in for them, though," Corstophine added thoughtfully.

Frankie had picked up on that right enough. Emma knew damn well who had attacked her sister-in-law; who it was might be waiting in the wings to attack her. What or who was she protecting?

They drove into the police station car park. Corstophine made straight for his crazy board to add Weasel as a suspect for Tunstall's murder, Frankie to her desk to fire up the computer. As she waited for the computer's operating system to creak into being, Frankie worried over the throw-away comment Weasel had made concerning the girl's suicide. Something about her not being able to see herself in the mirror. She headed downstairs to the cells.

Weasel was stretched out on the cell bench, hands comfortably behind his head. As Frankie drew nearer, she could hear the unmistakable sound of snoring coming from his slack lips. He looked like a weasel even in sleep: thin body, sharp face. It was a look she'd seen a hundred times before. Take yourself around any of the deprived areas in the country and you will see weasels aplenty. It must be the result of an impoverished diet: malnourished foetuses developing until some genetic failsafe decides this is the most optimum build for the indigent world that awaits. Prioritising survival against everything else. All born equal, aye, right!

She dismissed the thought. The police couldn't fix society, just try and prevent it all falling apart. She rapped on the door and Weasel was startled into wakefulness.

"Wha…?" His incoherence betrayed his confusion as

he struggled to understand where he was. He managed to focus on Frankie, the recognition that he was locked up in a police cell registering after a few seconds confusion.

"What do you want?" Some of his swagger had returned, safe behind bars.

"The girl that committed suicide at the train station..." Frankie began, only to be interrupted by Weasel.

"What about her? Dead, isn't she?"

Frankie held back from anger. "Yes, she's dead. When you said she couldn't see herself in the mirror, what did you mean?" She had a good idea what he'd meant but needed to hear it from him.

Weasel looked at her as if she was the village idiot. "She's blind, isn't she? Got the white stick 'n all. Shouldn't be allowed on a station platform if you ask me. Dangerous places."

Frankie left him before he'd finished speaking. She'd heard enough.

Back in the main office, Corstophine had added a question mark for Keith Tunstall's murderer. Weasel didn't strike him as having the initiative to have killed him and his story rang true. Tunstall took pole position along with Patricia and Jack McCoach. A faint green line joined the three of them together. Underneath their names, the rest of the McCoach family spread out, Emma, Robb and Phoebe. Bryan Cobb's name had been added next to Emma's as something more than just a contact, he just hadn't figured out what role he played. Frankie was put in mind of a family tree, a tree someone was dead set on pruning.

"I can't see what possible connection Tunstall had to the McCoach family. It makes no sense, and why start with Jack or Patricia?" Corstophine stroked his chin, an unconscious habit whenever he was in deep thought.

"We've missed something, sir. I don't know if it means anything but the girl who committed suicide, Sarah Keir, she was blind."

Corstophine's eyebrows raised in interest. "How do you know for sure?"

"I had assumed she was disabled, sir, but it was something Weasel said at the end of the interview. I asked him what he meant by the 'can't see yourself in the mirror' comment, and he told me the girl was blind. Her stick was a blind person's cane. The station staff must have removed it before we arrived."

"Can we check her medical records?"

"I'll get on it now, sir."

"Thanks, Frankie, although whether this has any relevance to Patricia's blinding or Keith's death...Try and find out how she lost her sight."

The reception door opened; PC Lamb entered carrying a full plastic shopping bag in each hand.

"Hello, sir. We've had quite a haul from Weasel's house. There must be several hundred wraps in these two bags." He held them up like trophies, a big grin splitting his face. Corstophine and Frankie took a quick look at the contents: this was the largest drugs haul they'd ever seen.

"Seal these in the large evidence bags before you lock them away in the evidence locker – and wear a bloody mask, Lamb, in case you inhale something you shouldn't!"

"Sir." PC Lamb replied smartly, turning on his heel and heading towards the row of lockable cabinets in the office corridor.

PC McAdam followed moments later, carrying a single carrier bag.

"We found this cash as well, sir. I'd estimate a good few thousand pounds."

"Good work, you two! That should keep the Chief off

our backs for a while." Corstophine allowed himself a moment of self-congratulation. It wasn't every day they managed to clean up an entire drugs operation in one swoop. "Well, I think that's our drugs problem sorted for the time being."

Frankie didn't share his enthusiasm. "For the moment, sir. It won't take long for someone else to move in, especially if the drugs world gets to hear the place is wide open. We still haven't worked out how they were distributing the product. We've been keeping an eye out for street dealers, making a nuisance of ourselves in the pubs and clubs, but we've not caught anyone in possession."

Hamish put his head around the office door, caught Corstophine's eye. "I've Stephen's legal here, sir. When do you think they'll be needed?"

Corstophine held up a finger asking Hamish to wait, before beckoning Frankie back towards him. "Time for another chat with our Weasel. Once he knows we've found him in possession of this little lot, he'll realise he's facing a considerable time behind bars."

He returned his attention back to the sergeant. "Can you accompany Stephen's legal representation to his cell, Hamish? Tell him he can have ten minutes, then we'll interview his client."

"Her, sir. She's a woman." He shut the door behind him, leaving Corstophine wondering if perhaps he should have attended the diversity training course as well. Frankie wisely kept her own counsel.

It was a subdued Weasel who sat facing them in the interview room. Frankie studied him as Corstophine ran through the prelim. He'd developed a tremor since they'd brought him in, holding one hand down on the table with the other in an effort to keep it still. She saw sweat beading his unnaturally pale skin. Weasel's eyes darted around the interview room until he caught her studying him, making him focus on the table. Frankie had seen the signs before, he was beginning to go cold turkey.

"Are you feeling alright, Stephen?" she asked as soon as Corstophine had finished speaking.

His solicitor looked up from the folder balanced on her knee, looked sideways at her client then back to her file with a total lack of concern.

Weasel engaged with Frankie again, "I'm fine, just get on with it." The pleading in his eyes betrayed the confidence of his reply. Frankie exchanged a quick sideways look with her boss, he'd also caught the tell-tale signs of someone abruptly denied their regular fix. Life was going to be become very uncomfortable for Weasel in the next few days.

"If you've been taking drugs, I'd advise you let us know so we can ensure you receive the correct medical assistance." Corstophine intoned. "Have you been a regular user of benzodiazepines or opiates? We can ask for a doctor to make you more comfortable."

Weasel looked to his solicitor for support. She exchanged a non-committal look, as if this was a subject they'd already covered and it was his call.

"No comment." Weasel spat at last, a tight smile on his face as if he'd just won an argument.

Corstophine shrugged, unconcerned.

"For the record, Stephen Currie has been advised to inform us of any drugs he may have been taking prior to his arrest so that the appropriate medical support can be put into place. He has declined to comment."

PC Lamb appeared at the interview room door, holding up three evidence bags in line of sight of the glazed section. Corstophine beckoned him in.

"PC Lamb is placing two bags of drugs and one bag

of used notes on the table. These were found in Stephen Currie's bedroom. Thank you, Lamb."

The PC left them to it, not before giving Weasel's solicitor a quick appraisal, which she studiously ignored.

"Would you like to explain how we found the drugs and cash in your bedroom, Stephen?"

Weasel shook his head, remaining silent until his solicitor prompted him to speak for the recording.

"No comment."

Corstophine nodded as if he expected nothing less. These legal aid solicitors always gave the same advice: if their client had a whiff of innocence and had a sharp enough mind then a few well-considered answers would serve them well in court. Anyone else, especially anyone with a paucity of functioning neurons, it was 'no comment' repeated ad nauseum.

"We'll be adding dealing with intent to supply to your charges, Stephen. Unless you're able to tell me how this quantity of drugs came into your possession you could be looking at eight years for this alone."

Weasel exchanged a panicked look with his advisor. She whispered something in his ear and he faced down the two detectives.

"No comment." This time he didn't look too sure about having won the argument.

His solicitor wrote on her hidden clipboard as the interview progressed. Frankie wondered if she'd taken her office work in with her, she seemed to have little interest in her client.

Corstophine could see where this interview was going. A sea of 'no comments' in reply to every question. He could wait until the drug dependency hit for real, the offer of a legal fix to alleviate the cramps and cravings could loosen the most obstinate tongue.

"OK, Stephen, I don't want to waste everyone's time." His solicitor's eyes flicked up from the notes she was studying, giving Corstophine a grateful glance before getting back to whatever she was doing.

"There are a couple of questions I would like answers to before you go back to your cell. With the drugs and money found in your possession, we have no alternative but to suspect you of the supply and distribution of class A drugs. Those were serious quantities found in your possession, and that will play badly against you in court. If you're able to tell me who supplied these drugs to you, and how you distributed them around town, I may be able to ask for a reduced sentence."

It was Weasel's turn to whisper in the solicitor's ear. Her expression made it clear Weasel's dental hygiene left a lot to be desired. She played with her pen when he'd finished, spinning it around in her fingers whilst she worked out his options.

"My client would like to make it clear that both the drugs and the money came from..." She sent an enquiring stare Weasel's way.

"Keith. Keith Tunstall." Weasel appeared exhausted at the disclosure.

"From Keith Tunstall who is a near neighbour. My client has no involvement, and never has had any involvement in the supply or distribution of drugs. He took those bags for safekeeping when he found the body."

Corstophine sat back in his seat. "Is your client willing to state that himself, for the record?"

Weasel repeated the statement as if he'd just learned it by rote, sulky word for word.

"Then you don't accept any culpability for Keith's murder?" Corstophine probed.

"I never killed him. I've told yer, I found him like tha', stretched out on the kitchen floor. It wisnae me!"

Frankie bit her tongue. The urge to say 'a big boy did it' almost too strong to suppress.

Corstophine wound the interview up and thanked the solicitor. Give him another few hours in his cell and he'd sell his missing mother for a doctor's fix.

Hamish came through to escort Weasel to his cell, holding him none too gently by his arm in case he tried to make a run for it. Frankie could see Weasel was rapidly approaching the point where he'd need help to stand, never mind run.

"The hospital's been on the phone, sir." Hamish managed to make the few words last as long as a performance poet. "It seems Patricia regained consciousness some hours ago and is fit enough to be questioned."

Frankie made a grab for her coat. "Shall we both go, sir?"

"No, Frankie. It's best just one person speaks to her for now. You go. I'll try and make some headway on these cases. Call me if she names anyone we need to know about."

"Understood, sir. I'll try and find out what she knows."

CHAPTER 37
Postman's Knock

Emma McCoach left the house an hour after Corstophine and Frankie had been to look at Robb's artisan distillery. Their visit had shaken her more than she liked to admit, particularly the confirmation that they'd found traces of poison in the water bottle. How on earth had that dim detective managed to find a half-empty plastic water bottle on a mountaintop? The wind up there was strong enough to blow people off their feet, never mind any litter that had been left behind! Then their interest in Robb's distillery – had they evidence to connect the two?

She had decided to carry on with her day's plans, drive the sixty-five miles to Inverness and meet with a friend, do a bit of shopping. God knew she needed the therapy of just doing normal things like everyone else. Emma fussed over her appearance, casting a critical eye over her hair before deciding her hairdresser appointment didn't require pulling forward and then had a word with the nurse before leaving.

The drive typically took her one and a half hours, just time enough to make the afternoon tea she had arranged. Robb should be back any minute now, he could deal with anything else whilst she was gone.

From the upstairs windows, two pairs of eyes watched as Emma drove the white Bentley Continental down the drive, silent except for the rattle of displaced gravel sounding like a gentle tide pulling at a pebble beach. Soon the car was lost to sight and the sound of the tide receded leaving nothing but silence. From one of the trees lining the drive, a crow cawed its displeasure at the car's passing.

The day nurse sent a heartfelt curse to speed Emma on her way before returning to her mobile phone, where the virtual world offered a far more interesting experience than humdrum reality. Headphones plugged in, she selected a soundtrack to while away an afternoon.

Phoebe imagined the Continental floating away to horizons unimaginable, as silent as a white feather. She liked hearing the crow's call and peered intently at the trees searching for a glimpse of the black-coated mourner. Crows could speak. She'd once watched a program about crows on the armoured TV screen in her room. Phoebe learned everything from the TV. Depending on the nurse, it was either left on or off. Nobody ever asked her what she would like to watch, and random channels sometimes appeared when a nurse handled the remote carelessly. It was an unusual education but informative.

The crow programme had explored the ability of a pet crow to vocalise words. The creature had been presented as a form of black parrot, and the narrator had marvelled at the creature's ability to say *good morning* or *good evening* depending on the time of day. Crows are some of the most intelligent birds, the narrator had explained, able to use tools such as sticks to prise bugs from under tree bark. There followed more and more complex mazes and puzzles that hid the crow's food, requiring huge feats of ingenuity and use of available tools as well as pattern recognition, until the crow was rewarded with a fat, wriggling grub.

Phoebe had laughed then, laughed so hard that day nurse had rushed in and forced another two pills into her mouth until she could laugh no more. Phoebe smiled at the memory. The crow had looked straight at the camera when it had swallowed the still-wriggling grub whole. Its bright, black intelligent eye almost filling the screen.

Let me out of this fucking cage, you fucking morons, it had said. Think you're so fucking clever? How come I can understand you, yet you can't understand me? Ever thought of that! I'll find a way out of here. I'll escape and then you'll pay. I'll fucking eat you, you bastards!

Phoebe gave up looking for the black mourner. If he didn't want to be seen, she wouldn't see him. She turned away from the window, only for the crow to call again. Intrigued, she looked out over the driveway once more. A red post office van slewed to a halt, spraying gravel carelessly as the driver spun the wheel. The driver was an older man, his uniform neat, his shoes polished. He opened the rear doors to pull out a parcel, seemingly at random, then marched briskly towards the front door where she lost sight of him.

In the depths of the house, the doorbell rang. Phoebe waited. The cleaner usually answered the door, acting as unofficial maid on the days she was in, but she'd finished an hour ago. She had left just before the nice woman who had smiled at her from the garden. They were police, the man and the woman standing with her mother. They looked everywhere even when standing still, heads turning, eyes probing. They were like the black mourner – intelligent, watchful, warning of danger.

In the absence of the cleaner/maid, Robb would answer the door. Robb wasn't at home. His sports car gleamed on the drive, red as the berries on the trees, but he was not here. Phoebe didn't wonder where he was; she didn't wonder where he wasn't. Robb came and went. Sometimes, he'd talk to her, sit in her room and speak without expecting an answer. It was alright, she couldn't answer when her body was full of pills. All she could do was dribble at him. Phoebe was glad she no longer dribbled; it made her chin sore.

Next in the strict hierarchy of doorbell responders would be her mother. Her mother...

Her mother wasn't her mother. Phoebe knew this in the way that a dunnock really, really ought to know that a cuckoo wasn't its hatchling. Was it through desperation that the parent birds ignored the fact that their strange offspring looked so different to themselves, had grown so much larger, was a danger to everyone else in the nest?

Nature programmes were Phoebe's favourites. She had learned all about cuckoos, that wooden clock call of theirs so innocent and soothing. Clever cuckoo. No, not her mother. She wasn't here either, she'd just floated away in her white feather – off to somewhere else, away from the black mourners and their inquisitive eyes.

The doorbell rang again, insistent this time. His finger must be sore from pressing so hard. In the next room she could hear a thud as day nurse's feet left the bed and hit the wooden floorboards. Day nurse cursed – *fucking maid* was clear in the hallway outside her door, other words indistinct. Footsteps fell away down the sweeping staircase. The door opened. Voices, quiet at first then louder. Day nurse screamed and then silence.

Phoebe listened with interest. This must be a most unexpected parcel!

She could hear heavy footsteps moving downstairs from room to room, searching. This postman behaved differently to all the others. Postman just knocks. Postman just passes the parcel. Postman doesn't walk around the house in his big feet.

Postman Pat was Phoebe's favourite postman. Postman Pat and his black and white cat. Postman Pat and his letters through the door. She'd never seen him put letters through the door but that's what he sang on the TV.

Footsteps came upstairs and paused outside her door. They weren't day nurse's footsteps, far too heavy. They came back to her door. Door rattled, handle turned – see, day nurse hadn't locked the door! Door opened.

Phoebe sat still in her chair and waited.

The postman stood in the doorway and looked at Phoebe. His eyes didn't look kind, or bored, or even angry. He looked at her in the same way a hungry dog looks at a meal, looking her off her chair.

"There you are, you fucking bitch!"

Phoebe accepted the words without emotion. She'd been called worse over the years. If he'd expected fear, or any sort of response, he was going to be sadly disappointed. Phoebe didn't really do emotion or at least, didn't do it very well. She did enjoy laughter though, laughing at things nobody else ever seemed to find amusing. It was quite amusing for the postman to stand in her doorway and swear at her. It was certainly an unusual, if not a unique occurrence. She really enjoyed unique occurrences; she knew they were what memories were made of. Everything else, the minutiae of each day, left no trace. She could go weeks without anything remarkable happening at all.

"You. You did this." The postman was finding it difficult to construct a sentence. He stood shaking on the spot. Phoebe wondered if he was about to disintegrate. Did people disintegrate? She couldn't remember if they did or whether that only happened in cartoons or films. Life can be complicated that way.

"You're coming with me." The postman pulled her to her feet, catching her in his arms as her body sagged unexpectedly. "Stand up. STAND UP!"

Phoebe knew better than to stand up. She needed help because of the drugs. She couldn't let anyone know she hadn't been taking her drugs. She couldn't stand up.

The postman half-dragged, half-carried her down the stairs and threw her into the back of his van. The door slammed on her. She was in a cage, a red cage. The postman sat in the driving seat and started the van, driving at speed back down the drive.

Phoebe had never imagined she'd be in Postman Pat's van. She was mildly upset not to find a black and white cat, but she knew truth from fiction, cartoon from reality – almost. The speed at which the postman took the corners made Phoebe slam against the van wall, so she braced herself against the sides and leant on a handy parcel to make herself more comfortable.

This was great. So much better than sitting in her room. Abducted by Postman Pat! She gave a fleeting thought for day nurse; she wouldn't be happy to find Phoebe no longer in her room. The only thing day nurse had to do was keep Phoebe quiet and in her room. Mother would probably sack her; she sacked all the nurses, eventually.

Meanwhile, she was on an adventure – she hardly ever had an adventure. The van flew along past streets and buildings she had seen on the very few occasions she had been taken anywhere. Postman didn't whistle or sing, and he didn't have a cat. Phoebe decided, on the balance of evidence and the weight of probability, that this most likely was not Postman Pat at all.

CHAPTER 38
Here, There and Everywhere

It was about the same time as a dejected Weasel was being led back to his cell that Robb finally reached the end of the track. What should have taken a couple of hours brisk walking had taken him six, long painful hours, one laboured step after the other. At least nobody had tried to attack him as he hobbled along, one foot swinging uselessly and hands raw from holding the stick that supported him. He rested on the final wooden gate, reaching into his pocket for his mobile. Still no signal.

Sandy's car was parked just back up the main road in the Craigag car park. With a final effort, Robb pushed through the walker's gate, back the few hundred metres up the main road, and limped the last few steps towards the car. It was only when he'd stopped to retrieve Sandy's keys from a pocket that he realised all the tyres were flat. The car sat down on its haunches like an abandoned scrap vehicle, knife wounds clearly visible in each tyre wall where they'd been slashed.

Robb rested his back against the car and felt his heart pounding. Red tracks crept along his arms where the blisters on his palms had opened to expose raw flesh, capillaries spilling their blood. He opened and closed each affected hand, dried blood unsticking from fingers until needle-sharp pain announced he was opening wounds that needed to stay closed. The top of the stick was stained dark where his blood had run. He had to peel the stick away from raw flesh, taking a fresh layer of skin with it.

There weren't any other cars parked, no walkers coming up the track. The sky had turned an ominous grey, signalling that good weather was being replaced by bad. That would explain why he hadn't met any hillwalkers on his way back down, there must be a storm coming. There was nothing else for it, he had to walk the last few minutes down to the road and flag a lift.

There was a lot of traffic, cars and lorries rushed past without anyone taking any notice of a dishevelled hiker holding out his thumb. The track joined the main road at a relatively straight section, providing good visibility so vehicles had a chance to stop safely. None of them were inclined to do so, and Robb stepped out more fully into the road in his frustration to catch someone's attention. Every time a car or lorry drove by, they had to suddenly swerve out into the centre of the road as they caught sight of him, sending back irritated car horn blasts as he struggled to avoid being blown off his one good foot.

When he finally managed to hitch a ride, the driver had eyed him suspiciously, finally accepting his story and offering to take him directly to the hospital. It was only a twenty-five minute drive back to town and the driver listened with ill-concealed interest as Robb called the police, reaching the lugubrious sergeant at the front desk.

Hamish listened to Robb's call, jotting down his particulars and almost driving him to distraction as he insisted that he gave his address, post code and phone number before being persuaded to put him through to the DI.

"Corstophine, you have to send a medical team to Gleann Dubh-Lighe bothy. Someone was up there shooting at us. Bryan's dead, shot in the stomach. Sandy's been shot in the shoulder and is bleeding out at the bothy. Someone might be there now, trying to get him." The words spilled over each other, forming a waterfall of noise.

Corstophine was on the other end of the line trying to make sense of the garbled message.

"Take it easy, Robb, slow down. You say Bryan's dead?"

Robb tried breathing more slowly. Now that he was safe, sitting in a car and on the way to the hospital, the adrenaline had nothing useful to do except fill him with nervous panic.

"He was hit last night. Someone shot him when he was out collecting firewood. We didn't see anyone, it was pitch dark by that time. Sandy was hit as he tried to shelter in the bothy with me. He's lost a lot of blood and needs urgent medical help."

"OK, don't worry. I'll make sure help is sent. You say whoever did this might still be there?"

"I don't know, maybe. I left the bothy early this morning to get help but twisted my bloody ankle, so I can't walk on it. It took ages to get to the car and then someone had slashed the tyres."

"Hang on a minute. Stay on the phone, Robb." Corstophine beckoned the two constables into his office.

"That's Robb McCoach on the line. He says they were attacked at the bothy they camped at last night and his car's been damaged. I want you to call in an emergency medical team. Bryan Cobb has been shot dead and Sandy McPhearson requires urgent medical help. You two need to provide assistance. He thinks that whoever did this may still be in the vicinity."

"Where exactly is this bothy, sir?" McAdam asked the obvious even as Corstophine pulled a map from the shelf above his desk.

"Here." Corstophine circled a small rectangle in amongst a sea of brown lines, the track Robb had laboriously inched down that morning showing as two innocuous dotted lines leading from the main road. "I don't know if the air ambulance is available but tell them it's urgent."

"Sir," they both chorused at once, McAdam grabbing the map out of Corstophine's hands as they went.

"And tape off the car in case there are fingerprints. I'll try and sort a forensics team."

They rushed out, grabbing coats as they went. McAdam was already calling the medical team, his voice indistinct as they left.

"That's two of our constables heading out now, Robb, and I'm trying for an air ambulance to collect Sandy. Where are you at this moment?"

"I'm heading to the hospital in case I've broken this bloody ankle. Look, never mind me. Whoever this lunatic is, he may be on his way to my place. There's only Mum and Phoebe there with a nurse, they can't be left alone. You'll have to go there, Jim. You have to make sure they're safe!" He was shouting now, the desperation to look after his family only too evident.

"Don't worry, Robb, I'll go there now." Corstophine's mind was in overdrive. Robb sounded genuinely frightened, worried for his family. That would tend to rule him out from the list of suspects. What if there was a madman intent on mutilating or murdering the family? He'd have to make sure they were safe until they caught whoever it was.

"Robb, DC Frankie McKenzie will be at the hospital when you arrive. I'll ask her to take a statement from you there, once she's seen Patricia."

"Aunt Pat's OK? She's come round?" His voice betrayed eagerness, hope.

"She's out of the coma. We had a call just now from the

284

hospital saying we can talk to her. I don't know how she is, I'm sorry."

A muffled sob came down the line. "Thanks. Thanks, Jim. Oh God, it's just too awful. Who's doing this?"

"We'll get to the bottom of it, Robb, don't you worry. What's important now is that I make sure your mother and sister are safe. We'll speak later. Wait for DC McKenzie and I'll get back to you as soon as I'm sure they're both safe."

Corstophine grabbed the keys for the police Land Rover, the other two patrol vehicles had been taken. The speed dial for forensics brought the usual sunny response which he cut short.

"I haven't time. Send a team out. There's been a shooting, one fatality and another person badly wounded. The desk sergeant will be able to patch you through to the constables heading to the scene, for the exact location, but the entrance track is near Glenfinnan on the A830."

He cut the call short, making a beeline for the front desk.

"Hamish, can you ask mountain rescue to liaise with McAdam and Lamb? They may need access to the Fassfern Estate, the gate to Gleann Dubh-Lighe bothy. Ask them to make sure the gate is unlocked, will you? There's been a murder, someone's been shooting at Robb McCoach and has killed Bryan Cobb and badly wounded Sandy McPhearson. McAdam's organising an air ambulance, but keep in the loop. You'd better call in the firearms unit as well, just in case. I'm going to the McCoach house, his family may be in danger."

The sergeant wrote infuriatingly slowly on his pad. Corstophine left him to it, they'd sort it all out between them. For now, he was the only one available to check in on the McCoach house. He found Emma's mobile number as he drove, breaking the highway code to key it into his phone. The phone rang three, four times before she picked up.

"Emma McCoach. Who is this?" She sounded as if the queen had just received an unexpected call whilst on the throne.

"This is DI James Corstophine, is everything alright?"

Emma frowned at her mobile with annoyance. The cheek of the man. He'd only just left the house and here he was bothering her again.

"What do you mean, is everything alright? You only saw me an hour ago!"

Corstophine heard the sound of a passing lorry in the background. "Are you driving, Mrs McCoach?"

"Yes, I'm on the way to Inverness. What's this all about?"

"Robb's just called. There's been a shooting at the bothy they stayed at last night and he has good reason to believe you're all in danger. You've not had anyone unexpected at the house?"

Emma frowned at her mobile. If this was some sort of ploy to make her return home, she wasn't having it.

"No, there's been nothing out of the ordinary. The nurse is at home, she'll deal with anything untoward, I'm sure. She's a most capable woman."

Corstophine waited for her to ask if her son was OK. A pregnant pause later and he decided that she just didn't care. "I'll make my way over, see if everything's alright. You've not had a call or anything?"

"The only call I've had is yours, Inspector. This all sounds a bit theatrical. It will be Patricia filling his head with all sorts of nonsense. Now, if you don't mind, I'm driving."

"This is serious, Emma. People have been shot." Corstophine heard the sound of a dropped call before he'd finished speaking.

"Bloody hell! How heartless can you get?" He wasn't expecting an answer.

The big house came into view as he emerged from the tree-lined drive. Somewhere behind him a solitary crow called out from its vantage point on one of the taller trees. Corstophine climbed the steps to the front door, immediately alert as he realised it had been left open.

"Hello, police. Is anyone at home?" He called out into the vast hallway, his voice loud enough to reach upstairs. A faint echo supplied the only response. Corstophine reached for the bell, only pulling back at the last minute in case he'd need it dusted for prints.

"Hello?" Nobody answered his call. "This is the police, I'm coming in!"

The house had that distinct air of being empty, an absence of comforting noises from any of the rooms. If that was a sixth sense he could feel, it was making the hairs on his arms stand up. Corstophine moved cautiously through the house, room by room, not knowing what to expect. A muffled squeaking made him enter the kitchen slowly, senses primed for whoever or whatever was inside. The source of the squeaking was easy to detect – a nurse lay trussed up like a turkey, gaffa tape wrapped around her mouth, underneath wild staring eyes. The same grey tape held her hands behind her back and bound her ankles together.

"Is there anyone here with you, in the house?" Corstophine spoke urgently, his voice low so it wouldn't carry. The nurse stopped her squeaking and shook her head.

"OK, this might hurt." So saying, he dug his fingers into her hair and underneath the tape, pulling away with a jerk. The tape ripped and he started to ease it away from her mouth, new noises coming from underneath the tape as strands of hair came away with it.

"He's taken the girl," she managed before gasping for air. Corstophine searched around and spotted a knife rack, relieved not to see any blades missing.

"Breath slowly. It's OK, I'm here now. I'll just have to cut you free, try not to move." The knife sliced easily through the tape, leaving her free to sit up and start working on removing it from her wrists.

"Who took her? Did you recognise who it was?" His voice was urgent. The woman was on the edge of a breakdown, he could hear the sobs breaking in her throat as she struggled with her bonds.

"Postman." Her voice broke under the strain before she started wailing. "I thought I was going to die."

Corstophine attempted to comfort her, desperately aware of precious time slipping past.

"You're not going to die. I'm here with you. You're safe now. You're saying it was a postman who did this?" He needed to radio for support, but everyone was already out. The two PCs at the bothy, Frankie at the hospital. Hamish was needed at the station to keep everyone in touch. She nodded vigorously in response, broken breaths punching the air as she tried to keep it together.

"He had a parcel. Threatened to kill me if I made a noise." She gulped for air, "I heard him go upstairs and take Phoebe out the front door." Her eyes flicked nervously to the doorway.

"Are you sure it was a postman? Not someone dressed as a postman? What was he driving?" The questions came too fast. He needed to slow everything down for her, calm her down.

"Post van, he had a post van. It was a postie!" The last word was emphatic.

"I'm just going to have a quick look around, make sure he's gone. All right?"

"NO!" The nurse shouted at him in pure panic. "Take me with you."

"OK." Corstophine held out an arm. "Are you feeling well enough to stand?"

She glared at him as if this was all his fault, then heaved herself up off the floor, leaving a trail of ripped gaffa tape behind. "I'll take you to Phoebe's room – you have to find her."

She held onto the bannisters for support, her breathing still ragged as if she'd been crying uncontrollably. Corstophine's offer of a supporting arm was shrugged off as he walked beside her, prepared to catch her if she collapsed. In front of them, a sparsely furnished room lay wide open, a solitary chair and bed provided the furniture. On the wall, their reflections stared back at them from a Perspex screen covering a blank TV.

"This is her room. He's taken her and you have to find her." She started crying in earnest then, huge racking sobs shaking her body.

Corstophine had seen the aftermath of shock before and knew the signs.

"Come on, I'll run you to the hospital for a check-up. Don't worry, we'll find her, and the man who's taken her." He spoke with more confidence than he felt. Short-staffed, no idea who or where her assailant might have gone and with who knew how many post office vans on the roads – how was he going to find Phoebe before…?

Corstophine decided not to pursue that line of thought. He called Hamish on the radio, explained what had happened and asked him to check if there were any post vans missing. As he hit the siren and sped down the drive, he realised he'd left the front door wide open. But that was the least of his worries.

CHAPTER 39
Bedside Manner

Frankie introduced herself to the ward nurse and was briskly marched to Patricia's bedside. As they hurried along the corridor, passing rooms where patients lay connected to tubing and scrolling display screens, the nurse told Frankie in no uncertain terms not to upset her patient.

"Patricia has suffered a major trauma. I don't want you to do anything that will put her under undue stress." She stopped outside Patricia's room, casting a practiced eye over her charge before adding one last comment. "I wouldn't normally allow any police questioning this soon after a patient has come out of a coma, but she insisted on speaking to you. I'll be monitoring her vital signs from reception, so at the first sign of any distress, you make your excuses and leave. Is that clear?"

"Perfectly." They locked eyes, Frankie and the ward nurse, sizing each other up and deciding to leave things there. Frankie took the chair next to Patricia's bed.

"Hello, Patricia, this is DC Frankie McKenzie. We met when you first came to the police station."

The bandaged head on the raised pillow tilted to face her. Dark purple bruising covered the flesh that wasn't concealed by the white bandage over her eyes.

"Frankie. Yes, I remember you." Her voice was quiet, querulous.

Frankie had the strong sense that the woman stretched out beside her was broken, her spirit crushed.

"I don't want to wear you out, Patricia, so tell me when you want me to leave. Is that alright?"

A faint smile lifted her lips, thin and colourless without the garish red makeup. "It's good to have anyone visit, even if it is the police."

Frankie smiled in return, glad that something remained of the woman's indomitable spirit. "You asked for us to come. Did you have any information that can help us catch whoever did this to you?"

One of the machines next to her changed tempo, the steady beeping increasing in speed. Frankie glanced guiltily at it, hoping it wouldn't attract the ward nurse's attention.

"She's my daughter, you know."

The DC struggled to make sense of Patricia's announcement. "Sorry. Who's your daughter?"

"Phoebe. She's mine. I gave birth to her."

Frankie stared at her, wondering if she was still living in a dreamlike state. "You're saying Phoebe McCoach is *your* daughter?"

The old Patricia flared up for a brief moment. "That's what I just told you, dammit!" She sighed heavily, reminding Frankie of the woman she had interviewed just six days previously. Frankie instantly felt guilty at the way she'd felt about her then, a madwoman wasting police time with her talk about séances and poisoning. She had been right about one of them.

The beeping reduced to its former speed as Patricia let out one long breath.

"Emma couldn't have any more children after Robb. She had a difficult birth. It ruined her womb. The only way Jack could have another child was through surrogacy, you see. He asked me if I'd have the child."

Frankie was unsure if she was understanding this

correctly, or whether this was going anywhere pertinent to the investigation.

"You had Jack's...you had your brother's child?"

"Yes." Patricia stated simply, as if having a child with your brother was the most natural thing to do. "Jack and Emma's child. It was a gestational surrogacy and the only way a foetus could be carried to term."

"Ah!"

"You didn't think?" Patricia attempted to laugh, then thought better of it. "I signed the papers to give them custody after the birth, but she will always be my baby."

Frankie sat silently, only too aware that she herself had been unable to conceive, painfully aware how much a child can be desired and the devastation that follows when that dream is cruelly taken away. She had felt hollow when she'd been given the news matter-of-factly by her doctor, told she would never be able to conceive – felt cheated.

"When she was wee, Jack used to bring her to see me almost every day. She was my sunshine." Patricia stopped, her mouth twisting around itself and her throat working to swallow. Frankie realised she was crying. Crying without eyes.

"Emma didn't like it. She put a stop to it. Phoebe loved me, you see, loved me as a child loves a mother. Emma felt insanely jealous and kept her away from me." She stopped, her arm reaching out towards a bedside table, sweeping ineffectually at the air. Frankie fetched the plastic glass that lay within reach, half-full of water, and placed it gently in her hand.

"Thank you." Patricia took small sips, her hand shaking so drips of water ran down her face. She held the glass for Frankie to take, childlike in her dependency.

"Eventually, she grew bored of her like I knew she

would. Emma has no staying power, instant gratification made flesh. It's a wonder the marriage held up so long, but she does like money." Patricia left that hanging for a few seconds, Emma's character dissected and laid out for inspection.

"By the time Phoebe started school, Emma was more than grateful for me to take on the fetching and carrying." Her lip started trembling again, mouth working to swallow pain. "Those were the happiest days of my life."

She spoke simply, those few words encompassing the entirety of her existence. Frankie felt a familiar constriction at the back of her throat as she fought to control her emotions.

"I'm sure the school all thought I was her real mother. It was my face they saw every morning when I dropped her off. Every afternoon I collected her, every school event. It was my face they saw in her." Her voice had dropped off such that Frankie had to strain to hear her above the background noise of the hospital.

"Emma couldn't be bothered with children, you see." Frankie noticed how Patricia's voice strengthened whenever she talked about her sister-in-law. "She found them irritating. Emotional vampires she said to me once – now there's the pot calling the kettle black." She managed a quiet laugh at that, encouraging the attached electrodes to transmit faster beeps to the monitoring equipment. There was a corresponding change in the scrolling displays of heartbeat and breathing. Frankie checked the corridor in case the nurse came scurrying back.

"She was only six years old. It was her birthday and Phoebe was desperate for a kitten, you know what wee girls are like! For some reason Emma had given her the idea that she would have one on her birthday, but Emma being Emma, she'd not even remembered it was the big day – much less given her a present. I'd turned up at the house as I always did, with an armful of presents before taking her to school, and she was distraught. I'd never seen her so upset. Emma just told her off for making a scene, and I had to try and calm her down."

Patricia's head tilted towards the overhead fluorescents as if she could see them, bandaged eye sockets seeking any kind of light in the permanent blackness.

"I hugged her, told her how much I loved her, kissed that mop of hair that always smelt so much of Phoebe. I don't think Emma ever touched the children." Her hand moved instinctively back towards the bedside table. Frankie moved quickly to prevent her from knocking the glass over, placing it in her hand again.

"Thank you, dear."

Frankie waited until the glass had been slowly emptied, half-filled it from the adjacent water jug and replaced it within reach.

"They had an art class that morning. I always think that Phoebe somehow inherited my love of art." She paused, taking a shaky breath before continuing.

"The school called me at ten. I'll always remember the time because the clock had just struck the hour. I like to count the bells, you see. Phoebe had been cutting coloured paper to make a collage. For some reason, the teacher was never clear, Phoebe had been given proper scissors, not those snub-nosed blunt things they usually hand out to the younger children. She was very precise about her art, you see. She really did have a talent! She probably fetched them herself so she could cut more accurately. I don't know the full story of what happened next. I don't think we ever will, but one of the girls was causing trouble. It may have been simple jealousy because Phoebe's work was the best in the class, but whatever the reason this girl kept banging into her on purpose. She was trying to mess up Phoebe's cutting, I presume. It was just too much for her. The birthday Emma couldn't be bothered to remember: the lack of any presents or love from her mother, the girl pushing and bumping into her until something gave."

Patricia paused again, breathing fast as if she'd just finished exercising. The chorus of beeping equipment reached a small crescendo before returning to more normal levels.

"Phoebe had lashed out behind her to push the girl away, pushed with all her strength. She'd forgotten the scissors in her hand. The girl was blinded."

Her voice became pleading. "She didn't do it on purpose, she wasn't even looking behind her. Imagine being Phoebe at that moment, hearing the screams and turning around to realise what she'd just done!"

Patricia let loose two long, broken sighs as Frankie started gathering strands in her head.

"The police were called. Social services, doctors, psychologists. None of them knew her, you see. None of them knew her like I did. They only saw the cold-blooded response, the lack of empathy. They immediately thought she was disturbed, psychotic, they said. I tried to explain that her mother had never displayed any affection to her, that this was how she was expected to behave when things went wrong, but they only listened to Emma. Emma was the legal mother, you see. I was just the working womb."

The beeping had increased in speed and Frankie caught the ward nurse standing at the end of the corridor with a determined expression on her face. A phone rang somewhere and Frankie was relieved to see her step back towards reception.

"Go on." Frankie encouraged. "You know who did this to you, don't you, Patricia?"

Patricia nodded imperceptibly, the bandaged head see-sawing on the fulcrum of her starched pillow.

"They took her to a special hospital, my Phoebe. Emma encouraged it, told all sorts of lies about her behaviour to excuse her own lack of empathy. I didn't see Phoebe for years until Jack was able to bring her home under strict conditions. He has shares in the private health company, you know, otherwise I don't think he could have managed to take her. She's been pumped full of anti-psychotics and sedatives ever since. The regular visits from Emma's tame psychiatrist just signs her into another year of chemical servitude. I couldn't do anything to help and Jack... Jack just wanted an easy life and let Emma have her way. I think he forgot Phoebe even existed."

"Who did this to you, Emma?" Frankie prompted again, concerned that the ward nurse would curtail her visit before she had managed to get the information she desperately needed.

"The girl's father." Her voice came as a whisper. "I've seen him staring at the house over the years. He blamed me for his daughter's blindness, even though, if anyone should be blamed for what was a terrible accident, it should be Emma. He'd seen me dropping off Phoebe at the school gates every day, seen her kiss me goodbye. He thought I was her mother – he was the only person who did."

"What's his name, Emma? We need to talk to him before anyone else gets hurt. Who is he?" Frankie already had a good idea who it was, she just needed Patricia to confirm.

"Sarah Keir's father, William Keir. I saw him in the garden at night quite recently. I painted him on the canvas. He had some sort of night vision googles that glowed in the dark, they made him quite obvious really, although I suppose *he* didn't know that."

"Thanks, Patricia, you have been a great help." Frankie made to leave but Patricia's hand grabbed at her coat with the unerring ability of the unsighted.

"I kept her collage, you know. It was really quite wonderful for such a young artist. She'd made the most beautiful little black kitten."

CHAPTER 40
GPS

Frankie's radio crackled into life as she left the hospital, mind whirling with the import of Patricia's words.

"Frankie, it's me. Where are you?" Corstophine's voice was clipped, urgent. Lacking any radio protocols.

"I'm just about to leave the hospital, sir. I've talked to Patricia, she's…"

"No time for that. See if Robb McCoach is in triage and take a statement from him. I'm coming in with the McCoach's nurse. Someone abducted Phoebe after Emma McCoach left for Inverness. Be with you in a couple of minutes."

The radio died as he killed the connection. She could hear the unmistakable sound of his siren in the background. Frankie swiftly turned back and made straight for the A&E department, sweeping her eyes over the assorted human flotsam that made up the waiting area. Robb was nowhere to be seen.

"Excuse me." Frankie held her warrant card in full view of the woman behind reception. "Can you tell me if you have a Robb McCoach here?"

The receptionist behind the Perspex screen peered at Frankie over the top of her glasses. "Who are you looking for, dear?"

Frankie held onto her composure. "Robb McCoach, he's had an injury?" She wondered if the last bit was surplus information but at least the woman bent down to her screen, tapping at her keyboard in a way that would make Hamish a speed typist.

"McCoach...McCoach. Yes, here we are." She looked up with a satisfied smile. "He's with a nurse now, twisted ankle. If you'd like to take a seat?" She indicated a row of plastic chairs, insufficient for the number of waiting patients who had no other option but to lean against walls or pillars.

Frankie didn't have the time to waste on niceties and headed straight into the curtained-off cubicles where the triage team worked.

"You can't go through there..." The receptionist's protestations came angrily from behind her screen. Frankie ignored her and marched up to the first medic she saw.

"Police." Frankie held up her warrant card. "I'm looking for Robb McCoach. Twisted ankle?"

A nurse pointed towards a curtained-off bed. She spotted an ankle being wrapped in a bandage through a gap in the privacy drapes.

"Sorry to interrupt. Police." A young nurse was taking her time bandaging up his ankle, turning in surprise at the interruption.

"Robb, I don't have long. Can you tell me what happened?"

Robb managed to convey the gist of his story in a few words, anxious to find out if his family were alright.

Frankie didn't see any way of sugar-coating this particular pill. "DI Corstophine is bringing in Phoebe's nurse. Your mother is OK, she's gone to Inverness – but Phoebe is missing."

"Missing? What do you mean missing?" Robb struggled to stand, the nurse holding him down with increasing difficulty as she wrestled with his bandage.

"Not now, Mr McCoach. I have to finish pulling this bandage tight. Please lie back down."

Her increasingly desperate calls for him to lie on the bed were ignored by both of them.

"Someone's taken her. We think it's the same man who attacked Patricia. Stay there, Robb, there's nothing you can do to help."

Robb collapsed back onto the bed, staring wildly at Frankie. "You have to find her. God, why is this all happening?"

The distinctive sound of an approaching police siren could be heard from the A&E entrance. Frankie tried a comforting smile to reassure him.

"That's DI Corstophine just arrived. Don't worry, we'll find her."

She left Robb wild-eyed on the bed, rushing out into the reception area where Corstophine was explaining that the nurse he was holding onto needed to be checked over.

"I think I know who it is, sir."

Corstophine had just removed a lanky youth from one of the chairs with a few well-chosen words, lowering the nurse into a sitting position. Her face had turned as white as a bandage, except for the tell-tale red rash across her mouth that had been left by the gaffa tape.

They left the hospital in a hurry, Frankie taking the spare seat in the Land Rover beside the DI.

"Who is it?" Corstophine's voice was tight, controlled as he manoeuvred the vehicle back onto the main street.

"Patricia thinks her attacker was the suicide's father, William Keir." She continued with a shortened explanation of the connection between Patricia, Emma and Phoebe and the accident that had blinded Sarah Keir.

Corstophine nodded as he searched the junction, unsure whether to head left or right.

"Do you happen to know if William's a postie?"

Frankie's blank expression reminded him he hadn't explained the link. "The nurse was attacked by a postie. He took Phoebe away in his van."

"He might be, sir. I never looked into it. He wasn't on the radar."

"I know, I know. Shit! How do we find the right bloody post van?"

Frankie sat in silence. How indeed? They couldn't chase after every post van they saw, and if they concentrated only on those they saw driving erratically and at speed, that didn't exactly reduce the field.

"Check with Hamish and see if he has any further information on missing post vans. I'll update Emma."

He called Emma on the mobile, Frankie listening with half an ear as she called Hamish on the radio.

"No, the depot says all the vans are accounted for." Hamish's measured tones were in contrast to the urgency of the situation they faced.

"Can you ask them if a William Keir works for them?"

"Willy? Aye, he works for them. He delivers here on Saturdays. Likes his overtime..."

Frankie interrupted the sergeant before he had a chance to tell her William's life story. "Did you know his daughter had been blinded?"

The pause on the other end of the radio was so extended, Frankie was beginning to think she'd lost the signal. Corstophine was still having a one-sided conversation with Emma and from what she could hear, Emma wasn't particularly worried that her daughter had been abducted.

"Aye, terrible thing it was, she was just a wee lass at the time. You've never seen so much blood..." The significance of the event that happened some twenty years ago when he was just a bobby had painstakingly filtered through Hamish's consciousness. "That was the McCoach girl that they took away from the school, mad Phoebe. Do ye think there's some connection?"

"Thanks, Hamish, let me know if you hear anything. We're looking for William Keir now, we think he's taken Phoebe in his post van." She decided to let the mad Phoebe comment go. Hamish's diversity training hadn't covered mental health. Come to think of it, none of them had ever had any training about mental health.

She cut the radio as Corstophine finished his call. "That bloody woman! Some people shouldn't be allowed to have kids. Can you believe she's more worried about meeting a friend for tea and cakes than she is about her own daughter?" His incredulous tone merely confirmed the character assessment Frankie had formed listening to Patricia.

"Hamish says he's a postie, sir. Delivers to the station most Saturdays." She hesitated before deciding whether to tell him that Hamish had known all along about the events leading up to Sarah Keir's blinding, that Hamish had been the first officer at the school when it happened. It wouldn't help, and Corstophine would fly off the rails in his present distracted mood. Also, to be fair, they'd not included Hamish in the investigation. They hadn't made use of his encyclopaedic knowledge of every event in the town for the last twenty, thirty years. She decided discretion was required.

"OK, so it looks very much as if he's our man. Do you suppose their vans are fitted with GPS trackers?" Corstophine was clutching at straws, strangely appropriate when searching for a needle in a haystack.

"I don't know, sir, I'll check with Hamish."

Corstophine's eyes rolled heavenwards at the thought of relying on the old sergeant for a fast response. "No,

Frankie, call the post office depot on your mobile. We need an instant fix on the vehicle if at all possible." He pulled into the side of the road. There was nothing to be gained in driving randomly around the streets in the hope of finding the right post van.

Frankie was listening intently to her phone. "OK, I see. Yes, this is important. He may have abducted a young woman. Yes, William Keir!" She shouted his name down the phone in exasperation, holding up a hand to forestall Corstophine's questioning.

"Are you sure? And it's been there for a while? OK, let me know the moment it starts moving again. On this number, thanks." She turned to the DI with relief. "They know where his van is, sir. It's parked in Glenfinnan, near the monument."

Corstophine spun the wheel, siren and blues kicked into life. Cars braked with a squeal of tyres as he cut across the traffic, the back wheels sliding on the tarmac as he pushed the Land Rover as fast as it could go.

"Try and raise McAdam and Lamb if they're in range, and tell them to get to the monument as soon as. They're almost on top of it, unless they've already started up the bloody trail to the bothy."

Frankie tried the radio, nothing but a burst of static. She reached Hamish, explained where they were heading and asked him to keep trying the PCs, get them to drop everything and head for the monument. She tried again on her phone, hoping against hope that the mobile signal might reach them when the radio couldn't. Nothing.

Corstophine exchanged a worried look with her. It was going to be down to the two of them. Even with the siren, it would take a good thirty minutes for the Land Rover to reach the monument, and a lot could happen in thirty minutes.

CHAPTER 41
Phoenix

When the two detectives had gently told him his Sarah was dead, William Keir had felt his sanity unravel, strand after delicate strand snapping. He refused to believe them at first, and had babbled desperately about her musical ability, had shown them her photograph as if offering incontrovertible proof that she was still alive. When they mouthed the lines 'so sorry for your loss,' words so inadequate yet so final, he lost any reason to live.

As he watched the two detectives walk away, the world he knew and understood stretched into a distance so profound that he was faced with the immeasurable void, a universe so large and uncaring it sucked every last morsel of sanity from his fragile mind. He had no memory of how long that fugue-like state had endured, he could have been staring unseeing through the window for hours. Then, like a phoenix rising from the ashes, he felt himself being reborn in fire – and this fire would exact vengeance.

He needed retribution in the way a flame needs fuel to survive – and the McCoach family were his to burn. They were the reason for his pain and suffering, and the girl was the reason for everything – but nothing had prepared him for seeing Phoebe just sitting there. She had given no indication of attempting to run, fight, or even plead for her life. Faced with the white heat of his rage she had calmly regarded him with those large, curious eyes. It was only then that he realised she was probably drugged. That threw him, how could he exact any real satisfaction for Sarah's death when the cause of it all remained unconcerned at her own fate?

In sudden confusion, he'd bundled her into the back of his post van where she lay quite contentedly. He hadn't even had to secure her before driving away. Phoebe was the perfect victim for a kidnap except he *needed* her to suffer, to feel pain. William drove without a destination in mind, fiercely blinking away the tears that blurred his vision as he remembered his daughter. Inside his mind the whirlwind gained strength, tearing the last vestiges of reason from their anchors until only rage remained.

William had been so proud he thought he'd burst when Sarah was accepted by the Glasgow Conservatoire. Her cello playing had brought unexpected tears to his eyes – seeing her so focussed, so happy as she played. He had the father to thank for that. You had to give him credit, Jack McCoach had taken care of Sarah. He'd been the one to suggest she learn an instrument. It would never have occurred to William that Sarah might be able to play anything.

She had shown promise from her very first lessons. Jack McCoach had found her a teacher from Dalwhinnie who drove the forty-five miles there and back, twice a week. It must have cost him a fortune. The teacher said she used to be in an orchestra; straddling her instrument in a way he initially found slightly offensive. He thought he'd stop the first lesson there and then, rather than have his blind daughter place herself in such an inappropriate position, but the way Sarah's face had illuminated when she heard the instrument's deep voice won him over.

On her fourteenth birthday, a full-size cello was delivered to their door. Jack had casually mentioned it had cost over £20,000, not boastfully but to impress upon them the need to look after it. It was held within a shaped metal case, soft and padded inside with red velvet that felt like silk. Sarah couldn't wait to play it and inhaled the instrument's scent like a sommelier sampling the finest wine. He could still picture the look of sheer rapture on her face when she drew the bow across the strings for the first time.

William realised eventually that this was how she could see. The vibrations filled the room, and Sarah had explained to him that the reverberation told her how large the space was, if someone was nearby, what the room contained. Jack McCoach had done all that he could to bring her back her sight. The entrance exam to the Conservatoire was a formality and Jack had set up some kind of trust fund that he had said would pay for her all her life, leave her in comfort no matter what. No matter what.

Then that little bastard had threatened them, threatened her. 'Go on, it's easy money,' he had said. 'You just have to post these envelopes through doors on your rounds.' William had refused of course. They all knew what those jiffy bags contained. Some of the other guys didn't care and took part willingly, doubling their income, trebling it on some rounds. They started driving flash cars, spreading cash around as if it grew on trees. He refused though. It wasn't for him.

The day the two heavies appeared at his door he'd felt afraid. These guys knew what they were about, pushed past him into the house as if he wasn't even there, to follow the sound of the cello playing. They had stared at her lasciviously, saw her sightless eyes, smiled evilly at each other and then at him.

"Be a shame if your girl had an accident." The words burnt into his brain. "Must be difficult, being blind, with the traffic and everything?"

They hadn't needed to spell it out. Sarah had heard

everything and implored him to call the police. He hadn't, of course. He knew the police couldn't be with her all the time. He couldn't be with her all the time – he wasn't with her at the end when she'd had enough of the threats, of not knowing who was waiting in the darkness. His life had ended when she died, it was as simple as that. How could anyone expect him to be capable of living when his only reason for existence lay dead on a mortuary slab? When her music died he felt his heart turn to stone. He'd heard people saying that before – about hearts turning to stone. He'd always considered it airy-fairy poetical nonsense until he felt a cold, dead weight in his chest where his heart once used to beat.

Jack McCoach – he was glad that he had died of a heart attack, it would have felt wrong taking *his* life after everything he'd done for Sarah. A father can't be held responsible for a daughter's actions, not really, not when he's busy every day and hardly ever sees her. No, William was glad that he had died on the mountains, it had saved him a job as well as salving his conscience.

William looked around him, wondering where he was going. This was the Glenfinnan road, the same road he had driven yesterday when he'd seen Robb in the back of that car. Was it the son he'd killed yesterday evening? The light was so bad he'd celebrated lining up the kill so successfully, but the other two… He was fairly sure he'd hit all three of them, but a doubt stubbornly remained. Then the mother who wasn't even in the house. It might be for the best, leaving her alive, leaving her to mourn for the rest of her life just as he had to.

The Glenfinnan Monument came into view on the left, a stone pillar stretching into the sky but falling short of any impressive height. It had always struck him as unfinished, a project with grand illusions and a fitting tribute to the waste of life it commemorated. He parked in the car park, waiting for the stream of tourists to exit the door in the tower base before marching Phoebe over.

"Is that everyone?"

The tour guide's confusion was clearly written on his face, wondering what the postman was doing with a young woman held so possessively in his arm.

"Yes, why do you want...? Is she OK?" He realised that he was being incoherent, not a useful trait in his line of work. "Why do you want to know?" That was better.

"I want you to give me the key to this door, then I want you to fuck off!"

The tour guide was affronted. How dare a postman speak to him like that, and what was wrong with the girl? He opened his mouth then closed it when he caught sight of the vicious blade in William's hand.

"Here, take it, I don't want any trouble." He threw a key down at William's feet before running, attracting the attention of tourists who reacted to the drama unfolding in front of them by reaching for their phones and cameras. William manhandled Phoebe to the narrow doorway at the base of the tower, ignoring the people staring at them as if they were part of the visitor attraction's entertainment.

"Get in!" William's terse command was followed by his pushing Phoebe through the tower door.

Phoebe found herself at the base of a stone staircase that wound upwards like the tower in her dreams. Behind her, she could hear William's urgent grunts as he forced the key into the lock, foot jammed against the door in readiness for a rescue attempt that never came. He pushed past her, roughly grabbing at her arm as he went.

"Up here, use your legs!" His voice was as harsh as his grip, pulling her up the worn steps so fast her feet threatened to trip her up.

Phoebe complied with her captor's instructions, feeling the rough stone against the palm of her free hand as they climbed the spiral staircase. The light was dim inside the tower, barely sufficient to see each step before he forced her upwards. The tower smelled like she had imagined: of stone impregnated with the patina of years. She tried to ignore the traces of scent left by the recent visitors, it spoiled the experience she was creating in her imagination. Phoebe felt excited, would the dragon be waiting for her at the top? As they approached the last stairs, the sky was revealed as a grey rectangle. A metal trapdoor had been left open in readiness for the next group of able-bodied tourists fit enough to climb the spiral and then lever themselves up onto the viewing platform. William reluctantly released her arm before glaring at her suspiciously in case she tried going back down the stairs.

"Stay there." He spoke to her as if to a dog before levering himself up onto the circular walkway. Phoebe stayed where she was, rubbing her arm where he'd been gripping so hard. There was a statue on top of the monument, she had seen it as he'd dragged her towards the entrance. The figure looked strange from this angle, foreshortened. She craned her neck to try and see around William's arms that stretched towards her.

"Hold on!"

Phoebe raised her arms into the air like a child waiting to be dressed. William grabbed her wrists, pulling her up bodily onto the viewing platform where they both staggered like drunks until regaining their balance. William slammed the trapdoor shut with a heavy metal finality, blocking any exit and leaving them both trapped in a circular prison in the sky.

Phoebe stared open-mouthed at the long silver finger of Loch Shiel, nestling between the still-green flanks of the surrounding hills. Grey cotton wall clouds pressed down, hiding the mountaintops under a veil of slowly shifting eiderdown.

"Look, isn't it beautiful?" Phoebe's voice startled him, so gentle a sound at complete odds to the violence he felt running through his veins, the immolating fire burning his mind from within. William hadn't even realised that she could speak. She had been silent, not even a cry of pain as he'd manhandled her into the van. She stood holding onto the inadequate safety rail that deterred visitors from falling off the platform, her dark eyes huge as they drank in the view. Phoebe breathed in each breath as if it might be her last, tasting the scents like a wild animal, running the tip of her tongue around her lips. She closed her eyes, arching back her neck to let the soft wind play in her hair, feeling the caress of the wind on her cheeks.

This was the perfect moment. William gripped the knife more firmly, angling the curved blade so it could slice her exposed neck. His hand trembled as the blade came within millimetres of her olive skin. Now! DO IT NOW!

Phoebe's eyes opened, unconcerned about the knife or the madness in the man wielding it.

"Isn't this just perfect?" She spoke with the simplicity of the innocent.

He froze as her eyes sought his, the knife falling uselessly away. This was never how it was meant to be. She should be crying, begging for her life, screaming for the mercy he wouldn't offer.

Phoebe smiled at him, so happy to be at the top of her stone tower where she had always dreamt she belonged – nothing could ever be as good as this.

In the distance William could hear an undulating police siren approaching; the panic and confusion building inside him until he felt he was going to explode. His mind was churning so fast that not a single thought could find purchase in the maelstrom in his head. William stared from Phoebe to the knife, from Phoebe to the trapdoor, from the sky to the ground; he listened to God and the devil inside him.

Phoebe gazed upon paradise.

CHAPTER 42
Glenfinnan

Hamish's slow voice came over the radio as Corstophine and Frankie approached Glenfinnan, weaving around cars and coaches too inept to clear the road in front of an approaching siren.

"I've had reports of a postman with a knife holding a woman captive at Glenfinnan Monument, sir."

"Thanks, Hamish, we're just arriving there now. Tell the firearms unit to meet us here – I think we've found our gunman." Corstophine pulled into the car park, catching sight of tourists gathering around the tower and the tell-tale sign of camera flashes angled upwards.

"There, sir, at the top!" Frankie had spotted two figures outlined against the sky on the viewing platform.

"Hamish, call the Royal Hotel and ask them if Sharmila Mallick is available and if she is, ask her to meet us here at the monument as quickly as she can. I think we may have a hostage situation."

Corstophine killed the siren, barely listening to Hamish's response as he opened the Land Rover door and stood looking up at the monument.

"Do we go up, sir?" Frankie stood next to him, slipping a pair of handcuffs into her pocket.

The tour guide approached, face still indignant at being accosted. "He took my key at knifepoint and locked the door!" The fear he'd felt had turned to anger; he pointed in the direction of the monument as if they needed directions.

"Is there a spare key" Frankie asked.

They both tore their eyes from the static figures at the top of the tower to look at the guide.

"At the centre. All the spare keys are at the centre." The finger swivelled like a weathervane to point over the road to the equally obvious visitor centre.

"Whatever keys are needed to get inside and up to the top, I need them, as quickly as you can. A young woman's life is in danger!" Corstophine spoke urgently, his focus returning to the two figures standing as close as lovers.

The tour guide stared blankly for a second until Frankie indicated for him to move with an impatient tilt of her head. He took off then, half-running until lost in the growing throng heading towards the tower. The crowd's excitement was palpable, urgent voices rising in volume until they resembled an agitated wasp's nest. Corstophine spotted a new wave of people exiting the visitor centre and moving towards them in search of fresh entertainment.

"We'll have to do something about this lot." He frowned at the gawping voyeurs, beside themselves to be involved in a real drama on their holidays.

"Frankie. Go over to the visitor centre, tell them to send as many of their staff as they can over here to help clear the car park, shut the bloody place down if they have to! We need the area cleared and cordoned off. You'd better check if the ambulance and fire brigade are on their way as well." Corstophine squinted up at the figures on top of the tower, cursing his eyesight. What if William Keir still had a gun?

"And radio through to the firearms unit. He may still be armed."

"Sir!" Frankie ran in the same direction the tour guide had taken seconds before, shouting at people to leave the car park as she went. The crowd backed away from her as she approached, then pressed forward again like mindless zombies.

Corstophine marched towards the tower, casting anxious glances at William and Phoebe. They stood frozen in place, the blade in William's hand too far away to be seen, except by the glint of reflected light as it caught the grey sky.

"Move back. Police. Back away." His shouts were ineffective. "Everyone outside the perimeter wall, he may be armed!"

The sudden realisation that this wasn't a movie and that they might be in danger persuaded those nearest the tower to back off. There was a sudden rush to leave the hexagonal stone courtyard that enclosed the monument, a small crush of bodies occurring at each of the exit points. Corstophine stood in the newly cleared space, onlookers forming a ragged perimeter on the other side of the low boundary wall and holding their phones in anticipation for the next act.

"William Keir. This is DI James Corstophine, you can talk to me. Can I call you William?" He shouted up at the statue of the unknown Highlander, hoping the sound of his voice would carry.

William looked down at him from the castellated circular wall, leaning over the metal barrier that reached just above his waist.

"Leave us alone! I'll kill her if you try anything!"

"Phoebe is innocent, William. I know the full story. It was just an accident. A terrible accident."

William shook his head. These were just words.

"I don't believe you. Leave us alone or I'll kill her now. I've got a knife, I mean it!" William waved the curved blade at Corstophine, letting him see it clearly.

"Don't do anything stupid, William, we can sort this

out. No-one else needs to get hurt." Corstophine searched beyond the crowd, trying to spot Frankie. The press of people was increasing with every passing minute, cars slowing on the main road in response to the unusual activity at the monument.

"You're one of the Black Mourners." Phoebe's voice floated down to him from her stone eyrie.

Corstophine looked up so quickly he felt a nerve twinge in his neck. The girl must have climbed up onto something as her body now leaned dangerously over the safety rail, quizzical dark eyes taking in the crowds. An expectant hush fell over the onlookers, their collective breaths held for the inevitable fall.

"Jesus, can't we do something?" Frankie's breathless voice announced her return.

"Get down from there, Phoebe, it's not safe!" Even as Corstophine shouted, the irony of his words hit home. Safe would be anywhere other than on top of that tower with a man who wanted to kill her.

William spotted her at the same time, switching his attention from Corstophine, and he flung himself at Phoebe with a mindless roar. They watched helplessly as he collided with her, saw her body jerk under the violence of the contact, and waited impotently for her to tip over the tower railing to certain death. The audience let loose a collective sigh of relief as they saw Phoebe being dragged back to the relative safety of the tower.

Up on the platform William held Phoebe close, her body as light as a rag doll in his arms. He felt the warmth of her, smelt her scent. It was so much like holding onto his own daughter he could not have released her if he tried.

Phoebe stood unresisting, pulled into the postman's body. She heard the crowd's pent-up fear escape as a single breath and their voices increasing in volume like a swarm of approaching insects. The postman was crying. Huge racking sobs tore his body as he convulsed. Phoebe followed her instincts, releasing her arms from his shaking hold and placing them around his shoulders.

"There, there." She'd played this game with her toys in a time before time, cuddling them, holding them close, giving them the love that her mother never gave her. It had been Patricia who had taught her how to hold and be held; how to be loved and give love in return. It was a lesson the years of drugs and isolation had never been able to eradicate. Over his shoulder she could see a single shaft of golden sunlight shine like a spotlight on the mountains. She wished the postman could see it too, but his head was buried deep in her shoulder in search of the impossible.

Down on the ground, Corstophine and Frankie grabbed the only chance they might have to unlock the door unseen. The noise of the crowd was increasing all the time, aided by those on the periphery who resented being told to clear the area by the visitor centre staff. In the growing hubbub and confusion, Corstophine twisted the key in the old lock and opened the door.

"See if you can distract him whilst I try and get to the top." Corstophine's urgent whisper fluttered around the inside of the stone tower like a moth. He started up the spiral staircase, treading softly to avoid alerting William to his approach.

Frankie returned to her vantage point outside. She could make out the two bodies joined together. Was he knifing her, holding her body as it bled to death in his arms? Her heart was in her mouth as she waited for Corstophine to reach the top.

Two sirens approached, a fire engine and ambulance

competing with each other for volume as they doppler-shifted closer and turned into the car park. Horns added a new note to the cacophony, forcing a path through the crowd of onlookers reluctant to lose their vantage point. Frankie attracted the fire tender driver's attention and beckoned them urgently towards her.

"What have we got?" The lead fireman had run from his vehicle, eyes taking in the two bodies on the top of the tower, the cleared space underneath.

"He's taken a young woman hostage. I don't know if he's hurt her but he's got a knife, maybe a gun. DI Corstophine's inside, making his way to the top. Have you something to break a fall or ladders that can reach the top?"

The fireman considered the tower's height, glancing from the top back down to the ground several times as if lining up a difficult drop kick. "I don't think the ladders will reach. We'd need the extended reach tender from Inverness."

"What about a safety blanket or something to catch them?" Frankie asked in desperation.

The fireman shook his head as his team gathered around him. "The only place where firemen use blankets to catch people is in the Beano – maybe back in the 80's but not now. There's more chance of a fireman getting injured than saving anyone jumping from height." They stood in a small circle, looking up at the tower. "Are they going to jump?"

Frankie gave him a look that would have withered a lesser mortal. "How do I know?" She took a calming breath. "Isn't there anything you can do?"

The firemen huddled closer, exchanging ideas and just as quickly deciding they wouldn't work. All the time they kept a watchful eye on the tower, just in case a body came down.

Frankie thought furiously. Corstophine must have reached the top by now, why hadn't he appeared? The crowd was being reluctantly ushered away by a small group of National Trust shopworkers. She spotted the tour guide amongst them and ran over to talk to him.

"Do the steps lead right up to the top, or is there another barrier or door to get through?"

The guide was perspiring, either from the running back and forth or from waving his arms energetically at tourists unwilling to leave. "There's a trapdoor at the top, you have to lever yourself up the last bit. It's not locked, there's never any need to."

Frankie ran back to the quorum of firemen, a plan forming in her head. If the trapdoor was shut, then Corstophine needed a diversion before he could open it without attracting William Keir's attention.

"Put your ladder up against the tower and make it as obvious as you can."

The lead fireman looked doubtful. "It won't reach to the viewing platform, it's about four metres short." He explained as if he was talking to a child, using his arms to describe an unattainable gap.

"I know." Frankie made a herculean attempt to keep calm. "I need to divert his attention."

The firemen looked doubtful but went back to their appliance parked outside the stone wall surrounding the tower. Whilst Frankie watched, the sound of the ladder turntable extending towards the tower was almost immediately drowned out by the siren starting up.

Up on the tower William let go of Phoebe, disentangling her arms to look over the side of the monument. The firemen were all action, running around and manning the ladder turntable which was already stretching towards them. Phoebe clapped her hands in excitement as she joined him. Postmen and firemen on the same day! A white ambulance parked near the fire engine added to the carnival.

"Firemen!" Phoebe exclaimed, holding William's arm in her excitement.

Hesitating under the trapdoor, Corstophine realised what Frankie was doing and cautiously opened the trapdoor. William stood mere metres away, his back to him as he leaned over the railing. Corstophine did a double take as he saw Phoebe hold onto William's arm, gesticulating at the scene underneath them in her excitement.

It was now or never. The trapdoor opened easily enough, but he had to strain as the weight threatened to drop onto the platform floor. It landed with a clang, just as Corstophine launched himself at William and reached for the knife.

William spun around at the sound of the trapdoor hitting the ground as Corstophine rushed him. The knife struck out in an automatic reflex, blade slicing at Corstophine's arm and cutting through jacket and flesh. Sheer momentum carried him into William, their bodies slamming against the guard rail. Corstophine realised he'd been wounded, the sting of lacerated flesh turning warmly wet under his sleeve.

William attempted to pull his knife hand free as they wrestled to the ground. Corstophine's hand was clamped onto his wrist and holding the knife at bay, but he was weakening by the second. God, the guy was strong! Corstophine could feel blood dripping down his sleeve, making his grip slippery as he held desperately onto William's knife arm. If that was an artery he didn't have much time before he bled out. Phoebe started screaming at the top of her voice.

Down at ground level, Frankie saw the knife plunge into Corstophine's side before the two men collided and fell. Without further thought she ran into the tower, powering up the stairs. The sound of Phoebe's wavering scream echoed down the stone steps and added fresh impetus to her legs. She reached the trapdoor to see William straddling Corstophine, his forearm pressing down on Corstorphine's neck and free hand raising the knife to strike at his blood-spattered face. Even as Frankie levered herself onto the platform, Phoebe lunged for the knife and held onto William's arm with all her strength.

"No more. Please let him go. Please." She started sobbing even as William tried to shake her free, the knife slicing air much too close to her face.

Frankie joined the fray, pulling William's knife arm so far back behind his back that he twisted awkwardly, allowing Corstophine to get out from underneath the arm that had been pressing down on his windpipe. Between them, Frankie somehow managed to cuff his knife hand, the weapon falling uselessly onto the stone platform. Corstophine held the newly cuffed arm behind William's back until Frankie was able to cuff his other wrist.

"Are you alright, sir?" Frankie asked fearfully, not sure how badly Corstophine had been wounded.

Corstophine saw the blood soaking his sleeve, dripping in a steady stream from his outstretched fingers.

"He might have hit an artery, there's a fair bit of blood in my sleeve. Best leave it for the medics." He panted from the exertion.

Corstophine's face was pale, she could see that he needed medical assistance. Frankie quickly checked that Phoebe was alright. She had stopped screaming and now just stood there like a mannequin, fascinated at the blood dripping from Corstophine's sleeve. William lay face down and unresponsive on the platform floor. It took her a second to realise the sounds he was making were sobs.

"I'll keep him down." Corstophine stood over the postman, holding his wounded arm above his head to reduce the flow of blood.

Frankie leant over the rail and shouted at the ambulance crew to beckon them up. "The DI's been wounded, get up here now!" She shouted to make herself heard over the siren, watching to make sure the medics had understood before turning back to Corstophine – her eyes taking in the blood pooling on the floor.

"Don't worry about me, look after the girl." Corstophine spoke tersely, his attention focussed on William's inert body.

The sound of the two approaching medics convinced her. She briefly nodded to him, checked that William didn't look as if he was in any mood to kick off again and went to comfort Phoebe.

CHAPTER 43
Dragon Slain

Whatever fight had been in William had been extinguished. He allowed himself to be led down the spiral staircase like a docile child, accompanied by a couple of the larger firemen who took positions above and below him as he descended. Corstophine climbed through the trapdoor as best as he could, his wounded arm held close to his body. Frankie followed with Phoebe, guiding her down after Corstophine. As they exited the tower Frankie was relieved to see PCs McAdam and Lamb running towards them. She shook her head at PC Lamb, his hand reluctantly leaving the ever-present Taser on his belt.

"Take him into custody." Frankie stood in front of William, waiting until he raised his head at the sound of her voice, his eyes wet with tears. "William Keir, I'm arresting you for the abduction of Phoebe McCoach and assaulting a police officer in the execution of his duty. You do not have to say anything, but it may harm your defence if you do not mention when questioned something which you later rely on in court. Anything you do say may be given in evidence."

PCs Lamb and McAdam held William in a firm grip, heading back to the patrol car. "Tell the firearms unit to stand down," Frankie called after them. She was about to ask for an update on what they'd found at the bothy, but Corstophine's sharp cry of pain stopped her.

The ambulance crew had removed the emergency

tourniquet they'd fitted high on Corstophine's arm, cutting the sleeve off his jacket to reveal a deep red slice up his bicep. His blood started flowing again in earnest before the medics applied another bandage, and Frankie watched him for long enough to reassure herself that he was going to be alright before turning her attention back to the girl.

Phoebe stood watching the medics as they wrapped a white bandage around Corstophine's arm, curious eyes drinking in the scene. For a young woman who had been abducted and just witnessed the violence at the top of the tower, she appeared completely at peace, almost serene. If it hadn't been for the banshee scream she had made from the tower, Frankie would have thought her untroubled by the day's events.

"Can I help?" A woman had approached Corstophine, laying what Frankie considered a proprietorial hand gently on his shoulder as the medics continued bandaging.

"Hello again." Corstophine smiled weakly at her. "I think we've got it all under control, thanks, Sharmila."

The woman offered Frankie a fleeting smile before focussing on Phoebe.

"Is she alright?"

Frankie realised the question Sharmila had issued was directed at her.

"I'm sorry, who are you?" She felt as if she'd missed something, who this woman was, what her connection was to Corstophine.

Corstophine spoke up. "Frankie, this is Dr Sharmila Mallick. She's here to offer her forensic psychologist expertise."

Frankie remembered the name. Corstophine had asked Hamish to try and contact her as they drove into the Glenfinnan car park. The woman left Corstophine's side and stood in front of Phoebe, her hand stretching out in slow motion to rest on Phoebe's shoulder.

"Are you OK, love?" Her voice was low and soft, the sort of voice you might use when trying to calm a wild animal.

Phoebe's eyes followed the hand as it lay on her shoulder, then met with Sharmila's.

"I was at the top of the tower." Phoebe's eyes were wide and wondering, leaving Sharmila to gaze up at the statue of the anonymous Highlander above them, smiling wryly over the calm waters of Loch Shiel. "He slew the dragon." She said this with impassive finality, closing a chapter on her life.

"Come on, love, I'll go home with you, if that's OK?" Sharmila directed the question at Corstophine and Frankie.

Corstophine glanced down at his newly fitted white bandage, already staining red. "I'll be off in the ambulance, Frankie. I think this will need a few stiches. Can you and Sharmila take Phoebe back to the station in the Land Rover and I'll see you there as soon as I can?"

He directed his next comment directly to Sharmila. "If you've the time, can you check her over?"

Sharmila nodded, aware of what Corstophine was asking. She had picked up enough of Phoebe's story to have concerns, and the girl's apparent lack of reaction to the violence of the last few hours was reason enough for her to want a closer look.

One of the firemen had joined them, holding a bloodied knife towards Frankie.

"Left this up there, love. I thought it would be safer with you."

Frankie retrieved a latex glove from her pocket, slipping it on before gingerly taking the bloodstained handle. "Thanks." She exchanged a tight smile with him, catching the absence of any ring on his hand. *Well, isn't this romantic?* The thought that followed that observation was banished as quickly as it had appeared, but she watched his departure with a lingering eye.

The ambulance left for the hospital with its siren now silent. Behind her, the fire crew attended to their vehicle. Snatches of conversation and laughter came her way as they dealt with the aftermath as they knew best. She headed towards the Land Rover, looking back over her shoulder at the two women.

"Come on, Phoebe, let's get you somewhere nice and warm." Sharmila climbed alongside Phoebe on the back seat, helping her on with a seatbelt, whilst Frankie dropped the blood-spattered knife into an evidence bag.

"You've not been harmed, have you, Phoebe?" Frankie caught the girl's eye in the rear-view mirror as she started the engine. She'd been so involved in dealing with William and Corstophine that the girl had been all but ignored. Phoebe certainly didn't appear to have any injuries.

"I'm fine, thanks." Her voice sounded as calm as she looked, relaxed in the back seat and looking for all the world as if she'd been enjoying every last minute.

"I think we're good." Sharmila commented from the back. "He didn't hurt you in any way?" She interrogated Phoebe, using the same quiet tone she'd used when she'd first approached her.

"No." She looked out of the window as they moved off. The more persistent tourists held mobiles up to them as they passed by, following their progress with panning arms. "He's sad."

"Who's sad, Phoebe?" Sharmila asked in such a low voice Frankie had to struggle to hear her over the noise of the diesel engine.

"The postman. He's sad because he's lost his girl. He told me."

"He may be sad but that doesn't excuse what he did, taking you away and threatening you up there."

Phoebe laughed happily. Frankie caught glimpses of her in the mirror as she drove.

"Silly, he wouldn't hurt me!" Phoebe answered with conviction, the laughter still evident in her response.

"Why do you say that?" Sharmila was analysing her responses, treating her as a patient.

"Because he loved her." Her face turned serious. "He held me when he cried," she stated simply. "I reminded him of his daughter. He couldn't hurt me, not then." She returned to her contemplation of the road, completely unconcerned.

Sharmila watched Phoebe closely, trying to reconcile the psychopath she had expected with the empathic young woman sat beside her.

"Phoebe, do you hear voices in your head?"

Phoebe turned away from her contemplation of the moving scenery, head tilted towards Sharmila.

"I used to." She swung her head around as if to hear more clearly. "No, they've gone away now." She searched Sharmila's face, saw compassion and understanding and decided she could be trusted. She whispered quietly so Frankie couldn't hear. "They went away when I stopped taking the tablets."

"How long, Phoebe? How many days since you stopped taking the medication?"

Phoebe considered. It wasn't easy counting days when they were all the same. "A lot," she said simply.

"I see." Sharmila watched her face, searched for guile or any hint that Phoebe was having an internal conversation. "That's good. That's good, Phoebe."

Phoebe beamed at her, delighted to have received any praise at all, then returned to watching the world speed by.

"I need to give her some tests." This was directed at Frankie.

"She'll have to be returned back home if there's no medical treatment required." Frankie wanted her delivered back safely to the McCoach house as soon as possible. There were going to be two prisoners at the station needing processing and she was still worried about Corstophine. He'd lost a lot of blood. The viewing platform had been slick with it when they left.

"This *is* a medical reason." Sharmila spoke in an authoritative voice. "I don't believe Phoebe needs the medication she's been on, and once I've worked out what they've been giving her and for how long, I'll be in a better position to make a diagnosis. In the meantime, I want to take her in for observation."

"I don't know if I can let you just take her..."

"Do you really want me to spell this out? I suspect this young woman has been clinically misdiagnosed as a young child and then repeatedly submitted to a regime of drugs that she should never have been given in the first place." Sharmila spared a quick glance towards Phoebe, satisfied she was unconcerned about their discussing her immediate future in front of her. "Someone, or some people, may have been guilty of an incorrect psychiatric diagnosis, then perpetuating that wrong diagnosis ever since. Whatever her assessment results are, she may require years of remedial counselling and specialist care to undo the harm that's been done. Home is the last place she needs to go."

Frankie thought hard. If Phoebe went back to Emma, then chances were she would be imprisoned back in her bedroom. It was fairly obvious from talking with Patricia that Emma had minimal maternal instincts towards either child, and the private nurses would ensure Phoebe took her drugs once they realised she'd been fooling them.

"Where do you propose taking her?" Frankie played for time, the decision too complex for any snap decision.

Sharmila delayed answering. There weren't that many options, and the one that was easiest for her might not work out best for Phoebe.

"If I can take her back with me, to the hospital …?"

"Carstairs? Once you're in there, they never let you out! That's what I've heard." Frankie decided this wasn't going to happen.

"It's true we have patients in there that should be back home or in less secure hospitals. That's the fault of an underfunded health service, not down to us. We get used as a dumping ground for anyone who's found to have behavioural problems that can lead to self-harm or be a danger to others." She paused, realising she wasn't selling Carstairs as an attractive option.

"Look, a lot of the patients we have to look after have been sent to us by the courts. The system is broken, we all know it. The doctors and psychiatric staff such as myself have said time and time again that sending kids with ADHD or similar disorders to an institution such as Carstairs only causes them to deteriorate further. I promise you, Frankie, I'll not let that happen to Phoebe. She needs care, we both know it, and this is the only way I know to get her seen immediately – before they drug her again."

Frankie didn't know what to do. She understood the rationale, even supported what Sharmila wanted to do, but how did this stand legally?

"OK, we'll go to the station and you can call for an ambulance, but I'll have to obtain the agreement of her mother or Robb before I can let her go."

Sharmila nodded in acceptance. "I just want to help." She focussed attention back on Phoebe. If she was unmedicated and rational, Phoebe was old enough to make her own decisions.

Frankie drove on. She would try and contact Corstophine. It was his call.

CHAPTER 44
Rosmary, That's For?

Corstophine left the hospital after his wound had been cleaned and stitched, clutching a paper bag containing painkillers and antibiotics. He'd managed to grab a lift with an ambulance, one advantage of the ambulance station sharing the same complex as the police on the industrial estate. Corstophine headed straight for the cells when he reached the station, waving aside Hamish's concerns about his injury and calling it 'just a flesh wound'. He wasn't sure if the sergeant had seen any Monty Python, but he appeared reassured at Corstophine's passing remark. William Keir was curled into a foetal position on the cell floor, unmoving. He watched him for long enough to detect his chest rise and fall, then moved on to see Weasel flat out on his bed, snoring.

Returning to his office and acknowledging the two PCs' congratulations, he opened his office door to find Phoebe sitting peacefully at his desk, drawing on a notepad under Sharmila's watchful eye.

"How are you feeling?" Sharmila asked the question before Frankie had a chance to speak.

"My arm's a bit sore where the stitches went in. They hurt more than the knife." He smiled grimly, seeing the relief in both women's faces. "What's with William Keir? He's curled up in his cell as if he's catatonic. Did he give you a statement?"

Frankie and Sharmila exchanged a meaningful look.

"Come on, out with it." Corstophine knew something was up, he just couldn't work out what.

Frankie opened. "No, sir, he's not said a word since we arrested him." She looked towards Sharmila with an air of desperation.

This was a new double act. Corstophine's eyebrow started rising. "What's up?"

Sharmila motioned towards the door, her eyes indicating Phoebe. "I think we should discuss this outside your office."

They left Phoebe contentedly drawing on her pad, oblivious to her surroundings.

"I believe William is suffering from a brief psychotic episode," Sharmila volunteered.

"What does that mean, exactly?" He felt his patience wearing thin. The pain in his arm and the adrenaline-fuelled fight on the top of the tower were beginning to exact a toll.

"It's not unknown for someone who's suffered from extreme stress or trauma to develop temporary psychosis. The death of his daughter may have been the trigger, especially if he's been under stress for months beforehand." Sharmila spread her hands like a supplicant. "What it means is that William has not been functioning rationally. He may exhibit paranoia or believe things that aren't real."

Corstophine didn't like the sound of where this was going. "Are you telling me he's insane?"

Sharmila pursed her lips. "William gives every indication of suffering from psychosis. His wild mood swings or the way he's behaving now, curled in a ball on the floor of the cell."

Frankie interrupted. "What Sharmila is saying, sir, is that in her clinical judgement we can't hold William Keir accountable for the crimes he's committed."

"You know he's going to be charged with murder?" Corstophine's exasperation was clear. A gash in his arm, a kidnapped girl, at least two murders and two grievous body assaults. "Unless I'm completely mistaken, it will be his prints and DNA at the scene of Patricia's attack and Tunstall's murder. Now I've locked him in a cell, you're presenting me with a get out of jail card?"

"I've raised a section order on William, and he'll be taken to Carstairs for treatment." Sharmila touched his shoulder. "If my diagnosis is confirmed then a murder conviction wouldn't hold against a plea for temporary insanity. He needs help, James, not a prison cell." She glanced through the office window at Phoebe, still busy with her drawing. "They both need help."

Corstophine's arm was beginning to hurt in earnest now where the muscle had been cut. He crossed over to the kitchen, leaving the two women outside his office, and struggled to release a painkiller from its packaging. As he chased it down with a glass of water, he considered his options. He could keep William locked up, interview him and present a winning case to the Procurator Fiscal, or let Sharmila take him off to Carstairs state hospital for assessment and treatment. If he was confirmed to be in a psychotic state, then that's where he'd probably end up anyway. He returned to the two women, his arm aching in its sling.

"OK, let's get William seen to by the professionals. Are your ambulance crew equipped to deal with someone who can turn violent?"

Sharmila gave him a look that reminded him so strongly of his wife that he had to tell himself this wasn't her. "I think you'll find our staff are equipped to deal with the most violent individuals society can offer, yes."

That was stupid. Corstophine held up his good hand in

acceptance. "Frankie, can you put the transfer paperwork in place?"

Frankie left them to sit at her desk, exchanging comments with the two constables as they discussed the events of the last few hours.

"What about Phoebe?" Corstophine watched the young woman through the glass, busy drawing at his desk.

"I'm not happy about her returning home." Sharmila hesitated. "If she's put back onto anti-psychotic drugs and sedatives, she'll just deteriorate. Phoebe needs a completely fresh assessment by someone who knows what they're doing."

"Someone like you?" Corstorphine ventured.

She gave him a tight smile. "Anyone other than whoever's been responsible for her so-called care up to now."

Hamish interrupted, calling over from his front desk position. "That's Robb McCoach arrived, sir. Shall I bring him through?"

"Thanks, Hamish, I'll see him in the interview room." He turned back to Sharmila, "Can you sit with Phoebe for a while until I've seen Robb?"

"Of course, take as long as you need."

Corstophine took his seat in the interview room, watching as Robb hobbled into sight. He was leaning heavily on an NHS walking stick, foot immobile in a bandage.

He lowered himself awkwardly onto a chair, his bandaged foot stretched out to one side.

"Can I get you anything to drink, Robb?" Corstophine registered the hand holding onto the stick was also heavily bandaged.

"I'm fine. How's Phoebe, where is she?" His words were urgent, worry written on his face.

Corstophine interrupted, catching Hamish as he made

slow progress out of the room. "Can you ask Frankie to join us?"

Robb's bandaged hands clenched on the table, his patience exhausted.

"Phoebe's fine, Robb. She's here, in my office with a psychologist. She's being checked over but she hasn't been hurt."

"What about Sandy, did you manage to reach him in time?"

Corstophine nodded. "The constables managed to call in the air ambulance." He shot Robb a brief smile, "I think Sandy is going to be OK. They told me the bullet went straight through and clipped the bone. He's lost a lot of blood but it doesn't look as if any major organs were hit."

"Who's been doing this? Have you caught anyone?"

"We have someone in custody, yes. I don't think you need to worry about being attacked anymore."

Robb collapsed in his chair as if a massive weight had been taken off his shoulders. "Thank God. Thank you, Jim. Thanks for everything." The relief was quickly followed by a desperate urge to know who it was they had arrested.

"I'd rather not say, for the moment. Not until we've had a chance to process the prisoner."

Frankie joined them, taking the seat alongside the DI and shooting him an enquiring glance.

"Do you mind if I record this conversation, Robb, just so I have something to refer back to if necessary?"

Robb acquiesced, puzzled as to why Corstophine needed to question him.

"I want to know more about the bottled water your father took with him the day of his heart attack."

"What about it? I made several flavours of water for him to taste. He always found something that wasn't right about them, too strongly flavoured or too bitter. He didn't see that offering flavoured Highland water could be a commercial success."

"Do you have any other samples of the same flavoured water? The same batch that your father's bottle came from?"

Robb blew his cheeks out in a way that reminded Frankie of his aunt. "No, I make around six bottles every batch, but the cleaner had been in and cleared all the other bottles out."

Corstophine made a note in his pad. "What flavour was this one?"

"Rosemary. Why are you asking me this? You don't think I'm the one who poisoned my own father?" Robb's voice increased in anger.

Corstophine held up a hand to forestall him. "I don't think that at all, Robb. We're just trying to find out what happened, how it could have happened. You said rosemary flavoured water, that's a bit strange, isn't it?"

Robb sighed in exasperation. He was desperate to see Phoebe and irritated at having to sit through these inane questions. This was a repeat of the conversation he'd had with his parents as they tore his ideas to pieces. "Rosemary has many beneficial uses. It can be drunk as a tea, or as an infusion. Its antioxidant properties are well-known, but now medical science is beginning to suspect it may be of use against some types of cancer. There's evidence it slows many age-related illnesses, protecting eyesight, brain function, it may even help with weight loss."

Corstophine looked impressed. "How do you go about making rosemary flavoured water?"

Robb looked at the detective to see if he was humouring him. Corstophine appeared genuinely interested, so Robb continued.

"You take the leaves and either boil them in water or soak them in alcohol to release the essential oils. I have a supply of alcohol that I was going to use for gin production, so I steeped the leaves in that before passing them through the still to concentrate the oils. Then it's just a case of adding the concentrate to the spring water until it tastes right."

"Did you taste that particular batch, the one your father took in the bottle?"

"I taste all the finished flavours otherwise how do I know if they're any good?" His eyes widened to express how stupid a question it was.

"What happens to the leaves when you've finished?" Corstophine continued probing.

Frankie started to take more interest in proceedings, she could see where the DI was going with this.

"I throw them out." Robb couldn't understand why Corstophine was labouring the point.

"Where? Can I find the used leaves in a bin, or compost heap?"

Robb thought for a minute. He never cleared up after himself, that's what the cleaner was for.

"I suppose they go on the compost heap. The cleaner sorts all that out."

"Thanks, Robb." Corstophine made to close the interview down. "One last thing. Who else has access to your distillery?"

"Well, the cleaner. In fact, I wish she wasn't so efficient. I never would have wanted her to scrub down all the equipment and throw out my samples. God knows what was in her head when she used bleach on the still. I'm still not sure if I'll ever be able to use it again." He returned to the original question. "My parents as well, they both know where the key's kept."

Corstophine finished writing his notes and formally closed the interview and recording. "Thank you, Robb – let's take you to see your sister."

He led Robb to his office, keeping him focussed away from the crazy board.

"Phoebe! You're safe, thank God!" He threw his arms around his sister then rocked back onto his one good foot in surprise as she spoke.

"Hello, Robb. Have you had an exciting day as well?"

"You said something!" He stared around Corstophine's office in astonishment. "She hasn't spoken for years!"

Sharmila introduced herself. "There's something you ought to know about your sister, Robb, and the treatment she's had. Then I think we'd better speak to your mother." Corstophine noticed a hard tone enter her voice that he'd not heard before.

They returned to the McCoach house, Frankie driving the Land Rover this time with Corstophine sitting beside her with his arm in a sling. In the back, Robb sat awkwardly with his bandaged foot stretched out and an incredulous expression as the previously silent Phoebe chatted her stream of consciousness to everyone.

Emma's car was back in the drive when they arrived back at the big house, and Sharmila marched purposely towards the door with Robb and Phoebe following more slowly in her wake.

"Do we need to go in there with her, sir?" Frankie asked doubtfully.

"No need, Frankie, I think Sharmila is more than capable of handling Emma on her own."

Frankie observed the DI out of the corner of her eye, seeing him focussed on Sharmila as she walked away. Frankie smiled to herself, that was a look on his face she'd not seen for a while.

Corstophine waited until she was lost to view before turning towards the craft distillery. "Right, Frankie, have a look for a pile of rosemary leaves, anything that might have been thrown out by an overzealous cleaner."

Frankie found a small pile of thin, needle-like leaves on top of a compost heap at the back of the shed, carefully scooping them into an evidence bag with a gloved hand as Corstophine watched.

"Time to have these looked at, Frankie."

Chapter 45
Mistaken Identity

Corstophine sat at his desk, typing up the report on the McCoach case. It had been three days since the events that had taken place at the Glenfinnan monument and his arm was still sore. He had dispensed with the sling they'd given him, some hours after leaving hospital, following the doctor's strict advice to go home and drink plenty of fluids and rest. Whether the doctor had expected his fluid of choice to be a 12-year-old single malt was a question Corstophine was content to leave unanswered. His arm itched continually from the fresh scar resembling a red zipper running up his left bicep, and he rubbed at it through the dressing under his shirt to alleviate the itch for another few minutes.

Sharmila's initial clinical report lay on his desk. She had confirmed William Keir's psychosis and had encouraged the full story out of him: the pressure to deliver drugs, the threats against him and his daughter. Sarah's death was almost certainly the final trigger that had sent him on a murderous trail of revenge. He would be held in Carstairs until his trial could be arranged, with a strong probability of being returned there afterwards although Sharmila was hopeful of his making an eventual recovery.

Corstophine sighed heavily. Despite the attacks, and his own injury, he couldn't help but feel sorry for William Keir. The guy had been placed in an impossible situation – if only he had come to them for help. Would they have been able to stop Keith Tunstall and Bryan's murders and Patricia's blinding? Prevent William from having a psychotic episode and exacting his own revenge? Corstophine didn't have an answer. There was only so much they could do.

Weasel had been only too keen to tell them everything he knew, once Corstophine offered to call in a doctor to relieve his withdrawal symptoms. He had identified the individual posties being used for delivering wraps, giving out names like a canary frightened of being sent down a mine. It didn't help him. He still faced a stretch inside for having the drugs and money in his possession. For the time being, his legal had managed to arrange bail, leaving Weasel back home with an electronic tag clamped around his ankle and dreading every knock at the door.

Robb had provided an update on his sister, letting him know she was no longer being administered anti-psychotic drugs. Phoebe was spending a few hours each day in a local unit with people her own age, where she would have the best chance of catching up on the lost years of her life. The rest of the time she lived at home with a dedicated team of therapists and teachers that Robb had arranged, with help from Sharmila. He was just happy to have a sister back that he had thought was lost forever. There had been a few changes at the private healthcare hospital as well. Several senior clinicians and managers were facing disciplinary action. Corstophine suspected Sharmila might have had an involvement although Robb now had a specific interest in the healthcare company – and as a major shareholder he had the clout to make changes. The family solicitor had also been in touch, letting him know that the 20% of shares that had been allocated to Sarah Keir's trust fund were being returned to the family.

Corstophine wondered whether Phoebe would ever manage to become a fully functioning member of society. After so many years of isolation and misdiagnosis she was also a victim in all of this. He never had much time for philosophical constructs, but he could appreciate how the butterfly effect had spread from the thoughtless actions of one child to result in the events of the last week. As far as Corstophine was concerned, Phoebe deserved as much of the McCoach money as she could get, but money was a poor substitute for love.

The one item Corstophine had been unable to bring to a satisfactory conclusion was Jack McCoach's poisoning. He had no doubt his death was a deliberate act of murder, and he had a good idea who was behind it, just no proof.

The phone rang. Corstophine checked the screen and recognised the forensics number straight away.

"Morning, Corstophine. How's your arm today?" The questioner was too cheerful to have any real concerns for his health.

"I'm fine. What have you got?"

"Straight to business, how like a detective. That bag of compost you sent us, rosemary and yew leaves. We looked again at the water bottle analysis and sure enough, there were some compound chemical signatures that indicate rosemary as well. I think you've found the source of your poison."

Corstophine listened impassively. The result wasn't a surprise. "How easy is it, do you imagine, mistaking yew leaves for rosemary?"

There was a pause. "Good question. Once the individual leaves are removed from the stem, and assuming no yew berries are in the mix then yes, they can look quite similar. Not that anyone handling the plants would be likely to make such a mistake, the leaves are quite different in feel and smell, but once softened in boiling water or alcohol then a good case could be made for mistaken identity."

"OK, thanks for your help."

"No problem, glad to help out. I'll send the official report over to you."

"I don't suppose there's any possibility of finding any genetic markers, no way of finding who picked them or handled them?" Corstophine asked hopefully.

"Not now, not when they've been boiled or steeped in alcohol and then distilled down. If you had the fresh leaves then we might have been able to help. Sorry, Corstophine."

He put the phone back down on his desk, rubbing at his arm in irritation and then cursing as the phone rang again.

"Yes, Corstophine. What is it?" His voice held more than a trace of impatience.

"Good morning, this is Chris Mullen from R&T Mutual. Am I speaking to DI Corstophine?"

Corstophine belatedly checked the number, realised it wasn't forensics phoning him back. "Yes, how can I help you?"

"We understand that one of our life assurance policies, one with a Mr Jack McCoach, has flagged up as a suspicious death? I was hoping you may be able to confirm the circumstances as we have to follow an investigative procedure in the event of possible malpractice."

Corstophine's eyebrow took its well-trodden path northwards.

"I can confirm that the cause of his death is under review. Can I ask why you're considering an investigation?"

There was a pause, as if the person on the other end of the line was studying chess pieces brought into play. "He had a life policy taken out by his wife, Emma McCoach, earlier this year. We were about to authorise the transfer of the sum assured when our underwriters advised that a police investigation had been instigated into the circumstances of his death."

"Can I ask how much his life was insured for?"

Another delay. "In strict confidence?"

"Of course." Corstophine replied.

"His life policy pays out £1,000,000 in the event of his death. A policy of this size requires certain criteria to be met, namely death by natural causes." There was the unmistakable sound of a keyboard being used, the random clatter clear down the line. "We were provided with a medical report stating the deceased had died of a heart attack. Is that correct?"

Corstophine's mind was working through the implications of the call. "Yes, that's right, that was the initial finding. Then we discovered evidence to strongly suggest he died of poisoning. Can I get back to you?" He took down details of the caller and promised to send all the relevant paperwork as soon as he could.

He called forensics back immediately. "The autopsy on Jack McCoach. Do you still have his clothes?"

"His clothes? I don't know, I'll see if they've been collected. His family were asked to collect all his personal belongings. Hang on."

Corstophine waited, drumming his fingers on his desk as the phone stayed silent for minute after minute.

"You still there?" Eventually a disembodied query came down the line.

"Yes, do you have any of his clothes still in your possession?" Corstophine almost shouted in his urgency to know.

"Yep, still have his clothes bagged. No-one's bothered to pick them up. Another day and we have the waste disposal van doing a collection so if they don't collect…"

"Test his jacket." Corstophine interrupted. "Test any of

his outer clothes. Wouldn't he have been sick if he'd been poisoned?"

"Well, yes. That's a possibility."

"Good, then test his jacket and trousers to see if there's any vomit. Then tell me if it contains the same poison and do it fast."

Corstophine slammed the phone down, calling through to Frankie to come into his office.

"Sir?" She stood in the doorway, surprised to see the DI so energised.

"The forensics lab still has Jack McCoach's clothes. They're testing them now for any traces of poison."

Frankie made the leap instantly. "That would be definite proof he was poisoned, not just the circumstantial proof from the water bottle!"

"Exactly!" Corstophine looked at her triumphantly.

"And we can tie the poison to the leaves the cleaner tipped behind Robb's shed," Frankie continued. Her face fell, "but it's still circumstantial – there's not enough to put Emma or Robb in the frame."

Corstophine played his trump card. "There is now. I've just had a call from a life assurance company. Emma took out a policy on Jack's life for a million, shortly before he died. She's tried collecting using the original death certificate."

"And conveniently forgot that his cause of death has been updated to suspicious." Frankie filled in.

"I think it's time to have Emma in for questioning, don't you?"

The focus of Corstophine's investigation stood on her doorstep and informed him she was leaving for good. Emma McCoach explained she was moving to Inverness and now was not an opportune time to waste on some fool's errand at the police station, especially whilst she had to oversee the removal men packing her personal items into the van parked on the driveway.

Corstophine listened impassively as a small audience of removal men clustered around them, listening to every word.

"That is inconvenient, and I am sorry, but you'll have to accompany us to the station, Ms McCoach. You can come willingly..." Corstophine left the threat hanging, turning to the assembled removal men. "I think you'd better come back another day, this might take some time."

Emma was almost incoherent with rage. He caught the words 'solicitor' and 'Chief Constable' as he walked a few steps away and left Frankie to hear her out. He selected Robb's number from his contacts.

"Robb? Your mother appears to have arranged a removal van to collect her belongings. I suggest you come straight here and sort out any misunderstandings." He listened as Robb expressed disbelief before having to advise him that his mother was about to be taken in for questioning. "I'm sorry, Robb, but we have a job to do. You can contact the family solicitor to meet us at the station, unless your mother wants to arrange her own legal advice?"

He placed the phone in Emma's hand, ceasing her rant to listen to her son.

The trip back to the police station proceeded in what could only be described as an icy atmosphere. Emma had decided she wasn't going to say a thing until she met with her solicitor, and they left her in stony silence in the interview room

They gave her an hour with the solicitor before Corstophine and Frankie took their seats, waiting for the solicitor to shuffle pages of handwritten notes before allowing the interview to start.

Corstophine ran through the preliminaries.

"Emma McCoach, can you confirm that you took out a life insurance policy on your husband, Jack McCoach, for one million pounds earlier this year?"

Frankie caught the surprised look on the solicitor's face before he was able to conceal it.

"No comment."

"And did you pack Jack's rucksack on the day of his death?"

"No comment."

Corstophine's attention was taken by PC Lamb's face filling the small window in the door, beckoning him out.

"Interview paused at 13:20. DI Corstophine leaving the room." He rose from his chair in irritation. One thing that was guaranteed to piss him off was someone interrupting him during an interview.

"This better be good!"

PC Lamb pointed to reception. "That's Robb McCoach to see you, sir. He said he's got information relevant to Jack McCoach's poisoning. I thought it might be urgent."

"Bring him to my office. And thanks, Phil, you made the right call."

"Thank you, sir." Phil Lamb almost saluted before heading briskly to reception.

Corstophine sat down, scratching his arm until the itching stopped, and watched Robb as he hobbled into the office. He still had the walking stick and the bandaged ankle, but his spare arm clutched his father's urn close to his chest. He looked furious, catching Corstophine's eye with an angry glare.

"What can I do for you, Robb?"

Robb slammed the urn down on Corstophine's desk. "You've got my mother in there?" Robb pointed to the interview room, his finger shaking.

"Yes. I'm sorry, we have to ask her a few questions." Corstophine started to try and calm the situation down.

"She did it!"

"I'm sorry, what are you trying to say?" Corstophine was confused. He'd expected Robb to be angry with him. It was only natural when the police had taken his mother in for questioning.

"Mum gave me the rosemary. She said she'd picked it all herself and put it in a plastic bag." He lifted the lid off the urn, revealing a clear bag containing green needles. "This is what she gave me. It's been mixed with poisonous yew, hasn't it? She made me poison my own father. She could have poisoned me, and now she's trying to clear the house of valuables!"

Corstophine looked from Robb to the inside of the pewter urn.

"This is the bag of rosemary she picked for you?"

"Yes, a few days before he went on the hill walk that killed him. I've just been on the phone to the cleaner. She confirmed Mother told her to throw out the other water bottles I'd filled and then clean everything in the shed with bleach." He looked steadily at the DI. "The cleaner said she's willing to swear in court that Mother gave her specific instructions to clean the distillery equipment and floor."

Corstophine spoke softly. "You realise that if you repeat this under caution it could convict your mother for murder? You do know what you're doing?"

Robb's expression hadn't changed.

"I know what I'm doing, Jim. She's destroyed my life. She's responsible for Phoebe being how she is. She killed my father, and if you hadn't turned up today she would have taken everything she could from the house." He shook his head in disbelief. "If I hadn't asked the removal men to take everything back inside…"

"What do you mean?"

Robb composed himself before replying. "My mother had started filling the van with the most expensive antiques and paintings, that's why I noticed it." They both stared at the brushed pewter urn standing on the table between them, reminding Corstophine of the pub table almost two weeks ago. "She had taken his urn. It made no sense. His ashes weren't in it anymore and Mother isn't one to waste time on sentimentality. When I looked inside the urn, I saw that she'd hidden this bag – waiting for a convenient time to dispose of it, I suppose."

Corstophine nodded, holding onto his aching arm. "Stay here, Robb. I'll have to ask one of the constables to sit with you, otherwise you'll have to wait out in reception, is that alright?"

"Aye." His head bent down towards Corstophine's desk before the tears showed. "I just want it over."

Back in the interview room, Corstophine repeated her son's allegations to cause the maximum impact. Emma attempted to brave it out whilst her solicitor looked more and more uncomfortable before eventually recusing himself, stating possible conflict of interest.

It was all over at that point. Corstophine knew it and so did Emma. Hamish led her to the cells until they could find alternative legal representation. In the interim, Robb gave a full statement and identified the bag of innocuous-looking green needles as those supplied by his mother.

It was almost too easy in the end. Forensics found vomit on Jack McCoach's jacket which contained the same poisons as the water left in Jack's plastic bottle. They found sufficient DNA traces on the needles and plastic bag to state with a high enough probability that they'd been handled by Emma, tying her into the supply of the yew leaves mixed with rosemary. The cleaner confirmed Robb's statement that Emma had insisted she clean the craft distillery with bleach and confirmed the location where she'd dumped the botanicals, behind the shed.

Emma made a last desperate attempt to avoid prosecution by putting her own son in the frame, but it was her greed and the life assurance policy that proved her undoing. It would only be a matter of due legal process before Emma was convicted and given life. As a result, she faced being struck out of the Will. Corstophine thought there must be a moral there somewhere, but he was just a cop, not a philosopher.

EPILOGUE

Life returned to more of a normal footing at the station following the McCoach case, but Corstophine had noticed a few changes. Frankie had turned up with more makeup than usual yesterday, and he could swear he'd caught her humming a tune to herself when she'd brought him a coffee. That evening he'd caught sight of one of the firemen waiting in the station car park before Frankie drove off with him. He was a good-looking fella. Alex McKay, if he remembered correctly. The same fireman who had collected William's knife from the tower and handed it to Frankie. He sent them a silent toast through the window, not that they would have seen him. Sometimes even detectives have problems focussing on anything other than what's directly in front of them.

He checked his watch, wincing as the freshly healed scar stretched in response to the twist of his wrist. Some scars take time. Physical scars were the easy ones – mental scars could take a lifetime. All of them left some trace behind.

A message chimed on his mobile. Corstophine glanced down at the screen and smiled as he saw Sharmila's name. 'I'll meet you at nine, Saturday. You sure you can manage a Munro with a sore arm?' It was followed by a kiss.